release

a novel by

HOPE RUSSELL NUNKI

*Mary,
with much gratitude,
[signature]*

Published by
Noon Key Productions LLC

RELEASE. Copyright © 2014 by Noon Key Productions LLC

Cover design by Lindsay Megahed / lindsaymegahed.com

All rights reserved. No part of this book may be reproduced or transmitted in any form or by any means, electronic or mechanical, including photocopying, recording, or by any information storage and retrieval system, without the written permission of the author. For information, contact:
Noon Key Productions LLC, P.O. Box 68193, Schaumburg, IL 60168.
hopenunki.com

This book is a work of fiction. Names, characters, places, incidents, and dialogue either are products of the author's imagination or are used fictitiously. Any resemblance to actual persons, living or dead, events, or locales is entirely coincidental.

Grateful acknowledgment is made for permission to incorporate the lyrics of "Be Still" in this work. © 2005 Sarah Marie McSweeney. operamantra.com

ISBN 978-0-9908434-0-5

10 9 8 7 6 5 4 3 2 1

To Tom

To Erin

and, most especially, to

F Z L T

1

Friday, November 11

Everyone knows how it feels to be caught. Sweat dampens your forehead when flashing lights appear in your rear-view mirror. Palpable dread descends when the teacher taps you on the shoulder. Your stomach sinks when you hear Mom or Dad holler from the porch.

As I crossed my threshold that night, nothing in my home felt level or square. The parallel and perpendicular lines of tables and picture frames, of banisters and stair treads, all felt askew. The dogs didn't meet me at the door. The light was all wrong, and my vision wavered at the periphery. Sleet pelted against the window, yet the room felt silent.

And there he was, with my laptop open, the screen facing me. Henry sat motionless, facing away.

"Where have you been?" he rasped without turning around.

"The storm, traffic," I mumbled. The drive back from Chicago had taken more than three hours—a distance that rarely takes a third of that in good weather.

He looked my way. His eyes were dead and forlorn. "Mandelyn, where have you been? Come and tell me," he said, patting the cushion beside him.

I shed my long black parka over the railing and my bags at the foot of the steps; then I circled the sofa to sit beside him. "Where are Frank and Lloyd?" I asked, but as soon as the words were out of my mouth, I remembered. "Oh, shit. Day care."

Unfazed, he continued. "I had to use your computer. I caught an early train to avoid the crowds. I didn't want to haul an ice-crusted backpack through the train station. I needed to work, but I couldn't find the tablet."

"I have it," I said, beginning to rise, but he stopped me with his right hand over mine.

"What is CVC, who is Morgan, and, one more time, *Where. Have. You. Been?*"

My eardrums began to vibrate as if a church bell had been struck inside my head. My hands felt icy, and my knees started to shudder. My intestines filled with sand, and my jaw locked. As much as I wanted to look away, I stared into Henry's dilated pupils.

"You know what I found, obviously," he continued. "I still want your answer."

"CVC is Chevalier Virtual Counseling," I managed to say, finally. "Morgan is the screen name of a CVC counselor. I started the program a month ago. I write to Morgan, and Morgan writes back with questions. No advice, just questions."

"Enlightening," he answered in the same detached tone. "Tell me more about Morgan."

"I know nothing about Morgan," I stammered. "It's not even a single person. It's a gender-neutral screen name that's used by whoever's on duty when my message arrives."

"A stranger—actually a team of strangers—knows more about you than you have allowed me to know for nearly four years. Fascinating," he droned.

I began to say, "Please don't think of it that way..."

"*Don't you dare,*" he said without raising his voice, yet each word abraded his throat so coarsely that I grasped my own in sympathetic pain. He coughed to regain his composure. "I will not be told what to say, what to do, or how to feel about this."

I was silent, so he continued.

"I read, online, that my wife—for whom I would do anything, for whom I have been patiently present and available as you meander through near-clinical mania and depression, even as you cast off every offer of kindness and support—that my wife has maligned and rejected me, preferring to pore over the memories of a gay high school boyfriend's best friend and a college hook-up, instead of living in the present. Then, I learn that your pen pal is an androgynous internet avatar. How do you think I feel, Mandelyn?"

That's when I said the thing I shouldn't have said. "You'd be right at home feeling like a martyr, I think."

He deserved to be furious. He deserved to be wrathful. I wanted him to be. That, I could handle. I knew how to respond to rage. All he did was purse his lips, exhale, take a slow sip of his Koval white rye, and set it on the table. He wasn't using a coaster.

"Why do you hate me so much?" he finally continued. "What have I done to deserve this much loathing? Not take Frank and Lloyd to the vet when I work downtown and you work five minutes away? Clean up after you? Handle the finances? Build you a house?"

"This house has been here since 1856," I argued.

This flustered him. "You're right, Mandelyn. I didn't build you a house. I made this house our home. We came here to be a family. Children, no children—we came here to move forward together. I thought that's what you wanted. What we wanted. What we planned for."

"What you planned for, Henry. Where was I while you were making plans, when you were holed away in your office fussing with magazine clippings, architectural drawings, budgets, and to-do lists?"

"That's what I'm asking you, Mandelyn. *Where have you been?* You checked out almost four years ago. It will be four whole years in February. I understand why. I grieve our loss, too. The way I grieve doesn't look like your way, but I lost Theodore that day, too."

That took me aback a bit. I couldn't remember the last time I had heard Henry say our son's name.

"How could you possibly know how I feel, Henry?" I asked, "Mine is real, actual loss, for which I am solely responsible. I'm so sorry that your charts and your graphs didn't give you a son. I really am.

"I should really give you credit, in fact. There isn't anything else you could have done. You did everything right. But what about me, Henry? How would you feel if you could have read some article, or if you could have analyzed some report that would have kept your son from dying inside me?"

Henry rose and walked into the kitchen with his glass. I thought he was going to refill it; instead, he threw it against what sounded like the stainless steel refrigerator. Shards of glass and cubes of ice skittered across the tiled floor. With perfect calm, Henry returned.

RELEASE

"Thank you, Mandelyn. For so long, I've wondered whether it was me you couldn't stand, or yourself. Thank you for solving that mystery."

"How do you expect me to respond to a statement like that?"

"God forbid that you—the preeminent public relations professional who knows exactly what to tell the world on behalf of anyone else, no matter how complex the issue or dreadful the circumstance—that you respond with a simple statement about yourself. I really used to admire your courage, Mandelyn. I adored how fearlessly you stood up to injustice. How you would conceive an idea and run with it. Commit to it. Sell it. Persuade the most obstinate, set-in-their-ways, sticks in the mud of—the power of dreams. The power of passion. You set your intentions and pursued them against all odds. Where did she go, Mandelyn? Because she isn't here, and she hasn't been for a long damn time. I miss her so much, I ache. What can I do to bring her back?"

"I don't know," I said, choking up. "I'm not entirely sure she exists anymore."

"No. That's not true. I… I don't think I can live in a world where that's possible. You still have ideas and dreams inside you, waiting to be discovered. You have great things yet to accomplish if you could only believe in yourself again. I won't be a party to a waste of so much potential.

"I don't know where you've been or where you are," he continued, "but I can own my part of the responsibility for you being lost. I sat back and watched this to happen, letting you subsist on routine and complacency. We're partners. No matter what happens, I'm always going to be a partner to you. From the moment we met, you challenged me to get outside of my comfort zone. You taught me that it is okay to imagine, and to build my reality from the products of that imagination. I've always wondered what you saw in me. I was just happy that you let me stand in your sunshine."

He turned away, addressing empty space, speaking to himself.

"The underpinning that my care and devotion were supposed to provide hasn't been enough to bolster you. I don't think that where we've found ourselves has much to do with Theodore, even. He isn't the reason I have failed you. Our losing him just brought that failure into stark relief. I don't know if I have it in me to give you what you need.

God knows I've tried.

"I've made a decision. I have to release you, Mandelyn. I have to let you go."

My muscles ached from how stiffly I had held myself upright as Henry poured himself out before me. My circulation had stopped, my breath was shallow, and my core temperature was, I was sure, five degrees below normal. I opened my mouth to speak, but there was no sound. I cleared my throat and finally managed to say, "Can I ask you something?"

"Sure," he said.

"How many entries did you read? Did you read them all?"

"I stopped after you finished mooning over your first time with Sam. You have a real penchant for detail, Mandelyn. I have to hand it to you. It felt like I was there.

"In all honesty—and I can't believe I'm saying this," he continued, "I think that this virtual counseling may actually be doing you some good. I could tell that you had begun to sort some things out for yourself. But here's the thing, Mand. I don't want to read those things about you. I want you to tell me yourself. If you're not able to give that part of yourself to me, I think we may be through. If you can't be your genuine self with me, then nothing else can really follow.

"I release you. Go. Find yourself. See if something or someone—in your past or in your future—holds the keys to your happiness. Maybe you'll find that you have what you need somewhere inside you. If you don't live this life fully, Mandelyn, it won't be on my account. I think you know I love you, but if the character of my love doesn't fulfill you, I don't have anything else to offer.

"I am going to bed. Think about what I've said. Stay here tonight, of course, but I don't think it's a good idea for you to remain for very long. You have a lot of work to do, and I will just get in the way."

As he left, I sat statue-still. Looking at my reflection in the picture window, I could see that my hair was limp, my face was gaunt, my eyes were haunted, and my shoulders were stooped. I didn't look like a person with potential for anything but mediocrity. I sure as hell didn't look like someone who'd inspire people to pursue dreams of their own.

RELEASE

Henry was right. I was lost. Adrift. And the last mooring in my life had just been taken away.

I wanted to cry. For all the fits and episodes of the last several weeks, when tears had come without warning, why couldn't I cry now? I needed a release. Henry was right about that, but I didn't need it in the way he had given it to me. I needed to escape the walls that I had built around myself and stop behaving like a defenseless coward. Not tonight, however. I laid myself down, reaching for the oatmeal wool blanket across the back of the couch, and, in a fetal ball, rested my eyes and willed sleep to come.

2

Leap Day, almost four years earlier

Henry focused on the statistics at first. "Doesn't the chance of something like this drop to nearly zero after being this far along? How could this happen?"

The doctor's voice sounded as if it had traveled through a foot of water. "The statistics do show that the likelihood of losing a baby drops after twelve weeks' gestation. What happened today is exceedingly rare."

I felt like my limp frame was being tossed about by the waves and currents at a seashore. My head sank against the stiff, fiber-filled pillow, and I stared at the ceiling.

"As it is, we need to discuss final arrangements for…" The doctor trailed off, either having forgotten his name or not wanting to say it.

I couldn't take it. I needed Henry to have that conversation elsewhere. I needed to not be a part of it. "Please, can you go someplace else to talk? Henry, you know what's best. Let me know what you decide." Even as I said the words, I knew that I couldn't simply ignore the situation. I just didn't have the fortitude to make the choices that needed to be made.

"Theodore. Theodore's arrangements," Henry added to complete the doctor's sentence. "Let's step into the hallway."

I was supposed to be safe. I was supposed to be in the clear. Not because of dates or statistics, or anything else that could be measured or tracked. Miscarriage just couldn't happen to someone like me. It happened to waifs—thin, anemic ghosts. I was too substantial, too fit, to be subjected to this. Ever since puberty, I had withstood supposedly good-natured teasing and outright malicious ridicule about my height and my build. After overhearing two of my seventh-grade gym teachers during a volleyball game, I had to endure the most mortifying principal-teacher meeting I could imagine at the time. I was actually assured by those grown, male, education professionals that being "built like a brick shit-house" was a compliment—that I showed real potential for collegiate volleyball and that the high school coaches should be notified.

I embraced my natural athleticism, warding off the thick-waisted, doughy-assed, flabby-armed silhouette typical of those in my family tree. Thankful as I was to stay slim and toned through high school and college, I never filled out more than a B cup. This invited more teasing from my more amply-endowed relatives and friends. I was the only pear-shaped person I knew with twelve percent body fat. I avoided strapless dresses, plunging necklines, and anything form-fitting well into my twenties, even though I was built to wear daring looks in almost every respect. I looked forward to getting the boobs that were supposed to come with pregnancy.

An upside of having "birthing hips" was, I presumed, the chance to use them. As it turned out, my so-called "good breeding genes" were, in fact, so much fraudulent insurance policy. The promise of safety through physical strength was a promise broken.

Henry felt like another broken promise. I'd taken his careful, exhaustive planning and his nearly obsessive research as insurance against the risks of pregnancy, to the point where I couldn't see what could possibly go wrong. He seemed to know a way to prevent or counteract every possible risk. Sleep on your left side to prevent heartburn. Rub your belly with coconut oil to prevent stretch marks and to benefit from the medium-chain fatty acids. Wear wrist braces prophylactically to prevent the onset of carpal tunnel.

He'd actually gotten upset with me just six weeks before, when he realized that the dog-earring and highlighting of *What to Expect When You're Expecting* was entirely his doing and not at all mine. He was encyclopedically aware of every last concern, from sushi and soft cheeses, to the "wrong" prenatal vitamins, to unsubstantiated worries I swore he fabricated in his mind. He cancelled our autumn trip to Ireland as soon as we found out we were pregnant. "Flying isn't restricted until the third trimester," I protested, but he didn't see the point of taking any chances.

From the evening we returned from the first obstetrician appointment, Henry set to work remapping our whole life plan. This baby was already a part of our family. He insisted that we find out whether we were having a boy or a girl as soon as we could. He pored through *Consumer Reports* ratings of every last piece of baby accoutrement. He started full-scale baby name research. He even got up to speed on the local organized sports teams and coaching opportunities.

The name Theodore, however, didn't come from research. One cold January morning, I was obstinately pulling my favorite kelly green sweater over my emerging baby bump. I was only thirteen weeks along. I had just begun to show, but I had also started to retain water. My face was puffy, or at least I insisted it was. Henry, to his credit, denied that he could tell. I referred to myself as "The Chipmunk" and, by extension, started calling the baby "The Little Chipmunk." To make light of feeling ugly, I would make little chipmunk faces at Henry now and then, making him laugh by curling my top lip under to buck my teeth and making little chittering noises with my tongue.

Henry was never one to comment on my appearance, for better or for worse, which is why what he did that morning was so unexpected. There I was, pantless, in the sweater that barely covered my navel. The usually-flattering knit rolled up over my newly-bulbous midsection whenever I raised my hands above my head, which is where they were when Henry came out from the shower.

Henry took one look at me and, with a mischievous grin, grabbed my brush from the bed and began singing into it.

I stared, mouth agape, at my usually staid, somber husband. With a towel around his waist, dripping wet, there he was, singing the *Alvin and the Chipmunks* theme song.

"What the hell are you doing?" I bellowed over his song and dance.

"Oh, come on! The Chipmunks? Your sweater?" He gestured at my belly. "The cheeks?" He imitated my chipmunk sounds. "You are a dead ringer for Theodore! You're hilarious!"

I experienced two kinds of humiliation at once, which, thankfully, Henry sensed, causing him to drop his hairbrush-microphone. I couldn't decide which was worse—being compared to a chubby musical rodent or being married to a grown man who could drop the lyrics of an 80s cartoon theme song at will. Who remembers stuff like that well enough to—with choreography!—sing full-volume at six o'clock in the morning?

Despite some residual hurt feelings, snickering at his expense won out over the insult to my vanity. The levity didn't last long, though. "I, uh, wish I was playing a joke," I said sullenly. "I haven't bought any maternity clothes. I didn't think I was ready for them. Is there any chance I can borrow a sweater of yours? I don't think any of mine are going to fit." The admission made a tear roll down my cheek.

"Noo… Oh, no. Oh, Mandelyn. I am so sorry. I didn't mean…" He rushed to me and held me close. "I was only… You've been making all the jokes, and…"

"It's okay. Really. I get it," I sniffed. I hated what pregnancy was doing to my usual emotional impenetrability, but I didn't mind burrowing my head into Henry's wet, bare shoulder. "But maybe, could you maybe not sing anymore? Ever?" As much as I tried to sound lighthearted, the undertone of bitterness was palpable.

"Never will I make that mistake again," he soothed, kissing the top of my ear softly as he began to rock, almost imperceptibly, back and forth.

With his next kiss at my ear, I pulled back a bit to look up into his eyes. With a wry smile, I purred, "Promise? Because your singing voice is awful." That achieved the tone I had been hoping for. I kissed him lightly. Henry returned my kiss with unexpected ardor. His hands, consolingly rested on my shoulder blades, began to glide down my back. Grasping the sweater, he gently pulled it over my head. Obligingly, I raised my hands, childlike. Henry tossed it into the laundry basket in the corner.

"I love you, you know. I love you so much," I cooed as I circled my arms around his waist, loosening his towel and letting it fall to the floor. He gave me a look that I couldn't quite read as sincerely or playfully askance. For the first time in weeks, I felt a stirring in my core that wasn't heartburn or indigestion. As I felt Henry rising and hardening against me, I was pleased, but I was also a bit surprised to see that his thoughts were heading in the same direction as mine.

"What about the baby?" I asked. "I thought the idea of… you know… made you nervous."

"You're past the first trimester," he assured me. "I'm sure it's okay. I'll be careful," he said reassuringly. I wasn't sure if the reassurance was for him or for me, but I thought it was sweet.

"How do you like the name Theodore?" he asked as I reclined onto the bed.

I gave it a little thought. "I like it. But what if the baby is a girl?"

As he crawled towards me, he said, in his deep masculine voice, "Oh, it's a boy. Our baby is a boy."

Running late, we shared a cab downtown instead of taking the Blue line like we usually would. We stopped at Iguana Café on our walk through the bitter, biting cold toward Grand Avenue. He didn't say a word when I ordered the chai latte, despite the caffeine, and I was thankful. The scent of Blommer Chocolate floated on the air as the nearby factory's production began for the day, and it became part of the memory. Whenever I would smell chocolate, I would think of Henry and me and the good days before everything changed.

~ ~ ~ ~ ~ ~ ~

I first noticed the bleeding on the morning of the Super Bowl. Plans with the neighbors across the hall were instantly forgotten. We spent the day at the hospital, scared out of our minds. The doctor did an ultrasound, and everything appeared to be fine. Theo, as Henry called him, had a strong heartbeat. I just had to take it easy.

On Valentine's Day, without any bleeding in the interim, I had another OBGYN appointment. We had finally reached the point when we could hope to learn the baby's gender. Henry came with me to the appointment, and we planned to celebrate afterward at Blackbird.

We never made it to dinner. During what was supposed to be a cursory follow-up, the doctors discovered a subchorionic hematoma, a blood clot between the placenta and the uterus. We were assured that nothing I had done had caused it, and nothing could have been done to prevent it. Subchorionic hematomas disappear on their own most of the time, we were told, so there wasn't any risk to my baby so long as I continued to take it easy. In all but a few rare cases, clots would either be absorbed back into the body, or they would bleed out and resolve themselves. Hearing the words "bleed out" was enough for Henry to insist on bed rest. The doctor seemed to hesitate but didn't disagree. Bed rest couldn't cause any harm.

The way in which I was discussed as if I wasn't even there—as if my opinions, my schedule, and my questions were immaterial—enraged me. "How dare you assert your completely home-taught opinion over that of my doctor?" I hissed at him while my doctor was out of the room. "How dare you insist that I put my life on hold for what is barely a complication?"

Henry was stone-faced in response. Arguing was useless. Deep down, I agreed with him. No risk was worth the potential downside. There weren't any therapeutic interventions, so if bed rest was what I could do to keep Teddy, who we now knew was a boy, safe, of course I would do it. I had to hand off a few work projects, but my teammates understood. I just resented being told what to do, having my choice and my doctor's advice usurped by my husband.

For the next two weeks, I lay around our condo for most of the day. Every now and then, I would check Teddy's heartbeat on the fetal Doppler machine I had purchased online. I would talk to him and sing to him all the time. I did crosswords and Sudoku until my eyes were dry. I caught up on every trashy daytime soap opera I'd ever watched during college. I watched every black and white movie I could get my hands on, feeling intellectually superior about my newfound knowledge of classic cinema.

I was in the bath, reading my Sara Paretsky and tolerating the lukewarm water instead of rinsing and getting out, when it happened. Without so much as a pinprick of pain, the water was suddenly the color of rubies.

"Placental abruption" is the term for what happens when the placenta begins to tear away from the uterus. In the hours that followed, my head swirled with medical jargon, which, thankfully, Henry devoured as if every new term gave him power in a situation neither of us could control. The subchorionic hematoma had caused a Class 1 placental abruption and an amniotic membrane microperforation.

Theodore was still alive and no fetal stress had yet been detected, but a number of issues were presenting themselves all at once. I was losing amniotic fluid more quickly than I was producing it. Without amniotic fluid, Theodore's lungs couldn't develop and his body could become deformed in the cramped space. Anytime I shifted in the wrong direction, I would bleed, taking nutrients away from both Theodore and myself. As if the situation wasn't complicated enough, any amount of blood present in the uterus could trigger cramping, leading to contractions and early labor.

I was admitted to the hospital, put on fluids, and given a catheter. I took the doctors' direction for the optimal position to assume, and then I had to stay perfectly still as long as I possibly could. The only slim chance we had was to minimize further amniotic fluid losses, help my body restore the amounts I would inevitably lose, and keep the placenta where it could continue transmitting nutrients through the umbilical cord. I sat with my left leg extended, my right folded beneath me, and reclined about twenty degrees.

"Micropreemie" was a term we learned in the early morning hours, once I was finally stable. Theodore was nineteen weeks along. That was nothing like being in a safe zone, but statistics improved with every week of gestation. Every day that I could hold on was another day Teddy was in the safest place he could be, except that there was yet another problem. The break in the amniotic membrane was now a site at which bacteria could infiltrate. After all of the positioning and immobility, I could still contract infection, putting Theodore and myself at grave risk.

"We need to talk about arrangements, Henry," I said with my head in a fog. "We need to talk about wishes and possibilities."

"No, Mand. We can't give up hope. You're situated now. We can do this. I believe in us."

The role reversal taking place between my husband and me made the fog around my head thicken all the more. "I'm not talking about surrender. I'm talking about being realistic. You need to get a hold of Nadja."

"I called her late last night. She will be on a plane this afternoon."

"That's premature," I said, and immediately rolled my eyes about the poor word choice. "I mean, my mom shouldn't come before we know what's going to happen. She only needed to be told that we don't know what's going on right now, but that we'll let her know what's happening once we do."

RELEASE

Henry's usually placid face contorted as he sought the right words to say. It took him a minute, at least, and felt like an eternity. Carefully, slowly, he began, taking my hands in his and looking into them, joined together, instead of my eyes. "At no point in the hours and days to come will we ever know exactly what is about to happen. I'm not sure we're ever going to know what our future holds from this point forward."

Then he looked up into my eyes. "I need your courage now, Mand. You have never been afraid of the unknown. You see it, acknowledge it, and face it. For all that I love in you, that may be what I love about you most of all. I need that from you, now. Be courageous for me."

I withdrew my right hand from his and stroked his cheek, holding his face in my hand. Henry's head collapsed onto the three remaining hands on the bed. I rested my free palm on the crown of his head. The shudders of his sobs were silent. It was the first and last time I have ever seen him cry.

No one else was saying so as the morning wore on, but we both knew the situation could not endure. Henry knew it, and, hearing him say it, I had to admit it, too. Looking back on that day, it was as if we were tied to the track of a morbid race between amniotic fluid loss, bleeding out, infection risk, and preterm labor. In this grotesque metaphor, preterm labor was what finally ran us down. I felt myself let go in the moments before the first contractions began. I knew, no matter what the fetal monitor said, that Theodore was already gone.

Labor can't be any harder than it is when delivering a stillborn child. Theodore was due on July 22nd, but instead our baby boy was born to us on the afternoon of Leap Day. The day was brilliantly clear. Snow crocuses had broken through the last melting drifts. The winter had been the coldest and snowiest of the last two decades. Dreary weather would return, kill the crocuses, and persist through the month ahead, but that day, in that brief moment of time, it seemed like spring was on its way.

I never felt my son's heartbeat. I never saw the true color of his skin, mottled blue by the trauma and asphyxiation. I never saw the light in his eyes. I did get to cradle him in my arms, though. I did get to hold his hand in mine. I got to speak to him, even if the words I shared were only heard by Henry's ears and mine. "I'm sorry, Teddy. I'm so sorry.

I love you. I have always loved you. I always will." For what could have been a minute, an hour, or a day, I rocked his perfect, tiny body as if lulling him to sleep. I kissed his delicate forehead, which a nurse had covered with a white hand-knitted cap.

Henry stroked my hair, Teddy's cheek, my shoulder, and Teddy's arm, and then repeated the pattern over and again. I eventually surrendered the body of our son to him. If Teddy had looked tiny in my arms, he dwindled all the more in Henry's. The expression in Henry's eyes as he looked upon his baby's face is the clearest image I take away from that day. No other person on this earth—no one—has ever looked upon the face of any other with an expression of more tragic, profound devotion. It's the image of that expression that both shatters and restores me every time I think of it. I think about it every single day.

3

Sunday, October 9

"You're crazy to wear those out on a night like this," I mumbled, pointing to Colette's Lucchese hand-tooled riding boots as she took her seat in the booth as elegantly as if we were taking high tea at the Drake Hotel Palm Court.

A sardonic smile snuck across her face. "Maybe don't toss the word 'crazy' around so casually. I left halfway through tonight's new *Dexter* to see you."

I acknowledged her sacrifice with a half-hearted shoulder-shrug and an eye-roll while doctoring my stale coffee with another creamer. "Thank you. I'm sorry," I whispered.

"Look, Mandelyn," Colette started, looking around the dingy diner to gauge our privacy. Except for a high-school-aged couple in the opposite corner and a tired man at the counter, we were alone. "I understand crazy, honey. I chair the Crazy Town welcoming committee. I just never thought you'd be the one I'd bring a basket of muffins."

My sniff was my best attempt at a laugh. "The latest straw on the camel's back is ridiculous," I said.

"Your hair's ridiculous, but I can let that go, too," she said with a wink.

The scrunchie offended my sensibilities as well, but it completed the look: hoodie, yoga pants, and Crocs. "Okay," I resolved, taking a deep breath. "Henry re-washed my sour cream container."

"Is that code for something?" Colette asked, nonplussed.

I shook off her attempt at a joke. "We rinse the recyclables so they don't draw bugs."

"And your cleanliness didn't pass muster? *Your* cleanliness?" Colette had given me more than a stab or two over the years about my fixation on germs, proper organization, and squaring items on tabletops—even when they weren't my tabletops or my items. "Didn't think they made people more orderly than you."

Shelly, as it read on her burnished brass name tag, arrived somewhat sullenly and refilled my cup as she asked if Colette wanted anything besides coffee.

"Sustenance, yes, but no coffee, and no more for this one, either," Colette quipped as she nodded her head in my direction. Glancing over the menu, she sneered, "Carbs… Carbs… Ah, here we go." My friend was carefree about a lot of things, but her diet was pretty much sacrosanct.

"I could use some hot water, a few lemon slices, and… this Denver scramble. Only could you leave out the ham and throw some turkey in there instead?"

"Denver… turkey, no ham. Sure, darlin'. And a pot of water. Any tea?"

"Nope, just the water. No, wait. Bring the tea. Chamomile?" She pointed at me, indicating that I would drink it, voluntarily or otherwise.

"Sure thing," Shelly said over her shoulder as she turned to leave.

"Chamomile will put me to sleep, Col," I complained. My state of mind was muddled and artificially alert at once. Colette was right. More caffeination wasn't a good idea.

"Tea will bring you back into focus. You're eating, too," she said.

I didn't have the energy to resist.

"So, your rinsing was inadequate," she continued.

I shrugged my shoulders in response as Shelly returned with a kettle of water, some lemon wedges, and an unexpectedly charming presentation of loose-leaf chamomile tea in a lightning jar, an infuser ball already filled for use. She removed my half-empty coffee cup and the litter of empty plastic creamers and sugar packets. She grabbed a fresh cup from the next booth and set it down before retreating.

Colette filled each of our mugs and tossed a lemon wedge in hers. She dropped the infuser ball into my cup and began to dip it as she spoke. "They always say that, 'It's never about what it's about.' Baby, there's gotta be more to this. I get that there are straws, and that there are camels' backs… but what is it, really? What is really going on?"

She reached out to steady my hand, which I was surprised to see was fidgeting manically with the edge of a paper doily. I jolted as if awakened by her touch. I could feel my throat tighten and took a sip of the half-steeped tea.

"I just felt, all at once, like a child. No," I corrected myself. "I felt like a… guest. A guest in my own house. Someone who'd overstayed her welcome. Like a well-intentioned visitor who was trying to help with the housekeeping, you know? Whom he didn't wish to offend. It was like he had crept into the laundry room to get the container and rinse it out without me noticing."

I couldn't read Colette's expression. Her tanned skin, botoxed forehead, and preternaturally plumped smile lines didn't always convey expressions in a conventional manner. She kept her right hand on mine while she fished with her left in her tawny Hermès hobo bag for a tissue. After a bit, she abandoned the effort and pushed a napkin in my direction.

"That realization just about knocked me over," I sniffed, dabbing a bit at my eyes. A single tear slid down the side of my nose. I was shocked I was crying at all. Tears only came about once a year for me. I get as emotional as anyone, I think. Emotion just doesn't manifest for me in the ways it does for other people.

"I started to think about all the times he'd made me feel… inconsequential, you know? Dumb stuff, like accepting or declining invitations without letting me know until after the fact. Or the way he just assumes that I'll take Frank or Lloyd to the vet, like my job doesn't have the importance to schedule around, like we shouldn't share that responsibility."

"That is bullshit," Colette stated with the somber tone of an adjudicator. "What else?"

"I don't know… Oh, the way he answers, 'It's complicated' or 'Don't worry about it' when I ask him to explain something. The dismissive attitude, like anything in his world is beyond my comprehension. Aah! And television. Somehow, watching a reality show once in a while makes me an idiot, but an *It's Always Sunny* marathon is what, high art? *Ultimate Fighting Championship* is 'escapist,' but *Grey's Anatomy* is brainrot?"

This keyed Colette's attention. "He did not call you an idiot. Tell me he didn't do that," she demanded.

"Well… no, he didn't. It's the way he exhales when he comes in the room if I'm already there. His barely audible moan has more criticism in it than any words could."

Shelly arrived with the scramble. It smelled deliciously greasy in spite of the meat substitution. The onion and green pepper aroma stirred my hunger, making me realize that I hadn't eaten since lunch, ten hours earlier. Colette pushed the plate to my side of the table, but not before disdainfully removing the buttered Greek toast by tweezing it with a thumb and forefinger and transferring it to a napkin, covering it quickly as if it were toxic. Once it was safely quarantined, she turned and put her hand to my forearm in comfort.

"I'm starting to get the picture, chica. I am. Now, please don't take this the wrong way, but you're talking about symptoms. I'm not saying you don't have every right to be upset. Things do not sound good. What I want you to do is talk to me about the diagnosis. What's at the heart of the matter? None of this by itself sounds like anything other than typical marriage… funk."

"You're right," I said blankly. It's the same conclusion I'd reached before Colette had arrived. It's the same conclusion I'd reached at least a dozen times over the last year—maybe longer.

"Have you thought about going back to therapy? Do they offer some sort of counseling services through the Laboratory? Maybe now that you have some distance from the loss of…" She trailed off while I shook my head.

"I don't want counseling. It didn't work three years ago. It's not going to work now. Psychiatrists are useless and prescriptions only addled my brain. You're the only shrink I'll ever need," I said, pointing at her with the tines of my fork.

Colette stirred her lemon water thoughtfully. "What a pickle. What. A. Pickle," she said with some reproachful-sounding clicks of her tongue. Then she gasped. "What about virtual counseling? I was just heard something on the radio about it. Do you know about this?"

"Is it like the psychic hotline?"

Colette gave a half-joking, half-antagonized sneer. "A little jokester, huh? No, funny pants. It was on WGN the other day. There's this woman. What was her name? Chevalier! She's looking for case studies for her books, so she invites people who need a sounding board to journal online."

I interrupted her, shaking my head. "Are you serious? That doesn't sound weird to you? Sad, crazy people posting anonymous cries for help on a website?"

"You're not sad, and you're not crazy. You're frustrated, maybe depressed. I know it feels the same, but it's not. Anyway, no. You sign this waiver of indemnity, saying that you understand that this is basically self-care. She tracks people very closely and contacts authorities and medical help if she has any reason to think a participant is in trouble."

"You remember all of this from drive-time news radio?"

"Who knows why some things stick in this brain and others don't?" she laughed. "Doesn't it intrigue you, though? The program has been so successful that the founder has other people in her practice helping, too. Oh, this was interesting! They all use these gender-neutral screen names. She saw that her site was becoming this magnet for pervy people bragging about their deviant sex lives and other nonsense, just to get a rise out the person on the other end. Men, women—didn't matter.

"So the virtual counselors all use names like Pat, Alex, Dakota, or Jess—whatever. She's found that it tones down the perv quotient significantly. And because they're screen names, her staff can respond to participants on each other's behalf. While you're writing to, say, Jamie or Casey the whole time, you're probably talking to any one of several people throughout the course of it.

"This was another thing they said: no one seems to notice the difference between one counselor or another, anyway, because they don't actually write that much in their responses. Their focus is on open-ended questioning. Socratic counseling, they called it."

I grunted. My mouth was full of scramble, so she continued.

"So that's another thing. She promises not to reveal your real name, except to the nice young men in the clean white coats if it comes to that, but you surrender the rights to the stories you tell. She can use the stories you write in any academic journal articles or textbooks she produces. That's how she can keep the service free."

Maybe it was because it was late. Maybe it was because my blood sugar had been low. Maybe it was the chamomile tea. Whatever it was, this was starting to sound like it could be an interesting idea. "I'll Google it. It can't hurt. Venting could be cathartic, if nothing else." I was nodding as I talked myself into it.

"Well, good. I'm glad. If my long-ass commute and talk radio addiction helps just one person, then great."

I welcomed a change in subject. "So, how long before you're done with that commute and are back in your home office? Your project was supposed to be done by the end of second quarter, I thought."

Her throaty, perturbed grumble was incongruous with her stunning, if slightly overdone, façade. Colette was the quintessential woman in a man's world. Growing up an Air Force brat, she spent the majority of her childhood on bases throughout the Southeast. Raised by her father, a widower, she became less a daughter and more a military wife at a young age. With few role models around, she patterned her life perspective from a conglomeration of *Charlie's Angels*, the officer's wives who'd babysit most Saturday nights, and her dad's *Playboy* magazines.

Her father ran construction projects on the Air Force bases, Colette told me when we met at my office three years earlier. "The combination of construction ego and military ego is pretty potent, especially without a mom around to balance things out," she said. "You get a pretty clear picture of what to expect from men, being raised that way, and a nothing-left-to-guesswork understanding of what men expect from us. The best part, though, is that you know how the sausage is made." Those were her exact words. The double-entendre was entirely intended, yet it didn't make you laugh, the way she said it. "You either learn how to beat boys at their own game or… I don't know what the other alternative is, obviously, and I sure as shit don't want to know. Growing up like I did made me fucking fabulous."

Colette parlayed her military connections and her construction know-how into a business development consulting practice. In the last several years, people like her prospered while every other facet of the construction industry flailed. She helped architects, engineers, and builders gain traction with the Army Corps of Engineers, the Department of Defense, the General Services Administration, and other agencies when almost all of the construction in the country was federally-funded. She used her network to connect like-minded firms for joint-venture pursuits, taking percentage cuts of any contracts secured by her clients. "I'm a pimp for the ugliest, most pompous group of assholes you'll ever meet. It's about time a hardbody chick like me made some money off their desperate asses. Let the chodes get in line."

I caught myself drifting out of focus, despite Colette's engaging, if indelicate, storytelling. It was easy to get lost in my befuddled awe of the life she led while she continued. The anecdote involved Patrón shots at Zocalo after a trade show and the hot reflexologist she visited the next day to relieve the pain brought on by new Louboutins. "Would it kill Christian to put some anti-skid on those red soles? Because someone's going to wrench a back falling off a table one of these days."

The tapping of her French-manicured acrylic nails against her teacup broke my trance. I'd let her take charge of the conversation because I owed her the chance to talk after dominating the evening's dialogue. I wasn't holding up the listening end of the conversation, though. I didn't want to let on that I hadn't been tuned in, so I did my best to laugh with the appropriate timbre. She saw right through me. To her credit, she didn't call me out on it.

"It's time to get you home," she said, rising from her seat and sliding into her Burberry trench. "Come on. I'm driving you. I'll bring you back in the morning to get your car. Are you going to the office?"

"Yeah. I'd love to take PTO, but we have the Joint Experimental Theoretical Physics Seminar tomorrow," I said with affected flair. "Someone from Brown is coming in to talk about the first results from the LUX Dark Matter Search."

"Riveting," she yawned. "Oh, well. Hang tight. I'll be back after I settle up with Shelly."

Years of experience kept me from even feigning a reach for the bill, which she swept from the tabletop as she pivoted and whisked toward the front of the restaurant. She had long, swift strides not typical of someone of her stature. Colette only broke five feet because of her vast collection of impractical footwear.

While she paid, I tried to put myself together. I yanked the sweatshirt sleeves down from my elbows to my wrists. I didn't recall pushing them up; I really wasn't messing around while stuffing myself with scramble. I caught sight of my ragged cuticles and recoiled at the grime under my peeling, unkempt nails. I looked as if I had been replacing an engine block. The dryness of my skin exaggerated the age it appeared to be. Tendons and veins rose from beneath the surface of my skin as if it were that of a woman twice my age. I blanched at the sight of my beautiful wedding ring on my jaundiced, ugly finger, which was crowned with a nail streaked with two nutrient-deficiency white marks. The east-west set oval solitaire, nestled beside the ultrafine microchannel-set Möbius wedding band, was truly stunning—elegant and unpretentious. It deserved better carriage.

During my engagement and for the first year or so of my marriage, I did such a nice job keeping my hands pretty. I spent an inordinate amount of money on nail polishes and hand lotions. I frequently got lost in admiration of the diamond's facets when they shone in the sunlight. Just over six years later, I eschewed the too-obvious metaphor—that I'd taken the ring's presence for granted, letting cleanings go by the wayside and allowing a perceptible film to coat the platinum's surface, clouding the stone.

Colette's bawdy laugh snapped me back to attention. I scooted from the booth and shuffled to meet her. Shelly and Colette were making little attempt to conceal their amusement as they stared at the high school couple in the corner booth. He had his hand up her shirt, and she, reclined on her right elbow, was grasping furiously at his neck with her left and moaning with theatrics far exceeding any pleasure she could possibly be experiencing. Both of them were oblivious to their audience. She, in her skinny jeans, responded in kind to each dry-humping thrust he delivered, his wallet chain clanging against the table's metal trim.

"Someone should stop them," I said vacantly, even though the absurdity of the tableau was the first thing to bring an authentic laugh to my day.

Shelly was unfazed. "I draw the line at cock play. She makes a move for his buckle, and I'll throw 'em both out into the rain."

RELEASE

The tired man spoke from the counter. "Let them have their fun. Youth is fleeting. I wish I'd done more necking back when I had the chance."

~ ~ ~ ~ ~ ~ ~

Driving up the winding riverside road toward home was like traveling a timeline, with schools, churches, old haunts, and landmarks imbued with memories from my childhood lining the way. Unlike many of the people in my life, I had lived in Weston almost all my life. For a suburb that otherwise looks and feels like Grover's Corners, it's actually pretty cosmopolitan, due in large part to the highly educated people drawn to the area by the specialized employment opportunities. Some of my elementary school friends and their parents had left when the furniture, cosmetics, and other manufacturing companies had faded away, but new families came, attracted by specialized contract employment at the companies—mostly foreign-owned—that stayed. Work would last three or four years, and then the families would leave when projects concluded. People came to work at the Irish-owned educational publishing company, the German-owned grocery store headquarters, any of the American-owned global companies with outposts in the area, or the Laboratory, where I had found a job after leaving my agency position in the city.

As we drove by a newer, nice-enough, nondescript subdivision, I broke the silence by asking, "Have you ever heard about what was once on that property, Col?"

"It's dark, it's late, and it's raining. You're not about to freak me out with some haunted graveyard story, are you?"

"Well, when you put it that way, maybe I should save the story for another time. There is a graveyard up there. It's all that remains of the Illinois State Industrial School for Delinquent Girls."

"Try putting that school name on a resume or a college application," Colette responded. "Jeez, could they come up with a name that sounds creepier?"

"I know, right? It had a bunch of names over the years, like the State Home for Juvenile Female Offenders, or the Training School for Girls—that's another good one. It was the Illinois Youth Center when they closed it down, just a few years after I was born. Most locals just call it The Girls' School. Girls who'd committed some crime or were just considered wayward were sentenced there to be rehabilitated."

"Who is in the graveyard—the girls who failed rehabilitation?"

"So much worse. Many of the girls were sent there by their families because they were pregnant. Loose moral character, you know." I sniffed cynically before I continued. "Oftentimes, there weren't doctors or even nurses available for deliveries. Teachers and social workers did what they could if no one else was around, but many of the girls and their babies died."

"God," Colette said, astonished.

"And there are the stories of beatings, restraints, starvation—all forms of punishment for girls who wouldn't 'reform.' Really awful stuff."

"Not exactly something you put on a real estate flyer for the people who built their houses up there, either."

"Exactly. Most of the inhumane stuff happened at the turn of the century, not long after the place was founded, but it never did enjoy the best reputation, you can imagine. The rumors of what happened there were obscured for decades, until historians and genealogists started to research and document the stories. There are all kinds of books and blogs about what happened there.

"In high school, the main thing I knew about the site was the cemetery," I continued. "Like a bunch of jackasses, we'd sneak onto the property, freak each other out with ghost stories, and couple off into the woods to make out. Most of the ghost stories were made-up nonsense, of course, but there are a few that people seem to agree upon. There's the one about the young woman in a flowing dress who wanders the cemetery on moonlit nights. I never heard or saw anything, but plenty of people talk about hearing crying babies, girls singing, pianos playing, or seeing red eyes watching from the shadows—fun stuff."

"Man alive," Colette said in wonder. "But you know, being scared produces the same chemical reaction in your body as being aroused. The adrenaline rush, the endorphins. Of course high school kids would go there."

"Don't I know it. I had my first kiss up there in that cemetery. Might have lost my virginity there, too, if Joshua hadn't had the good sense to put on the brakes. How messed-up is that?"

"What, that your first kiss was in a cemetery or that a guy decided to put on the brakes when you were just about to bang?"

"The kiss, weirdo. The stopping's easy to explain. Ah, Joshua Maines. Beautiful Joshua Maines. Turns out beautiful Joshua Maines was gay. I think part of me knew before he did, not because we didn't do it—just a bunch of telltale signs I willingly ignored because he was cute, Ivy-League smart, totally popular, and a top-tier athlete. Kind of the perfect package, except he liked boys. He lives downtown with his husband, Reynard, now. They're the ones who got Henry and me into Pit Bull rescue. All's well that ends well."

"So your first kiss… Was it with this same guy—this beautiful Joshua Maines?"

"Same guy."

Colette gave me a look of impressed approval.

"Not the same night—come on, Col!" I laughed. "The kiss was after a football game sophomore year. The sex—or not-sex, really—was the summer between junior and senior year." I smiled at the memories while drifting off into other reminiscing, until I realized that I hadn't seen Joshua and Reynard for too long and resolved to make a double date for the four of us. Colette derailed my train of thought when she pulled up in front of my house.

"Well, that sweet little story begins to redeem your spacing off while I told you about Zocalo and my favorite new reflexologist."

"I'm glad. You really are the best. What time tomorrow? Six-thirty?"

"Nah, make it quarter-till. That's about as late as I can get on the road and beat traffic. I'm going to need every minute of sleep I can get tonight, and so will you! Don't stay up. Go to bed, or… couch… or floor. Just get shut-eye. No excuses."

"I'll try. Love you, babe."

"Love you, too. N'night."

We hugged in that awkward way you have to in a car these days, now that all of them have consoles and gear shifts in between passengers and drivers. "Don't you miss the old days, when you could slide across the front seat and hug people properly, Col?"

"Not right at the moment. I love you, sweetheart, but if you think I'm putting out just because you told me your high school non-sex story and got me a little mushy, you really are nuts."

"No one makes me laugh like you do," I said, ironically not laughing in the least bit. "See you tomorrow morning."

I squeezed her a little tighter right before I broke away, grabbed my purse, and shuffled through the blowing mist, up the walkway toward my front door. I turned to wave, she tapped her horn in reply, and she left. When I put my key in the door, I could hear the dogs, Frank and Lloyd, rushing to meet me. Somehow, they always knew the difference between me and a stranger outside. The shuffle of their paws lifted my spirits a bit, easing me over the threshold.

4

Punctual as ever, Colette was in front of the house with her Mustang the next morning at six forty-five. I was feeling more presentable than I had the night before, wearing vintage embroidered jeans, a jade-heather kimono-style yoga wrap over a cream lace-trimmed camisole, and an obi belt. I almost never wore any jewelry except my cubic zirconia studs, but, feeling the need for a little extra femininity for a Monday, I added a bib necklace of amethyst, blue agate, and white quartz stones. Having spent too much time in the shower, my hair was still wet—usually unacceptable by my standards but excusable today, considering. I brought my makeup bag along, counting on time at stoplights to throw on a little concealer, mascara, and blush during my commute from the restaurant to the Laboratory. Concealer was imperative.

Sleep had been, not surprisingly, evasive. Henry had already gone to sleep by the time I got home, and he left while I was in the shower, calling through the closed door, "See you tonight, I hope. Love you!" I had spent the night on the couch, ostensibly to keep from waking him with my tossing and turning, but truly, just not wanting to share a bed with him, let alone give any explanation for where I had been. He hadn't woken up to see if I had made it home okay, which would have frustrated me a few years before, but now it was par for the course. It would have been stranger if he had woken up to ask me questions, or worse, if he'd been awake, lounging on the couch, watching some game on TV, and not asked me anything. The mutual avoidance, while clearly dysfunctional, was at least comfortably familiar.

Cuddled in my oatmeal wool blanket, I scrolled mindlessly through Facebook on my phone for a while after getting home, absentmindedly petting Frank as he dozed beside me on the floor, Lloyd lying nearby and snoring loudly. After a while, I opened the Diana Gabaldon novel I'd begun the week before, but I found myself reading the same page over and over again without engagement or comprehension. I even took a turn through the cable directory, but nothing piqued my interest. By about one in the morning, I finally summoned the courage to go to my office and look up Chevalier Virtual Counseling. The dogs followed, their claws clicking on the wide-plank hardwood floor.

Judging by the website, Chevalier Virtual Counseling appeared to be legitimate. As Communications Director at the Laboratory, I am highly suspicious of any company or organization with poorly-designed marketing materials. I was prepared to be met with flagrant use of stock imagery, animated GIFs, and Comic Sans. Instead, the site was as well-considered and assembled as any other counselor's or psychiatrist's.

"Chevalier Virtual Counseling (CVC) Frequently Asked Questions" appeared at the top of the screen. I clicked through, and several questions followed.

What is CVC?

Chevalier Virtual Counseling, or CVC, is a free service offered by the practice of Dr. Riley Chevalier. As part of Dr. Chevalier's full complement of counseling services, she and her staff offer virtual services that equate to guided self-care.

Who provides CVC?

Dr. Chevalier guides her staff in the practice of Socratic counseling—the minimal, open-ended questioning method that prompts program participants to explore their thoughts and feelings constructively, to make discoveries about personal strengths, and to understand the roadblocks between present circumstances and self-actualization.

What are Dr. Chevalier's credentials?

Dr. Chevalier is a board-certified psychiatrist. The only statements made on the CVC website that are the responsibility of CVC are her own and those of her staff.

RELEASE

Who Benefits from CVC?
We can help with a variety of lifestyle issues, such as:
- Occupations and Careers
- Personal Development
- Marriage and Relationships
- General Stress Management
- Self-Esteem and Confidence

If professional, confidential, simple, and free were what I sought, I was looking at it. I found this "wide variety" list to be rather limiting, but seeing that my needs were covered, I continued.

How does CVC work?
CVC is offered in a "Journal-Response" format. The benefits of live, in-person interactions cannot be understated, but we are unable to offer the 24/7 staffing that this option requires. However, we have found that the anonymity and pace of Journal-Response offer benefits, as well.

CVC is self-care through virtual dialectic. What some participants call "Candid Venting" counseling often leads to discoveries that live conversation may quell. Stream-of-consciousness narrative writing, without counselor interruption, keeps control of the conversation primarily in the program participant's hands. Knowledge that neither the possessor nor the counselor might have thought available to find is often unlocked this way.

Who can see what I write?
CVC is confidential, in that participants will not have access to anything submitted by any other program participant. However, any and all correspondence posted to CVC becomes the intellectual property of Dr. Riley Chevalier, for the expressed uses described in the Waiver of Indemnification.

When shouldn't CVC be used?
This is not the appropriate resource if a participant seeks detailed responses to questions. Chevalier Virtual Counseling is not a replacement for crisis intervention or psychiatric help. It is not a substitute for meeting with a licensed mental health expert for issues that require professional care.

For whatever reason anyone decides to do anything after two in the morning, I clicked the button to sign myself up. The Waiver of Indemnity page loaded.

> "Chevalier Virtual Counseling does not provide any medical advice. This program is not intended, nor should it be used, to diagnose, treat, cure, prevent, or mitigate any illness, disease, or condition…"

I scrolled through the Waiver of Indemnity. Just as the FAQ described, CVC promised nothing in terms of results, protected itself against liability for any outcome, and described in detail the course of action to be taken should any diagnosable illness or a threat to self or others be suspected. I clicked the "I agree" button.

It was at that point that I realized that neither Frank nor Lloyd were lying at my feet any longer. Usually, my nights of insomnia were at least ones with the company of one or both of them at my feet.

Frank, the older of the two, was a chocolate brown with white patches around his snout, down his neck, onto his chest, and on the tops of his front feet. His pink skin showed through the fur in the white patches, especially where it thinned just under his nose and on his belly. He was about six years old, our veterinarian estimated. He was a sullen, gloomy, unresponsive dog when we had met each other in the fall after we lost Theodore, but he had grown to be a sweet, patient, and loyal companion.

Lloyd, on the other hand, can be summed up in one word: precocious. His entire body is covered with white fur, with pink areas similar to Frank's, except Lloyd's belly is spotted like a Dalmatian's. He has a dark patch over his right eye and the sweetest smile you've ever seen, on a dog or otherwise. Lloyd is about three years old, but he was all puppy. He ran wild and alone, starving and sick on a decrepit acreage west of Rockford before we rescued the summer after we adopted Frank.

Neither dog has any visible scars from their abuse. Frank's a little overweight, Lloyd's underweight, and each will probably always be. Both of their histories are about neglect, not the tragic tales you hear of dogfights, puppy mill breeding, and physical abuse, which, while very real, isn't the story of all rescue Pits. Even so, each of them was in rigorous training for about a year before his resocializing was complete. Frank and Lloyd are simultaneous reminders of the cruelty in this world and the power we all have to overcome it with the right support and a determined spirit.

I closed my laptop and went to find them. If they weren't by me, there was only one other place to look. Sure enough, they were crashed out on the couches.

"Boys…," I said in a clear voice, relaxed but firm. Lloyd perked up his ears and turned to look at me. "You know better," I told him. I couldn't help but say this with a smile on my face, but rules were rules. As I circled the back of the couch to sit down with them, Frank raised his snout from his crossed paws, the smallest acknowledgement of my arrival, before setting it back down and closing his eyes. I should have made them get down, but I couldn't stand to. I cuddled in among them and thankfully, finally, drifted off to sleep.

They woke me just a few hours later, around five o'clock. I let them out, watching them leap like husky deer through the accumulating piles of leaves. The honeysuckle bushes were growing wild, too, encroaching on the roses. Henry wanted to rip out the honeysuckle, but I liked it, even if it was basically a weed. I made a mental note that if we didn't get out to work on the lawn this weekend, we'd have to bite the bullet and hire a yard service before the snow fell.

~ ~ ~ ~ ~ ~ ~ ~

As Colette drove on, I thought about the time I had spent online overnight. I was, once again, too introspective to hear her ask, twice, whether I wanted to stop for coffee. "No, that's alright," I managed to sneak in before she did anything else to snap me to attention. "Since when do you drink coffee?"

"I don't, as you know. That sludge will kill you, but I don't need you driving off the road, either. Did you sleep at all last night, babe?"

"Eventually," I sighed. "I signed up for that Virtual Counseling you told me about."

"I'm glad, sugar. I'm looking forward to having my friend back. Except for your cute top and necklace, you look like hammered shit and are just about as much fun to hang out with."

We pulled into the diner parking lot as I grabbed my purse, briefcase, and gym bag before unlatching the seat belt. "Only you, Col," I said as I opened the door. "You alone get to say a thing like that and make me like you more. You are the best. I'll text you later."

She air-kissed my cheek as I hugged her as awkwardly as I had the night before. "'K, hon. Have a day!" she chimed as she patted my shoulder. I clicked the button on my car remote to unlock the hatch and tossed the bags in the back, waving as Colette peeled out of the lot.

5

My job isn't the glamorous public relations gig I had imagined while I was in college, or even the fast-paced, high-profile job I left in the city, but it's turned out to be a decent fit. Promoting the work of theoretical physicists has its appeal, even if it is a little egg-heady most of the time.

The Department of Energy is an unusual employer. It's the government, and some of what we do has military implications, so the utmost secrecy is maintained in some respects. We are, however, one of the most open and transparent organizations in the federal sector, on the whole. The amount of information we publish about the experiments conducted here is mind-boggling. Virtually the only limit on civilian access to information is the patience it takes to read and comprehend the bizarre vocabulary and dense technical language we speak. It's part of my job to write about our experiments and discoveries in a manner that is as accessible to the general public as possible. That's a tall task when you're writing about fermions, leptons, quarks (who can't appreciate the names of quarks like "charm" and "strange?"), and now bosons and muons. It has taken me a long time to tell my baryons from my neutrinos, and I still learn something new every day, after almost four years.

The focus is on the science, but our campus offers so much more beyond that. Several books have been written about the sculptures and architecture on the property, including the sleekly interpreted, Gothic cathedral-inspired Laboratory headquarters. The two office towers open to a soaring atrium between them. Fully-grown trees, koi ponds, and a full array of seasonal plantings give the building a botanic garden atmosphere. Only the outermost offices have walls and doors, a design feature that is supposed to impart a spirit of openness, breaking down the cloistered barriers limiting human knowledge. Actually, I believe that the openness is meant to keep people on task through positive peer pressure. It's hard to daydream when you can clearly see your chief competition at the next desk, hard at work.

We host all kinds of cultural events that are open to the public. Under my leadership, my department promotes these events, which include the full gamut of scientific symposia, but also include dances, blood drives, debates, and classes ranging from creative writing to martial arts. We have a wildlife sanctuary where nature walks are led year-round, a dog training field, a model airplane flight area, and a working farm that is home to a herd of bison. School field trips are scheduled a few times each week, and we host all kinds of competitions, exhibitions, and even concerts.

It is a wonderful place, but that is not to say that times have been easy. It has been as tough for us here at the Laboratory as it has been for anyone else in the last few years. At about the same time as a new particle, the bottom Omega baryon, had been discovered, the economy tanked and funding quickly evaporated. I had only been there a few months when I was asked to add a section to my newsletter that addressed involuntary separation and workforce reduction issues. Separations were handled with respect, including paid administrative leave, outplacement counseling for career transitions, and full insurance benefits for six months. This would be meager consolation for the non-technical staff, whose accounting, human resources, and administrative positions were among the best-paid jobs of their kind in the suburbs. For the scientists, most of whom were contractors from around the world, the situation, while unwelcome, was anticipated and not altogether unusual. Projects come and go, and no one enters this field with a high expectation of job security. As it stands, we are currently dismantling two facilities, but funding has recently been approved for four new projects. For a place dedicated to studying the beginning of time, there is, surprisingly, always something new going on.

It is practically impossible to walk into the building in a bad mood. By the time I pass beneath the arch at the entrance, drive through the groves of oaks and maples, and circle the reflecting pond where a towering obelisk stands at the center, the grandeur usually washes away most of the outside world.

Such was the case, thankfully, that Monday morning. It was supposed to be an easy day. All of the logistics for the visiting professor had been confirmed, the audio/visual equipment requisitions had been submitted, and the signage to direct the BattleBots students had already been posted when I walked inside.

I didn't make it very far before the Chief Operating Officer, my boss, flagged me down. "Mandelyn! Mandelyn!" She was clearly giddy about something which, while not out of character for the small, spry Indian woman, still had her in pretty boisterous spirits for a Monday morning, right out of the gate.

"Good morning, Dr. Adiraju," I said with genuine cheer. It was natural to address the doctor with joy almost any time we had the chance to speak, but especially so given her present countenance.

"I have incredible news. I couldn't be more excited."

I could see that. "Please, come in and tell me all about it! Just let me put down my bags."

She practically skipped into my office, a cube with hip-height walls around the perimeter and a lovely view of the autumn-tinged trees outside. I set down my gym bag and briefcase in their usual places and offered her a seat on a blue exercise ball that I had brought in to replace the Lab-issued knock-off Aeron chair. I perched on my own silver ball and turned my attention to her as she jovially bounced in place.

"You won't believe who is coming to speak at our Lab! Guess!" She put the palms of her hands together and tapped her fingertips to one another as if she were deviously scheming world domination.

I desperately wanted to avoid dimming her enthusiasm, so I guessed with care. "Um… is it any of the *New York Times* bestsellers?" We extend about ten invitations each month to all manner of recently published scientific authors on the list.

She deflated a bit. "No, but ever so much better. Guess again!"

I really didn't want to disappoint her. "Give me a hint. Is it a physicist?"

"He is *the* astrophysicist. The very one we've all dreamed about hosting!"

I almost fell off my ball. "Not…"

"Yes! Can you believe it?" She giggled, and I joined her with a scream of excitement.

"You can't be serious. This is magnificent!" Now, I was bouncing. I could have kissed Dr. Adiraju. I'm not at liberty to tell you who it is we booked for this event, but I can tell you that he is the preeminent science communicator of our time—basically, the John Lennon of the scientific world.

"I am serious, and because I am serious, you must be serious with me for a moment. You see…"

"What is it?"

"The Doctor will be here on twelve December. We have less than two months to plan."

"The keynote for Muon g-2?"

Pronounced "Moo-on Gee Minus Two," the soon-to-begin experiment and the facility built especially for it had occupied a lot of my time and energy over the last year. The experiment was designed to identify theoretical, unnamed subatomic particles that mysteriously pop in and out of existence for fractions of milliseconds.

By shooting a stream of muons, a kind of subatomic particle, through a vacuum, we hope to learn about the other unnamed particles by observing how the muons react. Picture a child's toy top spinning on a table, and then turning on a fan to blow at its side. The top would wobble while skidding away, skipping over imperfections in the table's surface. The top, in this analogy, is the muon. The fan is an electromagnetic accelerator. The imperfections that cause the wobbling are the unnamed subatomic particles.

The experiment had been launched at a Department of Energy facility in New York a decade before. Because the technology at our facility is more precise, the experiment was moved to us. The media ate up the press releases we issued about moving the equipment across the country. The 50-foot-wide particle storage ring—basically, an enormous magnet—had to travel via a custom-fitted barge. Over the summer, it had gone down the Atlantic seaboard, around Florida, through the Gulf of Mexico, up the Mississippi River, onto the Illinois River, and along the

RELEASE

Des Plaines River before traveling over land during three overnight-only road trips, to finally arrive a month after its initial departure.

I got little sleep during the summer, having spent every waking moment coordinating media interviews, feeding official photos to reporters, and responding to every inquiry both internal and external. For a magnet, it was a pretty big deal.

"I will get you the contact information for the Doctor's publicist and agent, Mandelyn," Dr. Adiraju said.

"I have it in my files, but thanks."

December twelfth was just nine weeks away. The logistics didn't frighten me. Several times during my tenure, we'd arranged lecturers' itineraries, visas, and receptions within forty-eight hours. The problem was PR. We already had our hands full with the Muon g-2 grand opening. The addition of an acclaimed keynote speaker meant we would have to work twice as hard to properly promote this event through all available channels.

I straightened my posture, realizing that I'd dropped my elbows to my knees and begun to clap my hands together in a scheming pose of my own. "My team is equal to the task. I will begin the preparations this afternoon, after the school tour is complete and the BattleBots competition is safely underway."

"I know you will, Mandelyn. IM me later, when you have the outline of your new campaign together." She said this with such warmth and ease, as if altering the multi-channel campaign that had already been months in development was as easy as snapping my fingers. I would have to delegate the tour and the BattleBots to my team or to a Laboratory intern, but nothing else mattered as much as this.

~ ~ ~ ~ ~ ~ ~

I arrived at home that evening after eight o'clock, laden with my bags and a box full of Muon g-2 architectural renderings and DVDs of past lectures given by the Doctor. Frank and Lloyd rushed to the door, so I set things down in a hurried mess to nuzzle their faces, scratching their ears and cooing.

Henry was half-dozing on the couch, feet resting on the reclaimed wood coffee table, his standard Koval white rye in hand, watching the

Blackhawks game. His backpack was open next to him, laptop and folded plans protruding from the top. "Hi," he vacantly tossed over his shoulder.

"What's the score?" I asked as I plodded into the room, standing behind him and leaning into the couch.

"Two all," Henry muttered, eyes fixed to the screen.

"Who's playing?"

"The Blackhawks," he said.

"I know that. Who are they playing?"

"The Stars," he responded in the same monotone.

"Where are they from?"

Henry sighed. "Dallas."

I took a long pause. "What period is it?" I asked, getting irritated. Did every conversation really have to be this hard?

He paused the game, as if providing an answer of more than two words required undivided focus. "Five minutes left in the second," he said.

I couldn't tell if he was just annoyed or something worse. I grunted an ambiguous response. Watching sports on TV really wasn't my thing. He knew that. I was making an effort, however feebly, to have a conversation with him, though, and he wasn't meeting me halfway. I thought I'd give it one last effort. "How was your day?"

Henry had already unpaused the game. "Fine. Busy," was his robotic response.

"Oh. How interesting!" I said sarcastically. I was done trying. My spirit felt small. I didn't want to be the kind of person who channels frustration into passive aggression. I went to pour myself a glass of wine and reheat some leftovers, if I could find any.

It wasn't fair that a simple exchange with Henry flattened me after such a good day. His actions weren't intentional. It was just that the crushing weight of his indifference was becoming harder and harder to bear.

Just as I had one hundred times before, I evaluated my will to say the words that one of us needed to say: We Need to Talk. Could I articulate my worries, my needs, and my feelings? I considered how much mental energy it would take to handle Henry's response. Was I prepared for the consequences? What if I got his signature stone face yet again? What if he said, "Fine. Looks like we're through," and he forced the conversation down that path? What if he had grievances of his own? Was I prepared to defend my own shortcomings?

Having been out for two evenings in a row, I knew my dinner prospects were bleak. While Henry did more cooking than I did, he prepared most of his meals in single servings. Our work schedules were too unpredictable to make dinners together happen very often, and making meals for two led to a lot of wasted food.

Thankfully, there was leftover beef stew, which, with a large glass of Shiraz, would reestablish some emotional equilibrium. At the least, I hoped, it would give me the fuel for some creative ideas for the campaign.

~ ~ ~ ~ ~ ~ ~

I awoke in my office at two-thirty in the morning. I'd fallen asleep on my folded hands, elbows splayed wide across strewn papers. My laptop had gone into sleep mode. Spirals of color looped lazily about the screen and lit the room with an eerie glow. The last remnants of stew had congealed in the bowl sitting just out of reach, and the last trace of wine had stained the bottom of the balloon goblet.

Frank slept at my feet, stirring to stare at me with a look of confusion before emitting a blustery, horse-like snort and resting his snout back onto his paws. Lloyd lay in the corner of the office, curled in on himself like a cat. Knowing I wouldn't be able to sleep if I didn't clean up the dishes first, I rose, collected the bowl and glass, and headed downstairs. In a zombie state, I rinsed out each, set them in the dishwasher, and, after taking a moment to wipe down the counter and square the canisters back into their proper places, I headed up to bed.

On the nights that I decided to attempt sleep in my bed, I did so with trepidation. Ignoring this added evidence of our flawed situation, I moved on to the next decision: what to wear. Ever since graduating from college and living on my own, I preferred to sleep in the nude. It wasn't an attempt to be sexy or anything, just comfortable. I'd even woken up some mornings as a kid, finding that I'd pulled off my pajamas in my sleep. To me, sexy meant something silky, pretty, and simple—like my go-to indigo satin chemise.

Henry was down for the count, thanks in part to the Koval. I wouldn't have to contend with his reaching over for me, I felt sure. Still, to avoid that scenario, I decided that sexless, impenetrable attire was called for. I pulled on sweatpants, a ratty college t-shirt, and large wool socks before tiptoeing to the bathroom to wash my face and brush my teeth.

Once done, I quietly snuck in under the covers. On cue, Henry, who typically sleeps on his back when I am not there, flopped away onto his right side. Just as always, I was simultaneously offended and relieved by this unconscious rejection. For all the women out there with insatiable husbands, mine was not one of them. This simple nocturnal gesture reminded me of something he had said several times over the years. "I like your sexual aggression, Mandelyn. It turns me on that I turn you on." I lay there, barely able to close my eyes, entirely unable to sleep, afraid to toss or turn for the hours until the sun rose again.

~ ~ ~ ~ ~ ~ ~

My CVC counselor assignment arrived by email the next morning. I would be writing to "Morgan," and an https address was included with the welcome message. Under the auspices of breaking through a mid-afternoon mental block, I closed my files, clicked the link, and began.

> Dear Morgan,
>
> I wonder if everyone in the CVC program feels as self-conscious as I do when they begin. I feel like someone is looking over my shoulder while I type. I actually backspaced and re-typed these opening sentences a few times before just surrendering to the idea of getting my thoughts on the page, no matter how scattered and raw they may be. Here we go.
>
> I learned about CVC from my friend, Colette, who heard your founder on the radio. I called Colette after nine o'clock Sunday night, frustrated about so many things, and asked her to meet me at a diner near my office that I correctly assumed would be vacant, a place where we wouldn't be disturbed.

I told her that I felt like a guest in my own home. I told her that my husband, Henry, made me feel inconsequential—no, I should correct myself. I *let* myself feel inconsequential in reaction to what he says and does. For whatever issues I have to work out, I own my emotions. No one makes me feel anything—I choose how I feel—but I find his comments toward me, his attitudes toward me, and, most of all, his pervading indifference about me, to be ample reason to justify my feelings.

I think I'm getting ahead of myself. I should tell you about Henry. We met on New Year's Eve, when he was a semester away from completing his dual Master's in Architecture and Civil/Environmental Engineering. I was impressed, but not nearly as impressed as I would be when I realized how hard he'd worked to earn it.

He is one month younger than I am, but because I skipped kindergarten, he was a year behind me in school. He graduated from Milwaukee South Division High School and started college part-time, putting himself through school by working as a laborer through the union hall for two years, earning money while taking night classes. His mother raised him on her own, working two jobs, sometimes three. I wish I could have met her. She died suddenly, from an undiagnosed glioblastoma, while he was a junior at Iowa State University.

I thought that I was sitting down to vent about all of the ways that Henry has let me down—rag about all his bad habits and the things he does that drive me crazy. Trust me, there's no shortage of things I could complain about, but having just written a synopsis of his background, it makes me feel petty to dwell on them. Sure, he doesn't communicate very well. He's a man, and not only am I a woman, but I am also professionally trained in communications. Not exactly fair. Sure, he doesn't show affection very well or handle intimacy in the way I'd like him to, but geez... What kind of role model would he have had for seeing how that's done, while growing up? His neighborhood wasn't the best, he had no extended family to speak of, and most of all, he had no father figure.

Henry has a fascinating family tree. In a word, he is Dutch, but he doesn't look like any Dutch man you've ever seen. I had never heard about it before I knew Henry, but there is a significant population of Cape Verdean people in the Netherlands. His mother's father was among the first immigrants from the small West African island to Rotterdam. Many more arrived in the 60s and 70s, but he was among the first itinerant Cabo-Dutch sailors to immigrate in the early 50s. He met his tall, blonde-haired, blue-eyed bride in the Netherlands when she was touring during college. The Cabo-Dutch family disapproved of the match, so they eloped and moved to her hometown of Chicago, soon giving birth to Hendrika, Henry's mother.

His father's mother was from Sint Maarten. She met her tall, blonde-haired, blue-eyed groom while he was on vacation there. They married and settled in the Netherlands, delivering Henry's father, Igmar, about nine months to the day after they met.

Henry's paternal grandparents, wishing for Igmar to see the world, reached out through their Catholic parish—a small, tightly-knit community in the Netherlands—to find host families in the States. Hendrika and Igmar fell desperately in love and soon conceived Henry, much to the chagrin of their parents. A marriage was imposed, and the couple moved north to Milwaukee, following a factory job for Igmar, but neither the job nor the marriage lasted past Henry's first birthday. Relations soured between the families, the marriage was annulled, and Igmar returned to Rotterdam, never to be heard from again. There are lots of things to point out about all this:

- Watching people try to figure out or ask "what Henry is" is an endless source of amusement, at least for me. Guesses range from Italian to Inuit, from Cherokee to Cuban.
- People assume that Henry got ahead in life because he's a minority, but he never "checked a box" or received any special treatment because of his ethnicity.
- Henry tells me that his mother was one of the most racist people he's ever known, despite her own mixed heritage. As Henry described it, she "passed" for white, her Caucasian

- genes being more prominent in her appearance than her Caribbean ones.
- Hendrika never remarried and, to Henry's knowledge, never even dated again after Igmar left her. Henry chalks that up to bitterness over the divorce and abandonment, although I have to imagine she had little time or inclination to date after working so hard for all those years.
- Henry didn't date until college, and even then he wasn't exactly prolific—at least I don't think he was. He says he never really had time, which I believe, except that I also think his mother's experiences poisoned his outlook on romance and intimacy.
- It hasn't escaped my notice that I bear a passing resemblance to his mother, surprisingly enough, given our different heritages. While I am the fourth generation of my family in the United States, I am 100% German. Unlike Henry's international ancestry, mine can be solidly traced to the island of Fehmarn in the Baltic Sea.

That may be enough for now. I've already blown off an hour of my afternoon and need to get back to work. I look forward to seeing where this goes. – M

It's hard to describe how I felt after I had written that down. Seeing it on the screen, it helped me to think about things from Henry's point of view. Who really thinks about someone's parents or grandparents when, for instance, they're angry that the shoes they left by the front door have been moved, yet again, to the mud room? Who gets all Freudian when they can't agree on keeping the furnace set at sixty-seven or seventy-two? Maybe I needed to be a little more understanding of Henry's upbringing when dealing with his foibles.

That is why I was surprised, as I drove home, to get an email from CVC with a one-sentence response from Morgan.

> It is my understanding that you seek assistance with your marriage. Thank you for the background information on your husband, but let's focus on you. How do you feel about the state of your marriage?

I was frustrated by reading that, at least at first. I thought I had been taking the high road by not criticizing Henry, and I didn't like that my words of respect and admiration had been so summarily dismissed. Later that evening, I sat on the couch under my oatmeal wool blanket while Henry watched the Ken Burns *Baseball* documentary and fiddled with his new tablet. I typed on my work laptop.

> Hi, Morgan,
>
> It took me a while to decide how to describe the state of my relationship with Henry. Here it is: if opposites really do attract, then Henry and I are the best-suited people for each other in the history of marriage.
>
> Here is just a summary of how our views and backgrounds are divergent:
>
> - Henry is Catholic, a relic of his Cape Verdean grandfather and Sint Maartener grandmother. I am a rather lackadaisical non-denominational Protestant.
> - Henry moved seven times growing up, never leaving Milwaukee. I lived in the same house all my life, until the day I left for college. I have only lived three places since.
> - Henry's home life was fractured, obviously, while mine was halcyon. My parents, Niklaus and Nadja, were high school sweethearts and loved each other every day of their lives until the day my father died. Although he ate more than his fair share of red meat, didn't exercise as he should have, and enjoyed cigars and drinks with friends multiple times a week, his passing was entirely unexpected—an acute myocardial infarction that took him in his sleep.
> - My father was buried on Leap Day, the first of my two tragic associations with that day. I'll describe my other association another time. Suffice it to say that the other reason I have to dread Leap Day is at the root of my disgust with the entire field of psychology.
>
> No offense, but as long as I'm on the subject, you should know my skepticism about psychiatry, from the most casual pop psychologist to the most venerated doctor. I haven't found one yet that doesn't fall into one of two camps—the "everything

you think or feel is a product of something your mother, father, camp counselor, or dog did to you" defeatist camp, and the "everything happens for the highest spiritual good, even when we can't possibly imagine what that is" camp of deluded Pollyannas. Neither type of shrink pays any heed to free will or self-determination, and every one of them jumps to pharmaceuticals—magic pills that promise to solve everything. I don't have time for people who blame their failings on circumstances in their pasts or capitulate to divine providence, fortune, karma, or what-have-you.

Anyhow, within the year of my father leaving us, my mom retired from interior decorating and moved to New Mexico. She couldn't bear how "haunted" Weston was, she said. She saw my dad everywhere she looked, and while she didn't want to forget about him altogether, she wanted to gain control over which memories would come to her and when. "Embrace the best and forget the rest," she said.

Even though I had been living on my own for years, my parents' sudden departure from my everyday life put my relationship with Henry on fast-forward. Until that point, we had both prioritized our careers. We were happy to see each other a few times each month, have a fallback date for parties, and have someone disease-free to sleep with without the hassle of seduction. I, especially, was happy to have someone to claim as my significant other when out with friends. "Nope, sorry, I have a boyfriend," was a very convenient thing to say at the end of a night out, and I preferred that it be true.

I've gotten off track. You asked what I thought about the state of my marriage. I could continue to describe the opposites, like that he is a morning person and I am a night owl, or that he went to Iowa State and that three generations of my family went to the University of Iowa. (This is a much bigger divide to bridge than you'd think). It's not the point. The fact is that I crave intimacy, and he is cold and distant. Over the years, I have grown, maturing in the face of life's challenges. Henry is exactly the same person as he was the day we met. Nothing fazes him.

> I don't know why that bothers me. It just does.
> It's late, I haven't taken the dogs for a walk, and God knows Henry won't do it. – M

The next morning, I checked my email while I drank my coffee and waited for an English muffin to toast.

> I would like to see more description of your emotions regarding your marriage, not just the superficial description of your qualities and his. How do you really feel about Henry?

I spat out my coffee and pounded my fist on the granite countertop. Morgan was one more email response from getting shitcanned, I decided. This was useless. How dare this lackey, wannabe shrink not read between the lines? It was all there. We were opposites in a lot of ways, but we'd found a respect, even a fascination, in one another that, if it hadn't died completely, was surely on life support. How was that not clear?

"You really do get what you pay for," I said aloud to Frank and Lloyd. I slammed the lid of my laptop shut, not bothering to turn off the computer properly, shoved it in my briefcase, grabbed my coat and purse, and, leaving the half-empty coffee cup on the counter and muffin in the toaster, stormed out the door.

6

All through high school, my boyfriend Joshua, his best friend (and mine, by extension) Sam Tierney, and I worked at Polly Ester's, a 60s-themed restaurant on the more rural but developing west side of town. Joshua's parents owned the place, which they opened when the end cap of the strip mall, which they had built as part of their real estate development company, Maines Street, couldn't find a tenant. Joshua said that their intention was to show the marketplace that the location could attract customers, and then they would sell the restaurant to anyone who showed interest.

Polly Ester's first neighbors included a fly-by-night nail salon, a cigarette outlet, and a pawn shop. It opened at a challenging economic time, Mr. Maines said, which neither Sam nor I really understood. It was a risky time to be in real estate, Joshua explained later. "Let's just call a spade a fucking shovel," he said. "The economy's for shit. Restaurants are risky, but real estate development's riskier." We had no reason to disagree.

It was pretty remarkable, then, that as traffic increased on the county highway, the nail salon made way for a full-scale higher-end salon, the pawn shop was replaced by a jewelry store, and the cigarette outlet became an independent bookstore, all within just a few years' time.

We loved Polly Ester's because we could eat there for free and the Maineses paid us under the table. We were able to schedule ourselves whenever we pleased, leaving the less desirable shifts for other servers.

By the time Joshua's parents should have been selling the place, Harry and Marcia Maines had come to love operating the diner. Rather than sell, they began phase two of the development. Construction was nearly complete on that autumn day when Sam and I went to get a bite before he had to be back at school for basketball pre-season conditioning and I had to be back for volleyball practice.

Sam and I had found ourselves alone together dozens of times. Joshua, in addition to football, basketball, and track, wrote for the school newspaper and served on the student government council. He was almost never free on weekday nights. That was the reason it hadn't seemed odd to me that Sam said we should get dinner together, even when he asked in an uncharacteristically humorless tone.

We sat at the restaurant—me, sipping on my favorite banana-chocolate-peanut butter shake while Sam let a plate of cheese frenchie and fries get cold. For some reason, conversation lulled.

"So what's up? How do you like your teachers this year? Is Mrs. Hooker as bad as everyone says she is? Man, can you imagine a last name worse than that? If I married Mr. Hooker—well, first of all, I'm pretty sure that I wouldn't marry a guy named Mr. Hooker, but if I did…"

"Manny, I have to talk to you about something."

"Duh, duh, duhhhhh," I sang in an ominous tone. "You're not sleeping with Mrs. Hooker already, are you?"

"Stop and let me talk, alright? Look, have you thought about Homecoming at all?"

"Well, yeah, of course I have. I bought my dress this summer when my Aunt Marcy and my cousins were in town. We went to the city to go shopping. It's three weekends away. Wait—have you asked anyone yet?"

"Has anyone asked you?" Sam asked.

"Joshua and I will go, of course. Who are you going to make our fourth? I sure hope you upgrade from Little Miss Overbite Thin Lips from last year. I spent the entire dinner wondering whether she'd manage to keep food in her mouth or if it'd tumble out."

"Joshua isn't going to Homecoming this year. That's what I need to talk to you about."

"Don't be a dumbass. Of course he's going. Pictures at the river gazebo, Polly's for dinner, the dance, and downtown after."

Every year, we went to the Tierneys' after Homecoming, because their basement was built out with cozy couches, a papasan, a big projection screen, and a pool table in the other room if we weren't in the mood to watch TV. This had been our routine since freshman year. The first time, it was a big group of people who all went as friends. Sophomore year, Joshua asked me, presumably as friends, although, as I found out later, he had just been too shy to make the leap from friends to more-than-friends. Sam took a freshman, the manager of the sophomore basketball team, a girl who moved back to Boston that next January when her dad was transferred. We went with two other couples, which made getting from place to place difficult. No one would get their license until second semester, so we had to get two sets of parents to haul us around in minivans. The other two couples ditched us at the dance, and so it was Joshua, me, Sam, and the Boston girl back at Sam's. That year, Joshua and I cuddled in the papasan and watched *Gigi* while Sam got to third base on the pool table.

Junior year had been the best Homecoming of them all, except that Sam's date was a last-minute pick. Right before the dance, he crashed and burned with his summer fling, a lifeguard named Annie who, I can admit, drove me crazy with jealousy. She was ridiculously beautiful, and the way Sam looked at her when she sat in her chair above the water was the way every girl wants to be looked at at least once in her life.

Over the summer, we all agreed that we'd make senior year the best ever, hiring a limo and going into the city to visit the Sears Tower or catching a Second City improv show after the dance. I was actually a little put-out by Sam dodging my question about finding a date. I couldn't believe he hadn't asked anyone yet.

"None of that is going to happen, Manny. Joshua doesn't know how to tell you. I gave him an ultimatum this afternoon. If he didn't tell you, I would." Sam was upset, and he wasn't trying very hard to hide it.

"Well, this is bullshit," I said with milkshake still in my mouth. "Since when can't he, the king of blunt honesty, just come right out and say anything to anyone?"

Sam looked to his left, toward the open kitchen and the counter area. Mr. and Mrs. Maines were hardly ever around the restaurant anymore. Since construction on the second phase of the development was wrapping up, their focus was there, and the restaurant had become stable enough over the years to hire full-time managers who resented our blasé attitude toward work and the degree to which we took advantage of the free food.

"Would you look at me, Sam? What is it Joshua can't tell me? I'm his girlfriend, for crying out loud, and I've known him even longer than you have."

"I can't tell you that. That is something I can't do for him. But you know, if you don't want to go with anyone else, I could take you. We should still go."

"What am I, some sort of charity case, Sam? I can find myself a Homecoming date. I'm not one of your dumb sluts, that you can take off your buddy's hands because he can't honor his commitment and won't bother to tell me about it." I could feel the milkshake solidifying in my stomach, and my hands had started to shake.

"He never asked you, Manny. We talked about some plans, but he never came right out and asked you."

"He didn't ask me last year, either, unless you count, 'Hey, we're still on for this year, right?'"

"Not the most courtly of invitations, but yes, that does count as asking, Manny. That's not the point."

"'Let's just call a spade a fucking shovel,' as Joshua would say. You're just hard-up for a date. Well, go find some other girl to put her feet in the air for you. Stop trying to do me any favors."

"I hate that expression of his. Anyway, I'm not trying to do you a favor, here. I think we'd have a good time, and there isn't anyone else I want to spend my last Homecoming with but you. You're my girl, Manny," he said, reaching diagonally to take my left hand in his.

"I am not your girl, Sam," I said, shaking free of his grasp. "I see how you treat your girls. If that's the way you think all girls operate, you've got a lot of growing up to do." I was done talking. "Let's get out of here. We have to get back to school."

"You're right. But the offer stands. You can't miss your senior Homecoming. Let me know what you decide."

I should have had more empathy for his position, but he had pushed me too far. "Oh, I'll let you know right now!" In a fit I regret to this day, I flung the last, milky, chocolate-chunky remains of my milkshake at his face and stormed out of the restaurant.

What seemed like a badass gesture in the movies was not a good idea in real life, especially when the person whom you've coated in milkshake is your ride. I was coming to that realization when I stepped off of the curb and started walking toward Sam's car, a Ford Crown Victoria that I called The Millennium Falcon—the fastest hunk of junk in the galaxy.

I also began to realize something else. Joshua wasn't just backing out of Homecoming. The look on Sam's face, as he told me what Joshua didn't have the guts to tell me, revealed it all.

My stomach bloated suddenly, and my legs felt wobbly. Without much time to spare, I sprinted around the corner, dropped to my knees, and vomited milkshake in the weeds. When Sam came up behind me, brushed my hair from my face, and held it at the nape of my neck, I didn't resist. I crumpled, my hands on my thighs, sitting on my heels, leaning into Sam's solid frame. He stroked my back, over my shoulders, down my rib cage, and down to the small of my back before tracing a strong, sure oval back to the top.

"Take me home, Sam. I can't go back to school. I don't know what's going on, but… but…"

"It's alright, Manny. Here." Sam handed me a napkin. I wiped my mouth. "I know."

~ ~ ~ ~ ~ ~ ~

I was home on Wednesday afternoon when Joshua came to see me. I had skipped school that day, pouting about not being able to play in my volleyball game after missing practice the night before.

Joshua must have headed to my house directly after the final bell. "Let's go for a walk," he said as soon as I answered the door.

"Sam told me," I said, standing motionless in the doorway.

Joshua was instantly livid. "He said he'd only tell you about Homecoming. I can't believe he would…" Something on my face must have told him that he had misunderstood what I had said. "Wait. He did only tell you about Homecoming, right?" He was squinting, and he seemed short of breath.

"You need to start talking. Yeah. Let's go for a walk," I said, my voice bereft of any emotion.

We headed south down River Lane to the trail entrance, continued along the path suspended under the railroad tracks, turned to pass the dam, and followed the river toward the old windmill. It was a walk we had taken together at least a hundred times over the years. Sometimes, even as kids, we held hands, but most of the time, like now, we just walked side by side.

"Where do you want me to begin, Mandy?" He never called me Mandy. At least, he hadn't called me that since first grade, when I threatened to punch him in the gut if he didn't stop. Manny, Man, or M were his standards.

"Oh, I don't know. When did you decide not to go to Homecoming? Why did you send Sam to do your dirty work? Maybe most important—what else is going on, J? You two are acting so strange, all of a sudden."

"Well, if you really think about it, I've been acting weird for a while," Joshua said, with a distance in his voice that made me look his way. He didn't make eye contact.

"You're not talking about Labor Day weekend, are you?" I admonished him. "Joshua, it's forgotten. Can you imagine how gross it would be to have that be the story of our first time? I can't believe we even got that far."

"So it doesn't bother you that I couldn't manage to get it up when we were that far into it up there?"

"Up there" was the Girls' School cemetery, the site of our first kiss and a dozen or more thrilling and frightening weekend nights with friends through junior high and high school. That night, as much out of habit as anything else, we had gone there just to be alone and talk.

We talked about senior year that night—how we'd each ascended to the leadership positions to which we'd always aspired, and how we'd finally be able to do the things we'd always wanted to do. Joshua hadn't won the student council presidential election, but he was a captain of the football team and an editor of the school newspaper. I was a captain of the volleyball team and, once debate season began that winter, I would lead that club, as well.

Each of us was feeling overwhelmed by the AP classes on our schedules. I had English and U.S. History. Joshua had Calculus, Biology, and Chemistry. The teachers usually didn't allow students to take two AP science classes at one time, but Joshua's parents had petitioned for an exception and won. Joshua was sure that the teachers were singling him out to make an example of him, so he was determined to prove them wrong with straight As through the rest of the year.

We talked about college applications and wondered whether our parents would allow us to go on school visits together, without them there to chaperone. We reasoned that if we arranged for separate housing on campus, they would probably go for it. Our parents were close friends, and even after we had been together for two years, they never acknowledged it as a romantic arrangement. As far as they were concerned, he and I were still the dirt-smudged kids who spent every free moment riding bikes up and down the street and fishing in the river.

Neither of us wanted to go very far away for school, and neither of us wanted to go anywhere too big, but that is where the similarities ended. We had already determined that we'd probably end up at different schools. I was getting pressure to go to the University of Iowa like my parents, but I wanted to go where I could get a lot of time playing Division III volleyball and also prosper in a highly-ranked marketing and communications program. Joshua wanted either a pre-med or engineering degree from a Division I-A or strong-showing Division II school, but hadn't decided which sport he'd choose. Football and basketball coaches from more than a dozen schools had been in touch.

We reminisced about the summer—the concerts, the pick-up softball games, the trips to the beach, the carnivals, the shifts at Polly's, and all the walks, movies, card games, cookouts, and other little things. We laughed about elementary and junior high school memories. We remembered the people we'd known—especially those who'd moved away.

We discussed our future, how safe we felt with one another, and how we would always be there for one another. We kissed. I melted into his big, strong, safe arms, and everything in the world felt perfect. Feeling like the opportunity was presenting itself, I made a move past our usual make-out routine, reaching to unbuckle his belt.

"What are you doing? Here? I don't know if it's dark enough, yet. Someone might see."

"Not through the honeysuckle. It's grown so high and thick it's like a castle wall," I assured him.

"Funny about honeysuckle. It's invasive. People leave it because it smells so nice, but it doesn't take long before it grows out of control—starves and kills everything else around it."

"Less botany, more chemistry… Come on…," I begged.

He seemed to relax a bit as we continued to kiss. I opened the clasp of my bra for him, removing it from under my loosely-fitted sundress. Raising the stakes, I decided to slide my panties off, as well.

"Mandelyn… I don't know. On the ground? Without a blanket? Sounds uncomfortable."

"The night is perfect. Can you think of a better way to commemorate the summer?" I guided his hand up my thigh and placed it so he couldn't mistake how eager I was to make this a night we wouldn't forget.

I reclined on my right elbow and pulled him to me with my left hand. As I opened my legs to receive him, he set his knees between them with obvious trepidation. I took my hand from his neck, and, letting a single finger trace down his chest, arrived again at his open buckle. I rotated my wrist to slide my hand into his jeans.

This time, Joshua really did pull away, not abruptly, but definitively. "I'm nervous, Mandelyn. This isn't right. Not here. It's not how I want to remember you. This is not how we should have this moment etched in our minds."

He could see that I was disappointed, but I finally agreed. The sun had just set, and lights in the houses nearby had begun to appear. The grassy ground, overgrown and weed-choked, was beginning to feel damp as the temperature fell. We left the cemetery without a lot of conversation, and Joshua drove me home.

I reconsidered the events of that night, just one week before, as we continued walking toward the windmill. Fall had already begun to set in since then. The air was cooler, and the leaves had begun to lose their emerald brilliance. A few had fallen to the ground. I thought about the contrast between that night and the afternoon before answering his question. "Of course, it doesn't bother me. I didn't know you couldn't manage to… You don't remember. You pulled away from me before I noticed anything about you being ready, physically or otherwise."

Joshua shook his head. "We have been together for almost two years, Mandy. Haven't you ever wondered why it hasn't happened before now?"

"What are you trying to say, Joshua? I'm tired. I don't have the patience to draw any more out of you."

"I'm gay, Mandy."

I was silent for a moment as my mind jumbled. "That's derogatory. I think you're behavior is stupid, too, but…"

I stopped. We stood there, motionless, as the full weight of what Joshua had said finally sank in, for both of us. His face relaxed a bit. Mine stiffened.

"What do you mean?" I knew exactly what he meant. To Joshua's credit, he didn't answer my question, but steadfastly locked me into eye contact.

"Oh, my God, Joshua. Is this what Sam meant when he said there was something only you could tell me? Is this why he was the one to tell me…? Is he?"

"No, no, no, no, no… Come on—Sam?"

"But you? How? With the football and the basketball and the… girlfriend, Joshua?"

"I don't have any good answers for you," Joshua said, holding his hands out and shrugging. "It's the reason I've waited so long to tell you. I thought that if I could figure out the right words to use when explaining it, if I could really understand it myself, then it would somehow be easier. The thing is that there is no explanation, Mandy. I just am."

"Stop calling me Mandy. Don't use that name. My parents are the only two people in this world who get to call me that. You don't get to use that name with me."

"Mandelyn…"

I looked up at the windmill. It had fallen into such disrepair. The historical society women were always throwing bake sales, jewelry shows, craft fairs, and a seemingly endless stream of other fundraisers, hoping to pay for its restoration.

"How long have you known?" I asked, not looking at him.

"Forever, I think. When I was little, I knew I was different; I just didn't know how. When every other boy in second grade thought girls were gross, I thought girls were alright. When every other guy in seventh grade thought girls were awesome, I didn't see what the new appeal was about. When I wanted you to be my girlfriend, it was because I loved you. I've always loved you, Mandelyn. I admire you, I respect you, and you make me so happy. It was because of you that I was able to deny who I am for so long."

"Oh, gee. Thanks. Or, I guess I should say, 'You're welcome.'" Sarcasm was not my strong suit, but it was the best comeback I had at the moment.

"I tried everything to make this go away, but nothing works. I kind of hate myself for it. It's beyond my control."

"Of all the people who seemed to know themselves, Joshua… Shit, most of the kids in our class have no idea what they want to do with their lives. They're lemmings, following one another to the University of This-or-That, or to St. Whoever College." I was shouting, now. "You're one of the few people who seemed to get it—'to thine own self be true,' and all that. Don't you see? It's the reason I love you. You're not like anyone else I've ever known."

"You've got that right."

"Don't joke. I'm angry at you. If you denied who you are, it wasn't because of me. You can't put that on me. That's all on you." As I heard the words out loud, I could hear how hollow they were. I wasn't angry at Joshua, except about not feeling comfortable enough to tell me sooner.

"You've never been any good at staying mad at me for long," he said.

"I have so many questions. I really have no idea where to start," I mumbled.

"You wouldn't be Manny if you didn't."

"Do you… have crushes or… something?"

"Well, let me ask you this. Do you want to get on every single guy that walks the halls of Weston High School?"

I laughed in spite of myself. "No! Honestly, if it weren't for you, I don't know who I'd want as a boyfriend at our school. There's a lot I'm going to miss about high school, but the dating pool is not on the list."

"Then you know what I'm dealing with."

"Who else knows?" I asked. "Have you told your parents yet?"

"Just you and Sam. I was going to tell you first, except Sam called me on it before I had the chance."

"When was that?"

"Labor Day. I was telling him about our Saturday night at the cemetery. Don't get mad, Man. If you haven't figured out by now that we talk about you all the time, you're not as smart as I thought you were. He really laid into me, asking what could possibly be wrong with me for not, um, consummating things with you."

"Those aren't the words he used. Come on. What did he say?"

"It was really eloquent. You would have been impressed. Let me see, it was something along the lines of, 'Every guy in school would kill to nail your girlfriend, and you can't seal the deal. You're even gayer than I thought.'"

"Classy."

"Yeah, but I know an opportunity when I see one, especially when it comes to a set-up for a punch line. I said, 'Yeah, I thought I was just regular gay, but you know me—overachiever—turns out I'm actually super-gay.'"

I punched Joshua in the shoulder. "You are not supposed to be cracking me up right now! I'm supposed to be all heartbroken, or devastated, or something."

"You're not, though. I see I'm very easy to get over. I don't know how to feel about that."

"I don't know how I feel yet. I feel lied to, but I don't exactly feel betrayed, or anything. Wait a minute. Have you… done, you know, anything… with anybody?"

Until that moment, we had been standing, facing one another, close enough to touch, except that my arms were folded across my chest. Joshua unwound my hands and took them in his.

"Never. I would never do that to you. Cheating is cheating, no matter the circumstances. For all of the stuff that is hard about this, breaking up with you is going to be the hardest thing of all."

"Your mom is going to be pissed. She loves me."

"Believe me, I know."

We stood there for a while, in the shadow of the windmill, before I spoke again. I looked at our intertwined hands and thought that it would probably be the last time we'd touch each other exactly this way. I looked up into his eyes to see that he had been just as transfixed by our hands.

"You know, just because of… this… we can still go to Homecoming together, you know, as friends. Lots of people go as friends."

"I thought about that. The thing is, I feel like I've already wasted enough of your time. I don't want your memory of senior Homecoming to be with your gay ex-boyfriend."

"You'd rather give me a memory of going with my gay ex-boyfriend's best friend?"

"Wait. What? What are you talking about?"

"Sam. He told me yesterday that he thought we should go together. Sam and me, I mean."

"That dumb slut." He dropped my hands and began to pace. "What, has he been waiting in the wings all this time for his chance, like some sort of first runner-up?"

"Beauty pageant terminology. Really original, Joshua."

"Don't joke. Seriously. Just because our break-up isn't exactly happening in a traditional way, that doesn't mean that he gets to sweep in and take his best friend's girl."

"I don't think it's like that."

Joshua got himself worked up about this. "When, in all the time that you've known Sam, has he ever been just friends with a girl? Besides you, of course."

"That's not even the point. What are you, jealous?"

"Damn right, I am. Look around, Man. Do you see a lot of gay men wandering around Weston? I don't personally know anyone else who is gay. Do you? I'm losing you, Manny, and I can't help it. My best friend doesn't get to pick up the pieces."

"Okay. For one, I'm not in pieces. I'm not saying that I've fully processed this news yet, but I'm going to be just fine. Don't you worry. Second of all, I was never 'your girl.' I'm not anyone's to own, just like you were never 'my guy.' That's why you and I worked, Joshua. We didn't lord anything over one another. We weren't that awful couple with our hands in each other's back pockets during passing periods, or that couple making out in the parking lot after school. We were two independent people who cared about one another, and supported one another, and made each other laugh."

"We are still those people, Mandelyn."

"Maybe we will be something like those people to each other again sometime in the future, but we don't get to be those people to one another right now. Everything is going to be different between us. I'm not going to spend my senior year moping around waiting for something to happen, wondering if you're going to change your mind, or wishing I'd done anything differently. What did you say earlier about wasting my time? You haven't wasted anything, Joshua, but I'm not wasting my time with your opinions about who I should go out with after you. You never had that kind of say-so in my life. It sure as hell isn't going to start now."

"So let me make sure I understand this. Within ten minutes of hearing what, I think—not to pat myself on the back too much—think must be pretty devastating news, you make the super-independent, feminist, self-sufficient decision to seek your comfort in the arms of the first guy who offers you a little kindness. You could be on the cover of *Ms.* magazine, Manny."

"Fuck you, Joshua. That's not what I'm doing. All I'm saying is that you don't get a say in this. It's my decision." I took a moment to catch my breath. "Besides, I didn't leave things very well with Sam yesterday. He's surely moved on to finding someone whose legs are double-jointed or whose boobs defy physical law."

Joshua, much to my relief, smiled. "Well he is a dumb slut, but he's our dumb slut. Don't be too hard on him. You're right. He was probably at a loss for words after delivering my news to you. God, I'm such a coward."

"You're not a coward. What you've done has taken a lot of courage." I couldn't believe what I was saying and, looking at Joshua, could see he couldn't believe it, either. "I'm still a little shell-shocked, but I'll come around. There are a lot of courageous things you're going to have to do in the next few weeks and months. This news isn't going to stay quiet for long. You're going to need someone to be there for you through it all. I'll be there, and so will Sam. It's what we do."

We hugged each other fiercely for a long time before Joshua whispered into my hair. "What did you mean when you said you didn't leave things well with Sam yesterday? What did you say to him?"

"I accused him of treating me like a charity case and a slut, and then I threw my milkshake at him."

"That's my girl. I love you, Mandelyn."

"I love you, too."

It was getting late. We walked, watching as sparks of red and orange light shimmered over the ripples in the river while the sun set. For the first time in a long while, we held hands the entire way home.

7

Thursday, October 13

Morgan,

It took me a few days to process your directive. It made me mad, but I finally see that you're right. I was talking left brain instead of right, head instead of heart. The closest I got to talking about my feelings was at the end, when I said that I find Henry to be cold and distant and that I have needs.

I do have needs. I need passion. I need a partner. I need what my college friend Dante called a *simpatica*.

Ah, Dante Abatangelo. Now that was a guy who understood passion. He was not the kind of guy you could bring home to Mother, but he sure seemed to know how to get to home base.

Dante came from a prominent family on the south side of Des Moines, Iowa. For generations, his family ran a produce and meat distributor that supplied every good restaurant within two hundred miles, as far as Kansas City, Omaha, Minneapolis, and the Quad Cities. A few of his cousins had attended college, but they had earned degrees intended for use in the retail, office operations, or agronomy sides of the business. Dante intended, he said, to make his own way.

Before I knew him, however, "his way" seemed to be drinking, playing intramural rugby, blowing off class, and charming an impressive if nauseating number of girls out of their panties and self-respect. At least guys like my high school friend Sam had wit to back up their boasts. Dante seemed like the kind of guy who skated by on movie quotes, filthy jokes, and pick-up lines so lame your IQ would drop a point just to hear them.

You are probably wondering how a guy like Dante would end up a friend of mine. Needless to say, we ran in different circles in college, which is pretty hard to do on a campus of fifteen-hundred students. We didn't meet until my junior year, when I reluctantly accompanied Mary, a teammate and friend from my dormitory floor, to a fraternity party where she wanted to find Ben, a guy who she liked from our American Lit class.

I had nothing against the fraternities, specifically; many of my friends were affiliated. The system had its appeal, but volleyball, debate, and the radio station occupied so much of my time that sorority life seemed more like a distraction than anything else.

It wasn't going to the party that I minded; it was Mary's ulterior motive. I knew that Mary and Ben were bound to hook up, and I would be ditched to either find others to hang out with or, preferably, walk home before eleven o'clock. I had a self-imposed curfew because I had a game the next day and a lot to read for class on Monday.

So there I was, in Ben's room, arguing with him about the new Radiohead album, getting the "get lost or at least tone it down" stink eye from Mary, when in sauntered Dante. He was shirtless, wearing only silk boxers and a frighteningly short azure and chartreuse tie-dyed silk kimono, barely closed and belted between sternum and navel.

"Hi, Ben. Ladies," he said, as if nothing at all was unusual. He collected a bottle of Bombay Sapphire and a box of Macanudos from Ben's closet and, with a never-mind-my-interruption wave, turned and left like a psychedelic, pantless White Rabbit.

"To the victor go the spoils, MVP," Ben called after him. Dante waved in acknowledgment but without turning back or breaking stride.

"Winner?" I asked.

"Rugby. 23-19 over SAE today," he replied, surprised that this appeared to be news I didn't know.

As good a lead-in as that is to a story I should share another time, I have gotten off track. The prurient details of what followed in the night, weeks, and months after my first encounter with Dante aren't germane to the purpose I had for bringing him up. Without a doubt, Dante was easily the sexiest man I had been with to that point, despite that, from all outward appearances, he was absolutely not my type. Joshua was lanky and graceful, long mousy brown hair swept across his brow. As for Sam, it's still a mystery how his orange-red mullet and freckled ivory skin didn't repulse girls back in the day. His charm, not to mention his brawny Scot frame and stormy green eyes, carried him until hormones let his hair evolve to auburn, the freckles faded, and good sense prevailed with the party-in-the-back.

Dante was dark Southern Italian, pretty much the opposite of the Iowa farm boy whose clones dominated campus—the boys who would two-step you in one song and grind up on you in the next. Not that that couldn't be a nice, if slightly sordid, way to spend an evening... Dante was a frat guy through and through, yet he wouldn't have been caught dead in the basement where such dancing, if you could call it that, occurred.

The gin, cigars, and the kimono stirred a curiosity that drew me into the hall, much to my surprise and Mary's delight. I wasn't much of a drinker, especially during volleyball season, but the only other place I'd seen Macanudos was in my father's humidor, and Bombay Sapphire was as unexpected as Dante's attire. I was drawn by the absurdity more than the desire to partake of any of it.

I've gone off on a tangent again. My point is that Dante was circuitous and forthright all at the same time. He was familiar and exotic simultaneously. His spontaneity had a strategic undertow, which he used to pull many people under his spell. When you felt the intensity of Dante's attention, everything else just faded away.

So how do I feel about the state of my marriage, Morgan? I feel sad that I don't think I'll ever have that kind of spark with Henry. By this stage of my life, I should be satisfied with stability, maturity, and sincerity, but celibacy is not going to cut it for the rest of my days. Sex with Henry is always fine, just not sheet-rippingly passionate. He is considerate and selfless in bed. I'll give him that, at least. Is this just my dirty-thirty mid-life crisis? Let me know so I can budget for a sports car and a boob job. – M

The response from Morgan only took about an hour.

> Describe your first sexual experience. When did you lose your virginity, and to whom?

Morgan had to be a dude, I thought. No woman would ask another woman a question like that. I finally understood why CVC used gender-neutral names. Once I had the picture of a male reader in my mind, my writing would inevitably slant to that audience.

What difference did it make—how I lost my virginity—to the state of my marriage, anyhow? I have to admit that I was a little aroused by the idea of anonymously describing my first times to someone I would never have to see in real life.

Henry and I never talked about our first times. It occurred to me about four months into our relationship, and I meant to bring up the subject at the right opportunity. As time went on, I never got around to asking. It became too awkward.

I was being blatantly irresponsible with my time that workday afternoon, but the temptation to respond right away was too strong to resist.

> Dear Morgan,
>
> Which story do you want?
>
> Technically, my first time was with Sam, who I haven't spent a lot of time describing to you. In a nutshell, he was my high school sweetheart's best friend. Joshua, the sweetheart, came out to me before Homecoming senior year, after we had been together for almost two years. Joshua and I attended the same preschool and lived two doors down from one another for our whole lives. We met Sam in first grade, and the three of us were pretty much inseparable from that point on.
>
> In a long story I can write another time, Sam and I ended up going to Homecoming senior year as friends. He took me to River Run for dinner, a fancy place that hosted a lot of weddings and banquets. All the previous years, we had gone to Polly Ester's,

a nostalgia joint owned by Joshua's parents that was known for its burgers and old-timey soda fountain. We figured that it was just as well not to have dinner right under his parents' noses, even though they had been really cool and supportive of Joshua's revelation.

We watched *Joe Versus the Volcano* afterward. I won't spoil the movie for you if you haven't seen it. It's a movie about taking chances and finding love when pushed to extremes. Sam, Joshua, and I watched it together the spring of sophomore year, so we already knew the storyline. Sam and I talked more than we watched the movie.

The problem with going to a fancy place, as we found out, was that the portions were tiny. By the time the dance was over, we were famished. We cleaned out Sam's parents' cupboards of chips, popcorn, cookies, and everything else we could get our hands on. The picnic lay strewn across the table, which we faced on adjacent sides from our seats on the sectional couch. I sat, shoeless, legs askew. Sam sat, tie untied but still secured beneath his collar buttons, with his shirt half-open to a faded sleeveless Weston High School Sophomore Basketball shirt, his suspenders off his shoulders and around his haunches.

We steered clear of talk about Joshua, although his absence loomed over the whole evening. Most of our conversation dwelled on petty gossip, namely the apparel and the behavior of the other dance attendees. At a time between disparate fashion trends, we were finally beginning to get some perspective on the fads of the last decade, but that wisdom hadn't yet reached the majority of our classmates. Tall hair, lace, and puffy shoulders abounded for both genders.

Sam was the one with the guts to finally broach the subject of Joshua. "I just want to make sure you had a good time tonight, Manny—I mean, Mandelyn." I had insisted earlier in the evening that he had to call me by my full name. I thought it'd be weird for people to overhear my Homecoming date calling me something you'd sooner call a plumber or a mechanic. "You deserve it, after everything you've been through."

"What I've been through? Jeez, it's nothing," I assured him. Sure, Joshua and I were still a little awkward, but I was totally fine. I had quit my job at Polly's, though. Joshua's mom seemed sad to see me, and I didn't know how to act around her.

Sam had left soon after, too, what with basketball season approaching, or at least he said that was the reason.

I remember being swept up in the moment and blurting out, before I thought better of it, "You know, it's a little too early to ask, but have you thought about prom at all?"

"I gladly accept your chivalrous, debonair proposal, my liege," Sam said with a hilariously pompous English accent.

"Those words all describe dudes, dumbass," I teased.

"You are practically a dude, if you haven't noticed, M. Have you looked at how you're sitting right now? Is your junk hangin' free? You comfy?"

I made an impossibly unfeminine gesture, reaching up into my crinoline to grab my phantom "junk" in response.

"Always a lady. Oh, speaking of bad behavior! Did you see how Jim and Darcy were dancing over on the far end of the cafeteria?" Sam hopped over the table and into the open space on the floor, tearing his button-down shirt off and flinging it against the back of the couch. He lay down, lounged seductively, and said, "They reminded me of that scene in *Dirty Dancing*. The one in the studio when Johnny's wearing that undershirt and jeans, you know? 'Oh, Sylviaaaa...'"

"Yes, Mickey?" I laughed so suddenly that the Coke I was drinking went up my nose and burned my sinuses.

"How do you call your loverboy?" Sam sang.

I stood, pantomiming Baby's little seductive dance by the screen. "Come 'ere loverboy!"

Sam was getting up onto his knees. "And if he doesn't answer?"

I walked toward him. "Oh, loverboy..."

Sam was standing now. "And if he still doesn't answer?"

His voice had changed. He wasn't playing around anymore. A little bewildered, I continued, "I simply say..."

Sam stopped me with a kiss. Maybe because it was unexpected, or, more specifically, because he had different expectations than mine, but it was not a good start to a kiss. Our teeth banged together, and with him in his dress shoes and me without mine, I was a good five inches shorter than he was. He held my head in his left hand as he stooped to reach me. My head was tipped back uncomfortably. Slowly, we adjusted, and I realized just how soft his lips were against mine. I let my lips part and my mind go, kissing Sam back as he stroked my hair with his right hand.

He walked me back toward the couch. It was when he made the move to unzip my dress that I finally got some sense back in my head. "We can't... I mean, we shouldn't."

"Mandelyn, I love you." I must have stiffened against him in opposition, but he continued. "I know that sounds crazy, but I have loved you for so long, it hurts to think about it. I didn't think it would ever happen, so I tried to move on and forget about it, but it's always been you."

I couldn't form a sentence. "But you, and... We don't..." I had to sit down, sinking into the couch. Sam knelt before me.

"Tell me you don't want to, and we won't. Tell me you haven't thought about it, even once, and we'll stand up, go upstairs, and I'll take you home." He sighed, seeming to come to the conclusion that that was my inevitable response. "I know this isn't how you pictured your Homecoming, Mandelyn," he said, sounding dejected and looking away.

Something possessed me, and I turned his face back toward mine. "You're right. It's not how I pictured it, Sam. It was better. You made me feel like a princess tonight. You made me feel..." I paused to think of exactly the right word. "Desired. At dinner, and while we danced. How you looked at me. It was... nice."

Then things started to happen. We were kissing again, he was unbuckling, and I was getting out of my panties, which was no easy feat with the taffeta and crinoline splayed out all around me. He reached up under my dress and touched me with his fingertips, but I flinched at the contact. "You know that I haven't… I mean… Joshua and I did stuff, but we never…"

"Shhh," he said soothingly. "It's okay. We can go slow. I want to go slowly with you." Sam glided his hands over my thighs, and I shivered.

"Are you on the pill?" he whispered.

"Of course I'm not," I whispered back. "Why would I need to be on the pill?"

"A lot of girls take it for acne or to control headaches, or at least that's what they tell their parents."

"Well, I don't get headaches, and I don't have acne."

"That's why I assumed you were on the pill."

"I'm not," I said and began to straighten up.

"No—wait. I've got a condom." He jumped up, finding himself hobbled by his pants around his ankles. He pried his shoes off his heels without untying them and shuffled out of the pants before leaping into the other room like a gazelle. In an instant, he had returned, waving a gold coin in his hand.

"Look at you, Boy Scout, all prepared," I teased.

"Well, you have these ideas about how something might happen someday, and getting ready for the possibility is part of the fun."

"How many rubbers do you have stashed around here? Is every little nook in your house filled with gold coins, like some dirty Mario Brothers game?"

Sam laughed, but he quickly recognized the disgust on my face and rapidly recanted. "No! No, no, no. It's not like that at all. Look, as much shit as you guys give me about the girls I date…"

"Your use of the word 'date' is pretty loose. Come to think of it, so are your girls," I said.

"That's not fair, and it's not true. If you don't want to do this, I really understand, but don't turn your decision around and blame it on me being something I'm not."

"That's not what I'm doing. I don't know. Maybe it is." I thought for a moment before continuing. "How many girls have you been with, anyway? I mean, how many have you actually had sex with?"

"One," he whispered. "Annie. Last summer, at the end of the season. She broke up with me a week later."

"Oh, I'm so sorry. Really. I didn't know."

"Joshua is the only one who knows, and I told him I'd nail his ballsack to a tree if he told anyone."

"Descriptive," I said.

It was a combination of the fancy dinner, the dance, and, more than I acknowledged at the time, me wanting to one-up Annie. It was also, I think, some way of reaching closure with Joshua, as weird as that sounds. I kissed Sam, fumbling with his boxers to take them off. He was trembling as he pried the foil wrapper off the condom but put it on quickly enough. I reclined onto the couch, still in my dress. He planted his left hand to my side as he jostled through the skirt to reach me. He stroked my clitoris with the tip of his penis for a little bit, and I moaned reflexively. Sam smiled as he carefully guided himself into me.

Then, the doorbell rang. Sam withdrew just as slowly as he had entered and began to press into me again when the doorbell rang a second time.

"It could be those jerk neighbor kids ding-dong-ditching you again," I reassured him as I put my right hand to his chest.

"Yeah, or it could be those tools who said they were going to teepee tonight. If my parents come home and our yard is trashed, they are going to kill me." He pulled out and was on the floor, trying to find his pants.

"Don't worry. I'll go. I'll just go tell them to get lives and fuck off."

"You've got such sweet pillow talk, Manny," he said. "Okay, sure—I'll be here."

I ran upstairs as the doorbell rang a third time. Passing a mirror in the foyer, I glanced to see that my makeup was smeared a little bit but passable. On the other hand, my hair was a wreck of tangles.

I looked through the peephole and couldn't believe who was there. "Joshua?" was all I could manage to say once I opened the door.

He looked desolate. "Hi. I knew you guys would be here. Did you have fun tonight?"

"I, um, well..." For just a moment, I wondered whether Joshua had noticed my hair or smudged lipstick before I decided to take a different tack. "Of course I did. You were right. It was better that we didn't go as friends."

Joshua looked from side to side, fighting back tears. "I'm glad, Mandelyn. That's what I wanted for you." He began to step away from the door before I realized how cruel I probably sounded.

"Joshua. Stop. I'm sorry. That wasn't nice. Of course I would have rather had you there, too. Sam and I got on alright without you, though. That's all I was trying to say."

"What are you watching?" he sniffed.

"*Joe Versus the Volcano.*"

"Oh, yeah? Say, I know this might be a little weird, and you can totally say no, but do you think it'd be alright if I came in and watched it with you guys?"

I panicked, thinking of my panties on the basement floor and Sam sitting half-erect and pantless, waiting for me to return, but didn't know what else to say. "Sure, I guess."

"Where's Sam?" Joshua asked as he came inside.

I closed the door behind him. "He was, um, messing around with some of the wires in the TV. The tint on the screen wasn't quite right."

"Oh, yeah. I hope we didn't screw up the system when we were messing around with roundhouse kicks last week."

I didn't have any idea what he was talking about. The days of the three of us hanging out together were coming to an end.

"Could be," I said as I opened the door to the basement and called out loudly, "Guess who's here. It's Joshua! I said it was alright for him to watch the movie with us."

As I scanned the scene, everything seemed back to normal. Sam had his pants back on, the foil wrapper was nowhere to be seen, and his shirt was not only fully buttoned, but his tie was tied, and his suspenders were back on his shoulders.

"J! Hi! I'm glad you came by!" Sam said with almost too much enthusiasm. "Manny and I were just talking about how it wasn't right without you here."

"Geez, bro, loosen up. Party's over," Joshua said as he loosened Sam's tie and snapped his suspenders.

The rest of the night was among the more awkward I've ever experienced, sitting there between the two of them, watching a movie we'd all seen together just over a year before under very different circumstances. I could swear that the hint of spermicide was still in the air. Otherwise, not only was the evidence of anything happening gone, but neither Sam nor I ever spoke of it again. I never did get those panties back, however.

Now, does that count as a true first time, Morgan? I used to vehemently deny that it did, to myself. Having written it out, however, I have reevaluated the play. The player was over the goal line. Touchdown.

The time I always counted as my real first was with Dante just before my twenty-first birthday, but since I've answered your question and it's already an hour past quitting time, I'm going to leave it at that. — M

8

I remember being infuriated with the first words he said to me in that fraternity hallway. "Had enough third-wheel-dom for the evening?" Dante quipped, not looking up as he unlocked his door.

"What? Oh, Ben and Mary. Yeah. I kind of anticipated it. Why she can't manage to walk over here on her own, but has to drag me along instead is something I'll never know."

"She's insecure, which means she's a good match for Ben. A confident girl would walk all over him."

Dante pinpointed what had eluded me about my dislike of Ben, but I had to defend Mary. "What makes you think Mary's insecure?"

"Unless she has scoliosis, her posture has nervous and withdrawn written all over it. Her eyes were darting around the room like she was following a fly. And she chatters on about nothing in particular like she has to fill the silence."

"You don't know her, and pretending like you do is just pathetic. I'm going to go."

Dante called after me. "It's nice to finally meet you, Ziegel."

I spun on my heel and stomped back to confront him. "We haven't really met. I don't know who you are, and you don't know me." That wasn't entirely true. I'd seen him once or twice, bartending at the townie dive on the square. Sure, he was cute, but I wasn't impressed by the way that girls seemed to orbit him and how he seemed to relish it.

"I'm Dante," he said, extending his hand.

"Delyn Ziegel, although I guess you already knew that."

Two years earlier, I had decided on a whim to introduce myself at college with the new moniker and gratefully, it had stuck. I was done with being called Man or Manny.

The handshake, a good one, was just as incongruous as the bottle and box that were still cradled in his left arm. College students don't shake each other's hands in greeting unless you count the handshake/half-bro-hug combo endemic to fraternity brothers.

"I do," he said, and I recoiled a bit at the abrupt remark while withdrawing my hand. He rushed to explain. "I'm in American Lit with you, Ben, and Mary."

"I've never seen you there." That was true.

"I'm not there as often as I should be. Eight o'clock class and all. Besides, you're always so focused, almost like you've got blinders on."

"I don't have time to mess around."

"Everyone has time to waste. You just choose not to squander it. That's a great thing about you."

"Are you always this direct? You don't know anything about me."

"You're Mandelyn Ziegel. You play opposite for the volleyball team. You guys came in second in conference last year. You were key to last year's national championship-winning College Public Forum debate team, and you are on your way to being named Pi Kappa Delta All-American. You're from the Chicago suburbs, and your Saturday morning radio show kicks ass."

I was speechless. "How long have you been stalking me?"

"You can't hide at a school this size. Look, we can keep standing in the hallway while you despise me, or, if you want, you can come in and continue despising me, so long as you don't mind if I smoke one of these."

"Not if you don't put some pants on."

"Decorum. Right. Can we compromise with gym shorts? My jeans stink from the bar, and I don't have any others until I do laundry tomorrow."

To indicate that I'd accepted the terms, I walked into his room. While beer bongs and prairie fire shots were being consumed to the beat of Sir Mix-A-Lot and House of Pain in the basement, Dante's room stood in stark contrast. It was part Café des Amateurs, part museum, and part—there wasn't any other way to describe it—lair.

Dante didn't have posters; he had artwork—museum-quality prints framed and suspended from the ceiling by piano wire. The first print I noticed was a welcome reminder of home. Used to promote Chicago as a Columbian Exposition candidate two years prior to the 1893 event, the image features an ethereal woman sitting beside a globe on a high-rise rooftop. An eagle and a torch of liberty are over her shoulder, and she holds a crimson banner that reads "Art Science Industry." She looks out over a burgeoning Chicago skyline, no evidence of the fire that had leveled it just twenty years before. The slogan, "Chicago of To-day" blazes across the sky. The C and part of the H are charred, with flames licking and cresting against the rest of the name, red like the glow of embers. "The Metropolis of the West" scrolls in gold across the bottom of the composition.

The next print on the wall was *The Sin*, Franz von Stuck's most famous work. I had written a report about von Stuck a year before, when we were studying mythological and Biblical allegory in Ancient and Medieval Literature. *The Sin* had made its international debut at the Columbian Exposition. A woman's alabaster torso dominates the composition. Her right breast is in profile. Her left is front and center, the nipple partially obscured from view by her Lady Godiva-length raven hair. In many prints, it is difficult to discern what drapes over and above her, shielding the rest of her body from view, but once you see the leering, bloodthirsty face, it is unmistakable. Your eye is all but forced to circle around her, tracing the form of the serpent entrapping her. The painting is essentially black and white with the exception of the woman's lips, her left areola, and an amber glow to the upper right side.

Not wanting to let my astonishment show, I carefully said, "You're a Columbian Exposition guy, I see. Most people gravitate to the 1933 World's Fair. Art Deco over Art Nouveau."

"Ferris Wheel? Midway Plaisance? Illuminated Egyptian Temple?" he scoffed. "Tesla? Burnham, Olmsted, Sullivan? No contest. 'Science Finds, Industry Applies, Man Conforms.'"

"I thought it was 'Man Adapts,'" I corrected.

"I'd trust your semantic recollection over my holistic one." His words were simple enough, but I found them condescending. Vowing quickly not to forget the slight, I changed topics.

"You're a von Stuck fan. That is interesting. I'm full-blooded German, you know. I saw this at the Neue Pinakothek when my parents took me to Munich after I graduated from high school."

This impressed Dante. "That had to be amazing! Monet, Van Gogh, Cézanne. All there. What was your favorite?"

How the hell did he know that, I wondered to myself. Dante was a worthy opponent, I could see. I summoned my best game face and redirected the conversation. "Not von Stuck. He was Hitler's favorite painter."

"Von Stuck preceded Hitler by a generation. He wasn't a Nazi. He can't be associated with an evil like that."

"His paintings are evil. Mortal sin is the body of his work."

"Good cannot exist without evil. Hiding in the light empowers the darkness."

I turned to Dante. "Who are you, Obi-Wan Kenobi?"

Dante laughed. "Oh, my God, Ziegel. If you are a Star Wars geek on top of everything else, I am going to lose my mind."

"'Geek' overstates it. Settle down," I warned, even as I smiled in spite of myself.

His furniture drew my attention. While other bedrooms' desks were formica, plastic, or severely debilitated, penknife-graffitied wood, Dante had a pristine antique drafting table for a work surface, paired with a stool like the ones in shop class that swivel to raise and lower the seat. While others had futons, he had what I had to assume was a reproduction Mies van der Rohe Barcelona couch. From where I stood, I could see a basket with blankets and a few pillows at the foot of the bed.

"That's where you sleep?" I asked. "Not exactly the cuddly type, I take it."

"I wouldn't say that, exactly." He blushed. "More like I'm not the sleeping type. I've suffered insomnia since puberty. Not much sense in looking at a bed that gets little use—for sleep, I mean."

An overstuffed burgundy microsuede loveseat completed the seating accommodations. "Make yourself comfortable," he said as he set the bottle and box on the drafting table and started to fill the glasses.

I sank into the plush seat and immediately melted, realizing how uptight I had been and how grateful I was not to be called on it. It made my skin crawl to hear the words "Don't be so uptight," or anything to the effect, and it happened more often than I would like to admit. I had never been called uptight in high school. I thought the new accusations had something to do with the more easy-going posture of most Iowans. My Iowan friends worked harder than most of my peers in Weston, but they were less ostentatious about it.

I continued my scan of the room. A blue and green "Rue Mouffetard" sign was affixed to the back of the door, adding to the Fitzgerald-Hemingway vibe. The room's only anachronistic decoration was a H.O.R.D.E. poster that listed all the bands who had played the festival that year. The poster read like a playlist from my radio show. I had to change topics quickly or risk showing vulnerability.

"Alright, so what is with the kimono?" I asked.

"It's a smoking jacket," Dante said.

"It's not."

"Well, it's not one in the traditional sense. It's sort of an award that goes with the cigars."

"And the gin?"

"The gin is mine. Ben picked it up at the store for me when he was out earlier. Seemed a waste to quaff rotgut with one of Dominican's finest, don't you agree?"

"Not rum?"

"Meh. Too sweet. I like my potables to be more complex than that."

"I cannot refute your constructive," I said, immediately regretting how snooty it sounded.

"That is some sophisticated terminology there, Professor Ziegel."

Busted, I thought. "I was just messing with you. Debate jargon," I said.

"I thought you didn't have time to mess around."

"Yeah, I'm a wild one. Just wait until you have a few drinks in me, and I'll dazzle you with my analysis of attitudinal versus existential inherency."

"Give it to me in the simplest terms you can," he said as he set a glass—not a Solo cup, but an actual rocks glass—in my hand.

"Thank you," I said. "Okay... Attitudinal inherency describes something that is essentially a fact, but only because everyone accepts it as true."

"For there is nothing either good or bad, but thinking makes it so."

"Hamlet. Nice."

"So existential inherency is different how?"

"Actual, real fact. Reality—'it is what it is.'"

"The difference between attitudinal and existential inherency, then, is the difference between *a posteriori* versus *a priori* knowledge."

"What is that?"

"Epistemology." I must have looked a little blank. "Philosophy of knowledge," he explained.

"I couldn't say for sure."

"2+2=4 versus 2+2=5."

"*1984*. I'm impressed. You didn't strike me as literary or philosophical."

"I can see how my present outward appearance might be deceiving."

"It's not just that." It was hard to believe, but I'd almost forgotten about Dante's ridiculous outfit. "I get that bartenders pick up a lot of useless information on the job, but epistemology, let alone Orwell and Shakespeare, aren't the usual Trivia Tuesday fare."

"I thought you said you didn't know me."

"I don't know you. I've seen you before. That's not the same thing."

"You couldn't have been to the bar!" he said in mock astonishment. "You're not twenty-one."

"Like that's stopped anyone before. Wait. How do you know I'm not twenty-one?"

"Your hand isn't stamped from downstairs, and you didn't bring beer."

I took a defiant drink. "I didn't get my hand stamped because I hadn't planned to drink. I didn't bring beer for the same reason—not that I would have, anyway. I don't drink beer."

"You don't drink the swill that passes for beer. It's called The Beast for a reason. A good doppelbock would turn you around, I think. Are you twenty-one?"

"My birthday is coming up—All Saints Day. I like gin, good gin especially." I indicated that I'd already finished the first drink, clinking my glass to his.

"Oh!" he teased. "'I hadn't planned to drink. I didn't plan to stay,' she says. Using me for my alcohol. I see how it is, Ziegel." He refilled my glass, barely floating tonic over the surface.

"A cigar, too, if you're willing to part with one."

"I'm afraid I can't oblige. The MVP is only entitled to one of these."

"Then why do they give you the whole box?"

"It's a trust thing, maybe. Or maybe it's just a matter of storage. We don't exactly have a humidor here, so the box travels around. Everyone knows how many are in there."

"We could share one. I don't have cooties."

"Famous last words. Oh, alright. I would have offered, except that I wouldn't have supposed you wanted one," he said, cutting the cap with the guillotine from the box.

"My dad owns a tobacco and gift shop back home. He left his corporate job when I was in junior high school. I practically grew up on the scent of pipes, cigars, and incense."

"I wonder what Freud would say about that," he said with a louche wiggle of his eyebrows.

"Don't be gross," I said as he cracked a cedar spill from a remnant in the box and began to toast the foot of the cigar, rotating it methodically. That surprised me. "I have never seen anyone under the age of fifty light their cigars that way."

"I'm an old soul," he said, and I gave him a look to call his bluff. "Okay, I'm just fucking with you. I like the way the cedar makes it taste."

"So do I," I said distantly. Changing the subject yet again, I turned my attention to the door poster. "Did you make it to H.O.R.D.E. last summer? I would have killed to go."

"Me, too, but no. Maybe next summer, although I'm not sure I'll be around."

"Where will you be?"

"I haven't decided. I have it narrowed down to Muang Khoun or Jaipur," he answered nonchalantly.

"Oh, that's too bad, because I am either going to be at the North Pole or on the moons of Venus."

"There's no land at the North Pole, and Venus doesn't have moons," he said as he let the tip continue to dance above the flame.

RELEASE

"Well, I was misinformed," I did in my best Rick Blaine.

"Your Bogart impression needs work." He checked the light and drew.

"Is there anything you don't know?"

"The townie bar is more culturally illuminating than you might think," he deadpanned.

I paused. "Do I owe you an apology?" I finally asked. I was at my wit's end, confounded by Dante's unexpected brilliance.

"No," Dante said warmly as he handed the cigar to me.

"What's in... Where did you say?"

"Muang Khoun and Jaipur."

"Where are Muang Khoun and Jaipur?" The taste of the cigar was magnificent. I drew again.

"Laos and India, respectively. What's there is what I want to find out. I haven't ever traveled outside of the United States, and I am dying to. These trips are put together through service organizations. They're not cheap, but they're a lot less pricey than tourist packages.

"In Muang Khoun, you work on a mulberry plantation. In Jaipur, you build. This summer, the project is a library," he explained.

Now it was my turn to be impressed. "That sounds absolutely amazing." I gave the cigar back to Dante.

"We should go together," he said nonchalantly as he drew.

I laughed. "We just met," I said as I sipped my drink, letting a shard of ice roll around on my tongue after I set the glass down.

He laughed, too. "I'm not proposing marriage, Ziegel. I'm not even asking you to be my girlfriend, or anything. This is an entirely chaste offer to be a part of a trip of a lifetime. Which destination sounds better to you?"

As ridiculous as it was, hearing him hedge his offer deflated me a bit. I shook it off. "Well, I think I'd prefer swinging a hammer to working a field. How long is the trip? What does it cost?"

"You can go for as little time or as much time as you want. The main cost is the ticket to get there, which is, like, a thousand dollars, and that's if you get the ticket well in advance. Once you're there, accommodations are humble but are provided for a song, and a restaurant or a hotel is pretty reasonable for a break now and then. So you want to stay long enough to make it worthwhile."

I thought about my two previous summers at home in Weston, which made a trip to India sound like an even better idea than it had from the start. Nothing had been exactly wrong with home, but nothing had really felt right. My friends and I were growing apart. Joshua was really embracing his homosexual lifestyle, getting a job in the city at some niche bookstore on Halsted Street, leaving little time to spend with Sam and me. Not that Sam had any time, either; he and his two older brothers had launched a painting business that kept him busy during the day and exhausted by nightfall. I had interned at Leo Burnett, an experience that was humbling—a challenge both intellectually and socially. I had come away wondering if the world of corporate PR and advertising was really for me.

"I could go the whole summer, I think."

"You're pretty spectacular, Mandelyn Ziegel. I see a real *simpatica* in you. I had read you all wrong. I'm glad," he said as he put his left hand on my right knee.

"Wait. What do you mean by that—'had me all wrong?'"

"No… No, no, no. I don't mean that as a bad thing," he said as he patted my knee soothingly.

I took his hand from my knee and tossed it back into his lap. "How else could you mean it? What did you think of me before we ever exchanged a single word?"

"Don't do this. I said it all wrong." He seemed a little panicked. I liked it.

"No, tell me," I pushed, putting my empty glass on the table, which I noticed was a worn wood crate with "Encyclopedia Americana Vol 1-15" branded into the side. "I'd really like to know what kind of horrible person I turned out not to be."

"I'm ruining the whole evening," he said, more to himself than to me. He set the cigar in the ashtray, inhaled deeply and exhaled before he began. "Honestly, when was the last time you talked about the Columbian Exposition, art history, Star Wars, inherency parsing… literature? When was the last time you talked about third-world humanitarian aid during a frat party? I can't remember the last time."

"I haven't even gotten to your Mies van der Rohe bed, Rue Mouffetard sign, or your taste in music," I agreed.

"See, there are still plenty of topics on which you can despise me."

"I don't despise you," I said. "What was the other thing you said—about seeing something in me? What was the word you used?"

"*Simpatica?*"

"Yeah. So what, is that Italian for 'nice person?'"

"Not exactly. It starts there, but it's so much more than that. It's like we're sympathetic to one another at a deep level. You get me. I think I get you. This feels like a third date, not a coincidental chat between new acquaintances. That's a rare thing, don't you think?"

"Like soul mates?"

"What?"

"What you described. You described a soul mate."

"Yeah, I guess I did," Dante said.

I reached for Dante's glass and set it on the table. His hand was chilled from the ice. I held it between mine.

"What are you doing?" he whispered.

"Something reckless, probably." I took his hand and placed it on my heart, which was racing, as much from the moments before, while I was arguing with Dante, as in the moments since, when the gin and stimulating conversation had overtaken my good intentions.

"You're forward," Dante said as he leaned toward me.

"Shut up, Dante," I said, putting my hand on his heart, his mouth nearly against mine.

He tasted, as I did, of cedar and juniper. He explored my mouth with the tip of his tongue as he took my head in his left hand and his right slid down to cup my breast. I slid my free hand along his solid thigh and felt my heartbeat skip and stumble.

"Wait a moment," he breathed into me. "There's something I want to do."

He rose, taking my hands in his to pull me from the trappings of the velvety couch.

"I want to know what you think. Will you listen to something?"

I was a little discombobulated. "Sure… What?"

He was already across the room, flipping through pages of CDs in a case. He found one scrawled with Sharpie, words and a date I couldn't make out as a label. "I should have put this on earlier when you asked about H.O.R.D.E. A couple of the guys and I went out to Boulder last year, and one of them just tracked down this bootleg of the show." He fumbled with a few buttons, clicking ahead a few tracks to the one he had in mind. "Say Goodbye" began to play.

"This isn't what I wanted you to hear. I mean, it is—you've clearly got it bad for Dave Matthews, based on the content of your radio show—but I wondered if you'd listen to my poem for next week's Lit presentation."

"You want to recite poetry to me? Now?"

"Well, shit," he laughed, embarrassed. "When you say it like that, it makes it sound like I'm trying too hard. I wish I hadn't thought of it. It's just that you're in the inner circle with that professor, and I need to improve my grade. It'd mean a lot."

"What are you presenting?"

"'Chicago' by Carl Sandburg."

As he recited the opening stanza, I began to tremble, trying my hardest not to let Dante see. I was never one to be moved by poetry, but the power of those particular words cannot be understated. I sat down on the Mies couch as he continued, our eyes locked upon one another's as I reclined.

He never finished the poem. I violated my self-imposed curfew, waking up the next morning among sheets hastily cast out in the guise of bed-making, and then more hastily strewn as we writhed with one another until the early morning hours, giving and taking, surrendering and possessing. Over the next year, I became thoroughly codependent upon him, concupiscent despite how completely unsuited we were to one another in almost every respect.

9

Monday, October 17

    Dr. Adiraju was already sitting in my office as I arrived on Monday morning. Her serene manner felt portentous. I felt my shoulders rise with tension.

    Thankfully, her serenity was part ruse and part being plainly overwhelmed. She spoke without any introduction. "The Muon g-2 building has received a commendation from the Chicago Architectural Association. I knew that the project was deserving. I just didn't know if the outside world was going to realize it, too."

    I cheered with delight. It was all I could do to drop my bags before we embraced.

    "So much private deliberation, so many public meetings and media-fought battles. Without your savvy, this project wouldn't exist," she said. "This is your win as much as it is mine, the designers', or the builders'. That is why I would like you to represent the Lab at the award presentation next week."

    I released my grasp. "What? I don't know, Doctor. That sounds like a task well above my pay grade."

    "You are being too modest. Events such as these were your bread and butter in your past life. Besides, all we are talking about is attending. The architects submitted the application. They are the ones who will speak. It will be a lot of shaking hands, smiling, and nodding, perhaps some fielding of awkward advances from other attendees who would like to be a part of our future projects."

    "I think I can navigate that," I admitted.

    "I know you can. Now, do you have a few moments to talk about our campaign?"

Knowing that Dr. Adiraju usually comes out of the gate full-steam at the start each week, I had spent a good portion of Sunday getting prepared. I retrieved a folder from the credenza, another from my briefcase, and motioned to have her join me at the work table in the common area.

"I spoke with the speaker's bureau agent on Friday to confirm flight and hotel accommodations. We will be invoiced for both. They prefer to book hotels for their clients, and so long as I'm provided with a final itinerary one week prior, I am satisfied. The Doctor will arrive at 10:08 that morning at O'Hare. He prefers to drive himself, so he will arrive to check in and lunch at Atwater's with you and as many of the Directorate as accept the invitation. He will tour the facility at two o'clock, concluding in time for the press conference at four o'clock. CBS, Clear Channel, Cumulus, Newsweb, NBC Universal, and the *Tribune* will all be represented, as will be the *Sun-Times*, *Daily Herald*, WBEZ, and WTTW. U of C is going to have radio coverage and share it with the paper. There are a few stragglers, but to have this much commitment this early is pretty remarkable."

"I knew we were in good hands. Will the Doctor grant any individual interviews?"

"He will meet with writers for *Symmetry*, *Fast Company*, and *Chicago* magazines over breakfast, near the airport, on the thirteenth, before flying home that afternoon. Apparently, the three reporters were all in undergrad together and have been looking for a chance to co-author. The Doctor found the collaboration interesting, so he was game."

"Amazing! And the journals?"

"This is my draft of the release for the usual suspects: *International, Scientific & Academic, Libertas Academica, Bentham Science, IOP, Springer,* and *Elsevier*."

"Absolute perfection, Mandelyn. With all of this in hand, whatever are you going to do between now and the event?"

"I'll just have to get back to the rest of my job," I joked. On a more serious note, I added, "I'll let the team know how well they've done."

"Please do. And Mandelyn? For the Architectural Celebration? Get yourself something pretty to wear. These are architects, as you know.

They won't be as amused by your headbands, jeans, and yoga tops as we are."

"Fair enough, Doctor," I said, admiring her de rigueur Eileen Fisher ensemble. She giggled as she left, presumably to scare others into action before their first cups of coffee had kicked in.

~ ~ ~ ~ ~ ~ ~

That afternoon, I left in time to put dinner together at home. Henry and I had reached that stage in our relationship where we didn't do anything too spectacular to celebrate our birthdays. An evening home with a great meal was more our speed than a restaurant trip or a night out. I'd picked up a Châteaubriand and had a portobello bacon sauce under way, with maple-ginger roasted brussels sprouts, carrots, and cauliflower in the oven. A Napa Cab was on the counter, and salted caramel gelato was in the freezer for dessert.

When Henry arrived at home that evening, he was in unusually high spirits, literally. "Why are you so chipper?" I asked, noticing the distinct scent of rye on his breath. "Did the office throw you a party? I'm so glad you walk to the train."

"You know, ours is the only house without a wreath of leaves, a scarecrow, or any other autumnal decoration in the yard?"

"You didn't marry a domestic diva, just a culinary dynamo."

Henry swung his arm around my waist and dipped me. "I love you. You know that, right?" he mooned.

"What have you done?" I asked in reply.

"Any chance Joshua and Reynard could be free for your birthday?"

"What is going on?"

"How would you like to celebrate your birthday at Next?"

"The restaurant Next?"

"I got four tickets from the partners as a gift for my birthday. Friday the fourth," Henry said. "That, and a vaguely promising meeting scheduled for that same day. Something about the roll-out of a new plan, they said."

I had just been reading that the new Next concept was due to launch that week. A revolution in the culinary world, Next was breaking rules by selling tickets, like a theater, to its meals. Every three months or so, the restaurant would launch a new concept, and each new prix fixe meal would transport its revelers to a new destination. This was the restaurant's third iteration. The first, Paris, and the second, Thailand, had been unmitigated successes.

"They have an exchange if you don't want to go…"

I squealed. Grant Achatz's latest venue had only been open since the spring, but it already had *New York Times* coverage, reviews on NPR, and attention from every reputable critic in town. "This had to cost them a fortune!"

"Times must be looking up for the office. Let me celebrate you."

"Today is your birthday, and you're giving me the gift. I don't know what to say!"

"Then call it a celebration of us. We're long overdue."

"When you put it that way," I said, "I have something else to celebrate, I guess. Muon g-2 won a commendation, and I will represent the Lab at the Architectural Celebration."

"Dr. Adiraju is passing the reins?"

"Well, not all the reins," I laughed. "I think it is just standing on a stage and stroking the architect's ego."

"Still, this is magnificent news!"

"I guess," I said. I was surprised he was taking it as well as he was. His firm had never been recognized, and I knew it was a sore spot. "The Doctor was kind to point out how it never would have happened without all of the public meetings leading to the buy-in of the neighborhood and the municipality. Still, it's not like I designed the building, or anything."

"Don't dismiss the importance of this. This is the difference between being someone else's mouthpiece and being a direct representative. I am proud of you."

"Okay, then," I shrugged.

"Muon g-2? That's Antonosov and Colson, right?"

"You know it is," I said.

"I hate those guys," he said, as if on cue.

I laughed and patted his shoulder to acknowledge the old joke around town. "No one likes those guys. I'll call Joshua."

"Not yet," Henry whispered in my ear. "Let's enjoy dinner. It smells absolutely fantastic."

"Oh, it is," I teased.

"Want to join me upstairs before we sit down?"

"It's six o'clock," I half-scoffed, half-teased.

"We are both here, awake, happy, and not preoccupied, all at the same time. How long has it been since all those things happened at once? Where is that lingerie that you look so good in?"

"My chemise? Ready and waiting upstairs." I flinched with a bit of guilt about how long it had been since I'd worn it.

"I love how you look in that. I love it because I know how you feel when you're in it. I take no issue with how you look out of it, either."

I smiled. "Give me a few minutes."

While I changed, I thought I heard Henry talking downstairs. I was giddy, even as I actively pushed questioning thoughts from my mind. Where was this sudden ardor coming from? Why the sudden change of heart? Did I even want this?

I looked over my shoulder as he came into the room. He took me by my hip bones and kissed my neck. He slid his right hand downward and stroked just inside my legs. "You seem ready. You know I love how you respond to me," he groaned.

"I do respond." I kissed him, breathing in his familiar, musky scent and feeling tension roll from my shoulders.

~ ~ ~ ~ ~ ~ ~

Dinner was successful. Feeling a little brazen, I stayed in the chemise for our meal. We made quick work of cleaning up and reconvened upstairs soon after for bed. We settled into our once-familiar spooned arrangement after Henry turned off the light. Soon, Henry pressed the palm of his hand against the small of my back, then slowly glided it up, just above the ridge of my spine.

I jumped, remembering the tickets. "I forgot! I need to call Joshua before it gets too late."

"I already took care of it. I called before I came upstairs earlier. I supposed that we wouldn't be in any mood afterward. Was I right?"

I stiffened. This was straight out of Henry's playbook. I had said I would call Joshua. This was Henry's persnickety nature: a dictator in one moment, a sumpter-mule in the next. I inhaled, determined not to ruin the placid joy of the night. "Maybe you were," I conceded, "but I'd told you I'd call."

"Don't be mad. I just thought I'd help. I'd be off the phone faster than you, after all."

In this day and age, men like Henry didn't deserve much credit for—what was the word? "Tolerance" wasn't right. Tolerate is what you do to persevere an annoyance, withstand an otherwise unbearable situation. Henry did more than tolerate Joshua, but theirs wasn't a friendship in a genuine sense, either. Without my intercession, neither would have sought the other's company. In the sense of their gender, they were a pair of conspirators and also rivals of a kind. As much as I didn't want to believe it, there was a certain quality to Henry's regard for Joshua as a sort of vanquished opponent, and even a bit of conciliatory regard on Joshua's behalf toward Henry. Talking about it once, Joshua and I both saw that, with Henry's strict, conservative upbringing, his acceptance of Joshua and Reynard as fixtures in my life required an evolution past the prejudice instilled by his church and redoubled by his mother.

Henry was right. Their conversations were rarely more than transactional, even a bit curt. Joshua and I would have jabbered for over an hour. "Fair enough," I said. "So, they're able to make it, I guess?"

"He even offered to pick up the premium wine pairing for the night. Oh, let's talk about the Architectural Celebration, instead. Are you going solo?"

I had worried a bit about discussing this aspect of the event. Henry's firm felt that my employment at the Laboratory represented a conflict of interest, so they chose not to pursue the Lab as a client. Even though I had no role to play in consultant selections, the partners thought that I could, unscrupulously or even purely accidentally, feed inside information to Henry. The possibility of even the perception of impropriety had offended both of us equally. I couldn't tell if Henry was needling me for an invitation. "The architect only offered one ticket. I could probably get another one…"

"No, no. You shouldn't bring a competitor to their table. What I meant was whether anyone else from the Lab would attend."

"Just me. The design principal, the project manager, a few of the engineers, the contractor, some subcontractors, and me."

"As it should be. It's good to see the hard work rewarded." If there was a hint of envy in his voice—or jealousy, even—it was faint.

As we talked, Henry's fingers outlined my shoulder blade before he moved upward to trace the curve of my right shoulder. Then, he slid his touch down onto my oblique before reaching my breast, first from beneath, then moving toward my heart. Then, with the care he might take if he held my actual heart in his hand, he remained, holding my right breast as he gently grazed my nipple with his thumb.

I conscientiously soaked in every sensation, feeling his heart beat against my back, its pace quickening. I listened to his breath as he began to set the lightest of kisses along the ridge of my ear. I sighed involuntarily and became amazed, as well, at the aching sensation inside my thighs. I felt him harden against me, and a Cheshire cat-like smile rose at the corners of my mouth.

I turned my right hand, navigating to the root of him, my right foot hooking in between his calves to separate them. Parting them further—up his knee, then his thigh, voluntarily trapping my calf between his—I turned to lie on my back, prone. Locking my eyes with his, grin widening, I affected a coy tone, asking, "Really? Again?"

All Henry had to do was smile in return and agree, "Really." As he rose above me, deftly placing his knees between mine, I spread and raised my calves, embracing his waist with the full length of my legs.

He entered me, and I drew a breath sharply, exhilarated by the fulfillment. His eyes locked on mine with an unmistakable expression that I hoped I returned to him.

And then the floodgates opened. His lips parted and his head tilted in a beat. In the next, he was ravenous, as was I, consuming one another as he thrust with a force equaled by mine as I met him with my pelvis, as I rocked to meet each return in perfect time. He stroked my face with his right hand as I wrapped my arms around his shoulders, as much to grope him as to steady myself as our pace continued to accelerate.

Then, still as one, we rolled across the bed, Henry buried deep inside me. Once I was atop him, his hands slid down beneath my seat, and my thighs, burning yet powerful, led my rise and fall as I sought balance and purchase with my hands on his chest.

My eyes remained steadfastly engaged on his deep blue eyes, wild yet familiar, like the color of Lake Michigan as a spring storm approaches. Slowly, his eyelids began to flutter. They rolled back as they finally closed and he drew in a long, deep breath. It was at that moment I felt that exotic calm settle over every inch, from my belly down to my thighs. Then, the emerging… from clitoris, to groin, back to belly… and my release.

I collapsed over his chest, my thighs involuntarily tightened against his hips, and I bucked, first with slow, rhythmic bolts, but soon with a frenetic energy. I could hear my own voice, unworldly cries and moans cascading. Henry came with a hungry, urgent force, holding me desperately as each pulse wracked our bodies like an electrocution.

As the waves eventually subsided and we melted back into reality, I nestled into his side, head into his shoulder, my hand over his heart.

10

Friday, November 4

 The night of our dinner at Next had finally arrived. I drove in from Weston and picked up Henry outside his office, which was in the old London Guarantee & Accident Building. I drove south on Michigan Avenue before heading west on Randolph, through the Loop, across the expressway, and north on Halsted Street. I parked in our old neighborhood.

 Something had felt off-kilter with Henry from the moment he had gotten in the car. His meeting at work must not have gone well. His was a constitution slow to rise in temperature—a long simmer stage and a high melting point. He took days to silently process setbacks, rejections, and even challenges overcome. If he was in the throes of dealing with something, the best thing to do would be to let it play out.

 I was wearing the perfume I reserved for special occasions. I hoped the fragrance might trigger an olfactory response for him, as it always did for me. I had bought it from my father's shop not long before he passed away. I was wearing it the night Henry and I met. I wore it when Henry graduated, when he proposed, on our wedding day, and all the best occasions in between. The primary notes of the scent were, of all things, frankincense and myrrh. It was the scandalous novelty of the idea of wearing a fragrance called *God's Gift* that I had found hilarious and had made me give it a try, but it had been the scintillating fragrance that had sold me.

 Fulton Market had barely begun to gentrify, if you could even call it that, before we moved to the suburbs. Gentrification implies disrepair. While it wasn't ever tourist-friendly, Fulton Market was an area with consistently robust industrial activity, with manufacturers flanking distributors of everything from foodstuffs to machinery to furniture. A few galleries, niche retailers, and loft rehab condos were now stuffed in between. The restaurant was hardly distinguishable from the other storefronts, except that it lacked a rolling metal overhead door on its façade.

I finally decided, against better judgment, to ask about Henry's sullen state and try to set it aside before Joshua and Reynard arrived. "Is something wrong?" I asked.

"We met to talk about new ways to market the firm. 'Diversify the portfolio.' 'Extrapolate our expertise.' 'Explore correlated market silos.' I don't even know what that last phrase means, except that we are going to be chasing work we're not qualified to do." Henry sounded exasperated.

"I really thought that the reorganization would mean I have some sort of control over my destiny," he continued, "but nothing's really in my hands. I am proxy to aged fools who never knew good design but, by doing nothing more than continuing to wake up for the last fifty years, hold me over a barrel."

Henry has a deadly composition when it comes to self-promotion: hubris and innocence. He is better at customer service than most of his peers; he sours when discussing the topic of prospecting. He thinks that his design aesthetic and the value of his services should be self-evident, and that if he does good work, then the right kinds of projects should just naturally fall in line. He serves on juries a few times a year, is frequently quoted in the journals, and talks about the value of publishing all the time—always meaning to get around to assembling a firm monograph. His firm's website had finally been updated earlier in the year, but it was little more than an online portfolio. The idea of cold calling, direct mail, press releases, networking, and the rest is still anathema to him, especially for projects out of his realm of expertise.

Counseling Henry on this subject had always been complicated. He seemed receptive to my suggestions at the beginning of our relationship, but I noticed over time that he was merely tolerating them, that he never put any of them into action. I gradually stopped volunteering any advice, and for a while it was as if he either didn't notice the absence or was relieved by it. In a tough period we had soon after I left my agency job, right in the midst of the recession's darkest days, he accused me of withholding my support from him. I accused him of ignoring my ideas and of lording condescension over my life's work. He'd dismissed my job as a poor application of my talents. Needless to say, tonight was not the night to resurrect the issue.

Thankfully, we walked up to the nondescript door just as Joshua and Reynard walked around the corner and toward us from the opposite direction. Joshua looked dapper as always, his blazer fitting as if it had been tailored that day, his physique as noble as it had ever been in school. As we approached, I noticed that he wasn't wearing a dress shirt or tie. "What do you have on under there, Joshua?" I called from down the street.

With a flourish, he pulled apart his lapels to reveal an absurdly snug Superman shirt. "I am here to save you, miss. Fly away with me!" His embrace was as warm and familiar as always, transporting me back by twenty years, like it did every time.

"Hi, Reynard," I said over Joshua's shoulder. "Are you in costume, too?"

Reynard feigned a shyness before revealing his Cosby sweater. I laughed. "That is absolutely perfect. I wish I knew that dressing up is a thing!"

"I don't think most people do. I hope you don't mind. Rey wanted to wear his Lucky Star outfit, but I said no."

"Don't you be putting your cross-dressing shit on me, Joshua," Reynard snapped affectionately in his thick French accent. "Everyone knows who wears the pants in this relationship."

"You do, my love. Come, friends, let us away."

As we stepped through the door into the restaurant, the theme to *Star Wars* played, and the outside world drifted away. Henry handed our tickets to the waiting server as I checked my coat.

"Good evening," the server greeted us. "Welcome to Next 'Childhood.' I am Andrew and I'll be serving you this evening. Please follow me."

The new concept was just over two weeks into the run. I had actively stopped myself from reading any reviews so the surprises of the evening would remain intact.

As Andrew led us to our table, I wondered whether we had arrived too soon, or if we had been taken to the wrong seats. Nearly-empty glasses were strewn about our table, along with a half-finished cigar, an entirely completed crossword puzzle, and a pair of reading glasses. "What an amusing presentation," Joshua said. We sat, looking around to see whether someone would explain the gag. "Methinks Mom and Dad didn't clean up after last night's party. Their nightcaps become our aperitifs, perhaps?" he asked with a wink.

"Do you think that's what it is?" I wondered to Henry.

"Will these be filled?" Henry asked Andrew as he arrived.

"The presentation is complete, sir. This is the beginning of your experience. And what is your name?"

"It's Henry," I shared, deflecting the inquisition I felt Henry was about to launch. "What do we have here? A martini, a Manhattan, and… Is this a bloody Mary?"

"It is, and you are?"

"Mandelyn," I said, extending my hand in greeting.

"It's a pleasure to meet you. Enjoy," Andrew replied before swiftly retreating into the glass-paneled kitchen.

We each slurped at the remaining, rather strong, sips of the cocktails and nibbled on the garnishes as we surveyed the decor. Woven reed placemats sat upon our granite tabletop. Large dark wood panels were mounted over the caramel-colored walls that surrounded us. Beneath our napkins lay folded cards. An Ansel Adams-esque landscape of birch trees was printed inside each, with a dark screen overlay and green pixelated text on the right. "It's like the old green phosphor CRT monitors, like the early Apple IIs. Remember those in elementary school, Manny?" Joshua asked rhetorically.

The message read,

```
Wonder. Excitement. The feeling of the world
unfolding before you in unexpected ways.
Discover. And even fear of the unknown and
the future. There is a nostalgia we all carry
for childhood innocence and naiveté. As we
grow older, too often we lose the sense that
our lives are magical. This menu could have
been titled "Michigan 1985" and our memories
of childhood foods we ate and enjoyed. In
turn, these dishes are a product of Midwest
```

Americana. We hope to take these memories and these foods and bring them back to you, restoring a bit of the magic and wonder along the way. Enjoy, Grant and Dave.

"I wish you wouldn't speak for me. I'm not a child," Henry murmured as we read.

Henry usually wasn't one to overtly rebuke anyone, especially over something as simple as usurping an introduction. I hardly knew how to respond. "I'm sorry," I mumbled. "Andrew was standing beside me, across from you. I was just eager, I guess."

"Eager to shake the waiter's hand? Odd, don't you think?"

I could feel my eyebrows furrow as I gave Joshua a look of consternation. He shrugged his shoulders, understandably lacking an explanation.

"I've chosen to take the non-alcoholic pairing, if that's okay, Joshua," Henry sighed. "It's been a long week, and I don't think indulgence tonight is a good idea."

"That's exactly when indulgence is best, don't you think?"

"I try not to drink angry—well, not that I'm angry. I mean… I haven't put that the right way. I don't think that inebriation is going to send my mood in the right direction. Better to be sober and celebratory than down and dull. Don't worry. I'll come around. Besides, I'll be here to drive your lush asses home," Henry said, attempting a joke that fell flat. "Please. Everyone enjoy."

We were all silent for just a beat before Reynard chimed in. "'It is better to drink in celebration of surviving one's challenges than to drink trying to forget them,' I think the expression goes."

"'Well, I'm not to the point of having survived just yet, Reynard, so I'll stick with the virgin drinks if that's okay."

"Fair enough," Joshua interceded. "I'm curious to see what they do with them. I bet they're smashing."

Andrew returned with four gift-wrapped boxes. "I'll advise you not to shake these, even though that's usually the best way to find out what's inside. Oh, and do take the morsel in a single bite. You'll see why."

We all began carefully unwrapping the boxes but soon discovered that ripping the paper was really the only way to do it properly. The amuse-bouche inside was a tempura-fried ball set atop a scattering of peanut pieces and jellied bits. "It's pomegranate pâtes de fruits," Andrew shared over my shoulder as I investigated the contents. I fumbled with grasping at the bits with my fingers, noticing that Reynard poured his into his hand to eat them.

"Where are our utensils? Aren't we going to get forks or knives?"

"Eating with our hands is meant to be part of the experience for this course, Henry," Andrew assured him. "Go on and see what the dough has inside."

I ate mine as Henry ate his. The dough had been injected with a liquid peanut butter laced with more of the pâtes de fruit. "The flavor, and the texture… oh, my goodness. This is extraordinary!" I giggled, my mouth still half-full.

"Even the scent of the box. It's like the smell of a Cracker Jack box. That's astounding," Joshua chimed in.

Reynard had abandoned any attempt at propriety and upended the box, pouring the contents into his mouth. A huge grin took over his face.

"Did Andrew just say 'our' hands? Is speaking to us like children part of the experience, too?" Henry grumbled.

I wanted to retort, saying that I hadn't detected any condescension in Andrew's voice, but I withheld my comment, opting instead to taste the Madeira and maraschino liqueur cocktail that had just arrived. I hadn't considered what the proper pairing would be for a peanut butter and jelly course, but I could assuredly say this was just right.

Henry's beverage was an apple juice infused with cinnamon and nutmeg. He smiled. "This reminds me of the paper cups of the hot cider—so-called; it was really just warmed apple juice—that the volunteers sold from the concession stand at the sledding hill near my house, growing up," Henry said. He studied the glass as he said, absentmindedly, "I haven't thought about that place in years. It's where I got this," he said, motioning to a faint scar that lay between his temple and the ridge of his cheekbone.

"I have never noticed that," I said. "How'd you get that?"

"I was nine. I snuck over to the hill with two kids from down the street. None of us had sleds, but the others had laundry hampers that we took turns using. Not exactly the most aerodynamic things. It's a wonder I didn't bleed out. Another half-inch higher, and my brains would have been spread across that hill." Henry continued smiling, an expression totally out of sync with the morbid memory. "Hendrika was pissed about that!" he recalled, exaggerating the S sound as he laughed.

"Were you okay?"

"Oh, sure. She stitched me right up. You can't even see the marks anymore, just the line."

"She stitched your face? Hendrika?" I exclaimed.

"Right there in the kitchen. It wasn't as if we were going to go to the emergency room for a simple scratch."

"A scratch that needed stitches! Oh, my God! How did I never hear that story before?"

"I didn't ever think to tell you. We've all got scars. Most more obvious than this one. It hardly bears mentioning."

"But that one has a completely bizarre story behind it."

"Well, now you know," he said.

I sat dumbfounded. He didn't seem to understand why the idea of his mother suturing him in the kitchen would be that remarkable. You would think that story might have surfaced somewhere before five years into a marriage.

As Andrew cleared the boxes, he replaced them with massive white bowls that had delicate, shallow centers, along with soup spoons the size of average serving ware. At the center of each bowl were orchestrations of leafy celery, carrots in a variety of colors, red pearl onions, a noodle-like extruded white paste, a dollop of foam, a sprig of dill, and a smattering of other herbs I couldn't identify.

Joshua snuck a taste of the white paste. "It's chicken. It's chicken-noodle soup. Get it? The noodle is the chicken. It's mousse-like. Give it a try."

"Clever," Henry scoffed. "Molecular gastronomy. Guess we should have seen that coming." I couldn't tell whether he was chiding or merely observing.

Andrew returned and began to pour broth, first into mine, then into the others' bowls. Before I took my first taste, the steam rising from the dark, creamy liquid overtook my senses. The Pinot Gris paired with the course was equally full-bodied, buttery yet acidic enough to cut the richness of the soup and cleanse the palate.

"This big placesetting makes me feel like a kid sitting at the grown-up table," Henry noted dispassionately as he sipped his mint-thyme lemonade. I was starting to feel as if the Childhood theme of the evening was transporting Henry to a foreboding place in his past. "Thoughtful," he added.

"What work are you pursuing with your firm right now, *Henri*?" I felt, more than observed, Henry's cringe as Reynard's French pronunciation of his name grated his ears.

"It's interesting you ask that, Reynard. We had a meeting about that just today. It seems as if my firm would like to pursue more research and development facilities. They feel as if our experience with high school science rooms ought to translate." Henry's tone was unmistakably sarcastic. "I've been tasked with the pursuit of clients who, so far as I can tell, will laugh me out of the room. Happy Friday to me, huh?"

My heart sank. I feared where the conversation was headed. Joshua, usually more intuitive than anyone else in the room, didn't acknowledge the pall that was descending. "Who's on your list? I'd be happy to put you in touch with my pharma contacts."

"I have friends at Motorola," Reynard added.

"No. Thanks, guys. That's sweet, but I don't think that's the kind of R&D they have in mind." Henry lifted his bowl and let the remaining contents drizzle down his throat before shooting a knowing look in my direction.

I knew exactly who he was tasked with pursuing, but immediately repressed the realization. I willed myself back into the moment. Andrew, on cue, removed our bowls and set a pot of paintbrushes at the center of our table. Large square plates followed, a *mise en place* of three miniature school glue bottles replete with orange nozzles, a bowl filled with shaved pickled cucumber half-circles, a selection of flowers and greenery, a bowl of what appeared to be beer batter crispies, and a slice of fried potato, delicately perforated to resemble a kind of lace or netting.

Then a chef arrived. "Hello. I'm here to instruct an art lesson this evening. Feel free to make your own interpretations of this scene as I demonstrate the general technique." He tacked a sheet of paper on the wall with a few squares of tape and, wielding a felt-tipped marker, drew a large square, presumably representing our plate.

"Begin, if you'd like, with the sea. Let the cucumbers represent the undulating waves." He sketched a series of overlapping arcs over the bottom left corner of the field. While we followed his directions, he continued. "Follow that with the shoreline, for which we have provided the beer batter tempura and caviar 'soil,' which you can secure to the plate with the tartar sauce. Explore your own preferences with the flowers and the herb sprigs to give your beach some depth."

Each of us took a different approach to our painting. Henry's precise realism and Joshua's impressionist style stood in contrast to Reynard's somewhat cubist interpretation. Mine was purely infantile—my stick figure drawn with the balsamic reduction compared poorly with their more studied, artistic approaches. I drew my Meyer lemon coulis sun in the upper right corner, following directions, eating the remaining cucumber slices as I watched the others.

While we continued, Andrew arrived with four sashimi-grade walleye fillets, which we were to place at the composition's center and ensnare with the potato net. It was all I could do to sign my plate with the remaining balsamic and not suck the glue bottles of the remaining sauces before digging in, having never touched the brushes.

"Does anyone mind that this is difficult to eat? The vinegar syrup sticks to the plate. I'm not about to lick it like a dog," Henry complained.

He was really starting to get on my nerves. "Come on, dear. Play with your food," I chided.

Henry sipped his tea, a Darjeeling hojicha. The Darjeeling was Indian, the hojicha a roasted Japanese green tea. Henry exhaled with contentment, and I softened my stiffened countenance once again. "This tea is good, at least. Mandelyn, you have to try this."

A new wine hadn't been served, so I was eager to taste a beverage designed for the course. The tea was a delight, with smoky, floral, and astringent qualities pairing nicely with the fish.

"Darjeeling—was that something you drank much of while you were in India, Manny? Tell me a story from that summer. I love your anecdotes from that trip," Joshua begged.

"Chai's the tea of choice around Jaipur, actually. Anise, cinnamon bark, white peppercorns, and cardamom pods with black tea. Buffalo milk, and more sugar than anyone should consume in a sitting. You couldn't walk a block without passing a chai-wallah stand. They're like Starbucks—one on every corner, if Starbucks was a burlap-roofed stall on a dirt sidewalk that left only enough room to walk single file between the stalls and the passing traffic."

"How did I not know that you spent time in India, Mandelyn? How long have I known you? How has this not come up before?" Reynard said. "I have been to Mumbai, Bangalore, and New Delhi, but I've not made it out to the northern provinces."

"I don't talk about it all that often. It's really not that big a deal." The truth was that, over the years, I'd grown increasingly uncomfortable talking about my international travels around Henry. I could feel his jealousy, although I couldn't place whether it was a jealousy of the travel itself or of the people with whom I'd experienced it. Early in our relationship, we talked at length about how we should travel together. We took a few long weekend trips, to Savannah, San Francisco, and Seattle—all scheduled around architectural conferences, but nothing that was purely vacation and nothing international. We'd finally gotten around to planning our trip to Ireland as an anniversary celebration. After cancelling, and after all of what was to follow, we hadn't broached the subject since.

"Oh, come on. You're being modest," Joshua persisted. "Manny here built a library while she was on a summer-long trip during college." I couldn't tell if Joshua was stirring the pot or if he was truly oblivious to the atmosphere he was brewing.

"You're right. Single-handedly. I built an entire library. I even wrote and published all the books inside." My attempt at a joke rang hollow.

"For being a professional spokesperson, you're surprisingly uncomfortable in the spotlight, my friend," Joshua teased. He knew exactly what he was doing, and I was not pleased. "Come on. Tell us one thing you discovered while you were in Jaipur."

I could see that I wasn't going to get out of this easily. "Well, our work was in a slum outside of the city's core. The difference between the urban core, the slums, and then the rural villages outside the city… night and day doesn't do it justice. Anyway, the city's neighborhoods are each on a grid, for the most part—like Chicago—which is not at all the case in any of the other major Indian cities, I hear. I didn't really travel around the country at all."

I paused to assess how engaged the table was with my story. Unfortunately, everyone seemed rapt. "Jaipur is surrounded by mountains which, during monsoon season, can be treacherous to pass," I continued. "For that reason and for security reasons, you'd always need to hire a car and a driver, or, for shorter trips in town, an autorickshaw.

"The animals there were really extraordinary. Jaipurian langurs and the rhesus macaque—two types of monkey-like creatures that each have this creamy white fur and adorable dark little faces—are about as common as deer or foxes are here—maybe even squirrels, come to think about it. Camels are about as common as horses are here. Cows are everywhere.

"I don't know… what else? I went to a cricket match once. I was just about the only white woman—just about the only woman at all—in a crowd that numbered tens of thousands. I had a good time, but it's a game I will never, ever understand. I toured a few of the palaces and gardens—opulent, of course. Thousands of years old. Amazing architecture. What else is there to say?"

The arrival of the next course saved from having to continue. A simple cylindrical glass sat at the center of accoutrements about the perimeter. "Let me tell you about each of garnishes for your mac and cheese," Andrew said as he upended the glass and let the noodles disperse onto my plate. "From the top of the merry-go-round, you have a tournedo of Mangalitsa ham rolled with arugula," he continued as he stepped to Henry's plate and began to upend his glass. "A Manchego custard, a hot dog rock…" He paused for dramatic effect before continuing. "Apple, heart of tomato, parmesan cheese, and annatto seed oil-soaked pasta." Reynard and Joshua had already taken Andrew's lead, pouring their own pasta onto their plates. Seeing this pleased Andrew, it appeared. "Enjoy, then," he chirped.

The cheddar of the dish was unusually intense, made all the more so when paired with the Manchego custard. The tomato was delectable. The most controversial ingredient at the table was the hot dog rock. A powdery, crumbly reconstitution, the men couldn't agree on whether it was too chalky, tasted too much like beef jerky, or was too concentrated.

I found it to be so fun and imaginative that I couldn't be too critical. The spice and the notes of cherry and tobacco in the Matteo Correggia Roche d'Ampsej served with the course were unworldly. Henry's root beer, infused with fennel and vanilla bean, was pure joy.

"That'd be a great school report, Man, or maybe even a travel website review, but come on. What about the reason you were really in Jaipur?"

My heart skipped a beat, and not in the good way. By the time that summer had arrived, I knew on a logical, rational plane that Dante and I were bad news, almost addicted to one another. I hadn't figured out a way—or, more to the point, summoned the will—to extricate myself emotionally. Dante had barely passed classes, and I'd slipped from any chance to achieve cum laude. He had picked up fewer and fewer shifts at the bar, and I had dropped my radio show. I'd delivered adequately on the debate team, but was ousted from top positions by Bethany, an upstart freshman who never missed a chance to remind me about how aggressively our coach and I had worked to recruit her. Dante and I were together constantly. Once volleyball season was over, I practically never spent a night in my dorm, returning only to change, shower, and maintain some guise of respectability.

Jaipur had nothing to do with philanthropy by the time summer came. The trip had everything to do with remaining hip-bound with Dante, positioning myself however I could to get that marriage proposal I so desperately wanted, even though I knew it was a bad idea and probably would never come. I annoyed myself with all of the puppy love behaviors I'd picked up. I'd decided that I'd take his last name, feminism be damned, but possibly change my middle name to Ziegel in order to maintain some vestige of my maiden identity. I'd debated whether I could give up on my dream to work for a niche Chicago ad firm and live in the city, instead settling in Des Moines, knowing that the Abatangelo apron strings had already been stretched to their limits when Dante had enrolled in college just a county away.

Joshua knew all of this about my time that summer, so I found his forcing this subject to be the height of uncouth. "Is this what you really want to talk about?" I asked. "Are you sure there isn't some favorite childhood television show you want to trade trivia about instead?"

RELEASE

Reynard picked up on my apprehension. "Perhaps I never told you that before I moved to the States, my impressions of America were formed largely by Mike Seaver and his family on *Growing Pains*? My fellow countrymen are responsible for the launch of Leonardo DiCaprio's career, as I see it. The show never would have lasted as long as it did without the popularity of its French syndication. The humor of calling Mike's friend 'Boner' confused me for years."

Reynard's efforts to divert the conversation, however worthy, were for naught. As he continued, Joshua and I were locked in a deadly stare. "Why are you doing this?" I mouthed to him. "You know why," was his wordless response. The only course I had left was to dive in headfirst.

"Alright. So I went to help build a library. Indian children of Jaipur, especially girls, are more likely to be compromised—you know, malnourished, live in filth, be orphaned, run away, suffer from preventable and curable diseases, be sold into slave labor or the sex trade, and, in the end, die young. All of that is more likely to happen to girls from that region than to children anywhere else on the planet. It's a generations-old cycle founded in the caste system, misogyny, lack of access to basic medical care, and enforced illiteracy.

"The areas around the train station were the hardest. On any given morning, you can see kindergarten-aged kids picking through garbage to find anything of value to sell or eat. They call them rag-pickers because they sell scraps of cloth to people who recycle it into new textiles and even into paper. Kids who should be in school instead tote firewood from stall to stall in the bazaars, tend cows in the insanely busy streets, hustle some game of chance, or just spend the day begging."

I continued. "The only really encouraging development in the last several years is that Rajasthan has made investments designed to reduce poverty—implementing agricultural technologies, opening access to free healthcare, and opening new schools and libraries. The libraries are key because they're for everyone, not just the children, so the adults have a chance to break from the cycle, too."

I yearned to talk about anything else. "What more can I say? I washed my clothes in a bucket all summer long. I grew used to the monsoons and mosquito nets. I dealt with the wide-eyed stares from men in the street. I picked up some Hindi phrases that I've all but forgotten. I got my fill of chapattis, naan, daal, and chai. That's about it."

"With whom did you travel, Man? Were you there all alone?" Joshua asked.

I'd had it. I threw my napkin on the table. "Do you know where the washrooms are, Josh?" I asked, faking a smile through clenched teeth. "Would you show me where they are?"

"Sure, Man. Right this way," he taunted.

We had barely made it around the corner when Joshua started in. "Don't call me Josh. You know I hate nicknames. When have I ev…"

"What! The! Fuck! Josh?" I spat each word at him. I thumped him in the sternum with the back of my right fist with each exclamation. I noticed the man doubling as coat check and host look askance from his post. I continued, whispering. "You know what that trip meant to me, Josh-oo-ah," I emphasized. "Why are you dredging it up, and tonight of all nights? Can't you see that Henry is on edge?"

"When isn't Henry on edge these days, Mandelyn? That man is more tightly wound than anyone I have ever met. How badly do your feet hurt from walking on eggshells? Wait. Don't answer that. Let me ask you something else. Does Henry know about the trip to Jaipur? Really know, I mean?

"When you got back after that summer, I could see a fire in you unlike any I'd seen before and like nothing I've seen since. You had purpose, Mandelyn. Conviction. Of all the people who said they wanted to save the world, you seemed to be someone actually poised to do it. Where has that fire gone, Man? I know this isn't the right time, but when is it ever going to be? When are you going to wake up? The suburbs, your dull job, and your marginal marriage aren't going to sustain your spirit forever. I am watching it die by degrees, each time I see you. You are selling yourself short, and it's killing me to watch it."

Somewhere in Joshua's monologue, I abandoned any hope of keeping my composure. Tears rolled off my cheeks and stained my white silk blouse. There was only one thing I could say. "Don't you think I know that? But tonight isn't the night to solve my problems. Tonight isn't about me. It is only about all of us just having a nice time together."

"It is your birthday dinner, Mandelyn. Whose day is it if it isn't yours? And tomorrow, something else will get in the way. Another excuse, another procrastination. Another surrendered chance to live this life. I am trying to give you a gift here. I wish you would take it."

"Shove your gift up your ass, Joshua. I am handling things the best I can." I spun to leave, whether to the washroom, back to the table, or, damn it all, out the front door, I didn't even know.

Joshua grabbed me urgently. "That is exactly my point. This isn't your best. If it is, it just isn't good enough. You are better than this. It's like Nelson Mandela said: 'Our deepest fear is not that we are inadequate. Our deepest fear is that we are powerful beyond measure.' I don't remember it all, but he goes on to say, 'Who am I to be brilliant, gorgeous, talented, fabulous? No, who are you not to be? Your playing small does not serve the world.'"

I spoke plainly. "What if I'm not? I'm not better than this. Not anymore. And that scares the shit out of me. Thanks for bringing the worst of me to my attention, J. You're the best." I wiped the last tear from my face.

"By the way," I said, "that's not Mandela. Get your facts straight." Without so much as a glance at a mirror, I returned to the table.

I arrived to see Henry and Reynard cracking up, guffawing like two seventh graders who'd just seen a naked woman for the first time. The sight began to restore my mood. Lunch boxes had been placed for each of us. "I was just explaining the allure of Daisy Duke to Reynard. Apparently, short shorts work in any language and for any persuasion," Henry said as Reynard struggled to regain composure.

"I think I had this actual lunchbox," I said, examining the Strawberry Shortcake scene on its side.

"Who's Bobby Sherman?" Joshua asked, having followed me by a few paces, returning just as I had taken my chair.

"The Justin Bieber of his day," Andrew shared as he refilled water glasses. "We get that a lot. It's the oldest box we have in the collection."

"He kind of looks like you, Joshua," I teased. "At least it's how you looked when you were in your *CHiPs* phase."

Joshua smiled. "You were never a good Jon to my Ponch, but I can't say you didn't try."

"You wanted to be Ponch and Jon. There wasn't much space left for me." Finally, we all laughed.

The box contained an apple-brandy-port wine fruit roll-up, a homemade funyun, a tender piece of Wagyu beef jerky, a chocolate-banana-hazelnut praline pudding, and a Thermos filled with berry juice. Reynard's, Joshua's, and mine were port-spiked. The absolute highlight of the course was an Oreo-inspired truffle cookie.

If anyone noticed that my face looked a fright, no one said a word. Conversation continued on a far more innocuous path for a while, started by the notes in our lunchboxes signed by "Mom" or "Dad." What I supposed would be a sure-fire pitfall for our table's still-tenuous mood turned out to be easily sidestepped, due mostly to Henry refraining from sharing any more of his sad childhood stories. I would have been willing to bet he never got a note in his lunchbox in his entire life.

Reynard talked about his latest gallery exhibit. He was a freelance curator with exotic connections worldwide, and it didn't take long to feel humbled by his experience and wisdom. His passion for his work mitigated any feelings of envy or inadequacy his stories generated, however. It was impossible to watch him describe his discoveries—how they moved him, how he had seen people react to them—without getting caught up in his admiration and wonder.

Joshua, in turn, described the pharmaceutical research currently under way under his leadership. He had been recruited to join a multi-national conglomerate after he had achieved some degree of notoriety for his work on a cholesterol drug at a boutique laboratory the year before. While it would be years before his work would manifest for the general marketplace, his name had already begun to carry a degree of weight among professional circles.

Drug discussion continued as the next course arrived—a salad, Andrew said, that was meant to evoke the memory of an autumn walk in the Michigan woods. Service of the dish strained Andrew's forearms. Each of us received halved and hollowed birch logs, which served as a base, inside of which were hot stones roasting chestnuts, hay, and bits of pumpkin and apple. Atop the log and a clear plexiglas surface was a woodland scene crafted from broccoli, carrots, Swiss chard, and leeks, with garnishes of nasturtium, sorrel, sage, and thyme. Boulders of polenta that had been rolled in puffed black rice framed the dish, with roasted maitake rounding out the presentation.

"Is it just me, or does this smell like a Grateful Dead concert?" Henry asked.

"I wouldn't know. I never went to one," I said.

"Well, Dave Matthews, then. Or Phish. You know what I mean. This dish smells like weed."

We all laughed a little nervously. "Whatever do you mean, Henry?" I asked guilelessly.

Despite plenty of opportunities to do so, I had only smoked pot once, with Henry, on the night we met. Of all of the memories I supposed might be elicited during dinner that night, I never would have supposed that one so removed from my childhood would be one of them.

"No weed I smoked ever smelled this good," Joshua countered.

"How much did you ever smoke?" I asked. Strangely, I'd never talked about marijuana with Joshua.

"Not a lot—I don't know, a dozen times in college, maybe? How about you, Man?"

"Just once," I said, smiling a knowing smile at Henry.

A good amount of time passed between the salad course and the next. I was grateful for the respite, as I had become pretty full. Portions were more generous than I'd anticipated. I also didn't mind the time to regain a bit of sobriety, either.

When the next course was brought around, I was put off a bit by its composition. "This isn't just a hamburger, folks. This is meant to take you back to the time when McDonald's, Burger King, or White Castle was a treat."

"This looks like the aftermath of a food fight," I whispered to the table. Apart from the "burger," a sous-vide cooked, flat-top finished short rib, most of the other ingredients were liquefied to some degree and spread upon the plate. The sesame seed bun was, in fact, a sauce. If it hadn't been sprinkled with sesame seeds, it might have been mistaken for a pate. I found the ketchup off-putting—strong on Worcestershire, sugar, and vinegar. The mustard, pickles, and caramelized onion were more to my liking. I figured out what triggered me about the course.

"This smells like Polly's, doesn't it, Joshua?"

"That's exactly it!" Joshua exclaimed. "No wonder I gravitated to cholesterol pharmaceuticals. It's a wonder my blood type isn't Velveeta, after all the processed cheese food I ate back then."

"I love it," Henry said, his mouth full of food. "This tastes like childhood to me, more than anything we've had tonight."

"Did you eat a lot of hamburgers in your youth, *Henri*?" Reynard asked.

"It was all I could manage on my schedule. I'd run from school to work, and the only thing on the way was Mickey D's. It took going off to college for me to finally wise up about what I put in my system. I swear I had Big Mac nightmares and french fry withdrawal for a semester before shaking my addiction."

"What was your job in high school?" Joshua asked.

"Oh, work started in junior high. I helped my mom clean offices. It was the only way she could manage two jobs."

"Two jobs?" asked Reynard.

"Sure," Henry scoffed. "Most of the time, when she could hold onto the work. Sometimes three, if she could pick up a laundry job along the way. She cleaned homes for a service during the day, then I pitched in cleaning offices with her at night. The work got done more quickly that way," Henry said as he mixed the ingredients together on his plate. "It's really better if you stir it all together instead of eating each one alone, don't you think?"

Everyone's expressions were blank. Joshua and Reynard were busy processing the new information. I only realized then that neither of our friends knew that much about Henry's upbringing. My poverty stories earlier hadn't prompted responses at all similar to the ones Joshua and Reynard had now. I had described a distant land populated by people they'd never meet. Mine was a morbidly fascinating story, like something you'd glean from a *National Geographic*. Our friends pitied Henry, now. His poverty—even poverty that had been overcome, and not nearly as abhorrent as what I'd observed in Jaipur—was ten times more real because it was suddenly sitting at our table.

"You'd buy your own dinner every night, on your way to work cleaning offices after school? What were you, eleven?" Joshua stated more than asked.

"That's about right," Henry said, unfazed.

"Henry, I'm so sorry," Joshua sighed. "I had no idea."

"No idea of what? That I didn't grow up in the fairy tale idyll that the two of you knew?" he asked, motioning to Joshua and me. "Don't give it another thought." Henry was doing something that I couldn't quite comprehend. His tone was more jovial than it'd been all evening, but there was a saccharine quality to it that put my teeth on edge.

"Don't pity me. This isn't Dickens. I'm not Pip," he said dismissively. "Come on, let's continue to enjoy our conspicuous consumption, why don't we?" Henry took a big gulp of his caramel rooibos tea. In response to his command, each of the rest of us took generous swallows of our Spanish red wine, perplexed as to how to proceed.

The tone of the evening shifted in that moment, or maybe nothing changed and I had just managed to ignore recognizing it for a while. We had already been at the restaurant for more than three hours. Laughter could be heard throughout the dining room, but a stilted silence had fallen over our table. I found myself listening intently to the *Back to the Future* soundtrack. Andrew, possibly sensing the discord, returned to our table with buoyancy we hadn't previously seen. "I have a dish from the chef that he would like you to try. He wants you to eat your vegetables before dessert," he said with an almost forced yet entirely professional theatricality.

On each of our plates were five hollowed brussels sprout cups, each filled with a different sauce. "From the top, going clockwise, we have a Béarnaise pudding, bacon rillettes, truffle puree, bacon jam, mustard cream, and chestnut puree. Let me know which becomes your favorite, everyone." Andrew clapped his hands together, trying to manufacture a little mirth before retreating. We ate joylessly, the scrumptious pastes and gels lost in our thorny impasse.

"How does the flavor of the Béarnaise compare to the sauce you grew up with, Reynard?" I said to break the silence.

Henry interjected, "Don't fill the quiet with the frivolous or inane, Mandelyn."

"Come on, Henry," Joshua interceded, "don't be that way. Hey, I'm sorry. I just didn't know. It doesn't change anything."

"What you just said makes no sense at all. No kidding, it doesn't change anything—for me. I'm still a black man from the 'hood. Does it change anything for you?"

I had never heard Henry refer to himself as a black man. Why hearing him say it was shocking, I can't explain. On the surface, it was like calling an apple red or the sky blue. What made it strange was that Henry never identified with black American culture.

"What are you doing, Henry? You're scaring me," I said.

"Aryan princess scared by the black man. Well, princess, I am black. It's what people see. Might as well call this spade a fucking shovel, right, Joshua?"

I didn't care how awkward the rest of the night was going to become. No one was going to call me a racist. I opened my mouth to begin a rant in my defense but was cut off.

"At least I'm finally going to get some mileage out of it," Henry continued. "That's the other big news of the day. I got promoted. I am now President of the city's newest architectural and engineering Minority and Disadvantaged Business Enterprise."

"What? Why now?" I stammered, incredulous.

"I gave in, Mandelyn. They've wanted me to lend my name to the designation request ever since I got my S.E. I always resisted. Today, they named my price, and I took it. I sold out."

I was flabbergasted, desperately flailing for anything I could possibly say in response.

There was a long pause before Joshua finally spoke. "I know it isn't happening the way you'd probably want it to happen, Henry, but MBE or DBE is nothing to be ashamed of. It'll open up a lot of new opportunities for you."

Henry put down his fork with a little more force than was required. "Have I ever seemed like someone who is ashamed, Joshua?"

"No, you haven't," Joshua carefully replied.

"Do I come across as pretentious, or someone with anything to hide?"

"Not at all," Joshua assured him.

"I am a man who is concerned about many things, but the way you or anyone else perceives me is not on the list, Joshua. Do you know why that is? It is because I am not ashamed. I am not pretentious, and I don't have anything to hide.

"I never took a hand-out, Joshua," Henry continued. "I never hit from the short tees. I know I had more challenges than you while I was growing up. I don't judge you for your pristine childhood any more than you should judge me for my dire one. I see now that you made assumptions about me based on my achievements, like I wasn't one of 'those' black men because I'd managed to get out.

"My character was developed while overcoming my challenges, you see. You've surmised certain things about me. That I'm cold. That I'm distant. That is fine. Those suppositions are probably true. Just keep this in mind: your paradigm doesn't include the complications mine does. This new information doesn't change the truth. I'm still the same person."

Everyone was stunned, diffident in the face of Henry's declarations, which made the farcical irony of the next course's whimsy all the more acerbic. "Who likes Pixy Sticks and bubblegum?" Andrew sang as he set the plates and glasses down, disappearing as quickly as he had appeared. Set where a knife would belong was a pair of scissors to cut open each of the three tubes containing freeze-dried powders—strawberry, raspberry, and hibiscus, as we discovered. The frosted mug of pink soda arrived with a float of crème fraîche over the top. I engrossed myself in the course, actively deflecting the ominous mood from my perception.

"Are we okay, Henry?" Joshua asked timidly. "You two mean the world to me. I don't want a rift between us."

"We're fine, Joshua," Henry stated bluntly, eyes never leaving his plate, his behavior revealing his true feelings.

I dismissed him, reaching for Joshua's and Reynard's clasped hands, taking them in mine and kissing the back of each in turn. "Nothing you could do or say would separate us. Not ever."

While everyone had said and done the appropriate things, the situation still felt unresolved, but none of us had the energy to make any further amends just yet. Reynard was the first to take the reins, asking what plans were shaping up for the upcoming holidays. We hadn't really discussed ours yet, I shared, assuming that we would make Thanksgiving dinner for ourselves and save our trip to see my mother in New Mexico at Christmas time. Reynard said this was nonsense—that we ought to have dinner together at their place and bring the dogs so they could all play together. Segueing to the dogs, we continued talking about them until the next course arrived.

"Good Lord, it's foie gras on a beater. How precious is that?" Joshua cooed. "And hot apple cider doughnut holes? We got those at the pumpkin farm every year, remember, Manny?"

I had already begun to lick my beater, so I could only grunt and nod my reply. It was a perfect ending to the meal, or so I thought. Without menus, which, as Andrew explained, wouldn't be handed out until the end, I naturally assumed that two desserts were quite enough, but no. Not one, but two desserts still remained.

The campfire sweet potato pie course rivaled the Autumn Walk course's presentation complexity. Andrew revealed the vanilla and cinnamon-stewed sweet potato "logs" that were arranged on a slate slab before they were set ablaze, fueled by a powdered grain alcohol. While they burned, he prepared our plates with apricot puree, marshmallows, ginger pâtes de fruit, and bourbon ice cream. It was the only point during the entire meal when our quiet wasn't brought about by awkward tension. We were all mesmerized by the crackle of the flames.

"This is my favorite dish of all, I think," Joshua marveled. I looked at him over the red and orange glow. I knew what he meant. I was also thinking back to campfires at the Girls' School, and I smiled more warmly than I had all night long. Once the lights came up, we served ourselves, topping the entire concoction with a drizzle of warm butterscotch syrup.

By the time the hot cocoa arrived, I was beyond full. The chocolate was decadent, and the Armagnac, as Reynard explained, was oak-aged and distilled only once, making it more pungent and complex than typical brandies. "It is believed to have multiple healing properties, including the cure for hepatitis and gout," Reynard laughed, "so if you suffer these maladies, you're all set, my friends. It is also purposed to 'Loosen the tongue and embolden the wit, if someone timid from time to time himself permits,'" he recited as a quotation from memory. Henry helped himself to the majority of my serving. I hoped what Reynard said was true.

RELEASE

All told, we had been at Next for over five hours, and it had felt every bit of that. Andrew was swift and practically invisible as he processed bills and returned receipts. We walked with Joshua and Reynard to Halsted before parting ways. Joshua was brief, only whispering, "Remember what I said," in my ear before slapping me on the back like an old buddy and calling out, "Happy Birthday, ol' Man."

Our drive home was nearly silent. I thought about the Proustian moments we'd all experienced during the meal, especially Henry's. Of any of us, his was the childhood that was the most stark and pronounced. In comparison, ours seemed unworthy of comment—relatively unchallenged, undistinguished, and unremarkable.

I wished that we could spend the drive home talking about the balance of concept and execution of the meal; debate the idea of food as art versus sustenance; discuss the narrative, beauty, extravagance, and any number of high-level thoughts. As we followed the expressway home, I yearned to talk about the experience but didn't have the wit to navigate it without letting any of the other night's peculiarities infiltrate.

I finally summoned the courage to ask, "Your partners want you to get in talks with the Laboratory now, don't they?"

"Yep. I have fifty-one percent control of the subsidiary, but all my directives will come from the board. So fifty-one percent doesn't mean much."

"They think that the MBE/DBE will help you stand out, I take it?"

"Yep," Henry repeated. I lost my will to ask any more.

I thought about what Joshua had said about eggshells. At moments throughout the dinner, I had alternately wanted to conclude the night with Henry either with sex or with murder. As it turned out, neither occurred. We each stumbled our way to our bedroom, shed our clothes unceremoniously and, without so much as brushing our teeth or washing our faces, crawled into bed and fell promptly to sleep.

11

Thursday, November 10

Colette's advice in the days leading up to the Architectural Celebration was hilarious. "Live it up! You deserve this. Marketers at companies all over town attend parties like this once each month or more. Just because you are the face and voice of the geek elite doesn't mean that you have to behave like one of them. Rock your inner diva, and, for once, live a story that you can sit across a table and entertain me with, please?"

I needed to find a dress. I visited every shop in two suburban malls for something I thought would be both interesting yet understated. "Wear black, unless you have some incredibly bold statement to make and want to announce it with your outfit. Everyone wears black. I'm not saying 'be boring.' Be bold. Just be bold in black," Colette coached.

I didn't find a thing after a Saturday of searching. That night, in a panic, I Googled phrase after phrase—"black cocktail dresses," "pretty professional dresses," and even "edgy evening wear"—but couldn't find anything but eBay listings and soft-core porn. It was when I searched "sexy couture" that I finally had a breakthrough. Couture, it turned out, triggered an ad for a high-end runway rental website. Never in a million years would I dream of buying the Narciso Rodriguez 'Seek Expertise Shift' I selected, but for a fraction of the price, I could wear it for one night.

The train was the better way to get downtown for the evening, and it was common sense to get a hotel room. The Laboratory wouldn't reimburse the cost, but we weren't destitute. Taking the train meant avoiding outrageous parking costs, saving gas, and, most importantly, allowing me a drink or two at the reception—after joining the project team on stage for the award acceptance, of course—with an easy place to crash at night's end. I was almost as excited about the hotel as I was about the event. The online deal I found was, thankfully, where the event was taking place—inside the most exciting addition to the Chicago skyline in a decade, Aqua Tower.

So that's how I found myself on the all-stops afternoon train from Weston to Ogilvie Station at one-thirty in the afternoon, with a dress bag across my lap and my gym bag on the floor between my ankles. I had my new shoes (gold metallic Valentino Bow d'Orsay Pumps), thigh-high nylons (my go-to secret confidence-builder), Spanx (which utterly desexualized the aforementioned), and all manner of unfamiliar makeup (department store cosmetic ladies are surely the present-day incarnation of the Sirens Odysseus encountered), so I was prepared to give the dress its proper carriage.

The bottle-green glass in the windows of the train car enhanced the bleakness of the passing scenery, leafless trees and contrails transitioning to dilapidated factories and barbed wire fences over the course of the next hour. The leaves were the only things that were different about the view I remembered from the short period of time that I had commuted from Weston to my job at the agency downtown. The landscape, even while it was verdant, had been as dreary as the commute. When Henry had been promoted after getting his licenses, I finally surrendered to his persistent requests and abandoned the last vestige of my city life.

My only traveling companion that afternoon was a twenty-something on the upper-level in the last corner seat, wearing standard-issue hipster apparel, replete with a plaid fur-lined trapper hat. A yellow box of Natural American Spirit cigarettes poked out of the canvas messenger bag splayed on the luggage rack suspended beside him, over the aisle below. His feet, in blue Dr. Martens, were hoisted beside the bag. I could make out the cutouts of three white stars across the toes of the boots and another set of three stars along the ankle.

He caught me looking him over. "Nice shoes," I said.

"Yeah… they're vintage," he mooned as he looked them over in admiration. "You can only find them in the U.K., usually, except I picked these up at Goodwill." His tone implied that I should be impressed with him in at least a few different ways. Because I didn't respond with the appropriate amount of awe, he sighed and returned his attention to his worn copy of Pynchon's *Inherent Vice* and—no kidding—actually began twisting his mustache in contemplation.

The landscape and solitude did nothing to daunt my spirits. After weeks of directionless, self-involved navel gazing, I was finally feeling as if I was breaking through. "Directionless" probably wasn't a fair assessment of how I'd spent my time, actually. I had become fond of journaling with Morgan, and I felt like I had been guided toward some important discoveries. As we rolled on, I pulled the tablet from my bag and wrote.

> Morgan,
>
> "To what degree have I abandoned my sense of identity over time?" I find myself wondering this afternoon. In the last three years, I have devolved from being a determined yet free spirit to a risk-averse weakling. I find as much self-actualization in The Container Store these days as I ever did harvesting mulberries in Muang Khoun, building in Jaipur, or pitching an ad campaign. I had never been the type to settle down. How much mileage did I expect to get out of living halfway, or lately, living in the past?
>
> Henry used to tell me how courageous he thought I was. It's fair to believe that my changing so fundamentally could be a source of resentment for him but, being a good man, Henry continued to love me, however hard I'd managed to make it for him to do.
>
> Henry hasn't changed at all from the moment we met, like I said. He is focused, reliable, and unimpeachably ethical. When we lost Theodore, it was Henry who suggested we move to Weston and slow the pace of our lives, even though he hated the suburbs and we took a loss on the condo. Henry stepped it up at the office at a time when half our friends were losing their jobs. He got himself promoted, for crying out loud, making it possible for me to leave the agency and join the Laboratory. He was the one who bathed me—on those times that I couldn't see the point. He washed my hair and shaved my legs.
>
> I have been immensely ungrateful. I can see that now. I chose to see Henry's stalwart, emotionless behavior as foreboding instead of as a fortification for both of us. I can't blame

him for adapting his survival mechanisms into habits over time, especially since I validated them through my acquiescence. I chose to see him as a martyr instead of a rock. I chose to resent the anchor and safe harbor he provided, instead of treasuring their protections while the horrible storm swirled around and battered us.

I have projected unreasonable expectations onto Henry. With the whole idea of "soul mates" and "one person out there for everyone" mythology I embraced as a child, it's no wonder Henry isn't meeting my expectations! Who could?

Henry is a partner to me, giving everything he has to our relationship. Henry does not have strong communication skills. I have always known that. Should that condemn him—condemn us? How strong a partner have I been to him, on the whole? Is it fair to punish him—punish us, really—by withholding my ability to connect, just because it's harder for him to meet me at my level? Absolutely not. It's just not fair for me to expect Henry to be this be-all, end-all, perfect guy who meets all my needs. It's just not realistic.

If I'm thinking realistically, I have to admit that I'd sold Henry short when his tender, honest gestures of love didn't look and feel like fairy tale chivalry. He will never be the guy to hold my hand while walking down the street. He won't buy me flowers or tell me I look nice without an obscene amount of hinting on my part. He will never ask me to dance. What will he do instead? He'll do the most selfless, even debasing, work to care for me the best way he knows how.

It comes down to this: loving Henry means loving him for who he is, as well as who he isn't. I need to decide to do that if our marriage is going to work.

Maybe we get to have our trysts and escapades before marriage, so that whatever we give up in order to be with just one person isn't really lost. Our experiences still exist, at least in our memories. I treasure all of the Emma-Mr. Knightley, Scarlett-Rhett flirtations I shared with Sam over the years, before we lost track of each other. I don't think those coquettish exchanges could have occurred outside of the safe confines of a relationship that could never be anything more than platonic. Projecting any more gravity onto that period in my life, yearning to relive it, or seeking it in my present circumstances is nothing but quixotic impracticality.

Equally impractical is the yearning for the kind of chemical, hormonal, raw animal heat people find in college flings, like I had with Dante. Yes, I can safely say that my wild oats are sown. While I have to admit that the likelihood of, oh, say, screwing in a public place again or making another sex tape is absolutely not in my future, I'm glad I have the torrid memories. What am I to draw upon while fantasizing, after all? Hahaha. My dirty library is well-stocked with material. – M

The image of an actual "dirty library" began to take shape in my head. I pictured a saucy animated princess, gliding aboard a ladder past volumes of leather-bound books (because how else would books in a dirty library be bound?), seeking just the right story of light bondage and role play. The snorting laugh that erupted from me drew the eye of the hipster as he rose from his seat and slung his bag over his head and across his body. I gave him a wink.

As the train pulled into the station, I straightened my poise with resolve. A new chapter was beginning in my life, one of clarity. I knew who I was, or thought I was on my way. "Knowing who Henry is and who we are together is the firm foundation on which I will begin to build my life from this point forward," I thought to myself. The insipid longing to live in the past needed to stay safely behind me. I'd spent too many years pretending to be a grown-up. Actually being an adult—that started now.

As I strode through the station and out onto Canal Street, the brisk wind carried the heady scent of Blommer Chocolate, and it intoxicated me. It took me back to the days of waking up in Henry's bed, in his condo, the condo that would become ours, and where we would begin to build our life together. The message from the universe couldn't have been clearer. That was the day that I would try to begin again.

12

Friday, November 11

Just before five in the morning, I was startled awake by the sound of sirens on the street below. There were so many unfamiliar city noises I'd forgotten about, that I had grown unaccustomed to hearing since moving to Weston.

I wanted to fall back to sleep and put off contemplating what had happened the night before, but I knew that wasn't going to happen. I thought about gathering my things, sneaking out of the hotel room, and going home. The walk to the train station would be bone-chilling, and the thought of the all-stops reverse commute thwarted that plan. I gathered the sheets around me, unable to truly fathom what I had done.

But there he was—Sam, sleeping beside me.

My mind picked up some speed with that anxious acknowledgement. I thought about taking a taxi all the way back to Weston. Finding one that would do it would be practically impossible. I tried to calculate what a taxi to Weston would cost, imagining how large a tip I would need to promise to convince someone to go. And how would I explain that to Henry? I'd taken the day off of work to enjoy the city, or possibly nurse a hangover, which hadn't, thankfully, arrived. Yet. My swirling head told me that it was entirely possible I was still drunk.

So, I wasn't leaving. Besides, it was my hotel room. I'd have to go through the whole check-out process, and I couldn't just leave Sam here to wake up alone. I hadn't begun to think through how I felt about the previous night's debauchery, but I knew we couldn't ignore what had happened and act like everything was normal.

I knew I should have been guilt-stricken. A large part of me was. What had happened to my resolve to make an effort with Henry? What had happened to my resolution to "begin again?" A large portion of me felt like I'd broken a promise to myself, like I'd let myself down. Guilt and disappointment consumed most of my emotions, but there was a small part of me that began to rationalize. Maybe I needed to get this depravity out of my system before I could make a new start on my marriage?

Good Lord, I was the master of delusion. I was getting lost in spirals of thought and knew there was only one way to sort everything out. With the tablet in hand, I pulled a discarded duvet from the foot of the bed, wrapped it around myself, and snuck out onto the balcony.

First, I read the response from yesterday afternoon's entry.

> You are making progress, but consider sorting things out somewhat further. There are lessons to learn before you move on. There is past, there is present, and there is future.

On the one hand, this was a novel compared to the previous responses. On the other hand, there really wasn't any clear directive. As it was, I didn't have much time to contemplate what Morgan meant. I set to writing.

> Morgan,
>
> I have made a terrible mistake.
>
> I want to get these details down before sleep, repression, or alcohol take them away. I snuck out of my own hotel room and onto this beautiful hotel balcony. I can see my breath, it's so cold out here, not made any better by the fact that I don't have any pajamas. I planned to be alone in my room and didn't have space in my bag for them. Don't worry—I haven't become a completely uninhibited degenerate. I stole the duvet off the bed to keep me warm.
>
> Last night should have been a highlight in my career. If I limit my memories of last night to the banquet itself, maybe it'll be that again one day. As it is, I might have ruined everything.
>
> I will tell the story of last night with as much information as I recall. It would be easier, I think, if I would just put it behind me, but you have told me that I need to sort things out and learn from them before I can move on, so that is what I will do.

RELEASE

I'm already a little hazy on some of the details. If only I can black this out, now that would be something!

The night began like a fairy tale, except that instead of brainless princesses and impossible princes, there were artists, scientists, benefactors, humanitarians, and captains of industry, each more brilliant and accomplished than the last. The room glowed with more candlelight than you'd think the Chicago Fire Department would allow (exoneration of Mrs. O'Leary's cow notwithstanding) and globe chandeliers of twinkling lights suspended from the ceiling by imperceptible threads. Each table's centerpiece was arranged differently, with calla lilies, orchids, amaryllis, astilbes, pussy willow branches, and many other varieties of lovely white flowers and greenery I couldn't begin to identify.

Almost all of the attendees were, in fact, wearing black, which should have made the servers in white tuxedo jackets easier to find. I needed to find one—several, actually—and get food in my stomach before I could think about enjoying a drink. Every waiter I could see was carrying champagne, however. If there was to be some sort of toast, I didn't want to be caught empty-handed. I took a glass, promising myself that I wouldn't take but a sip until whatever we were getting ready to celebrate was announced.

My table was near the windows overlooking Lake Shore East Park, which afforded a wonderful view but was about as far away as possible from hors d'oeuvres, the bar, and the best socializing. Looking across the room from the doorway into the ballroom, I could see that the project team had already taken their seats. I knew that the right thing to do would be to join them, but, reasoning that I would spend the rest of the night at their table, I continued my search for a stuffed mushroom, chicken satay skewer, or even a canapé.

I have to tell the truth. I put myself together pretty well last night. The dress, which I had chosen as much for its artsy features as I had for the fact that it seemed like it'd be figure-forgiving, still required industrial-strength Spanx, a torture device I have long since surrendered to wearing on nearly a daily basis.

I was glad to have had the foresight to make an appointment at the hotel salon for an up-do and mani-pedi. I knew that I'd twirl and fuss with my hair all evening if it were down, and the whole ensemble would have been for naught if I hadn't given my bedraggled nails over to professional intervention. This got everything set in place and off my mind. Best of all, I managed to find some darling Kate Spade gold bow earrings, a matching pendant, and a pair of Valentino pumps on eBay. I looked at the shimmering metallic gold heels with these so-not-me ostentatious bows across the toes and paraphrased Colette. "I look fucking fabulous," I said to my reflection.

No amount of primping, however—the primers, powders, contouring, lining, and filling—would have prepared me for what happened just after I walked into the "pre-event lounge." (I'd called it a bar a few times, to the disdain of the concierge and restaurant hostess I asked for directions through the sprawling first-floor complex.) I was meandering through the crowd, looking for a familiar face, or at least a mini quiche or a spring roll, when someone whispered in my ear from behind me.

"I've never seen you looking any hotter. How about we ditch this place and get out of here?"

I knew exactly who it was the instant he'd begun to speak, which is why I took a generous drink of my champagne to brace myself.

"Sam! What are you doing here?" I exclaimed my question more than asked it as I swung around, knowing who I would see but having no idea why or how.

I hadn't seen him in over a year, since a co-worker's wedding reception at River Run, where he'd returned to work as a manager after college. I gave him the hug of an old friend. A few weeks ago, when I was still waxing nostalgic about relationships past and what might have been, I might have been more coy or flirty. For the moment, though, I only had two things on my mind: relief for finally finding a familiar face, and food.

I stepped back and held Sam at arm's length. He was in a black tuxedo, something I'd only seen him wearing once before, at Joshua's wedding.

"Man, you clean up well. How much did your 'date' pay for you?" I asked. Okay, I could flirt a little if it was in the language of innocent, backhanded compliments, right?

"You like what you see?" he asked. He spun on a heel, ran his hand down the left lapel, and gave me a wink. "I think I'm even above your pay grade now, Manny. It's only high-class prostitution for me these days. Speaking of prostitution, you're probably here… Let me think." He tapped his left index finger against his lips in thought. "I've got it. You are either here shilling for one of these chumps freelance, or you are filling in for one of the nukes at your Lab who cancelled at the last minute."

"It has been a while since we last saw each other," I said, nodding in mock admiration of his supposed shrewdness and taking another sip, "but it's nice that you remember my line of work. No. I'm not here freelancing, and I'm not filling in. I'm the director of communications for the Laboratory, now. I'm here to represent them when Muon g-2 wins its award tonight."

"So when a dozen people traipse onto the stage to look admiringly at the architect's back, you, the most articulate one of the bunch, will be standing there with the proles, nodding and smiling?"

"Well, yeah," I said, trailing off for just a pause while deciding whether to take the bait of his insult. "And I get to eat well, drink well, and partake in delightful banter for an evening away in the city. Speaking of which, I must be going." I feigned a turn to leave.

"Wait, don't go. Don't be cross. Here." He snagged a crab cake from a passing tray. I had noticed several trays pass as we talked but didn't want to be caught with food in my mouth during our repartee. He handed me the crab cake. "Here. A peace offering."

"I forgive you," I said, taking a bite, then continued, with my mouth full, "mostly because these crab cakes are unbelievable." I upended my flute to wash it down.

"Thanks," he smiled. "I'll be sure to pay your compliments to the chef."

I thought he was being cute, but something about the look on his face told me otherwise. I gestured at him, using the empty glass as a sort of interrogatory magic wand. "Wait. What do you mean 'you'll pay my compliments to the chef?'"

"This is my gig. I've been managing events here on contract for about a year, now. It was only part-time for a while, but it's almost a full-time job now."

I wanted to interject another snide comment, about how proud I was that he was making his way up the escort industry ladder, but Sam whisked his hand to the left and grasped another champagne by the stem and handed it to me, all without breaking my eye contact. I decided to let my snide comment go. "Why, thank you. So that explains the tuxedo. But what do you mean 'full-time?' What about River Run?"

"You really haven't gotten out much lately, have you? River Run has been 'Closed for Renovations' for about five months now, ever since the beginning of July." He had air-quoted and winked when he said "closed for renovations." "Either the owners were running a drug cartel out of the joint, or the place was about to fail structurally and tumble into the river. It was in such disrepair. I'd named some of the mice I saw on a regular basis."

I snickered, even as my stomach turned at the thought of mice in the kitchen.

"Doesn't matter," Sam continued. "I was done with that place. I was already contracting down here, now and then. I started around the beginning of the year. When River Run closed, I picked up a few shifts bartending at Meat, that new bar and smokehouse just down from where your dad's shop used to be, but the pace here was already picking up. The commute sucks, but the money's good. I may move down here after the holidays if it keeps up. I love it."

I began to respond, but an anxious man in a white chef's coat appeared at Sam's side. He whispered something in his ear, and then Sam gave him a clipped response. He turned back to me. "You're going to get me fired. I've been chatting you up while I should have been making sure the tables were set with soup spoons instead of salad forks." He kissed my cheek and squeezed my shoulder. "I'll find you again later on. Hopefully, you'll be drunk and in the mood to make some bad decisions," he winked. "A word of advice: load up on appetizers. The portions you're getting with dinner are for crap. Delicious but tiny, unlike me. I'm awful, but, well… you know…"

I knew. Sam was witty, but he was never subtle.

Oh, God. I've ruined everything. The sun is coming up over the lake, now. I can't see much of it because of the other buildings along the water, but the sparkles that are sneaking through the spaces between are still something to behold.

Just then, I heard Sam slide the balcony door open behind me. Like a guilty child, I closed the website window before he could see what I had been doing.

"Did I catch you getting a pre-dawn porn fix?"

I laughed what I thought would be a cute, but turned out to be a nervous, giggle. "Um, no!"

"Oh, that's too bad. I find that a good porn fix before breakfast can get your day off to a great start."

I tried to manufacture my half of our usual Hepburn-Tracy banter, but it just wasn't coming. I shrugged.

"It's freezing out here. Come inside. I want to see if nipples can actually cut glass."

I must have given him a look of shock. "I'm kidding!" he said as he approached. "I put a K-cup on for you. I hope dark roast is alright. I ordered a continental breakfast, too—hope that's okay. I told them to charge it to my house account." He bent down to kiss the base of my neck, and I involuntarily recoiled.

"You are shivering," he observed, and, as he looked down into my duvet, he saw why. "Fuck, you're saucy. Out here, naked as a jaybird for all of Lake Shore East to see," he teased in a juvenile sing-song tone. He eased the duvet off my left shoulder as he knelt down and began to kiss my shoulder. I resisted, easing the duvet back into place.

"You're right. It is cold out here," I said. I put my bare feet down onto the concrete and made a move toward standing, but Sam had come around to stand before me. I hadn't realized it before now, but he had nothing but a cotton sheet on himself, folded up awkwardly and wrapped around his waist like an enormous towel.

"Wait a moment. Will you let me do something?" He was barely audible. "Stand up," he said.

I did. He took the corner of the duvet I was clutching in my left hand. I released my grasp without thinking, once again letting myself be mesmerized. I had the other corner tucked under the same arm. Slowly, but deftly, he held it open, shielding the view that anyone else would have from any other direction. Without any rush, shame, or self-consciousness, he let his gaze travel every inch of me before returning to my eyes. "You're absolutely spectacular. Please tell me you're hearing that often enough. You're absolutely, astoundingly beautiful."

All I could manage was a steady, mute shake of the head. I knew full well that I should be shaking my head no to whatever was happening—whatever was about to happen, but let him believe that the response was to his spoken words alone.

"Take a seat, Mandelyn." After only a moment's hesitation, I did so. In part, I did it because I thought I might faint. I also had an irresponsible curiosity about what would come next. I sat upon the duvet still wrapped around my backside. Sam knelt and covered my shoulders and arms with the rest, leaving my legs exposed to the cold, which I couldn't feel. Adrenaline coursed through me, the residual alcohol in my system dilated my blood vessels, and numbness settled into my bones. I tipped my head back onto the top of the chair to look behind me. The balconies are quite open, with no exterior walls between the hotel rooms for privacy.

"No one is out here, Mandelyn. It's early, and it's winter. It's only you and me." Kneeling, he slid his hands around and beneath me, grasping me at the small of my back and pulling me toward himself. Running his sure hands over my thighs, he separated them. My tailbone was more than halfway off the edge of my seat, my head against the space where my shoulder blades should have been resting on the chair.

RELEASE

In a moment, his head was down between my legs, and I gasped with surprise. His head rose for just a moment more. "You'll need to be quiet out here, you know. Can you do that? Make the noises you made last night out here, and you'll get us both arrested."

Resistance, at this stage, was well beyond my grasp. I bit my lip and nodded.

~ ~ ~ ~ ~ ~ ~ ~

We went back inside when room service arrived. I looked around for the sweatshirt that I'd worn on the train, and that I would wear home later in the day. Finding it on the back of the bathroom door, I began to pull it over my head.

"No, stay just as you are," he begged. "I only have my tux stuff up here. I have nothing to wear. If I have to be naked, you have to stay naked with me. Please?" Still post-orgasmically addled, I found little reason to protest.

The continental breakfast belied its bourgeois title. The spread of artisan breads and pastries, fruit, yogurt, granola, cheeses, and cold cuts made the perfect picnic, which we arranged upon the bed. We sat across from one another and ate.

"So I need to ask you a question," Sam started as he spread cream cheese on a bagel. "Why didn't you want me to use a condom last night?"

I was really hoping that we wouldn't have to talk about that. I remembered being upset that he, as I took it, wasn't as wrapped up in the passion as I was. Still, it was inexcusable that I had insisted and, thankfully, failed to convince him to forget about protection. "I really don't want to blame the champagne… or the wine, the cocktails, or the laced coffee. Man, that sounds bad when you say it all at once!"

Sam wasn't allowing me to change the subject. I continued.

"The fact is I have no idea. I guess that in the heat of the moment, I thought about the fact that it's been years since I had sex using condoms. I really don't have all that much sex anymore. A diaphragm works well enough for my purposes. I hate condoms."

"No one likes condoms. But you don't have that diaphragm here, do you?"

"Well no, of course not. I didn't come here planning to have sex."

"That's good to know. I'm glad I'm not just the guy who could fulfill some sordid scavenger hunt you were on."

I couldn't read his tone. "You know me, Sam. What happened last night… I have never done that. I haven't ever been unfaithful to Henry."

"Then maybe that's my real question, Man. What did happen last night? That sounded stupid. I know what happened. I was there. We had fun. I had fun, anyway. Did you have fun? Of course you did. I mean, you did, right?"

I nodded reassuringly. Sam was all kinds of uncomfortable. While it wasn't anything I relished, I was glad, at least, that I wasn't alone in my awkwardness. I popped a strawberry in my mouth.

"Maybe I don't know what I am asking, Man. I just… God, I guess it's confession time." Sam sat up straight, cleared his throat, and rested his hands on his knees. He spoke slowly, over-articulating each word.

"I have thought about this—you and me—happening for far, far too long. In fact, it's been part of what I've thought about in some way, shape, or form every day since we met. Well… not since we met. Puberty, and then after Homecoming night… Now, I know that sounds weird and creepy and—with Joshua, and with you being married—just plain wrong.

"Look, I don't have these raging fantasies about you all the time. Okay—truth be told—sometimes I do! But it's been a while since that was a usual thing. I haven't seen you for so long, after all. Most of the time, it's… I don't know, some quality I see in a girl I meet. I think to myself, yeah, she's got a smile like Manny's. Her eyes sparkle like Manny's. She's smart like Manny. She makes me laugh like Manny. What I'm saying is, you were on some kind of serious-ass pedestal for me. Until last night, I didn't know how serious that pedestal was."

Somewhere in the midst of his soliloquy, Sam had shifted his hands from his knees onto my own. I took my right hand and placed it on his left. To my surprise, he withdrew both of his hands and placed them demurely back in his lap. Realizing how he had slighted me a bit by withdrawing, he gave me a sheepish smile of apology.

Then, he continued. "So last night, I tried to live it all out. All of it. The fairy tale and the exotic fantasy. And most of it was really great. Nothing about how we were together, you know, physically, failed my expectations," he assured me. "After decades of building up anticipation, that's a damn high bar I'd set. I have no complaints.

"I'm not trying to justify what happened. I'm only human, Mandelyn, but this isn't my usual style. I don't sleep around as much as I ever made it seem, and I definitely never fool around with married women. It just felt like, and this is the worst ethical argument I can ever imagine…"

The hemming and hawing had finally gotten on my nerves. "God, just spit it out, Sam. It's me you're talking to." If I sounded a little brusque, it was only because friend-me would never tolerate a story from friend-him with this much prologue.

He took a deep breath. "You're right. Okay. Somehow, it felt… okay to have you for just one night because it was the… fulfillment of a universal dictate. Like, yeah. It's all out of order in the chronology of our lives. It's wrong, just so very wrong on multiple levels. But I felt like this… connection between us had to be made, or this fantasy world in my head would continue to wreck every potentially good relationship I would ever have for the rest of my life.

"But here's the last part, and it's the weirdest part of all. Now that what happened, happened… now that it's over, I don't feel whole, or evolved, or even relieved. I feel kind of shitty. Yeah, a big part of that has to do with the adultery. Is that what it is if I'm not the one in a committed relationship? The moral failing, maybe? Whatever. But I think it's like what I was trying to ask you back when we sat down to our picnic here. I know why I did what I did last night. Why did you do what you did last night, Mandelyn? I'd really like to know."

I was stunned silent. Suddenly, I could really feel my nakedness and his. It wasn't sexy. It wasn't romantic. It sure as hell wasn't intimate. I felt like the light of interrogation was on me, even though Sam's questions weren't accusatory or anything that I should be afraid of. My flesh rose in goose bumps as I slumped away, leaning into my left hand on the bed behind me, and I stared out the window. I couldn't make eye contact. A long time passed before I finally managed to say the only thing that came to mind. "What time is it? When do you need to get downstairs?"

It was eight-thirty. "Shit," Sam said, "I have to be at work and presentable in thirty minutes. Okay. Listen. We aren't done. Let me drive you back to Weston this afternoon. I have my car here. It'll save you from having to take the train, and we can talk more on the ride west. Now, I can shower and change into my work clothes downstairs, but would it be too much for me to borrow your sweatshirt? The rest of last night's clothes won't look too crazy, but I can't be seen in last night's tuxedo shirt or coat between here and there."

"Sure," I said. "Wait. What will I wear? I need to check out by noon."

"I'll have someone run it back up here in a bag once I'm changed. Don't worry. Although, if you had to wear the clothes from last night again, it wouldn't be the worst thing. Any excuse to get you into that dress and those heels again is alright by me." He kissed me on the cheek, jumped out of bed, threw on his now-frumpy tux pants, my sweatshirt, and his out-of-place patent leather wingtips, and was out the door before I could say another word.

~ ~ ~ ~ ~ ~ ~

Morgan,

I am so hung over. Alcohol, for the foreseeable future, is my enemy. Loud noises, sunlight, and complex thoughts are also on that enemies list. The headache didn't hit me until just a little while ago, once Sam and I finished our screaming match in the breakdown lane of the Eisenhower expressway.

Sam did the gentlemanly thing by offering to drive me home. Thinking that taking him up on the offer would not only make things less awkward, but would also get me home faster, I accepted. I was wrong on both counts. It has been so long since I was stuck in Friday gridlock that I'd forgotten how awful it could be. The fact that it is snowing is making it so much worse. Being stuck in a small space beside someone I shouldn't have slept with, however, is excruciating.

Sam asked me an important question before he left for work this morning: "Why did you do what you did last night?" You'll probably ask the same thing, so I'll just go ahead and tell you. It took me a day of wandering the city to figure out my answer, and I really don't like what I came up with. How can something that only took one night to do take just as long or longer to understand? In any case, I started by telling him what I'd come up with so far.

RELEASE

I told Sam that I wasn't ready to give up on the fantasies I had created during my childhood. I still want to believe that there are soul mates out there for all of us. I still want to believe that there is one person on this planet who always says and does the right things, who always sees the beauty in what you say and do, and continues to worship the ground you walk on even after you, say, miscarry a baby, take everything in your relationship for granted, and withdraw from life in general out of fear.

"What do you have to be afraid of, Mandelyn?" Sam asked. His voice was so kind and warm.

"So many things," I replied.

I don't want to miscarry again. That's the main thing, Morgan. Sex became a scary thing to me for a long time. I went on Depo-Provera for about a year after we lost Theodore, but I hated how it made me feel. I couldn't sort out how much of my weight gain, my mood swings, and my utter lack of energy had to do with postpartum depression, the antidepressants, or the progesterone. Most of all, birth control seemed kind of useless, since I couldn't bring myself to let Henry make love to me, anyway. So, I stopped getting the shot.

"I still didn't want to get pregnant, so I raised the prospect of Henry getting a vasectomy," I told Sam. I thought Henry would be all in, since he worries about every little thing. I couldn't believe how Henry reacted. He absolutely lost it. It's the only time he's ever screamed at me.

"He screamed that I was supposed to be the courageous one, that I needed to use the courage he knew I had to get him past the fear of another miscarriage—to get past the fear for both of us," I told Sam.

"Whoa. What did you say to that?" Sam asked.

I told him that I thought it was unfair to put that on me. Since I'm the one who had to carry the baby, ultimately, the risk really only lies with me. "He became very dark," I explained to Sam. "He said that I clearly didn't understand what marriage was about if I thought I was the only one taking a risk."

"Oh, Manny. That is... a lot to sort out. And clearly you didn't get your tubes tied, unless the diaphragm is just something you're into," he said.

Clearly, Sam has never inserted a diaphragm, or else he would know that no one puts one in just for kicks. I thought about ligation, but I just couldn't do it. Mostly, I didn't want to mess around with my system any more than I already had, so an IUD or an arm implant—I didn't want anything foreign inside me. Really, though, if I'm being totally honest, I didn't tie my tubes because I didn't want to totally close the door on the possibility of having another baby someday, I told him.

"You'd have Henry get snipped, but you wouldn't do it yourself?" Sam asked.

I told Sam that I've become a pretty shitty person. I project all of my insecurities onto Henry. All my guilt, all my failings. When I said that, Sam gave me a look that put me a little on edge, so I argued, "Don't tell me I shouldn't feel guilty, and don't tell me I didn't fail. No one is ever going to tell me that I didn't have a part to play in what happened, and that I failed to fulfill some feminine obligation as a result."

"Stop right there, Ziegel. Stop it." I could count on one hand the number of times he'd ever called me by my last name. For as straight as we could be with one another, I almost never heard him speak in a tone as abrupt and admonishing as what he had when he continued. "I swear that, if it weren't for the snow, I would pull over right now to look you in the eye when I say this.

"You're telling me a lot of shit. A boatload of it. It's sad, it's raw, and it's obviously all true," he said. "I'm sorry you feel guilty, and I'm sorry that you feel like you've failed. You shouldn't feel guilty, and you haven't failed. Your miscarriage was not your fault. I don't think that anything I say or do is going to get that through your head today. The fact that you've been carrying this around for over three years, though—that's serious. You and I have another problem here, though. It goes back to where you started, when you said that you... How did you put it? 'Don't want to give up on your childhood fantasies?' Don't bullshit me, now. You're not talking about me, are you? I think I know what I am to you. I am not your fantasy."

"After everything you confessed to me this morning, don't make me answer that," I said.

Why does Sam have to know exactly what to say and do in every single instance? Why does he have to know me—the real me—going back to before marriage, before careers, before college, when hapless romances and homecomings were all that seemed to matter? How much valor did it take for him to cut through the self-deception and rationalizing and just call it like it is? Sam was calling this spade a fucking shovel.

"You don't have to answer. Don't sugar-coat what's happening here, Mandelyn. The fact is that you didn't fuck me last night. You wanted to fuck some fictionalized, unattainable, imaginary version of me."

At that point, he did pull over. "'Always says and does the right things?' Mandelyn, who is *that* person? The guy who opens your doors, or dedicates songs to you on the radio, or sends you chocolates? That's seduction, Mandelyn. That's artifice. It's the protocol for gaining panty access. The guy who does that may love you, but love has nothing to do with any of those moves. They're moves, Mandelyn. You do understand that, right?"

I was filling with rage as he spoke—at him as much as myself, for falling for his so-called moves—that I couldn't see straight. I went off. "Of course I do! I'm not a child! But you don't know what I live with! You don't know what it's like to be in a marriage where opened doors, or dedicated songs, or chocolates, or flowers, or handholding, or... touching?! Where none of that happens anymore. You don't know how starved I've become for any hint of affection, and you don't know how hard it is to resist taking the... the kindness, the most innocent of gestures, and... and making it into something it's not."

I stopped to catch my breath, although my meandering rant had landed on something I'd never realized before. "Oh, my God!" I exclaimed. "I've got it. I'm not a child, but I am a fool. It's like honeysuckle."

"Honeysuckle?" Who could blame Sam for being confused?

"I took the memory of our friendship and planted it like so much honeysuckle, like the bushes that used to grow at the Girls' School cemetery. Who doesn't love honeysuckle? It smells so sweet and it is attractive to wildlife. But honeysuckle eventually starves out every plant around it, destroys the soil, and can draw bugs and pests that are impossible to exterminate even after the honeysuckle is gone."

He took a moment before he spoke. I don't think he paused because he had to figure out his answer. I think he only had to determine exactly how to phrase it so that it would end the conversation.

"I don't know, Mandelyn. Maybe that is true. But honeysuckle only does that when it grows where it doesn't belong. I didn't do this to you. I'm not casting blame, but I hope you know the truth. You've done this to yourself. The sooner you own that, the sooner you might find true happiness again. You were happy once. I know it, and you can be happy again. You just have to, I don't know. Weed your garden, Mandelyn. Decide what's meant to grow there and prune the rest."

Both of us had reached our end. I felt my headache coming on. "Just drive me home," I told him.

Getting back into traffic wasn't too difficult, since it had barely inched forward in the time since he had pulled off the road. We sat in silence for a long time before he turned on the radio. That's when I pulled out the tablet and wrote all of this to you. Our exit is finally in view. It's after seven o'clock. Part of me wonders what Henry is going to say when I get home. Another part of me wonders why he hasn't called. Even though check-in texts or calls aren't typical, he should be wondering where I am, with the snow coming down as it is. Anyway, that's about it. Thanks as always. — M

As we headed north from the highway, the reality of what I had done had finally begun to sink in. Now, I really did feel guilty. I wondered if I looked any different than I had when I left the house the day before. I felt like the enormity of what I had done must have some physical manifestation I couldn't conceal. I wondered if it would be something dramatic enough for Henry to notice. It would be something that he couldn't place, maybe, but certainly hadn't been there Thursday morning when he gave me his usual peck and left for work.

I wasn't deceptive enough to keep this from him. While I was in no way prepared to confess my transgressions, I knew that I would have to tell him about this someday. Relationships don't survive infidelity and dishonesty. If I had any chance at all of making my marriage work, it couldn't be done from a foundation of lies.

As we turned onto my street, Sam finally broke the silence.

"Don't hate me, Manny. I don't know what we will be to each other after last night. Maybe we won't be anything at all. Not a lot changes, if you think about it. I'm almost never in town anymore. We've managed to stay out of each other's lives for the last—what has it been, a year?"

"Probably about that," I mumbled.

"I don't have any authority to stand on here. I don't have any similar experience to draw upon to know what people should do in a situation like this. I do know this is a much bigger thing to deal with for you than it is for me, though. I've been thinking about it the whole way back here, while you've been typing over there. For what it's worth, I think that last night did for me what I hoped it would. I feel, well, closure, if that makes any sense. I don't see you as an unattainable crush anymore. I think the best thing I can do for you now, as a friend, is to stay clear of you while you sort out your life and what you want it to be. How does that sound?"

My throat clenched, but I'd be damned if I'd let him see me get upset about this. "Sounds about right to me. It's weird to think that I won't see you around, but you're probably right. It's just as well."

When we pulled up in front of my house, I realized that I hadn't made a game plan. I didn't know what I'd say if Henry asked why I was being dropped off instead of walking from the train. I didn't know what I'd say if he asked who had given me a ride. I didn't know what I'd say if he asked why I looked different to him. None of that mattered, though. I was home, and I had to deal with whatever came my way. Ready or not.

13

Henry was gone when I awoke the next morning, presumably to get the dogs from overnight kenneling and pay the exorbitant fees I'd incurred. He had taken my bags to our room and left them in front of my closet door. My mind was blank. "Go," he had said. Go where? It wasn't as if the rest of the world would stop just because my life was falling apart. The Muon g-2 grand opening and lecture were less than a month away, so I couldn't take time off. In fact, the opposite was true. I had to be one hundred percent at the Laboratory for the next four weeks. After that, I could have whatever melodramatic breakdown I wanted. For now, everything had to stay business as usual.

Colette's, naturally, was the most logical place to stay. For whatever other few friends I still had in town, she was the only one who knew what I'd been going through—the only one who had probably seen this coming. I began to pack a suitcase, not knowing just how much I would need to take with me. "Find yourself," he had said. How long, I wondered, would that take? Would it ever truly happen?

The first step was to see if lodging was even available. I decided that texting Colette was better. She would surely be at some krav maga, aerial yoga, or bellydancing class—or she could possibly be sleeping off her previous night's Bacchanalia. In any case, I wasn't prepared to talk about what had happened just yet.

I threw trouser socks, underwear, bras, camisoles, jeans, and shirts in a suitcase. I tossed in a pair of nude pumps, a pair of brown flats, and my favorite pair of over-the-knee black boots. I counted on whatever was at the dry cleaners or a run to the mall for anything else I'd need. I grabbed whatever few random necklaces I happened to see from where they hung, and I checked my ears to make sure I was wearing my ever-present cubic zirconia studs. Right before I zipped the suitcase shut, and for no good reason I could discern after the fact, I grabbed my indigo satin chemise. My gym bag still had all my toiletries, so I reloaded it with my gym shoes, a few sports bras, and a couple pairs of yoga pants, pushing the Valentinos and other random pieces of Thursday evening's attire aside to make room.

That was about it. I looked around the room. The moss green walls, the jewel-toned comforter, and blonde furniture felt foreign already. Rather than try and figure out what that observation even meant in terms of the state of my psyche, I swept out the door, down the stairs, and, after finding my purse and my keys where they'd landed on the floor last night, headed to the garage, got in my car, and drove away.

About a block down the road, I whipped into a driveway, threw the car in reverse, and sped back home. I left the car running in the driveway while I ran back into the house, grabbed a piece of paper from the pad on the refrigerator, and wrote a note. Eloquence wasn't required. I kept it simple:

> *This doesn't have to affect the dogs. I'll walk them and feed them. Don't worry.*

I hesitated. How should I sign a note to my husband in a circumstance like this? Would an "M" too cold or too familiar? "Best?" "Love?"

"Fuck it," I said to myself. For all my transgressions, and there were many, I hadn't rejected him. He had rejected me. I was allowed to feel however I wanted to feel about him. In spite of it all, "love" was what I felt, so "*Love — M*" was how I signed it. I put the note on the fridge with a magnet, then hustled out the door and on my way.

~ ~ ~ ~ ~ ~ ~

By the early afternoon, I still hadn't heard back from Colette. I sat at a tea house in downtown Weston—one that locals never visited but that drew tourists by the dozens. I was getting unappreciative glances from my waitress when I finally felt my phone buzz.

"*Sorry the camel's back broke :(Call me ASAP,*" the message read. I decided I'd been enough of a drag on afternoon tea business already, so I quickly gathered my things, left a $10 tip, paid my bill, and walked toward the pedestrian bridge before dialing.

Colette was clearly harried when she answered. "Hi, babe… oh… I'm devastated by your news. Really and truly. You guys will find a way. I know you will. But I have to be quick. I'm in the lobby of the hotel in between breakout sessions. Did I mention that this client from hell insisted I come with him to beautiful, sunny Atlanta? Ugh, this conference and this city are as boring as fuck. I can't believe I'm giving up my weekend to spend my time with these geriatrics. But let's focus on you. Of course you can stay. In fact, this works out perfectly. I'm going to be here until Wednesday, so you'll have the place to yourself for a bit. Make yourself at home. Hit the liquor cabinet as hard as you need."

For the first time in weeks, I laughed without the assistance of inebriation. "Okay. You are the best, friend."

"I know I am. Now don't go forgetting the hazy details of your wild romp Thursday night. I want to hear all about it," she chimed.

"Oh, just wait," I cryptically replied. "I'll tell you all about it when you get back."

"Oooo, you tease. All right. Make me wait like a horny Homecoming date." It was amazing how close to home that hit.

"Enjoy Hotlanta for me."

"Don't call it that," she chirped back. "No one calls it that. Alright. Later, hooker."

I smiled and put the phone back in my coat pocket before taking a look around. Standing in the middle of an island in the middle of the river, I realized I had no destination. I wasn't in any rush to get to Colette's. I wasn't hungry, I wasn't cold, and I didn't have any shopping to do downtown. There I was, with no place to be, no one wondering about me, and nothing for which I was immediately accountable. It should have been liberating, but I felt confounded. I felt like a speck afloat in the overcast November sky. After thinking about the choices I had for my unexpected freedom, I chose the boring option: to stop for some groceries, rent some movies, and head to Colette's.

As I drove, I looked at my hands on the wheel. My wedding ring. What was I to do with that? Was I separated? What do people even mean when they say that they are separated? I thought aloud. Clearly, separation meant more than physically being apart. Separation was separation emotionally and spiritually, too. It always sounded like polite code for impending divorce when used in social situations. How was I supposed to identify, now that I had been "released?"

And who said "released?" Where had Henry come up with that terminology? The word made me feel feral, as if I had been cast out into the wild. Thinking of my behavior of two nights before, I felt as if I had certainly played the part of a cat in heat. Did I deserve to wear Henry's ring, having done what I had done? It didn't matter that he didn't know what had happened; I knew. Without another moment's thought, I pulled it from my finger and put it in the glove box. When I arrived at the grocery store, I used my key to lock the compartment before going inside.

Maybe you don't realize it, but a woman's wedding ring is single-man repellent. You can choose to interpret that statement however you want, but one thing is certain: you cannot know how powerful a deterrent gold and diamonds become when worn on your left hand until you go without them. I know I had no idea.

I started by looking for the pomegranates. Henry always fussed about the mess they made, so this seemed like the right opportunity to buy a few. I was scratching the surface of one with my fingernail, still manicured from Thursday, when a man approached.

"How can you tell if these are ripe?" he asked. "I've never known."

"They're all ripe," I answered. "The best ones have a little give to them, and you can scratch the surface with your fingernail. See, like this." I demonstrated the technique and then put the pomegranate in my cart. I picked up another one.

"You know, pomegranates symbolize fertility, prosperity, and generosity," he said with a purposefully pompous inflection, before chuckling under his breath. "I remember that from the mythology unit of sophomore English class."

I raised an eyebrow. "Persephone, I think—abducted and forced to live in Hades with… Hades. You know, until this moment, I never realized that Hades was the name of the place and the ruler of the Underworld."

"Beauty and brains. Double threat, I see."

"Wow. Um… thanks?"

"I'm Brett."

"Mandelyn. You look familiar."

"I thought I recognized you. You're a Lab rat like me. I'm in IT."

"Oh, no. Do you hate me? All my last-minute requests? My hands are usually bound with those eleventh-hour demands. The guest lecturers—they never know what they want for AV until they arrive, no matter how often we ask them to let us know…"

"No worries, really. I understand, or at least I am still an understanding person. I just started about a month ago. Also, I'm not in the group that gets to, uh, satisfy your needs."

I remembered putting the press release together. We post the names of new employees on the portal each week and send the news to a few local papers and trade journals. "Just a month, huh? I give you… three more weeks before you're cursing me behind my back."

"You underestimate yourself. I'm sure you could drive me crazy in a lot less time than that."

I may have been out of the dating game since before Bush was reelected, but I wasn't stupid. This was flirtation. "Um… where did you work before? Are you from here?" I stammered.

"Brand-new transplant," he drawled. "I was put on furlough at Oak Ridge when HFIR was on maintenance shutdown, and I tried like hell to transfer to ORELA. When the chance to work on the Long Baseline gear-up came, I went after it. I couldn't believe my luck when I got the call."

"Moving from Knoxville to Chicago just before winter sets in. There aren't a lot of people who'd call that lucky."

"I'm feeling lucky today, ma'am." He winked, and his smile was impossibly infectious, but I was in no state of mind for what was clearly happening.

"Oh," I giggled nervously. "That's, um… nice. Say, I don't mean to be rude, but I need to be on my way. I need to, uh…" All I could hear was Henry and Joshua, each chastising me for being unable to speak for myself.

"What, darlin'? Is someone waiting for you at home?"

"Well… yes. Sure. This pomegranate is for salad. For dinner. I don't want to hold up dinner."

"Okay. It's three-thirty, so I think you're safe. I'd sure like to give you a call sometime, maybe have you show me around town? The downtowns of the cities along the river are pretty little things, but I still haven't found a good barbecue place."

"I… should have said that it's my, uh, husband at home making dinner."

Brett blushed. "Oh, ma'am, I'm truly sorry. I hope I haven't slighted you. I just didn't see a wedding ring, and…"

"It's being cleaned. I just dropped it off today. See?" I showed him the deep impression and callous on the inside of my hand. "Off the market, just like this pomegranate here." I set the second fruit in the cart.

"Well, you have a lucky man, Mandelyn. Maybe I'll stop by your office sometime soon, and you can help me learn who's who. You can let me know if there's a barbecue place in the area that might measure up to my expectations." He put a pomegranate in his cart and began to head toward the bakery.

"Meat," I called after him.

"Come again?" he said as he turned back to look at me.

"Meat is alright, I hear. M-E-A-T, not M-E-E-T. It's a bar and smokehouse I've heard good things about. I don't know how it'll compare to what you're used to in Tennessee."

"Meat. I'll check it out and let you know what I think. Thanks, ma'am. You have yourself a good, um, dinner." Brett extended his hand, I shook it, and we parted ways.

I bolted to the check-out counter, determined not to cross paths with Brett in any other aisle. Surely there would be something at Colette's I could eat, and I'd find something to watch on TV. When I returned to my car, I opened the glove compartment, found my ring, put it back on, tore out of the lot, and made a beeline up the road toward Colette's.

14

Nine days passed. I had settled into Colette's guest room and buried myself in work and routine. I went to the Lab early and worked out on campus, still got to my desk before most of my cohorts, and, with the exception of driving to the house each day to visit Frank and Lloyd, I remained all business during working hours.

Unlike the weeks and months before, however, I generally left the office at a reasonable hour each night. My brain was hard-wired for the tasks on hand, rendering overtime largely inessential. I could attribute some of my midnight oil-burning habit over the years to the peer pressure of conspicuous busyness. I had let undisciplined choices distract me, and I let outright procrastinations eat away my valuable time. I was reminded that self-control was required when I worked downtown and my daily routine was dictated by the train schedule. External structures like that were nice to rely upon when the call of the next email, outline, brief, or other task lay as an enticement to keep working.

I had been leaving the office on time, but I hadn't necessarily been leaving campus. When I had first started at the Laboratory, I had made a point of attending as many of the hosted events as possible. Mostly, it was a matter of accelerating my learning curve, but it was also a matter of good will. Whenever I attended a lecture, or even a concert or dance, I carried myself as if I were still on the clock, intentionally keeping an impartial distance from the proceedings, not really engaging. Now, I participated out of sheer personal interest. I'd already been to a chamber music program, a poetry slam, and an art show opening. Colette had reluctantly joined me for a barn dance the previous Saturday night, but we soon faded when it was painfully, obviously not her scene. Despite the southwestern-inspired accents in her wardrobe and her penchant for country music, Colette was purely urban cowgirl.

It wasn't really my scene, either, without Henry there. My presence without him would have made for awkward conversations and explanations that I wasn't ready to make. As it was, I hated the milestones I was passing in terms of disseminating news of my personal life meltdown.

Dr. Adiraju picked up on the change in my routine within three days. She was kind in her sympathy yet professionally dispassionate, leaving her door open, she said, if I ever needed to talk.

The first two times I talked with my mom, I easily skirted the topic of Henry. She had a lot to tell me about upcoming Albuquerque Science Fiction Society events and wanted to hear every last detail about the Muon g-2 grand opening.

Since moving to New Mexico almost seven years earlier, my mom had become increasingly curious about scientific topics, particularly nuclear technology and all things related to the cosmos. She had visited the Albuquerque Nuclear Museum just after her arrival, which quickly led to a visit to Los Alamos with the ASFS, or the "SFers," as she called them. Soon dissatisfied with simply taking in the exhibits and reading about the history of discoveries, she began to visit significant sites around the state and region, starting with Roswell, White Sands, and Carlsbad, but continuing on to Farmington, Dulce, and, most recently, Sahuarita, Arizona. She also helped plan and run the annual Bubonicon Science Fiction festival. While I was happy about her new passions, an increasing number of our conversations involved sorting science fiction from science fact.

She had been discussing the local Winter Solstice events that she was a part of planning. We had never been able to accept her annual invitations because of Henry's busy year-end schedule. Truth be told, it just wasn't our scene. The geek factor of her SF friends exceeded even our reasonably high threshold. Besides, by traveling on Christmas Eve, our fares were far more reasonable, and we avoided the worst of the holiday travel volume, arriving just in time for the famous luminaria displays. We'd typically stay for a week, spending a day or two at Sandia Peak or Taos, skiing, before heading back to Chicago.

Mom had increased her involvement with a planning committee this year, and her pleas for us to travel earlier and attend had increased proportionately. It was when she broached the topic of coming to Weston and attending the grand opening, however, that I finally told her what was going on. I stuck to cursory information and avoided delving into any more detail than absolutely necessary. It was only by promising that I would come for the Solstice and Christmas that I was able to divert her focus from the subject, asking whether she'd indulge my customary Old Town pilgrimage for the green chile, mole enchilada, and sopapilla smorgasbord I always craved upon arrival. She agreed, but not before extending the hope that it'd be both Henry and me who'd be with her for the holidays.

Immediately after hanging up, I called Henry. If I knew my mom, she'd be in touch with him within the hour. As it turned out, she'd already beaten me to it.

"She called the office last week. I should have told you. I'm sorry," he apologized.

"Damn right you should have told me!" I exclaimed before remembering my surroundings and regaining composure.

"I know," Henry pleaded, "and it's not even logical, but in my defense, we only have one parent left between the two of us. I shouldn't have taken advantage of her open ear, but I've never been one to build a personal support network until I needed one. I should have listened to you. I sort of need one right now."

I was conflicted. Here he was, telling me and showing me that he had listened to me, and that he appreciated, finally, that something I told him had value. On the other hand, all I could wonder about was what he had talked about with my mother and why she hadn't said anything to me about their conversation. "What did you say, exactly? Did you tell her about CVC?" I finally managed to ask.

"No. I'm doing the best I can to forget I ever heard about CVC. Have you continued to journal, though?"

"I haven't written since the day I left, Henry. I'm busy as hell, here. It's all I can do to get back to Colette's after work, make some dinner, decompress a bit from the day, and get a decent night's sleep."

"I'm glad you're sleeping, at least. I can barely manage two or three hours a night."

"That's strange, since I practically never slept in our bed when I was there," I snapped.

"But I knew you were here in our home. I lie awake thinking about you."

"I'm sorry," I said, and I genuinely meant it.

"You know what would help put my mind at ease, Mand? Keep writing. To Morgan, if that's what works, but maybe to a real person instead, or just to yourself. Online, maybe in a real, physical journal, or even on the back of an envelope. It doesn't matter. Just keep trying to sort out your feelings. Or maybe you should get out of town. I know you can't right now, but after the lecture, maybe? Go see Nadja. If I could…"

"I knew it! She's needling you to get us down for the Solstice, isn't she?"

"That's not it at all. She and I just…"

"I have to get back to work. You're not the only one with a tough job, Henry," I said before hanging up the phone.

Immediately, I hated how our conversation had gone. I wished I could play it back and take note of all the places I had gone wrong. There had probably been five separate opportunities for me to be supportive or empathetic, or just to hear him out, and I'd thrown every chance away. To learn that Henry wasn't sleeping was particularly hard. Even in his most stressful times, I'd never known him to have a hint of insomnia.

I stared out the window. The sky was bleak, twilight in appearance even though it was still mid-afternoon. The final leaves had fallen, the silhouettes of bare branches like cracks in the opaque, overcast wall of clouds. On my screen, a blank page stared back at me, the blinking cursor like a taunting, ticking measure of time slipping through my fingers. I buried my face in both hands and sighed deeply enough for my exhaled breath to blow the wispy baby fuzz along my hairline around. I rubbed my eyes with the length of my thumbs, grateful to have had the forethought to skip makeup that morning.

Before returning to task, I looked at the palms of my hands, my right in particular. I remembered what a palm reader in India had said about the Mount of Venus, which on my hand was noticeably pronounced. "If this area is full, as yours is full, you have the capacity and yearning to love deeply, and you have a generous nature. You will find great happiness in romantic and creative pursuits," she had said.

"What a mess," I mumbled to myself, as much in recollection of that revelation as in description of my present circumstances. "What an absolute fucking mess."

~ ~ ~ ~ ~ ~ ~

When I told Joshua what had happened with Henry and me, our conversation was surprisingly brief. He didn't sound surprised. Neither did he say, "I told you so." We left our Thanksgiving plans open-ended. Neither of us had been in touch since, so I assumed that was off.

Colette had proposed several of the swankiest steakhouses and bistros in the city for Thanksgiving. I didn't have it in me to put together a meal for just the two of us, so I acquiesced to the idea of going out, but I couldn't bring myself to go anywhere too ritzy. Thanksgiving was supposed to be homespun, with lumps in the gravy and cracks in the top of the pumpkin pie. We finally agreed on the Palmer House Hotel. While incredibly posh, it at least was a classic.

No matter how many times I visit the Palmer House, it always takes my breath away. The country's oldest continually operating hotel, its French Empire architecture never fails to evoke my awe. While we admired the lavish features, a concierge shared that this was actually the third hotel to stand at the site. The first had been built by Potter Palmer as a wedding present for his wife, Bertha. It burned to the ground in the Great Chicago Fire, just thirteen days after it opened. With his investors strong-arming him under the guise of civic pride, Palmer not only rebuilt, but set about increasing the opulence and beauty of the original design, whose plans were saved by the grace of Architect John Van Osdel and his forethought to bury them for safekeeping.

Despite the sky-high cost of materials in the midst of the city's reconstruction, the new hotel was built entirely of brick and iron and marketed as "The World's Only Fire Proof Hotel." When it reopened four years later, magnificence was evident down to the smallest detail: marble sculptures at every turn, Tiffany light fixtures throughout, guest rooms that were the largest of their kind at the time, and even a barber shop floor that was supposedly inlaid with silver dollars. Just fifty years later, when Bertha, who ran the hotel and much of her then-late husband's real estate empire, decided that Chicago could support a larger hotel, she had the entire building rebuilt. Astoundingly, it was completed in three phases, without losing a single day of operation, and reopened at almost three times its previous size to commemorate its anniversary.

From the first day of the hotel's operation, food at the Palmer House was unparalleled in its decadence and served in the grandest European traditions. The brownie was actually invented by the hotel chef on Bertha's request. She wanted to serve the women attending the Columbian Exposition something that would taste like cake but wouldn't dirty their hands as they walked and ate. Upon our arrival, Colette and I each had one of the apricot-glazed, walnut-inundated treats, still made according to the original recipe, with coffee.

Both of us had been to the hotel several times before for work-related reasons, but neither of us had ever stayed the night. We made a day of it, scheduling services in the spa and getting a room so we wouldn't have to drive all the way back to Weston after dinner. After facials, massages, and a few glasses of champagne, she talked me into upgrading from a bikini wax to a full-fledged deforestation. Somewhere in the process, she nicknamed my newly shorn region "The Lonely Brazilian."

I think the hotel staff thought we were a couple, which, short of making out, we didn't do much to dispel. We even brought Frank and Lloyd, walking them around the hotel as we frolicked like children throughout the building, sometimes talking in more serious tones, but most times skipping through the hallways that circle and connect the grand lobby, lounges, banquet rooms, and meeting room spaces. Roaming the corridors, pathways, staircases, and niches throughout the facility imparted a feeling akin to roaming catacombs, only with fewer skulls and significantly more gilded urns and candelabras. Christmas decorations—soaring trees, swags of garlands, and vintage decorations like nutcrackers, toy soldiers, and French horns—were already displayed, further adding to the ambiance.

"Here's a question for you," Colette said as we walked. "Who's stronger, Melanie or Scarlett?"

"From *Gone with the Wind*? Scarlett. No question."

"Really? So Scarlett's better for having bucked the system than working within it. Scarlett ends the book alone—unloved, disrespected, and inconsequential."

"Well, Melanie ends up dead," I argued.

"Home with her King, untethered from mortal constraints. Everyone dies, babe. Melanie lived."

"You have a point," I admitted.

"Scarlett disgraced femininity and let her masculinity run rampant. She's to be pitied, not admired."

"Hmm... I'll have to think about that. But then I have a question for you: Ashley or Rhett?"

"For Scarlett or myself?" Colette asked.

"Either one."

"Scarlett let the best thing in her life go when Rhett walked out," Colette said. "She practically pushed him. Not that he was perfect, any way you look at it. If Scarlett had only told him what she needed him to be, not someone bent on changing her, spoiling her, or protecting her, but a partner or a confidant—that would have been something.

"And Rhett was right when he said that Scarlett wouldn't have understood Ashley," she continued. "What she admired in Ashley was the femininity she lacked. That includes her inability to honestly communicate. Scheming and manipulation were all she knew."

"What about you, then?" I asked

Colette sniffed. "Rhett or Ashley? Neither."

"Why aren't you married, Colette?" I asked. "Why didn't you ever take the plunge?" At the beginning of our friendship, I'd assumed that she'd divorced somewhere along the way. Later, I found out that she had never settled down, except that she'd moved to Weston to be closer to a serious boyfriend. I'd never found the right time or way to ask her why it hadn't worked out.

"I never found a guy with enough balls to ask, I guess. It, probably, has a lot to do with me never spending much time looking for him."

"Don't you wish you had someone to grow old with, though?"

"I've got plenty of people to grow old with, sweetie! In all my time, I've never wanted for company."

"I know, but I mean a partner. Someone you can rely on."

"Babydoll, I'm a handful, am I right?"

"Truth!" I exclaimed and raised my champagne glass to toast it.

"If I meet the man who gets electrified by that—who understands my whack-a-doodle self, and who electrifies me just as much—you know, gets me just as jazzed up, even about his crazy parts, his weird parts, his bad parts as he is about mine, then maybe I'd be game. I'm not waiting on the sidelines for that man to come along, though, know what I mean?"

"Clearly, you're not on the sidelines."

"I've got needs in the meantime, and so do a whole lot of people out there whose whole assortment of needs isn't going to be accommodated by the likes of me. If I want to go out and dance, I go out and dance, and I know just the men to call. If I want to pound shots and play pool, that's where I'm going, and I've got the people I need for nights like that. If I want to go lie topless on a beach, hell, I go alone, anymore. Even with surgical intervention, these tits aren't what they once were."

"You're spectacular," I assured her.

"You're spectacular," she replied, leaning over and tweaking my boob nonchalantly. "So, back to the topic of pairing off and happily ever after. Maybe it was watching my Daddy carouse with his spun sugar ladies as they'd melt all over him, trying to glom on and get a free ride. I used to think seeing all that saved me from a fate worse than death. Other times, I felt like it ruined me for the purpose God made us—you know, 'forsake all others, flesh of my flesh,' and all."

"I don't see you submitting to any man."

"Sugar, are you hung up on that one Bible verse? Is that part of what's got you all turned around?"

"I think that one Bible verse has a large chunk of society turned around."

"Damn straight it does. That's because it's cherry-picking, patriarchal, semantic bullshit."

"Tell me how you really feel," I joked.

Colette was uncharacteristically serious all of a sudden. "I can't cite chapter and verse, sitting here post-spa tipsy under the Palmer House frescos on Thanksgiving afternoon, but I can recite the phrase that comes right before the one you're talking about. It says, 'Submit to one another out of reverence for Christ.' Everyone always skips over that and goes right to the woman submitting to the man."

"Almost makes me want to go get the Gideon Bible out of the bedside table and reread it," I said.

"I can tell you something else, too. Between the time that lovely Bible letter was written and today, we've had two thousand years of Roman assimilators, well-intentioned Pharisee-battlers, crusaders, and power-hungry leaders of all types bending the Message to convert and evangelize by whatever means worked. In the meantime, languages have been lost, translations have been mangled, and all manner of unintentional and intentional distortions, misrepresentations, corruptions, suppressions, and outright falsifications have been made."

"Your drawl's coming out," I teased.

"I sure as shit hope so, because here's one more thing that Southerners still understand. We respect masculinity and femininity, but that doesn't mean we're a society of cavemen and delicate flowers. We understand that chromosomes give us more of one gender's characteristics and less of the other, but we all get both, and they don't work at cross-purposes."

"I'm not sure I follow you," I said.

"It's like Ashley and Melanie. She didn't just submit to him. They submitted to each other. Ashley was a leader in the war because his men respected his calm, reasoned strength, but when he came home? Melanie was in charge and everyone knew it, including him. Yet, she was dutiful to him until her last day. Scarlett and Rhett were doomed from day one because neither of them submitted to the other. Two mules in horse harnesses."

"I know there's a lesson here that should be sinking in. I just don't know what it is."

"I wonder if your situation is a matter of balance," Colette said. "The worst relationships of all are the ones in which one person submits to the other without reciprocation, with one person stalwart and the other just hanging on. Submissive behavior from both people is key to successful relationships."

RELEASE

"You're not getting political on me, are you?" Politics were just about the only subject on which Colette and I disagreed. Debate was fun at times; I just wasn't feeling it that day.

"Absolutely not," Colette said with a wink. "People who look to the so-called 'good ol' days,' when women were at home and men were at work, make me want to spit, too. That wasn't submissiveness. That was economic dependence endemic to a patriarchal system. What people dismiss, though, is that the creation and maintenance of house and home had greater value back then. Men submitted to their roles as breadwinners, too."

"So what, women working outside the home gave rise to the breakdown of society?" I asked, baiting her.

"The whole thing is more complicated than what we're talking about, of course," she conceded. "You and I can have the jobs we have and can be the people we are today because of feminism. Constrictive gender roles prevented women from even considering career paths like ours until half a century ago."

I agreed. "The women whose shoulders we stand upon—they had to assert their masculinity to compete in a man's world because that's what it was. It's taken this long for their efforts to change the rules of the game."

"Right," Colette continued, "but in the meantime, we diminished the value of domesticity and child-rearing, as if those roles were only assumed by women who were somehow less than the ones who chose the workplace."

"Years from now, we're going to look back on the path of feminism and realize these were all steps in the evolution," I said.

"I hope so," Colette sighed. "We're ruining generations of men in the meantime, I think. We told girls to play with trucks instead of dolls, and to play harder in sports. Hooray for that. We told them they could be anything, but what we meant was that they should become doctors, lawyers, engineers, and captains of industry. Women who chose homemaking, or traditionally feminine careers like teaching, nursing, or administrative roles were relegated to a separate class. That was a mistake that's only being rectified in this generation."

"How does any of that ruin men, though?"

"At the same time we demonized femininity in women, we also expected men to be more feminine—collaborative, expressive, less competitive. It's quite a mixed message. We women didn't take away their masculinity by embracing masculine traits ourselves. We are confusing them by telling them to exhibit the very characteristics we spent a generation degrading."

"I can agree with all of that," I reasoned. "I think it's an issue of nomenclature. Feminine is not synonymous with womanly, and masculine isn't synonymous with manly. A fully-actualized person can develop both sets of characteristics."

"See, and that's what I'm looking for. If I found the man with enough confidence to be vulnerable, the moral character to own his needs and desires, and the self-assurance to know that I, being his equal, would not diminish but enhance his worth—I'd submit to that, because that kind of guy would submit equally to me."

"So that's why you're single," I deadpanned.

"That's what I'm saying," she laughed as we toasted another truth.

"I'd rather have Melanie and Ashley's relationship, but I'd rather marry Rhett than Ashley. And I'd rather be Scarlett than Melanie, without the conniving or the extramarital yearning," I said.

"Melanie and Ashley were probably happier overall," Colette concluded. "I bet Scarlett and Rhett had better sex, though."

~ ~ ~ ~ ~ ~ ~

Oiled, buffed, and lacquered, we sat down to dinner at four o'clock. Carving stations were placed at each corner of the room, offering prime rib, mustard-glazed and clove-studded ham, lamb with mint sauce, and maple-honey-molasses-roasted turkey. Chicken was served with button mushrooms and bacon lardons in a red wine and pearl onion reduction. The Alaskan halibut was served pan-roasted in a lemon-dill and late harvest Riesling sauce. Shrimp cocktail, smoked lake trout, and lox were served on silver trays over ice. A full complement of cheeses, breads, vegetables, potatoes, and salads were dizzying in their variety and complexity. Standouts included the butternut squash soup with candied pecans and cinnamon cream, the rhubarb-cranberry compote, and the chestnut-pistachio stuffing. A platter of desserts towered at the center of the room, and the champagne never stopped flowing, but I retained a modicum of self-control throughout the afternoon.

"I usually don't get to places this nice, even once a year. Amidst all the craziness of the last month, I have dined like a queen at three of the city's most celebrated venues," I said. "Here's to celebrating at this one with you, friend."

"Happy Thanksgiving, doll. You deserve it," Colette replied.

"Did I ever tell you about the Thanksgiving I spent in Laos? It couldn't have been more different than the one we're having here."

Thinking of that first Thanksgiving after college, I felt a little self-conscious at the disparity. "After school, I was a little burned-out, or at least I'd convinced myself of as much at the time. I wasn't ready for the corporate world, as I pictured it."

"It's hard to picture you in a traditional corporate setting. No offense," Colette quipped.

"None taken. I never really did fit in. Too unconventional for the corporate side and too straight-laced for the creatives. Anyway, I'd had a rough go with a college... boyfriend. Senior year was sort of a drag, and I was ready for a gap year by graduation."

Things had not fallen apart with Dante as much as they had faded away, but it took a long time to truly internalize that fact. Instead, I repressed it, dedicating my senior year to no-nonsense ass-kicking. I made it to all-conference in volleyball and earned my Pi Kappa Delta All-American designation. By graduation, I was burned-out. Rather than return to Chicago, I got an apartment with friends in Des Moines' Sherman Hill neighborhood. More than I'd like to admit, I chose to live there so I'd be close enough that if Dante were to "see the error of his ways," I would be conveniently nearby.

"I picked up a waitress job at a new brew pub in town. I pushed for a bartender position, but they weren't open to anyone lacking experience. It was my first legitimate on-the-payroll job, not counting work-study, internships, or the under-the-counter work I did in high school."

"Bar wench. I can hardly picture it," Colette said.

"I felt bohemian. Compared to my white-bread suburban childhood and essentially rural college experience, I was. The restaurant lifestyle fit my nonexistent sleep schedule and my burgeoning new social life."

"Restaurant people kick ass. Artists, writers, actors, and drug dealers."

"Well, and grad students, housewives, retirees, and people just trying to make ends meet. You're right, though. Very few of them thought of themselves as servers, cooks, or bartenders. Work, for them, was a means to two ends: cash and a good time."

"*Laissez les bons temps rouler.*"

"Exactly. Every four hours on the clock came with a shift beer at the end, and that was almost always stretched into a second or third before going home, rarely alone."

"So many sluts. God, I miss it."

I laughed. "With friends, I mean. Jeez! I didn't take part in the seedier stuff."

"Surprise, surprise," Colette said, rolling her eyes.

I stuck my tongue out at her playfully. "I wasn't completely innocent. Give me some credit. At Polly's, I was always aware of the pot, the blow, the random hook-ups, and all the other soap opera stuff. It's all part of the lifestyle. I floated above it then, mostly because of my age and the fact that Joshua's parents owned the restaurant.

"At the brewery, I gravitated to the people that were pretty much drama-free. The best friends I had during my time there were older."

It was with that group of friends that I had traveled to Laos over the week leading up to Thanksgiving that year. With 20/20 hindsight, it's plain to see that going to Muang Khoun had been a way to maintain some manner of symbolic connection with Dante, however obscure. The planning began when Lily and I were doing our side work after the lunch rush waned.

"My one friend, Lily, had been cagey and distant for weeks. When I finally got the courage to ask her about it, she fell apart. She unfurled the story of how she had discovered her husband's affair and had just filed for divorce. It happened in perfectly melodramatic fashion: '…and there he was, in bed with his secretary! I should have known he wanted me to get out of the house and work for a reason!' she shared."

"Poor girl. How old was she?"

"Thirty-one."

"Jeez, she was just a baby!"

"Right? It didn't seem like she was all that young, considering that I was just twenty-two at the time, but I can totally see that now. Even then, I had a hard time sympathizing with a woman who had married young, for money and, with her whole life still before her, was also due to receive annual spousal support in the low six-figures. She was free from marital bonds to a paunchy, graying, perpetually greasy man whose lewd eye had stumbled across my own décolletage on more than a few of his restaurant visits."

"It's like the story's always the same."

"I guess," I said vacantly, fading out for a bit as I thought about my own situation and how it had some distant similarities to Lily's. Colette picked up on my moody expression and brought the conversation back around.

"So what's all of this have to do with Laos?"

"Oh, right. So I knew about this volunteering tourism program from my trip to India. I orchestrated the trip for two of us and two other server friends, a teacher and a grad student who were also due for a break and were able to take off for a few days. Lily even paid for our flights."

With far less time to invest, and with a distinctly different objective than my previous travel, this was an experience I felt on a deeper, more altruistic, spiritual level.

"We spent our first day touring the Plain of Jars, this field strewn with hundreds of these massive stone funerary urns dating back more than two thousand years. We also visited That Foun Stupa and the relics of Wat Piawat temple. I'll have to show you pictures sometime."

The region had been destroyed by centuries of ravaging invaders seeking treasure, concluding with extensive bombing during the Vietnam War, the unexploded ordnance of which is still being cleared to this day. Some of the struggling inhabitants actually collect the debris of crashed aircraft, melt it down into spoons, and sell them to tourists.

"From there, we took a songthaew, a jerry-rigged pick-up truck/taxicab contraption, to the farm," I continued. "Because of the chemical pollution, poor sanitary conditions, and generations of unsustainable farming practices like slash-and-burn, just a few crops grow sufficiently in the country, and only with a whole slew of pesticide intervention.

People are at work to bring new crops, that can grow more sustainably, to the region. We spent the week harvesting mulberries, caring for the farm animals, and making cheese."

"Why mulberries? Why not some kind of grain or rice?"

"I wondered the same thing. Turns out that silkworms eat mulberry leaves and produce silk, providing an industry besides farming for the village. The leaves are also used to make tea, and they're used in stir-fries and tempura. Goats eat the stalks, and then the farm sells the milk, cheese, and yogurt. The berries taste great on their own, but can also be used to produce wine. Nothing's wasted, and all of the components are incredibly healthy. The berries are a great source of phytonutrient compounds like anthocyanins and resveratrol; they have a ton of anti-oxidants and B vitamins; they are rich in iron, potassium, manganese, and magnesium… From then on, I always have a bag of dried mulberries on hand for smoothies, for pancakes, or just for snacking."

"Should have known better than to ask a science nerd that question," Colette joked before straightening her face and raising her glass in a toast. "I always knew there was more to you than suburban ennui. I'm glad you shared that with me. To knowing that it really takes a village."

"Hear, hear." Despite the volumes of food, the champagne was beginning to catch up with me a bit.

"Speaking of which, I have an idea for you and your situation. Have you thought about getting out of town? You know, give your mind and soul some space to wander?"

"Did Nadja talk to you, too?"

"Who's Nadja?"

"My mom. She's been bugging me to come to Albuquerque early this year."

"I haven't talked to her. Why wouldn't you want to do that, though? Isn't it usually Henry's schedule that holds you up from leaving sooner?"

"It's not just that. I don't know. My mom is great, but she's never been the best one to talk to about relationships. She never experienced heartbreak. She and my dad were together since puberty, basically. When he died, it was the first time she was ever alone, and she dealt with that by skipping town. Fine for her, but not exactly practical for the rest of us."

"So don't do that. What about going someplace on your own? I mean, completely on your own—somewhere you've never been before?"

"I don't know if trying to find my way around some new place is the best way to fix my problems. Sounds like I'd be distracting myself from them in favor of assembling the right sightseeing itinerary."

"You've never traveled alone, have you?"

"Sure, I have."

"I don't mean simply getting on a plane by yourself. I mean going someplace and not having someone on the other end expecting you. I mean no work, no agenda, no commitments, no responsibilities. Think about when you checked in at Chateau Colette. You were on your own for, what—two or three hours?—and with one innocent flirtation in the supermarket produce aisle, you freak out and sequester yourself in my living room for two days?"

I regretted telling her about Brett and the ensuing pantry pillaging that followed. I camped on her sofa, even calling off work on Monday, and ate nothing but what I could find in her house, a diet that amounted to cassava root chips, garlic-stuffed olives, beef jerky, and cashews. I watched every last cheesy romantic comedy I could get my hands on. I ran up an on-demand cable bill of over fifty dollars.

"That was different. I had just left Henry that morning. I was still all stirred up."

"And yet your ring is still on. I'd like to think you're wearing it as a symbol of fidelity, but I don't think that's exactly the reason, is it? You're using it as a pussy shield, aren't you? Fortification against the hordes of men intent on marauding and plundering."

"You think I should take off my ring? Play the single girl? I have to be honest. If you're looking for a wing man tonight, your odds are better solo."

"Much as I'd like to take The Lonely Brazilian out on the town, doll, I wouldn't be caught dead out on Thanksgiving night. It's just like New Year's Eve. I have no use for amateurs. In fact, let's go get into jammies, cuddle with the pups, and keep talking upstairs."

We rose and walked arm in arm out of the restaurant, through the grand lobby, and took the elevator to our room on the eleventh floor. We faced a "courtyard," which amounted to looking at the sets of windows facing our room from the opposite tower. A fire escape lay immediately before us, further blocking our view out onto what little we could see of Wabash Avenue, and a nondescript black tar roof lay below. Neither of us minded in the least, especially since being back in the cavern obstructed most of the noise from the passing L train throughout the night.

I took the dogs for a walk while Colette showered and got ready for bed. When I got back to the room, I washed my face and brushed my teeth while she played with Frank and Lloyd.

I could have bought pajamas while I was at Colette's, but I hadn't. I'd been sleeping in the blue silk chemise, nullifying the erotic associations I had with it virtually altogether. My nipples stood erect against it, a fact Colette called stark attention to the first time she noticed, of course. "Don't mind me if I stare. I love nipples. Wish I had a set. I have nipple envy. Mine are shy. Only thing about me that is." Colette's were inverted, which she shared was actually a blessing most of the time. As she put it, she never had "headlights" anxiety, no matter how cold the room, and she never had to worry about them giving her away if she was turned on and wanted to keep it a secret.

"So your two most exotic travels have been to lands with monsoons," she said.

"They have been, although in Laos, the season was over by the time we arrived."

"I'm just thinking—why not go to the desert? You've done warm and tropical. What about warm and arid?"

"I thought you said I shouldn't go to Albuquerque."

"That's not really the desert. That's still the high plains, weatherwise. Hot in the summer, no doubt about it, and drier than here, but I'm thinking Arizona."

"Sand, rattlesnakes, and cactuses? Meh."

"How about the woods? Oregon or Colorado, maybe?"

"Sounds treacherous. I don't want to go anywhere I'm going to end up stranded in until the spring thaw."

"Let's see… warm, dry, accessible… I've got it! You have to go to Sedona. I had someone just this week tell me about a condo he has there, on the north side of town, that gets booked only, like, half the time. You should go—I can hook you up!"

"Isn't that the desert?"

"Northern Arizona is nothing like Southern Arizona. It's vibrant and desolate at the same time. There are the red sandstone rock formations, a smattering of cacti, but also the cypress, juniper, cedar, and the sycamore. Oh! You're a jock—you'll love the hiking trails. This is exactly the place where you can go, be mindful, journal some more—get your brain, heart, and libido in conversation with one another again."

I was a little dumbfounded by her last justification, but I was already sold. I was also suffering from the trifecta of tryptophan, champagne, and a luxuriously warm duvet. I was drifting off to sleep, feeling very warm and happy.

"I'm so thankful for you, Colette. You've been an absolute Godsend to me these last several weeks. Without you, I don't know where I'd be."

"Probably at home, or out with your husband and gay boyfriends, having a home-cooked meal. If it hadn't been for CVC, Henry wouldn't have found out about your waywardness."

"That's right, and I would have been either miserable or faking happiness. It's not your fault that Henry found out. There are a lot of times I'm glad he did. I don't know how all of this is going to end, but at least the wheels are moving. I'm miserable a lot of the time, but at least it's real. I'll take genuine sad over fake happy any day of the week."

"Except when it comes to going under knives or lasers, my friend, I feel exactly the same way. It's the real deal for me or nothing at all."

"Wait, what are you saying?"

"My boobs aren't real. My lips aren't real. My hair is not this color, and it's not this straight or smooth without a shit-ton of formaldehyde. My forehead hasn't moved since Clinton was in office. Surely you've realized as much."

I stammered, "Well… yes…"

"You're a smart girl. Surely you've wondered why I go to the trouble."

"Even if I hadn't, I know you're going to tell me."

"It's my God-given body that's telling the lie to the world, not me. I want my artifice to tell the truth. I am youthful, vibrant, and desirable. My tits, lips, hair, and forehead have begun to disagree with that.

I won't let them misrepresent me to the world. When I feel old, I will dress old, and I will look old. Until then, it's silicone in my funbags, botox in my face, embalming fluid in my hair, and bleach wherever it's needed. I'm going to be the hottest old biddy in the home."

"You, with your Hermès and Burberry. I can see it now."

"Bet your ass, hooker."

I laughed. I'd laughed a lot throughout the day. This was gratitude, I thought to myself. For the first time in my life, I finally understood the meaning of that word. I used to think that thankfulness and gratitude were the same, but they're not. Thanks is the clothing of gratitude. We say words of thanks to express the sentiment of gratitude. Gratitude is the prospectus; thanks is the transaction. I was thankful for Colette being in my life, but I was grateful for what her presence had opened up to me.

"I love you, Colette."

"I love you, too, honey. Now go to sleep. Of all God's gifts, almost none is better than a good night's sleep with a full belly, cuddly dogs, a good friend, and a fading champagne buzz."

I lay in bed for a while, thinking about what Colette had said about my ring. She was right; I wasn't wearing it out of devotion. I was wearing it as a shield, and that phoniness degraded its appearance and its meaning. Until I knew what it meant to me, it couldn't symbolize anything to me at all. I got up, took off my ring, and stowed it safely away.

15

Sunday, December 11

Dante knew he ought to go right to her house, but five hours of driving in a rental across the prairie had left him feeling like he had been assembled from a kit of spare parts. He would have been smart to find the gym in town and work out the stiffness from his joints on the elliptical. He reasoned that he'd already called the gym while he was on the road and set up a personal training session (physical therapy, actually, but personal training sounded better than work needed to loosen up old rugby-ruined knees and shoulders) with a sugar-voiced woman named Stephani. "The one with the I," he remembered her chirping, "which is important, since there's also a Stephanie on staff with an IE." That would suffice.

Dante was hungry, and he was thirsty. A large beer and a sandwich were in order. Eight-thirty was the only appointment they had at the gym the next morning, which he felt lucky to find at all, but it meant that it'd need to be an early night. Fortunately, he'd been able to leave earlier than he'd planned, and he'd made good time. His cousin wasn't expecting him for another forty-five minutes. If she was smart, and she was, she'd consider Dante's track record for on-time arrival and not count on seeing him for another two hours.

As he drove along the main street, Dante scanned the awnings and windows for a restaurant or bar where it looked like the food would be worth the indulgence. He spotted the car backing out of the diagonal parking spot in front at about the same time as he saw the sign. By all outward appearances, he decided that the straightforwardly-named Meat would fit the bill. He parked, fumbling over the buttons and knobs on the unfamiliar dashboard to make sure the headlights were off before heading inside.

The place was vacant, which wasn't any real surprise, since it was three-forty-five on a Sunday afternoon. There weren't any TVs, which surprised Dante even as he was relieved. He'd listened to most of the Chiefs-Jets game on satellite radio as he drove, and he'd had about enough sports white noise for the day. It was the last game that anyone thought his Chiefs could win in the season, since the Jets' record was just as middling and unimpressive as theirs. No luck. Dante had turned it off in favor of a Dave Matthews Band concert recording he'd found while scanning the stations. An Alpine Valley show with "Crash Into Me," "Gravedigger," "Rhyme & Reason," "Stay or Leave," and a cover of Peter Gabriel's "Sledgehammer." Good stuff.

"Is the kitchen still open?" Dante called to the bartender, who appeared to be the only person in the place.

"Hard to believe, right?" the bartender joked in reply. "Yeah, they're in there. Your timing's good, too. We'll pick up in about an hour. You'll get the kitchen's personal attention from now until then."

Dante could have a conversation with this guy, he could see. "What's good?" he asked as he took a seat at the bar, shedding his leather jacket and tossing it over the barstool next to his.

"Pulled pork. The smell of it has been making me drool all afternoon. We smoke on property—none of that catered-in factory crap. Sandwich is on a pretzel roll."

"Great. Give me that. And what would you drink with it? What's on tap?"

"We've got forty beers on hand. Are you a pilsner guy, you like the weird stuff, or are you somewhere in between?"

"What's your weirdest?"

"We've got a coffee IPA you should try. Goes great with the pork. You won't regret it."

"Coffee?"

"Yeah. What'll they do next, right? It's not in-your-face. The flavor's there mostly to complement the smoked malt, and the hops are strong."

"Okay, let me try that." Dante looked around and made a mental note to chastise his cousin for not having brought him here before.

"How long has this place been open?"

The bartender answered over his shoulder as he put the ticket in the window. "About a year now. Why? Do you live in town?"

"No, just visiting. I'm here for the lecture tomorrow night."

"Oh, right… I heard about that. Kind of a big deal—with media here to cover it, even. Doesn't that dude give, like, two or three lectures a week? I've seen him on *Larry King Live* and *Colbert Report*, and all. He's a friggin' genius, but I'm not sure I get why another speech is such big news." The bartender set the deep amber pint on a coaster in front of him.

"He's the keynote for the Muon g-2 grand opening. I can't wait to hear what he has to say about it. He's great with taking that brainiac stuff and making it easy to understand. Besides, it's not every day you get to see a fifty-foot-diameter magnet. The work they do there blows my mind. I'm kind of a science geek."

Dante looked up and saw that the bartender had glazed over. Bored, probably, like almost everyone else became whenever Dante got on the subject of science.

"Besides," Dante continued, shifting away from the subject, "the road trip gave me an excuse to visit some family in the area. The timing was right, so I made the drive. I didn't know it was getting that much hype outside of the world of physics."

"I know the woman who does PR at the Lab. I think she sort of blew the doors off promoting it. I'm Sam, by the way."

"Dante. This is really good. What did you say it was?"

"I don't think I did. Aleman makes it, a company of a few guys starting to make a name for themselves around here."

"Coffee in beer. Who would have thought? Does it have any caffeine in it?"

"Negligible. I think the alcohol pretty much negates any caffeine buzz you could get. Let me check on your sandwich." Sam turned to walk to the window but continued the conversation. "Where are you here from?"

"Des Moines," Dante said, studying the logo on the pint glass. "And before you say it, yes, I get that's a long way to drive for a science lecture."

"Isn't that, like, eight hours away?"

"More like five. What can I say? It fit into my schedule, and my cousin will be happy I finally made it to town. She wasn't able to make it to the family Thanksgiving, so I thought I'd bring a little family to her."

"I gotcha. Here you go. Enjoy it." After setting the plate down, Sam half-leaned, half-sat on the counter behind him and continued to snack on a plate of fries sitting beside the end of the tap line.

"Damn, this is good," Dante said through a full mouth of food. "You can understand why my expectations weren't too high, but this is really good."

"Why wouldn't you think it'd be good? I'm not the only one who can smell the smoke, right?"

"No, it's not that. It's just with it being slow in here, and this place being in the suburbs… I'm from Iowa. Hogs… cattle… We take meat kind of seriously."

"Well, as someone who grew up next door to the hog butcher to the world, I thank your state's contribution to my high cholesterol and blood pressure."

"Oh, no, man, I don't mean to be a dick," Dante said, his mouth still full of food. "I meant to give a compliment, and it came out all wrong."

"No worries," Sam said dismissively.

"Like I know anything about farming. I mean, I know people who do. Family on my dad's side, mostly. I'm an accountant. The only thing I really know about meat is what I'm willing to pay for it and how I like it done."

"Me, too. Besides, Chicago hasn't been butcher of anything to the world for decades. I was quoting Sandburg."

"Tool Maker, Stacker of Wheat, Player with Railroads and Freight Handler to the Nation," Dante recited. "I've gotcha."

"Okay, you win. I've lived here all my life, and I've read the poem, but it takes a guy from Iowa to come into the bar on a Sunday afternoon to quote it to me."

"College English class assignment. I was trying to impress a girl from Chicago. It stuck with me," Dante laughed.

"Did you get the girl, though? That's the important part of the story."

Dante's bashful smirk said it all. Sam held his hand up for a high-five. Dante put his hand to Sam's, although with some reluctance.

"That's what I'm talking about!" Sam said.

They both laughed.

"So do you still know the whole poem?" Sam continued. "Takes that kind of incentive to commit things to memory long-term, at least for me."

"I don't know," Dante said. "I didn't know I had that one line floating around up there until I said it just now."

"Okay. So twenty bucks says you can't recite the rest. Fun times for a Sunday afternoon."

"Alright. Get ready to earn your tip. I'm going to lose," Dante said as he stretched his neck from side to side and cracked his knuckles. "Wait, how will you know if I do it or not? I could make up whatever I want and sell it as true if I wanted."

"Would you do that? I thought you weren't a dick."

Dante smiled. "Alright, here it goes."

> *Hog Butcher for the World,*
> > *Tool Maker, Stacker of Wheat,*
> > *Player with Railroads and the Nation's Freight Handler;*
> > *Stormy, husky, brawling,*
> > *City of the Big Shoulders:*
> *They tell me you are wicked and I believe them, for I have seen your painted women under the gas lamps luring the farm boys.*
> *And they tell me you are crooked and I answer: Yes, it is true I have seen the gunman kill and go free to kill again.*
> *And they tell me you are brutal and my reply is: On the faces of women and children I have seen the marks of wanton hunger.*
> *And having answered so I turn once more to those who sneer at this my city, and I give them back the sneer and say to them:*
> *Come and show me another city with lifted head singing so proud to be alive and coarse and strong and cunning.*

> *Flinging magnetic curses amid the toil of piling job on job,
> here is a tall bold slugger set vivid against the little
> soft cities;*
> *Fierce as a dog with tongue lapping for action, cunning as
> a savage pitted against the wilderness,*
> *Bareheaded,*
> *Shoveling,*
> *Wrecking,*
> *Planning,*
> *Building, breaking, rebuilding,*
> *Under the smoke, dust all over his mouth, laughing with
> white teeth,*
> *Under the terrible burden of destiny laughing as a young
> man laughs,*
> *Laughing even as an ignorant fighter laughs who has
> never lost a battle,*
> *Bragging and laughing that under his wrist is the pulse,
> and under his ribs the heart of the people,*
> > *Laughing!*

Dante paused to drink the rest of his beer before finishing, hoisting his pint and punctuating his words with gestures using the same.

> *Laughing the stormy, husky, brawling laughter of Youth,
> half-naked, sweating, proud to be Hog Butcher, Tool
> Maker, Stacker of Wheat, Player with Railroads and
> Freight Handler to the Nation.*

Dante set the pint down and shifted on his stool, reaching for his wallet.

Sam was reaching for his at the same time. "Damn, man, I hate to lose an afternoon's wages, but it's not so bad when I get a 'private performance of poetry' in exchange." Sam said the last alliterative words with a Falstaffian flourish as he took a twenty from his wallet and put it on the bar.

"What are you doing?" Dante asked. "I don't think I got that middle part right, with the smoke and dust and white teeth, and all. I owe you."

"You sold it, bro," Sam said. "Take the money."

"Buy this, and we'll call it even," Dante said, motioning to the plate and the glass. "It was fun to find I still had that rattling around somewhere up there."

"You got it. Man, I don't even really like poetry, but that's a good one. I'll have to look it up."

"Got me laid in college, anyway. Doubt it'd have that same power, now that women our age have wised up to guys our age. Takes a lot more than poetry to get some anymore."

"Don't I know it. Say, it was good meeting you," Sam said, shaking Dante's outstretched hand. "Stop by again if you're still around. I'm here a few nights this week."

"I'll try. At least, I'll let my cousin know that she needs to put this place on her list."

"Thanks, man. Have a good time while you're in town."

"Plan to. See ya. Thanks a lot."

When he rose, Dante put his wallet back in his pocket before heading toward the door. He fumbled around again for the car keys before he realized that the doors were already unlocked. The chip in the fob triggered the doors when it was close enough. Once inside, Dante pressed the start button, backed out, and headed up the road, over the river, and, turning right, headed up the hill toward Zara's.

When Sam lifted the plate, he saw that Dante had left the twenty tucked underneath.

16

Tuesday, December 13

Zara Groves learned that she took the same train as Hank Bevrijden on a day that had gotten off to a bad start. She'd slept poorly, and she had an awkward conversation with her visiting cousin in the morning, which put her on the road later than normal. She didn't need to speed to stay on schedule, so long as she skipped her routine coffee stop, but she had been speeding out of nervousness. The unsympathetic police officer made catching her train nearly impossible.

She lived south of the station; if she had been on the other side of the tracks, she would have missed the train altogether. Frustrated, she sprinted from her distant parking spot and arrived in just enough time to board the last car. She never sat in the last car. It meant that the walk along the platform toward the single egress at Ogilvie would be that much longer than usual.

At least the last car had seats available. As all rail commuters know, the front cars are always occupied by curmudgeons whose seat dibs go back to the Reagan administration, and the cars in between are full of impenetrable cliques. She had finally found a regular spot, where she didn't feel like she'd stolen someone else's God-given right. Her fellow seatmates were all women near or past the age of retirement, whose conversation centered on recipes, grandchildren, and medical maladies. One woman's methodical knitting had produced sweaters, scarves, and blankets in the short time since Zara had made her acquaintance. Her favorite knitting projects, the woman said, were the tiny knitted caps, which she donated to be worn by the preemies whose heads were too small for the ones issued by the hospital.

Just after Zara had flopped down into an open seat just inside the doors, she saw him. She hoped desperately that he wouldn't recognize her, but she quickly reasoned that he probably wouldn't. While theirs was a small office, it was a somewhat reserved one, and she had heard that there had been some turnover in her position prior to her arrival. She got the impression that people didn't really invest the time to get acquainted with the receptionists until after the breaking-in period.

Also, it'd be hard for Hank to recognize someone he couldn't see. His distant gaze out the window was unwavering, even with the bustle of boarding travelers shuffling along the aisle between them and in the aisles overhead. His iPad, loaded with the *Tribune*, sat idle on his lap. The apple cupped in his right hand looked as if it was just about to roll onto the floor, his fingers unclenching as his apathetic grasp slackened.

"Excuse me, Mr. Bev... ridden?" Zara whispered. She sat backward, with her shoulder blades to the wall and the stairwell behind her, and every person who walked through the adjacent vestibule door brushed her coat sleeve. Hank was facing forward, head leaning against the scratched, soiled window. The seat to his side and the ones across from him were vacant. Zara sat kitty-corner from him, out of reach. She'd either have to raise her voice or move to his side of the train to get his attention.

"Mr. Bev-ridden!" Zara said in a rasping, shouted whisper meant to be polite yet more effective. She wasn't sure she was pronouncing his last name correctly—whether she was putting the stress on the right syllable. Was it BEV-ridden or bev-RID-den? The apple was going to fall, which would surely snap him from his stupor. When that happened, he may glance around to see if anyone had noticed, and she would be the only other person in his direct line of sight. To avoid the embarrassment that could cause both of them, her choice was to either change her seat or get his attention.

"Hank!" Zara said urgently, but in a volume that didn't exceed a normal speaking voice. He reacted as if she had pricked him with a pin.

"Hi, ah, um. Oh, my. I must have been, uh, dozing off," Hank mumbled. His hand reengaged, and he took a bite of the apple, resting the fruit on the iPad before returning his stare to the world passing by. A single bead of juice trailed down the dappled red skin from where the flesh he'd just eaten had been removed. Zara, whose eyesight had always been keen, watched the juice droplet travel to meet the surface of the tablet, which had gone dark and dormant.

A minute passed before something occurred to Hank. He turned to look at Zara. "I'm sorry. Did you call me Hank? How did you know my name?"

"My name is Zara, sir. I work in your office. I started after Labor Day. I'm at reception."

"Ah. How nice. Well, thank you for bringing me back to life. I didn't sleep so well last night." He didn't look as if he had slept well for many consecutive nights, but she repressed this observation.

"I understand that. I have a houseguest that has turned out to be pretty incorrigible," she shared. "Late nights aren't a problem for him because he's on vacation, but he didn't seem to get that I still had to work in the morning."

"I'm sorry to hear that. You know what they say about houseguests. They're like fish."

"Well, he drinks like a fish, if that's what you mean."

Hank laughed. "They say that fish and houseguests smell after three days, but I like your comparison better. I'm sorry your hospitality is being taken for granted."

"That's putting it mildly," Zara sniffed. "Tell me, do you think it's appropriate for your cousin, who you hardly ever get to see, to ask for a place to stay, and then proceed to invite some old college crush to come stay with him his second and last night in town?"

Immediately, she realized she'd said too much. Hank's expression evolved from one of profound indifference to surprised curiosity.

"I can't believe I just told all of that to you, sir. I am very sorry."

"It's okay. You haven't shocked me yet. And 'sir?' How old do you think I am?"

"It's not age. The other principals are so formal. I supposed it was a company-wide thing."

"It's not company-wide." Hank smiled reassuringly.

"Well, that's a relief. I haven't worked any place where so many people insisted on such formality. It's like a throwback to another generation."

"Well, I get that the Mad Men vibe is a little strong around our office. Without the rye, of course, or at least not as much of it. Maybe a little more would loosen things up."

"I don't drink anymore," Zara said.

Hank was nonplussed. "Oh. Well. Um. I'm sorry."

"Sorry that I don't drink?"

"No, not that! I mean, I'm sorry to imply that alcohol would be something casual to joke about. Clearly for some people it's not the right, uh, solution… Well, not solution, but it's serious, and…"

Zara laughed. "Don't be nervous! Trust me, sobriety isn't, like, a taboo subject for me." She reached into the neck of her blouse and retrieved a silver disc pendant on a delicate chain. Hank strained to make out the inscription.

"One year sober last month. I told my sponsor that I didn't care for the traditional chips and medallions. They look a little… Masonic. This one spoke to me." As she leaned over to give Hank a better look, he could see the swirling filigree scripted "1" and, engraved along the perimeter in a tiny script, the words "One Day at a Time."

"Wow. I thought you people were supposed to stay anonymous."

Zara dropped the necklace back into her décolletage. "It's just that we don't reveal the names of other members to non-members. I'm not ashamed to talk about it."

"Well, there's no reason to be, I guess."

"That's generous, considering you don't know me. Of course I have a lot of regret and shame about the things I did when I was drinking. The twelve steps aren't there to take those feelings away, exactly. Receiving forgiveness helps, but it's not like you finish the steps and come out fixed at the other end. I work them every day. They're never truly done."

"You don't look like someone who's lived long enough to speak with as much wisdom as you seem to have."

"I'm not wise." Zara blushed. "I just have a pretty good understanding of the things I can control and the things I'm not able to control."

"That's more than I know."

"I'm not surprised. Almost no one walking around does. There's no reason for you to have examined yourself as closely as I have while going through this, and all I know for sure is that I still have a long way to go. Look, I won't get evangelical about the whole experience. Just one more thing about A.A., and I swear I'm done. The twelve steps? They're not just about alcohol or even addiction, exactly. I won't go through the whole spiel. Look them up sometime. There's a lot to be learned from admitting powerlessness over things that would otherwise control you, and from seeking the support of God, as you understand Him, through meditation and prayer."

"Well, so long as you don't get evangelical about it," Hank said, one eyebrow raised, but with a good-natured smile.

"It's just easy to get excited when I talk about it."

"Don't apologize. It's great to hear people talk about their passions."

"Well, I didn't apologize, and I'm not sure if 'passion' is the right word for it, but I know what you mean. Anyway… It looks like we're about to pull into the station. Time to prepare for our twenty-minute walk down the platform."

"It's not that bad, actually. I sit down here every day. The crowd disperses by the time you get to where you think the crowd is going to be, if that makes any sense. Just watch."

"Okay," Zara said. "If you say so."

The overhead announcements were droning on about vigilance against terrorists and collecting belongings from the surrounding area. They rode in silence for the next few minutes. As they wound through the Fulton River District, Zara watched Hank curl and uncurl the fingers of his left hand, as if it was arthritic or injured. He examined the back of his hand and his palm. He had no wedding ring.

Finally, Hank spoke again. "It's been a little while since I've heard someone speak with as much energy and vulnerability as you showed this morning. It's a refreshing thing to see."

Zara took a moment to process this before responding. "You're welcome, then. If there's anything else you want to know, just ask."

Hank was right about the crowds, as it turned out. The two of them walked without urgency down the platform, through the station, and out onto the street, never encumbered by the throngs of other commuters Zara usually became embroiled with on the way outside. Zara and Hank made little conversation between the station and the office as they rounded Wacker Drive. They commented to one another about little things—the weather, how Thanksgiving had been, and plans for the holidays. Hank was strangely evasive through all of the small talk, but Zara supposed that he was only trying to reestablish some degree of decorum appropriate for the workplace.

As the two rode in the elevator, Hank seemed to be weighing whether to say something.

"I probably shouldn't mention it, but I have to say, Zara, that whatever your fragrance is… it's really spectacular," he said shyly.

Although it was a rather innocuous statement in and of itself, the fact that it seemed to be so difficult for Hank to share gave Zara a moment of pause. She mulled it over, deciding that it was nice to finally have had something resembling a real conversation with a co-worker—nice enough that Zara had mostly forgotten about the speeding ticket, and even about the argument she'd had with Dante that morning about bringing Delyn home, keeping her up most of the night while the two of them talked in the next room until nearly sunrise.

17

Monday, December 12

The big day was off to a good start, with the minor exception of my attire. The business casual workplace had eroded my wardrobe, something that I only managed to realize on days when truly professional dress was required. I had a respectable-looking but fussy pinstriped suit from the dry cleaners, but I realized at the last minute that I didn't have a proper shirt or shell. I improvised with my blue chemise. This way, I jokingly reasoned with myself, nervous speakers wouldn't have to be too imaginative when picturing at least one person in the audience, me, in her underwear.

Dr. Adiraju was ravishing and commanding in a salwar kameez suit. She was the consummate master of ceremonies, greeting the assembled Laboratory leaders, government representatives, and corporate benefactors, making warm introductions among them. She shared exactly the right anecdotes at the appropriate times and asked perfectly-placed, open-ended, softball questions to her staff throughout the lengthy luncheon, setting them up to share their own pithy observations and stories of Laboratory accomplishments.

The Doctor was a delight from the moment he arrived. There wasn't a subject on which he wasn't studied and articulate. His eyes dazzled as much while he described the Kepler spacecraft and its hunt for alien worlds as they did while he talked about the previous night's tromping of the Chiefs by the New York Jets. He was joyous in his admiration of the Supernova Cosmology Project and the High-z Supernova Search Team, applauding their recent Nobel Prize in Physics and leading a spirited but polite debate on the ramifications of their dark matter research.

I was more than grateful for a seat at the table, but my attention was divided. I tried to stay engaged with conversation at the table, but I kept wondering what was going on back at the office, too. As much as I tried to be a delegating, trusting manager, I found my hand drifting back to my phone every two or three minutes, to send another text following up on some logistical quirk reviewed just moments before. Our department intern finally conveyed her exasperation when she added punctuation to one of her responses. I knew I had to lay off when I saw, "Yes. I. Got. It."

Each department head had been charged with leading a portion of the campus tour in the area of his or her expertise. I started the trip at the eastern end, showing the cluster of Victorian farmhouses, explaining how the Department of Energy had purchased the entire town back in the 1960s and relocated the homes to this area to serve as a set of dormitories for visiting scientists. Then, we headed westward to tour the Neutrino and Proton areas, to the Technical Division building to shake hands at several of the site offices, and then back to the main hall for the accelerator ring presentation. The Doctor nodded politely through each speech and interjected relatively innocuous questions at the appropriate intervals, but I couldn't help but think that he would have been able, if asked on the spot, to present the information he was receiving with greater specificity and aplomb, even unrehearsed.

As the afternoon wore on, reporters began to arrive and set up their equipment in the auditorium. It was decided that, with the volume of expected turnout, we would use the main auditorium and, upon conclusion of the press conference, break down the equipment in short order and reset the space for the evening's event. The press conference felt like a sort of homecoming for me, reconnecting with old friends and colleagues at the various media outlets and ogling various new faces whose names I only knew through email correspondence, bylines, or the television screen.

Caterers began to arrange the various warming trays and chafing dishes of hors d'oeuvres. Florists arranged the table decorations, and my staff displayed the nametags and directional signage. I double-checked timetables with the charter operator we had hired to transport the attendees between the Muon g-2 building and the auditorium, assuring that no one would be stranded at either building throughout the event's duration.

Everything felt too seamless, too placid. Two months before, assembling an event of this magnitude had seemed impossible. I almost wished for that one mission glitch to happen, so I would have something to contend with, instead of pacing between one end of the auditorium lobby and the other. I told myself to get it together and trust that everyone and everything was in place and functioning. Given the sum of all things considered, I decided to give myself a break, eyeing the bar but deciding that discretion was the better part of valor, at least while on the clock.

The Doctor returned from the hotel in plenty of time, trading his more scholarly tweed jacket with the leather elbow patches, chambray shirt, and jeans for a sharp navy suit, brushed silk oxford, and signature tapestry vest. One almost forgot, watching him in action, that he was the guest of honor. An animated, practiced showman, he was every bit the host.

The reception was in full swing when I looked across the room and saw someone entirely out of place and unexpected. I didn't want to get caught staring, just in case it wasn't who I thought it was.

His temples had begun to grey, but in every other respect, Dante looked exactly like he had more than a decade before. He looked every bit like a fan boy, waiting in the short line that had formed for an audience with the Doctor. I almost swallowed my gum, just then realizing that I'd been chomping, likely with mouth agape, throughout the entire day's proceedings.

As I walked up behind him, I hadn't formed any words to say. I willed my feet to stop in their tracks, to give me some respite as I devised something clever to say. As I opened my mouth, I looked forward to discovering what would come out.

"Of all the gin joints in all the towns in all the world, he walks into mine," I lisped, and rather convincingly, I thought.

Dante circled slowly, his expression evolving from one of profound confusion to utter disbelief. "Delyn Ziegel? What in the world are you doing here?"

We each stood motionless, staring stupidly at one another, in awkward silence, before I had the presence to respond. "I could ask you the same question. I work here. I live here. You don't do either."

"I just can't believe… Come here, you!" He clutched my shoulders and pulled me awkwardly into his chest. The embrace was further complicated by the book under his arm, which fell to the floor as his arms wrapped around me.

"What are you doing here? Did you come to town just for this?" I asked as I pulled back.

"Just for this?" he asked. "Mysteries of the universe will soon be revealed by the research conducted at this facility, the opening of which is being celebrated by the foremost science communicator of our time. That seems like it's worth a drive from the prairie for a simple country mouse."

I was reminded that Dante was a chameleon. He was the kind of guy who in one moment could sing every lyric of *American Pie*, describe Jeffersonian agrarian ideology in the next, go on to elucidate string theory, and finish by going Neanderthal while recounting a dump tackle from a rugby match.

"Whatever became of you, Dante?" I asked to fill the awkward silence. "I haven't heard a thing about you in years."

"I knocked around here and there for a while before I finally returned to the family fold. I work in the office at Abatangelo. Don't be too impressed. It's not as glamorous as it sounds. How about you, though? The last I heard, you were on the team for some ad campaign that won a Clio. That had to be pretty cool."

"Two golds, actually," I said. I was a minor player on an immensely popular light beer campaign, but I was destined to be no more than a mid-level writer at best. "I left that rat race about three years ago."

"What happened to working in a niche shop? I figured you'd be running your own agency by now," Dante said.

I didn't want to tell him that no place I had applied would hire someone who'd skated through school, worked at a brew pub for two years, and then limped back to her hometown, defeated, after her college boyfriend never got the sense to rekindle things, let alone pick up the phone. I had finally been able to convince a former Leo Burnett friend who'd moved to DDB to hire me as an entry-level writer.

"Ah, life is a funny thing. The long story short is that I'm the Director of Communications for the Laboratory, now."

"So it's been you whispering in my ear all this time. I read you almost every day. If I'd really been paying attention, I would have realized it long before now."

"What are you talking about?"

"Your blog or, rather, the Laboratory blog. I follow it. I read every entry."

"I don't write most of the entries. I only edit them. Why on Earth would you follow our blog?"

"I'm bored with keeping tabs on the small corner of the universe I understand. If I'd actually applied myself in school, I think I could have pursued astronomy. Sorted out real mysteries. As it is, I have to live out my fantasy in other ways. You really know how to explain the complexities of the Laboratory's work so even this Luddite can understand."

"More like erudite. Your geekery knows no bounds, truly," I teased, trying to disguise how touched I was by his compliments.

Dante moved to the head of the line. I hardly needed to intercede, but did so just the same. "Doctor, this is my good friend Dante Abatangelo."

"Please tell me you're not a Pluto apologist," the Doctor said with a motion to the book. "Any other day, I'm game, but I've got bigger things on my mind at the moment, Dante."

We all laughed, Dante more nervously than amusedly. "Oh, no! I loved what you had to say about Pluto. Anything big enough to have, well, four moons now, with the discovery of Kerberos orbiting it, is big enough for me, no matter how it's categorized."

"It takes a certain level of geek to be up to speed on new Plutonian moons, Dante."

"Oh, you have no idea, Doctor," I chimed in.

"All day long, and you're still so formal, Ms. Ziegel. Please use my first name."

I blushed.

"Because I think you'll appreciate the inside track, you two, I'll let you in on an astronomical secret," he continued. "We think Pluto may actually have a fifth moon. Look for it to be confirmed sometime next year."

"That's a pretty heavy burden to carry, sir. I'm not sure I can be trusted with planetary news of such magnitude," Dante gushed.

"Well, it's dwarf-planetary. I think the secret's safe with you," he replied.

Dante seemed to have forgotten about the book under his arm. "Did you intend to do anything with that book there, Dante?" I asked.

He snapped from his trance and nearly dropped the book again. "Oh, yes, I was wondering if you'd do me the favor—I mean, privilege, of…"

"I'd be happy to." The Doctor took the book, drew a fountain pen from his breast pocket, and began to write. "I am inscribing this to you, correct?"

Dante was captivated, managing only to nod as his eyes were transfixed on the book. The Doctor finished his autograph and, handing the book back, excused himself after exchanging warm handshakes with us both.

"That's the longest I've seen him speak with anyone all day," I remarked.

Dante grinned from ear to ear.

"Hey, I have a few things I need to do before the lecture begins, but save me a seat," I joked, rising on my toes to air kiss him, but in another feat of awkwardness, managing to plant my lips firmly into his cheekbone. I giggled with embarrassment. "I guess I'm a little out of practice."

"I find that hard to believe. Sure, I'll save you a seat." Dante's smile hadn't faded in the least.

I hurried around, checking in with each member of my staff to ensure that everyone who had visited the Muon g-2 building had returned. The nametags had reasonably accounted for our key guests' arrivals, everyone promised VIP seating had secured it, and the servers were circulating with appetizers and drinks. Everything was humming along like a well-oiled machine. I sidled up beside the Doctor to let him know that it was time for him to go backstage and prepare, and I escorted him to the green room. Returning, I found Dr. Adiraju talking with a state senator. I alerted her that the caterers would begin ringing the chimes for people to take their seats. Dr. Adiraju and her coterie made their way into the auditorium, taking their appointed seats in the front rows.

I exhaled, realizing that I hadn't truly processed what it meant for Dante to appear in the midst of everything else under way. I had, on the whole, taken what ought to have been a jarring development in relative stride. I resquared my shoulders, realizing that it was not time to pat myself on the back just yet. I located the head waiter, let him know we were ready to begin, and entered the auditorium. Just as he had said he would, Dante had saved me a seat, thankfully on the aisle and in the last row before the exit door on the audience's right side.

"Don't you want to sit closer?" I asked. "I have people, you know. I've got connections."

"Won't this be more convenient if you have any reason to jump up?"

"I guess. Among all the details, I'd never figured out how I fit into the scheme."

"You haven't changed. Here, take a load off." Dante patted the seat.

The lights lowered, and Dr. Adiraju took the stage. At the podium, she gathered her note cards and, delivering the speech we had so meticulously massaged over the last several days, she introduced dignitaries in attendance and thanked everyone graciously for their support.

As she began to describe the many accomplishments of our featured speaker, Dante put his arm over the back of my chair and started to give me an impromptu massage, making me realize how tense my shoulders had been, up nearly to my ears. I stretched my arms out before me, balling my hands into fists and re-tensing my shoulders before splaying my fingers and letting the last vestiges of stress dissipate. "Thank you. I needed that," I said.

Dante took my left hand in his own. "You're not wearing a wedding ring, Ziegel," he observed.

"I'm not," I whispered.

"Interesting," he said.

"Shhh. We're about to begin."

~ ~ ~ ~ ~ ~ ~

RELEASE

The lobby was abuzz for more than an hour after the lecture concluded. The Doctor had spoken for more than ninety minutes, addressing myriad topics sure to keep every attendee stocked with scientific and philosophical conversation fodder well through the holiday season. I roamed the lobby and could overhear impassioned tête-à-têtes on every subject from the space race to STEM funding, from the popularity of *The Big Bang Theory* television show to Moore's Law and singularity. The Doctor's talk about spirituality in science had drawn audible gasps from several members of the audience, to which he readily responded with such diplomacy that the whole of the group had returned securely to the palm of his hand.

Dante lingered as I shook hands and made introductions, keeping his distance as Dr. Adiraju introduced me to too many people to remember. She was effervescent, riding the high of the evening's success, secure in the knowledge of what it meant for the Laboratory's good reputation and continued success. I, in turn, continued to defer the real congratulations to my team, who continued to scurry about the facility, maintaining the food and drink service beyond our contracted time period. I willfully prevented myself from thinking about the premiums we would have to pay for going over our allotments. I was sure that it wouldn't matter to anyone signing checks, but I hated to exceed budget.

It was after ten o'clock before the last attendees departed. After shaking the head security guard's hand, I walked with Dante toward the parking lot, neither of us having broached the subject of where we were going or what we were doing. Ours were the last two cars in the lot.

"What's next?" Dante asked innocently enough. I could see his breath billow from his lips as he spoke.

"I don't know," I whispered. He'd put his arm over my shoulder soon after we were out of sight of the building's doors. I rotated to face him, letting his hand glide across the nape of my neck to land on my left trapezius. I looked up into his eyes. "What do you want to do?"

"I want to hang out and talk, Delyn. I want to catch up. You're kind of a mystery to me right now."

"I like being a little mysterious." I was working with little sleep and was coming off an adrenaline high. I wasn't making a lot of sense but didn't care much about it at that moment. I even started to rise on my toes and began to let my eyelids flutter shut.

"Not that I'm not intrigued or tempted by other notions," Dante said as he either chose to ignore or actually did not notice my advances, "but let's get a drink first. I went someplace downtown last night that I'd like to go to again. What do you say?"

"Chicago? I don't know. It's already so late."

"No, Weston! There's a lot happening around this little burg of yours."

"How long have you been here?" I was beginning to realize that Dante was something of a mystery to me, too.

"Not long enough. Why don't we take my car? I could drop you here on our way back."

I agreed, still a little deflated by the slight I'd perceived. "Seems silly to take two if we're going to be back by this way." The two of us broke apart and headed toward his sedan. "This is nice," I said.

"It's a rental. My Jeep is freezing in the winter when I take it anywhere out of town. It's fine for getting to and from work, but highway winds whip right though the plastic."

"You still have that old clunker?" I gasped, getting into the car.

"If it ain't broke, right? I've sunk some cash into it, but it's held up great, overall."

"It was a beat-up jalopy when I last saw it, almost twenty years ago!"

"Aw, come on! It's got character."

"Rust is not character. A busted AM radio is not character."

"You never seemed to mind, although some real doors and windows would have saved us from getting arrested on that trip to Okoboji. That poor family will be scandalized for life by what they saw."

He had me there. We had made a lot of memories in that old thing. "So long as it still has its name, I guess it's alright."

"Yep, the Falcon'll still make point-five past lightspeed. She may not look like much, but she's got it where it counts."

I smiled. "What was your favorite part of the lecture?" I asked. "What did you take away from it?"

Dante headed up the road toward downtown. "I can't stop thinking about what he was saying about quantum nonlocality. I wanted to ask him about his thoughts on tangled hierarchy and the connection between erotic compulsion and true love."

I'd written a little about quantum nonlocality and tangled hierarchy for work. The basis of this field of science is that subatomic particles can know about and communicate with one another instantaneously, over vast distances, kind of like E.S.P. at the level of the universe's smallest-known building blocks. I would never describe it that way professionally—Dr. Adiraju would have my head for invoking pseudoscience. It's one of the most baffling curiosities of quantum mechanics. Scientists are hard at work investigating what bearing quantum behaviors could have on classical physics. The implications for communications, for instance, would literally be astronomical.

Still, of all the things I thought Dante would say, nothing like that was anywhere in the vicinity. "What? I mean… huh?"

Dante continued. "I thought we wouldn't hear as much about the cosmos, given the occasion, the venue, and the audience, but it felt like he was leading up to a more metaphysical discussion."

"He's famous for his aversion to diluting science with superstitions and new-age nonsense."

"Yeah, I know. I've just been spending a lot of time, lately, thinking about where to draw the line."

You and me both, I thought to myself. "Give me an example."

"Like, he'll talk about time travel, for instance. If quantum nonlocality, which is science fact on a micro level, could be replicated on a macro level, time travel and even teleportation would be possible, theoretically. That's a pretty significant suspension of disbelief. On the other hand, he's an atheist."

"He's not an atheist. He denounced that label two years ago. Pushed into it, he accepted being called an agnostic," I clarified.

"I think that's a semantic distinction. All he was trying to do was end speculation about his religious beliefs. It's a non-issue to him, except for his disgust with fundamentalist beliefs being taught as science, or his dislike of the God of the Gaps perspective."

"Right…" I searched my memory to figure out what any of this had to do with anything erotic. "The God of the Gaps paradigm is a real problem, though. The scientific community's ego has grown to hubristic, omnipotent proportions. The arrogance of God of the Gaps arguments stymies scientific progress. It's a lazy scientist who throws up his hands and says, 'If I can't understand this, it can't be understood by anyone, so it must be part of God's mystery.'"

"It would be lazy, but I think that's a stereotype in our modern age—a dated caricature of the scientist who also believes in a personal God," Dante said.

"It's a caricature based upon thousands of years of religious and governmental resistance to scientific discovery. Think about the persecution of Galileo, or what the Doctor said about the age when Baghdad was the center of scientific discovery until—Who was it, al-Ghazālī?— decried mathematics and science as the work of the devil. Think about what George Bush said about it being 'Our God who named the stars.' We're all talking about the same thing: the fight against scientific ignorance."

Dante paused to consider his answer before speaking. "I think about what Einstein said, and I hope I don't butcher this, but he characterized his religious stance as an 'unbounded admiration for the structure of the world so far as our science can reveal it.'"

"'An attitude of humility corresponding to the weakness of our intellectual understanding' is another way Einstein put it," I quoted. "See, I took what the Doctor said as an evisceration of the God of the Gaps argument only as it applies to intelligent design. Did you hear the gasps from some of the people in the audience? Clearly, they took issue with the Doctor's opinion, like invoking God is an immediate excuse to discontinue all exploration and experimentation."

Dante was poised for debate. This topic appeared to be one about which he was really passionate. "People who react that way to the God of the Gaps argument live their lives teed up, ready to argue blindly against intelligent design, as if evolution couldn't have had the hand of God in it, directing its path. But no, that's not what I really got at all. The Doctor only worries about invoking intelligent design if it prevents scientists from making further discoveries."

"And you're trying to understand the connection between erotic compulsion and true love?" I asked, going back to his original statement.

"As it relates to quantum nonlocality and tangled hierarchy," he said. "The Doctor's a lover. No doubt about it. Did you know that he was an national award-winning ballroom dancer in college?"

"I did not, and while that is awesome, I'm not sure how ballroom dancing translates to... anway, that's all beside the point. Tell me how you understand tangled hierarchy."

"In the smallest nutshell I can fit it in, it's like envisioning the structure of the universe as a bundle of tangled yarn, not organized by any means that follow the laws of nature, as the general population currently understands them."

"Okay, I'm with you so far," I lied.

"Applying quantum entanglement to the social paradigm, envision timelines—your life, my life, the progress of the universe, all timelines—like yarn bundles, not clean, orderly, straight lines. It's a way of understanding why people, thoughts, and challenges are encountered time and time again. It's why we find ourselves revisiting the same memories, making the same mistakes, and going in circles."

I wasn't sure I liked where this was headed. "Uh-huh... and this has to do with erotic compulsions—how?"

"Quantum nonlocality explains that the practically imperceptible jumps between the strange loops of the tangled hierarchy happen all the time. They may seem haphazard, but they're really quite logical. Some people call these leaps coincidence; others call this phenomenon fate, depending on their religious leanings."

I interrupted. "What you're describing is the philosophical equivalent of a *Candy Land* board game."

"With the cards advancing you along the winding path, the trails and passes letting you skip ahead, the cards for the different candy lands... sure. Kind of crossed with *Chutes and Ladders*, though, too."

That's when I was sure that the conversation was going someplace silly.

"But leaps can also be initiated, to a certain extent, by choice—what the religious call free will," he said.

"Everyone calls it free will," I droned. I knew, then, for sure. His path of logic was pathological. While Dante's reasoning was generally sound, I instinctively bristled at his misapplication of theoretical physics to social interactions.

He didn't pick up on my unamused tone. "So, do you remember when he was talking about the ignoble drives of the masculine psyche and the power it craves?" he asked.

I finally had to interject. "No, I don't remember him using those words at all."

"Alright, fine. That is me extrapolating from his talk about the role of ego in scientific momentum toward the periphery of ignorance. Bear with me, though. Until well into the last century, the scientific world was absurdly chauvinistic, am I right?"

It still is. Men outnumber women at the Laboratory by at least twenty to one. I organize trips of women physicists to local schools to promote careers in science. Of late, Dr. Adiraju has been increasingly resistant to me pitching her story as a human interest piece for scientific journals. While she is proud of her achievements, she is growing weary of being the poster child for women in physics.

"And male ego just as often spurred scientific discovery as thwarted it," Dante continued. "On occasion, the choices of scientists led to fantastic discoveries; other times, discoveries were made by happenstance. Happenstance brought about by dutiful investigation and a prepared, alert mind, but happenstance nonetheless."

"Like the Big Bang Theory and nuclear fission." Both were discoveries accidentally made while in the pursuit of other objectives.

"Right on. So, what if one chose to compare the historically egocentric, masculine temperament of scientific work with the most ignoble of masculine drives, lust? If ego drives scientific breakthroughs, but it also makes failed scientists justify their failures with the God of the Gaps argument, then..."

"... the properly timed quantum leap could convert a carnal attraction to a complex emotional, spiritual connection," I said with deep skepticism, "or could just as easily devolve a fairytale romance into its so-called destined oblivion?"

"You just wrapped up my point better than I ever could."

Same old Dante, intriguing and infuriating at the same time.

"So God of the Gaps doesn't have to be a cop-out," he continued. "To me, a better way to invoke divinity is to let fate take a hand in scientific discovery, not oppose it. Instead of ignorantly accepting that some things are unknowable, what if scientists acknowledged the mysteries they encountered, then used that restored objectivity to refocus, even redirect and further motivate their investigation? I mean, if scientists didn't encounter mysteries, then I'd wonder whether their experiments were all that challenging. They should embrace mystery and seek conflict. That's the way to be sure they're truly on the periphery of the unknown."

"They should trust—have faith, so to speak—that epiphany and resolution reside on a higher plane of consciousness," I said. "Wow. You got a great deal more out of the lecture than I did, obviously. I must not have been paying attention as closely as you were."

"What were you paying attention to instead?" he asked.

"Your hand on my shoulder, mostly."

"Well, I was aroused. Intellectually, of course."

An awkward moment of silence fell. "Anyway…," I said. Thankfully, we had finally arrived downtown. "Where are you taking me, and can I say for a moment how funny I find it that you're taking me out in my hometown?"

"Have you been to Meat? It doesn't seem like it's been open that long."

My stomach imploded. "About a year, I think." I paused to clear my throat. "I haven't been, but I've heard good things."

"You'll love it," Dante said.

As we walked in, I furtively scanned the room. There wasn't any sign of Sam, and with the bar seeming to be fully-staffed, I supposed we were in the clear. Just the same, I found a more secluded table well away from the door, as Dante went to the bar to get us a round of drinks. For as few people as I knew in town anymore, I was feeling the absence of my ring nontheless. I didn't want to have to explain it, or worse, have someone notice and silently make assumptions.

Dante joined me at the table with a tulip snifter of deep golden beer for himself and a highball glass for me. "Sapphire Tonic still your poison?" he said as he set the drink on a coaster.

"You have no idea," I replied. "To old times."

He met my glass with his.

"What are you drinking?" I asked.

"The Hammer White Cedar Imperial Blonde," Dante said, examining the glass. "It's made by Aleman, these local guys who made this coffee IPA I had yesterday. It's citrusy and nicely bitter, yet malty." He took another sip, taking a moment to savor it. "And it has a hoppy, spicy finish."

"What's with it being served in such a small snifter?"

"The shape of the glass accentuates the flavor by bringing out the scent of the hops. It's a small glass because imperial blondes are pretty strong, as beer goes. 7.2 ABV," he said.

"Sounds great," I said. "So, to go back to that whole idea of embracing mystery and seeking conflict... The idea of surrendering control, trusting that epiphany and resolution reside on a higher plane of consciousness, makes me want to cry."

"What? It makes me want to jump for joy! It feels like gospel to me. For all the ages, science and religion posed themselves as if working at cross-purposes. This is the dawning of a new age, in which an encountered mystery isn't the end of the road, where the faithful of the world shrug our shoulders in acquiescence. It's the point at which we let our faith manifest in dutiful investigation, not by pretending to be God or seeking superiority over Him, but by letting Him work through us, revealing Himself to us and helping us understand Him."

"'All will be revealed' takes on a whole new meaning when you put it that way."

"Exactly! Revelation isn't something we wait to see happen, but something in which we take an active part."

"That's the part that makes me want to cry."

"You're not worried about the End of Days, are you?"

"Aren't you? Are you ready for judgment?" I asked.

"Now, wait. You haven't become an eschatologist on me, now?"

The conversation was making me feel like I was inside a pinball game with Dante at every spinner, bumper, and slingshot. "You didn't answer my question," I said.

"I'm more at ease with myself than I've ever been, but I have plenty for which I'm sure I'll be called to atone," Dante answered. "But I believe that we're talking about two different things."

"I wouldn't pretend to know when the End of Days is coming, but it feels like it's near," I despaired.

Dante paused for a long moment, drinking deeply from the snifter before continuing. "If that is really how you feel, what is there to worry about?"

I held up my left hand and pointed at my ring finger.

"Yeah, about that...," Dante began.

That is when I saw Sam and Brett walk in the door. My eyes must have popped out of my head. "Are you okay?" Dante asked. I couldn't tell if he was asking if I was okay with not wearing my ring or with what I had just seen.

I played it off. "Let's just say that I've been given the distance to study my life's mystery objectively," I stated as I used my cocktail straw to stir the ice in my otherwise drained glass. "And I'm anxiously awaiting that quantum leap to occur amidst my tangled hierarchy, so that I can ascend the strange loop to the higher plane of consciousness, where I can sort my shit out."

"So you're separated from Henry," Dante deduced.

"I've been released, encouraged to go out and figure out how I can be happy again."

"Wow. That sounds like my cue to get us another round. Hold that thought."

Before I could tell him to stay put, hoping to prevent the worlds of Dante, Sam, and Brett from colliding, he rose and, with glasses in hand, was already down the few steps between us and the end of the bar. I fiddled with my purse, checking my phone for any messages and wishing for any distraction from what appeared to be inevitable.

I finally got the nerve to look up and see what had become of Dante. Sure enough, there he was, giving a fraternity-style handshake/bro-hug to Sam, as if they were old friends, and shaking Brett's hand in what appeared to be a new introduction. Of course, Sam and Brett had met. I had sent Brett here, and anyone who meets Sam once is a friend. He could run for mayor if he had any ambition or ability to sustain focus.

Dante motioned to me, waving. I sat stone-faced, willing myself to awaken from the impending nightmare. I read Sam's expression. He was also in a state of confusion.

Dante slapped Sam's shoulder as an apparent invitation to our table. They approached, Sam's eyes lit with a fearful fire and his mouth contorting into a pursed frown.

"This guy listened to my meanderings the other day while I washed the dust of the road from my throat, Ziegel. Delyn, this is Sam Tierney."

"Delyn? Is anything I know about you real anymore? Where's your ring, Manny?"

Dante's smile dropped from his face as his eyebrows knitted for a moment. Then, a look of understanding replaced his look of bewilderment. "I'm an ass. Of course you guys know one another. I'm the out-of-towner here. What, did you guys go to school together? I didn't even think."

I had no idea how to proceed, but I did know I couldn't talk to all three of them at once. Brett, the least embroiled of the three men, graciously stepped aside but not before interjecting his own complication to the mix. "Ring still at the jeweler, there? Seems an awful long time for cleaning, don't you think? I'm going to go on back down to the bar, y'all, to find myself a pork sandwich. Nice recommendation on the place, Mandelyn. The barbecue's great. It was a pleasure meeting you, Dante. Sam, maybe I'll see you back down there in a bit, once… um, yeah."

Sam and Dante watched for a moment as Brett trailed off before stepping back and returning to the bar down below. The two of them both turned back to face me, expressions on their faces that I would have found amusing if I weren't so discombobulated.

"How do you two know each other?" I asked.

"Never mind that," Sam said. "Dante, would you mind giving me a moment to talk with our Mandelyn, here? There's a matter on which I need to satisfy my curiosity," he said ominously.

I looked at Dante, begging him with my eyes not to go, but either he didn't understand or didn't acknowledge my plea. "Sure, I, uh, never got that second round. I'll be right back," he assured me.

"Make it a sidecar. She likes those," Sam called after him.

Dante had barely stepped out of earshot before Sam practically snarled at me. "Just how deep have you dug into your little black book during your apparent sexual pilgrimage, Manny? Have you burned through all of your northern Illinois conquests already? Did you have to range back into the Hawkeye state to satisfy your hunger? Pick yourself up a Tennessee Volunteer?"

"You're disgusting. You have no idea what you're talking about."

"Don't I? I spend less than thirty minutes with that guy Sunday afternoon, and he waxes poetic about you, literally—to the point that he recites Sandburg he memorized almost twenty years ago, in the hopes of putting it to you. Then, it also appears that your good friend Brett has eyes for you. You are an efficient adulterer. I'll give you that."

Sam was being so ugly. All I wanted to do was put a stop to the situation before Dante returned. "Shut up," I said. "Stop it right now. Don't marginalize something you can't understand with your fetid accusations."

"Seems fair, doesn't it? My dreams of happiness in exchange for yours?" he scowled.

"You had better start making some sense. Get to your point, so we can end this before he comes back," I demanded.

"Start by telling me where your ring is," Sam said.

"Henry confronted me the night you drove me back from Chicago," I admitted.

"Don't you think I deserved to know that? What if I had run into him in town?" he asked.

"He didn't release me because of you—or, rather, not because of what we did that night. Your conscience is still in the clear," I assured him, somewhat sarcastically.

"Oh, gee, thanks. Glad you are allowing me that, oh holy one. Like you have the authority to make that determination," he said.

"You're out of line. Please, Sam. Don't make a scene," I begged.

Sam continued undeterred. "And 'release' you? What does that even mean? Like, you two are separated? The way you say it, it sounds like you're a free agent wide receiver. And what do you mean it's not because of what we did that night? How else would it have anything to do with me at all if it doesn't involve that night?"

"It's a long story and, the way you're talking to me right now, I don't think you deserve to hear it. My problems are between Henry and me."

"And Dante, and Brett, and who the hell knows who else."

"You need to leave before you say something you'll regret."

"Regret?" he scoffed. "My only regret is that you took the perfect night that was unfolding between us and ruined it with your wantonness. It was never in the stars for us, Man. I guess I know that. All I wanted was one night to approximate it. Shame on me for supposing that a cheap imitation could ever take the place of the real thing. Maybe it's just as well we didn't make love. By stopping you when I did, I probably saved us—or me… Who knows what it'll take to save you—from seeing the full depth of the destruction that your insatiable appetite would have on my soul?"

"What do you mean we didn't…?" I was too incredulous to comprehend his meaning. "We woke up the next morning… and the sheets… We were…"

Sam was in a sinister place. "Oh, my God! You think we fucked! Oh, Man… you blacked out, didn't you?" Sam laughed menacingly before redirecting his ire. "You are in a sad state, Mandelyn. I pity you. How pathetic is it that you don't know whether you spread your legs for me? You just assume you did, and I was just powerless to your charms. You're no muse, Mandelyn. You are not some irresistible nymph or goddess. For Christ's sake… you're a succubus. Worse; you are nothing but a simple, resistible, whore."

"I never claimed to be… I wasn't…," I started to say, though I was so thoroughly embarrassed by the growing attention on our conversation that I essentially said the words, incredulously, to myself.

Dante returned to the table halfway through Sam's soliloquy, without either Sam's awareness or mine. When Dante spoke, we both jumped. "You didn't strike me as the misogynist type, Sam. I read you all wrong."

I finally snapped to attention as I pushed the chair out from behind me with the force of my rage. "Get out, Sam. Leave my sight before I destroy you. You're nothing to me now."

"The minute I leave is the minute you're going to have to face the truth of yourself and what you've become."

I swung at Sam's face with my closed left fist. Bright, searing pain radiated through my arm as I connected with his substantial jaw. I pummeled him without a shred of self-awareness or restraint, my incoherent screams sounding foreign and ugly as blood pulsed in my eardrums. It took a moment for Dante to intervene and restrain me, catching my errant fist in his eye socket before finally locking each of my elbows in his hands, his shoulder shielding Sam from further attack. Brett had returned and pulled Sam back, both men with looks of astonishment and disdain on their faces. The music stopped, and the bar patrons were silent and staring in aghast anticipation.

"Have a nice life, Man. I hope you're happy." Sam turned and, as the crowd parted, he walked away and was gone.

I wanted to scream something horrible to Sam as he left, something decimating and final, but no words came. I panted, silent tears streaming from my eyes.

"Let's go," Dante said. "We're done here."

"We are," I blubbered. "It's all done."

18

I drove Dante's rental south, by his navigation, to his cousin's condo, while he dabbed at his split eyebrow with a paper cocktail napkin. The neighborhood was nice enough, if a little contrived. It was meant to look historic, but it was only a pretender to its authentic heirloom peers. Other than the vinyl siding and the pastiche finishes, the main giveaway was the landscaping, or, rather, the lack of it. Whatever few trees there were had been planted, not sown, and none were taller than the single-story rooflines along the street. The view over the frozen river was nice, though. Looking at the opposite bank, I could see the gazebo that had been the site of my high school Homecoming pictures. The lights decorating the structure sparkled across the ice.

The scent inside the house was splendid but a little overpowering. "My cousin makes scented candles and other hippie stuff. At least she used to," Dante explained. "She kind of got away from it for a while, and she has a regular office job now. The aroma never really goes away, it seems. Make yourself comfortable. I'm just going to clean up a bit, if you'll excuse me."

"Sure," I mumbled. Still feeling a little otherworldly, I walked down the hall past a galley kitchen and arrived in a modest living room. A shabby feather pillow in a yellowed case and a set of bed sheets lay half-spread, half-wadded into the corner of the brown threadbare sectional that dominated the room. A chipboard entertainment center housed various dated entertainment system components, and a tower half-filled with CDs sat beside it. I felt as if I was in my college apartment again, except for an oil painting above the couch, a rainy landscape that looked like it could have been from one of those starving artist sales at airport hotels. I never would have hung something so dreary on my wall.

I almost fainted when I heard the voice behind me. "I painted that a year ago," she said. I spun to see a dour yet prepossessing woman approach. "The colors are muddied, but the light on the horizon makes me feel hopeful. I know it isn't much, but I don't have the heart to let it go."

"No, it's... nice. I'm, um, Delyn," I said, extending my hand in greeting. "Really, it's nice. I came in with Dante," I rushed to explain, surprised by how nervous I seemed to be. Her deep brown eyes were jarring, especially without any other facial feature from which I could discern a clear emotion. "He's in your washroom. I'm a friend from college."

"Zara," she said perfunctorily. "You came here all the way from Iowa, too?" she continued, a skeptical tone emerging.

"Oh, no. I live here. We ran into each other at the lecture tonight, actually."

"I see. I'm sorry. I don't mean to be rude, but…"

The sound of a flush and the running of sink water could be heard from down the hall. The door opened, and I exhaled audibly with relief when he emerged.

"Hey, cuz. I see you met, um, Delyn. We went to college together. I knew she was from the suburbs, but I'd forgotten which one a long time ago. She lives just up the road. Small world, huh?"

"I see. Say, Dante, I was just starting to tell Delyn that I have work tomorrow. It's late. I was just getting ready to go to bed when you two came in. I wish I could stay up and visit with you, but…"

She gave us a hard, calculating look, trying, I thought, to figure out what the nature of our past or present connection might be.

"…are you heading home tomorrow morning, Dante, or will we get to visit after I get home from work? I feel like I barely got to see you while you were here."

He shrugged his shoulders in apology. "I have to head out mid-day. I want to get back and settled before I go back to work Wednesday."

"Yeah, I know what you mean. Alright. I'll see you in the morning," she said, giving her cousin a hug. "Delyn, it was, um, nice to meet you," she said, hardly seeming to mean it, as she walked dejectedly down the hall, turning into the bedroom just beside the front door.

"I'm sorry about that," Dante whispered as she closed her door. "She's particular about her sleep. I didn't realize it was past midnight. I think she was waiting up for me."

"Should I go?" I had no idea what the night could have in store. What I had wanted, or what I thought I had wanted, seemed so far out of reach at this point that the better option seemed to be to cut and run.

Dante appeared to panic. "No! Stay, I mean. The evening took a wild turn... or five...," he joked, "but I want to finish our conversation, don't you? We were just beginning to solve some of the world's problems before everything got turned upside-down."

I felt my cheeks flush. The sensation was bewildering. "I'd like that," I said.

"Sit down and make yourself comfortable. Can I get you something to drink? Some water, maybe?"

"Water would be great."

He searched a few cabinets before finding a couple of giant plastic fast food cups. He pulled a tray of ice from the freezer, cracked it, and put a few cubes in each cup. Looking in the fridge, he found a filtering water pitcher. He refilled and replaced the tray, filled each cup, refilled the pitcher from the tap, and brought the two cups to the thrift shop table.

"She's had a rough time. Her mom, my dad's sister, has been worried about her. Zara's sort of the only one who's flown the nest. I said I'd look in on her when I was in town. She hasn't accepted anyone's calls lately. I didn't have any idea of what I'd find. Believe it or not, this is much better than I thought it'd be. Zara doesn't know, but I'm meeting her mom for lunch on my way back home."

"To give your report?" I guessed.

"Something like that. Visit with her, of course, but yeah. Zara will probably be the subject of most of our conversation."

"Well, I'm sorry—that she's had a rough time, I mean."

"We all have our burdens. Speaking of which… where were we?" Dante asked.

"Remember our total honesty game from college?" I asked in reply.

"Ha!" he laughed. "Pity it was just a game. Where would the world be if everyone was as direct with one another as we were back then?"

"I think we should play it now," I said. "It'd make catching up with you so much easier."

"Haven't you been straight with me before now, Ziegel?" he asked.

"I have been, but it's all been just scratching the surface. Safe subjects."

"God, love, sex, and science are what constitute safe subjects in your world. Man, I've missed you."

"No, really," I redirected. "I've always wanted to know what went down between us—why we drifted apart. If we could talk some of that out, it'd go a long way toward sorting out my present circumstances."

"Not willing to just embrace the mystery, huh?"

"I've moved on to objective investigation," I said.

"You know, I think you're right. Let's sort out the facts you know and develop a hypothesis," he replied.

"I was asking about you," I corrected him.

"I know. We'll get to that. Do you trust me?"

"Sure," I said. I turned on the couch to face him straight on, kicking off my pumps, tucking my left foot underneath me and letting my right leg stretch long.

"So," Dante began, "let me ask you this: Do you think it's possible you've become oversexualized?"

I was stunned. "I really doubt it. I haven't had sex in weeks."

"That's not what I mean. It's not the same thing. I'm asking if you have become fixated upon or hypersensitive to sexual topics and issues."

"I haven't ever really been into discussing the details of sex. I'm not a prude, though. You know that."

"Do you think about sex a lot?" he asked.

"Not really," I started, but then I corrected myself. "More lately, maybe."

"When was the last time you had an orgasm?"

"Um... I said I haven't had sex in weeks."

"There's more than one road to the amusement park, Ziegel."

"You don't think I know that?" I said, shocked. "I'm well aware of... that. I've just never been into... it."

"Masturbation. You should be able to say the word, at least."

"I can say it."

"A corporal, intellectual, emotional release would do you wonders," Dante mumbled.

I laughed. "Is that a fancy way of saying 'orgasm?'"

"Not exactly," he said. "Let me ask you something. You haven't had sex in weeks. What, pray tell, happened between yourself and Mr. Tierney? His rant was about something that happened recently, I take it."

"That doesn't count."

"Would your husband agree?"

It took a bit for me to phrase my response. "It depends on what we're talking about. It was a carnal act, yes, but there wasn't any penetration."

"No penile penetration. So do lesbians not have sex, then?"

"Of course they do. The rules are different there."

"Gay men, then, as well? No vagina—different rules?"

I was really wondering where this was going. "I didn't mean different rules like that."

Dante let the silence hold until I finally clarified. "Alright," I admitted, "so all of that is basically in the same category. All are acts of lovemaking."

"More or less. Do you still love me?"

My brow knitted, but I was up for this challenge. "What are you getting at?"

"Go with me on this. Do you love me, Ziegel?"

"I guess I do. I'm not sure if I would have answered the same way if someone had asked me that before tonight. I am not in love with you anymore," I assured him, "but I care about you, sure. That's love."

"And I you. Describe the quality of love you had for me back when we were together."

"Well…," I took a long moment to consider my answer. "I admired your intelligence. I liked your Renaissance world view. I enjoyed our matches of wit. I liked arguing with you. You made me laugh."

"You didn't mention that I turned you on."

"I was trying to show restraint."

"Fuck restraint," he countered. "Life is short. Do you understand what an immeasurable gift it is to be sitting here, not only with your husband's consent but with his encouragement, with the express purpose of getting your head straight? It's time to lay it all out there, Ziegel. Did I turn you on?"

"Well, yes," I admitted.

"What about me turned you on?"

"Well, where do I start?" I teased.

"Stop flirting. Tell me. You need to be able to articulate these things."

"This is very difficult."

"Name one thing."

"Your... I don't know. Your eyes."

"Too easy. Don't plagiarize a teen romance novel. Make this real."

"Fine! Your... honesty. You faced life's darkness head-on and revealed its inferiority to the light. You were—are—startlingly brilliant. You don't suffer fools or phoniness of any kind."

"Alright, sort of obscure, kind of Holden Caulfield-esque. But nice. Did you like my cock?"

"Excuse me?"

"My penis. Did my genitalia ever give you pleasure? Don't make a joke of this. Just answer the question."

"You know I like it. Liked it, I mean. Your body still turns me on."

"Not my body. My penis."

"Yes!" This line of questioning was getting on my nerves. "I liked your penis. I liked how it felt in my hands. I liked how it felt in my mouth. I liked how it felt inside me. My vagina. Is that what you wanted to hear?"

"We're making progress. Did I ever bring you to orgasm?"

"Are you kidding me now? Why are you asking about that?"

"I wouldn't ask if I wasn't sure. When is the last time you had sex?"

"Two months ago," I said.

"I thought you said your last orgasm was six weeks ago."

"I didn't have sex six weeks ago."

"Did you masturbate?" he asked.

"No!"

"It's a fair question. If you weren't with someone else, it's a fair deduction."

"I was with someone else," I said.

"Sam."

"Yes, Sam."

"So again, you've parsed 'sex' to include only vaginal penetration," he said.

"Alright. It was oral sex."

"Given and received?"

"Given the night before, and received the morning after," I answered.

"And you climaxed?"

"Yes."

"Did you cry out?" he asked.

"I muffled myself."

"Were you ashamed?"

"Not in the moment, although I should have been," I explained. "I was on a hotel balcony in the early morning hours. I didn't want to wake the neighbors or get arrested."

"Not ashamed in the moment? So you're ashamed now?"

"It's not shame I feel, exactly, but I'm not proud of my adultery."

"Alright, Ziegel," he stated matter-of-factly, "that is a fair, academic response. I believe that."

"Well, bully for you," I said, sarcastically.

"I'm trying to help, you know. Do you still trust me?"

"I just want to know where this is headed."

"Here's my hypothesis," he said. "I think you're more concerned with your partner's orgasm, as some measure of your own sexual prowess, than you are with your own satisfaction. I think you are so accustomed to either embellishing or simulating ecstasy that you don't even realize you're doing it anymore. I think you do it just to stroke your partner's ego and to subconsciously reassure yourself of your own integration. I think you are out of touch with your own needs, of the flesh and otherwise, that whatever few orgasms you actually do have arrive by coincidence, and because they're not climaxes that also engage your mind and your soul, they're dissatisfying, like you don't honestly know what the fuss is about."

"How did you arrive at…? I mean, what does any of this have to do with…? This is ridiculous. You're an ass. I'm leaving," I said as I started to rise.

Dante grasped my arm. "Prove I'm wrong."

I shook his hand from me. "You're infuriating."

"And you're a classic Type A. Don't make it a competition, but I know you want to prove me wrong somehow."

"I can't believe we're actually discussing this. You won't talk me into doing anything like that with you tonight."

"That's right. I won't," he said. "Prove it or don't, but don't rationalize that I've made you do anything you don't want to do. This doesn't really involve me, if you know what I mean."

"You want me to masturbate for you? Is that what you're saying?"

"Maybe you should masturbate for you."

I made a sound of shocked surprise and began to protest. "So what, you'll just sit there and watch, like some perverted reality TV show judge?" I asked.

"I'm your *simpatico*, Mandelyn. Don't forget that. I think this could really be a key to your catharsis."

"I haven't forgotten. This is insane, though. You can't deny that."

"What's crazier: faking orgasm while denying yourself its fully intended expression—watching black and white TV for the rest of your life instead of full-spectrum color, so to speak—or taking the steps to make a change?" he asked.

"I don't fake orgasm."

"This is a circular argument. Surely I don't need to point that out."

"Alright! What happens here, then?" I asked.

"Control the situation. Decide what to do."

"I can't believe this is about to happen."

"That language separates you from the situation," he explained. "Own this, Ziegel. No schedule, no seduction, no salaciousness."

"Simple as that. Got it."

I sat down with a huff, but resettled myself. I lay back and reached up under my hair to distribute it across the pillow. I locked eyes with Dante in an attempt at daring defiance. I started to let my knees fall apart, letting my left leg stretch long as Dante sat forward to let it snake behind him. I began to shift the hem of my skirt up my leg, grazing over the lace at the top of my stocking.

Dante interrupted me, putting his hand over mine. "Stop. You were actually going to lie here and let me watch you get off, weren't you?"

"What were we talking about?"

"I accused you of faking it and, in response, you were going to, I don't know, lie here and let me watch you rub one out?"

"I thought… I mean…" I rose with a start, shaking off the fog that had begun to drift over me.

"I started by saying you could use a corporal, intellectual, emotional release. I didn't mean it in just a libidinous way. Blame my poor choice of words, if you'd like. I was trying to be glib. Maybe I was too deadpan. If you misconstrued my words, I apologize, but when you reacted the way you did, I decided to challenge you.

"What I was saying was true all along, though," he continued. "I think you've splintered the essence of your sexuality—hell, your whole psyche—into safe, encapsulated, easy-to-understand components as some means of compensation. To compensate for what, I don't know, but I want to."

I raised my hand to my mouth to stop myself from saying something vulgar. I didn't even know what it was that I would have said, but my temper was rising.

Dante seemed to backtrack. "Maybe it was irresponsible and manipulative, but to see if my suspicion was correct, I posited that you demonstrate your ecstasy, which is different from orgasm and far more serious. The implications for the rest of your life are far more severe than if you're just, I don't know… frigid."

"I am *not*…"

"No, I don't think you are, either. But here's the thing. I was really very careful not to tell you how to prove me wrong. You made the leap to demonstrating your physical ability to do so. That's pure Freudian id: carnality, sensuality. Back in the day, your psyche was far more balanced than that—a bit ego-driven, but balanced and in check, for the most part."

"Ego?" I asked.

"Brain. Reality. Pride. The Delyn I knew in school would have straight-up told me to fuck off if I'd pushed her around like this."

"The Dante I knew in school would have persisted. That Dante was a stubborn piece of shit."

"And you? I think you would have retaliated by describing an orgasm to me in such detail that there was no room to assume you didn't know from whence you spoke." Dante paused, considering. "Well, actually, I don't know..."

"What? Please tell me what you think I ought to have done. I haven't experienced quite enough 'mansplaining' yet tonight."

"'Mansplaining.' Good one."

"No, seriously," I demanded, "tell me what you mean—you 'don't know.'"

"I said that the Delyn I used to know had a balanced psyche. I don't think it is now. If you're still listening to me as a friend, if you still trust me, hear this: You probably wouldn't have told me just to fuck off in college. Your super-ego would have stepped in and, with head and heart collaborating, you would have crafted a comeback so sincere, and profound, and barbed I would have been put in place, new asshole ripped, and guilt-ridden as hell on top of it."

I was dumbstruck. He was right, and I wanted to hate him for it, but I couldn't. Would I have heard him? Would I have listened to all of what he'd just said, if he'd just come right out and told me all of this? This was classic Dante, telling by showing, 'catching the conscience of the King,' and all that. Finally, I just admitted it. "You're right. What's become of me?"

"That's something you're going to have to figure out for yourself, woman."

He winked; I smiled.

"Tell me this, though," Dante continued. "How long have you felt this way?"

"What? How long have I felt divided against myself, able only to process emotions through a single aspect of my psyche?"

"Do you think that's what's happening?"

"I don't know. You have me thinking here. I cry, like, all the time now, for the dumbest reasons. I scream and hit with almost no provocation, apparently. Before the last month, I had only hit one other person violently, and that was for good reason. And you were right to ask; I think about sex, like, constantly. I wonder who's doing it, how they're doing it, and what it's like for them. Also, I wonder—no, I feel sure that everyone around me is looking at me, wondering the same things. Logically, I know it's almost completely untrue, but I find myself supposing that if I'm thinking about it, everyone else must be, too."

"How long has this been going on?"

"I don't know, really. I've never been quite right after Theodore died, but I managed to get through. It's been harder, though, in the last—I don't know—two or three months."

"Who is Theodore?"

"He was my son. There were complications, and he died in utero."

"Oh, Mandelyn, I'm so sorry for your loss. I had no idea."

"How could you have possibly?" I asked.

"When was Theodore due?"

"July twenty-second. Feast day of Saint Mary Magdalene."

"Is that significant?"

"Not especially. Just that I was born on All Saints Day. I always liked the little connection."

"When was he born?"

"Leap Day."

"And the first Leap Day since it happened is coming up. It's the first birthday of Theodore's that the calendar won't let you skip. Do you think you worked through that grief in the right way—you know, afterward?"

"I really want to change the subject. Is that okay with you?"

"I guess. Okay." Dante went to the kitchen for more water. As he poured our glasses, he continued. "Have you been wondering about my sex life all night, then?"

"Pretty much all night," I laughed. "Not now. Well, not until just now."

"Then ask."

"I don't even know if you have a girlfriend."

"I don't," he answered.

"Have you had girlfriends?"

"Ever? Of course," he laughed. "Recently? Not really. Not since the summer. 'Girlfriend' is a much more malleable term now than it was when you were last on the scene, friend."

"I'll bet it is," I said lasciviously.

"No, it's not like that. It's like what we're talking about. It's like every woman I meet has a single encapsulated objective; everyone is so matter-of-fact. There is the woman who will not 'waste' even a first date unless the guy is independently vetted and declares a desire, if not an outright intention, to marry before the soups and salads are cleared. Then, there is the woman who picks out a guy at a bar and—I don't know; it's weird—kind of declares her need to fuck, like it's a clinical, life-sustaining prescription to fill. No preamble, no pretension, just 'Do you want to hook up?' The oddest of all, though, is the disillusioned romantic who, when you're out, you can tell is sizing you up against some unattainable ideal, keeping a mental checklist of all the aspects that she'll complain to her friends about later. Mystery, allure, trust—gone.

"And here is another thing," Dante continued. "Heartbreak is practically unheard-of anymore, because no one allows themselves to be open or vulnerable enough to let it happen. No one has any faith that love can be more than a means to certain ends. The thing of it is, though, that a stance like that basically yields this state of… perpetual heartsickness. Geez, I swear that I hadn't really thought it all out like that before. Now that I've said it out loud, it sounds bleaker than it really is."

"Where do you fall on that continuum, then? Or, is everything you described just true of women?"

"You know, I hadn't ever thought of it that way, but you're right. Most of this applies as much to men as it does to women, except the guys who are only looking to fuck still mask their intentions because they're ashamed of them, and should be. They're the poisonous ones who've jaded the romantics."

"It sounds pretty horrible out there," I said.

"No more horrible than your state of affairs, pardon the pun. Can I tell you what else I think?"

"What's ever stopped you before?" I asked in reply.

"I bet you're all three types of women I described, each in turn. In one moment, you just seek the sexual. The next, the sentimental. The next, the unattainable artifice of the ideal. I think that's good news."

"How could that possibly be good news?"

"It means all three parts are still there," he explained. "You just have to find a way to put them back together again."

"I forgot how well you see me, Dante. It's unsettling."

"When were you ever one to settle, anyway? We can stop playing the game if you want."

"You're not playing at anything now, though, are you?" I asked.

"I'm not, and I don't think you are, either," he said.

"I'm not."

We paused and just looked into one another's eyes for a moment before he continued. "So what else? What else are you thinking about tonight?"

"I'm wondering whether you really think I used to fake it with you."

"Orgasm?" Dante asked.

"Yes."

"The truth is, I don't know," he said. "I didn't used to think so, but as time went on and I got wise to the ways of the world, I started to second-guess."

"Wise to the ways of the world?"

"When I had more experience with women, I mean. I didn't know the first thing about what I was doing back in school. Surely you knew that. All this time, I always assumed you found my virginity charming and took some pleasure in deflowering me."

"Your what?"

"Virginity. You were my first, Mandelyn. I know I never told you that, but, I don't know. I hoped that somehow you'd intuited that somewhere along the way."

"How could I intuit something like that? It's not like I broke a seal, like on a gallon of milk or a bottle of aspirin."

"You're the one who made me a man."

"Ugh. That expression grosses me out. I'm guessing, since you haven't mentioned it, that you don't know about me, either, then, do you?"

"Know what?" he asked.

"That you were basically my first, too."

"Basically? What the hell does 'basically' mean? Please don't tell me you're parsing definitions again. Full disclosure, Ziegel. I'd had plenty of other experience—just not the coital act itself."

"I'm not parsing anything."

"What is your number?"

"Today? Now?"

"Now."

"What are we counting, exactly?"

"Whatever counts to you."

"Three. I count three," I said.

"Henry, me, and…"

"Sam."

"You're counting oral?"

"Not in this tally. Sam was my first, technically."

"Wow. That brings a whole new element to the episode at the bar. When did that take place?"

"High school. Senior year Homecoming. Disastrous."

"Say no more… I mean, unless you really want to. I feel like knowing any more about him is just going to bum me out. It would make me happy, though, to find out he had an Atari 2600 joystick, if you know what I mean."

"I'm not going to go down that path with you tonight," I laughed. "Be assured that you're quite well-endowed. No need for comparisons. Anyway, we've gone off-topic. You don't think you've ever brought me to orgasm, do you?"

"This would be a whole lot easier if you would just come out with it. No pun intended."

"Bullshit," I managed to say, still laughing. "Alright. The answer is no. I'm sorry. It wasn't any fault of yours. I didn't really know, exactly, at the time. I thought I wasn't capable of getting there, during intercourse, at least. Then, I was almost thirty, and it clicked."

"Well, now I am bummed out."

"It isn't that I didn't have a good time. We were hot together," I assured him.

"Just no fireworks. Gotcha," he groused.

"Hot, I tell you! Go back and watch the tape," I joked.

"Don't think I haven't. That's part of what clued me in."

I wasn't sure how I felt about that tape still existing, or that he would or could still watch it. Part of me wanted to see it, too. "Loud, huh?" I asked.

"The lady doth protest too much."

"Now I feel bad that I told you," I lamented.

"For everything else we've ever been able to talk about, you couldn't have clued me in back then, back when I could have done something about it?" Dante asked.

"I didn't want to bring you down or make you feel inadequate, because you're not. I mean, you weren't. I'm sure you're not now." I wished I wasn't rambling. "It had nothing to do with you.

"Besides… you and I, we connected on a lot of levels: intellectually, physically… But 'tough talk'—emotional topics, you know, were never really at the forefront. Didn't you ever notice that? We were always able to talk about our opinions and get worked up over them. We could talk about our passions and triumphs, for sure. But the vulnerable stuff—sadness, fear, even love—we always skirted those subjects, I feel."

"We traveled to one of the poorest, most desolate places on Earth together. We saw devastation and famine brought about by generations of economic injustice. That's sadness."

"That's not the same. That's observation and mutual visceral experience. It's not, you know, examination of what comes from inside you. It never occurred to me that we didn't relate to each other this way until I was telling Henry about that trip, not that long ago. I remember being torn apart by what we saw there, but the fact that you didn't appear to have similarly deep reactions made it… I don't know… too hard for me to approach sorting it out with you. It was a lot easier to escape it on those nights after the work was done."

"Those were some pretty hot nights."

"How did you feel about what we saw in Jaipur?"

"Come on. Of course I was shocked; I was despondent. But I also felt grateful—for what I had and for the chance to be able to do something to help. I felt guilty. What an embarrassment of riches we have in this country! It was out of that guilt and embarrassment that I shoved how I felt to the side. How would my guilt or embarrassment have served those people? What good would it have done to relish or wallow in emotion?"

"I can see your point, but I'm not talking about wallowing or relishing. Just acknowledgement and processing. Not just back then. Now. Don't you think that talking out emotions leads to a better-balanced psyche? How does repressing or dismissing your super-ego serve your needs, Dante?"

Dante glanced around the room. He seemed nervous, all of a sudden. "*Simpatica*, Delyn. You've always been able to get me."

"What? What is it?"

"It's just that… You know that saying, 'Be kind, for everyone you meet is fighting a hard battle?'"

"Yeah. Plato, I think."

"No. Lots of people think that, but it was actually said by this guy John Watson. He was a preacher and an author in the late nineteenth century, under the pseudonym of Ian Maclaren. I heard the quote and learned a little about him when I was in Mount Pleasant after college. Ian Maclaren died in Mount Pleasant while he on tour, preaching and promoting his literature."

"Mount Pleasant, Iowa? What were you doing there?"

"It's pretty twisted that they built an insane asylum in a town named Mount Pleasant, don't you think? An oxymoron on both counts. I never saw a mountain there, and it was far from pleasant for me. I was a residential patient at the Mount Pleasant Mental Health Institute—that's what they call it now—for six weeks following graduation, and I was a chronic outpatient for much of the next two years."

"What…?" I began.

"Just let me continue. I don't know if I'll ever be in a state of mind like this again—a state where I can just let it all come out. If you ever wondered why I fell off the map after school, and, let's be honest, most of senior year, that's why. It's not a proud episode in my history, so I let a lot of good people drift out of my life for fear of having it be revealed to them."

"There's no shame in…"

"You don't get to say that. You don't know. Just because I've made peace with it doesn't mean I'm even close to the picture of mental health today. If you wonder where I picked up all my psychobabble, that's where. I have come to accept the stasis I have achieved by letting my head keep hegemony over my heart. I always liked logic, as you know, but my coping mechanism of choice is the quantitative domain. Black and white. Right and wrong. Action and consequence."

"How did all of this happen? How did it begin?"

"No one can answer that. My childhood was as normal as they come. I had a reasonably stable family life filled with Rockwellian life events. You've met them; you know. No discernible history of mental instability, even. Zara and I are the only ones who've struggled; at least, we're the only ones who went public. Something just snapped, or, more like, slipped. I was in the process of slipping well before we met, I know now. I ran through all the typical subconscious efforts. For a while, I was the entertainer. Seriously regressive. I couldn't hold myself in a conversation without quoting Beavis, Butt-head, Ren, or Stimpy. Then, I moved on to aggression. I played rugby as if I were in contention for the World Cup. Didn't that ever seem odd to you?"

"I never thought your athletic aggression was a bad thing."

"Sure you didn't, because you were involved with a sanctioned competitive sport. Not that actual rugby players aren't athletes. Me, I was just looking for a legal way to beat the shit out of people.

"Anyway, I eventually started drinking way too much. It's a wonder I didn't end up on Zara's path, which is why I look in on her when I can. She thinks I check in on her because I don't want to see her end up in a hospital, which is partly true, but it's also because I identify with her in other ways beyond what I've let her believe.

"The next step on my path of dysfunctional compensation was seducing anyone I could. Not even sexually, necessarily; more in terms of grandiosity. I needed followers, people who admired me without knowing why. People who would behave as I wished without questioning my motives. The thing is that I didn't have any motive, except to see what I could get away with. That night we met—that's just another example of how I was pushing the edge. Remember the cigars? That was a real thing, but the stupid smoking jacket? That was vanity and conceit—me pushing the edge to see who reacted."

"I reacted; that's for sure," I tried to joke.

"I saw you and Mary in Ben's room and changed clothes with the specific goal of getting a rise out of either one, both, or all of you. What happened after that, though… That wasn't part of the plan. You proved to be the person who woke me up, made me realize that my malignant narcissism—that's what shrinks call it—wasn't going to cut it anymore."

"Dante, I have to say something. None of this sounds real. The person you're describing just isn't the person I know."

"I was on a path to becoming outright sociopathic until you came along. Italian-American Psycho. The element I lacked was sadism. You sparked just enough empathy in me to prevent me from wanting to hurt you emotionally. Because of that empathy, my growing superiority complex settled down. You kept me from becoming a full-blown Lothario. Before you, I was above having sex with anyone who'd fall for my schemes. They were prey too easily won."

"I don't know what I'm supposed to say to this, Dante. 'You're welcome?'"

"You were my drug, Delyn. You saved me from myself, and you didn't even know it. This is the heart of what I'm telling you. I couldn't be a good man to you back then. God, I wanted to be. I knew that I was standing in my own way, putting barriers up, trying to protect you from the broken person I thought I might be. I pushed you away for your own good, or that's what I reasoned at the time. It was stupid, but I couldn't stop myself."

Slow, silent tears were falling from my eyes. "I don't know what to do with what you're saying, Dante."

He continued, undeterred. "If you ever wondered why I didn't reach out to you after all these years, it's because… I've used you. Not just back then. I have this sentimental fantasy of us, borne from the time we had together, but it's evolved into something with a life of its own. That fantasy occupies too much of my heart to let any new reality take its place. Really, it's just about all that is there."

I sighed. "So what have we learned tonight? I have a psyche divided against itself, only able to handle life decisions through a single aspect at a time, and you have constructed an imaginary world that prevents you from having any genuine interactions. Where do we go from here?"

"Lie down with me."

"I don't know."

"Hold me. Let me hold you. Nothing else will happen. I'm tired. Aren't you? It's not just because it's three in the morning. We are two damaged people. If there's any blessing at all, at least we are finally able to see the world and ourselves without artifice. The thing is this, Mandelyn. We really only have tonight. When the sun rises in a few hours, you have a job to do, and so do I. Neither of us can be of any further help to the other."

By this point, Dante was crying, too. "You need to integrate your head, heart, and body in order to figure out what it is you really want in this life, where it is, and how to get it," he said. "Whatever that is, I don't have it. I'd love to pretend that I do, or that I could, but I don't, and I never will."

I shook my head, not because I didn't believe what he was saying, but because I didn't want it to be true.

Dante continued. "Me, I need to deconstruct the internal masquerade I've built and learn to be vulnerable. What you said, about how the descriptions of the types of women I meet—that they apply just as easily to men, to myself? You're right. I am heartsick and disillusioned. I need to cure that. Trying to be more vulnerable is a step in the right direction. All I know is that this is our last chance for a… how did I put it?"

"Corporal, intellectual, emotional release," I said.

"Right. Not orgasm, though." He took my hands in his. "Shared, centered calm. Escape, not from, but into ourselves, with each of us here to guide the other home. Intimacy with no endgame. It might be the last thing we can do for one another. Lie down with me."

The couch was not going to do. It was tolerable as a place to sit, but entirely unsuited for sleeping two. There was a large basket full of old comforters and fleece blankets to the side of the couch. Dante raided it, spreading several atop one another on the floor to assemble a not-altogether-uncomfortable bed. I considered apparel options as Dante pulled his shirt over his head.

"Do you want me to find you a shirt to wear? You can't sleep in your suit," he said as he fumbled through his phone, presumably to set some sort of wake-up alarm.

"It's okay," I said as I unzipped my skirt. "I'll be comfortable in this." The skirt fell to the floor, and I stepped out of it where it landed. Dante, now in boxers, had already nestled into the little burrow on the

RELEASE

floor and chivalrously half-diverted his eyes as I unhooked my bra and, wrestling out of it from under my chemise, dropped it aside. Finally, I slid the nylons from each thigh, put them with the rest of the day's attire, and settled in beside him.

    Tangled together, we drifted along in a twilight sleep for a long time. While our hands ranged, caressed, and explored, they did not grope or fondle. My groin ached, but the beat of my heart and his remained chaste. In time, we finally, if briefly, drifted to sleep. The intimacy I experienced that night was greater than any other I had ever felt. It was more intimacy than thought I had the capacity to know.

19

Saturday: Vacation Day #1

Hey Col,

I am on the plane to Flagstaff... well, Phoenix first, then a puddle-hopper to Flagstaff. Are they still called puddle-hoppers when you're flying over the desert?

You are eternally wise. Thank you for seeing what I couldn't see for myself and suggesting I get out of town. I haven't ever travelled alone except for work. That seems impossible, but it's true. Thirty minutes into the flight, and I'm apprehensive about being totally on my own, but it feels right.

More than anything, I hope the next few days bring some closure to all of this soul-searching, some meaning to this emotional suffering. I feel self-righteous and stupid to speak in such hyperbole with so many in the world struggling to achieve a basic means of survival and to secure human dignities. My meager trials are nothing when compared to the enormity of others'.

In a paltry defense of my own situation, I find the magnitude of this futility to be worthy of some small attention, if for no other reason than to serve as a cautionary tale. How absurd is the degree of wastefulness resulting from love unrequited, love misdirected, love misunderstood, or love that is false, fleeting, and failed? Where else could our energies be directed without the spiritual degradation that happens when we are not able or choose not—from a place of self-doubting, self-denying fear—to articulate our needs? When we do not or cannot discern true sources for their fulfillment? What else could we accomplish within our privileged lives if we could only manage to elucidate these needs to those from whom we require assistance, without reliance upon mystical intervention to have a hand in it all?

I re-read that paragraph, thinking that the metaphysical tractor beam of Sedona appeared to be pulling me in. It felt nice, as if I was on the verge of rising to that higher plane of consciousness where the answers might make themselves known.

I continued to write.

> I think I can finally tell you what happened on the night of Architectural Celebration. As it turned out, I didn't have the story straight myself until the night of the Muon g-2 event. I'm sorry that I couldn't bring myself to tell you any more than the most scant details before now.
>
> I told you about running into Sam, and how Sam had actually served our table when he saw that I needed a friend's support. That, at least, gives some context to how our innocuous flirtation escalated, but I didn't really understand the gravity or character of my adultery until I talked to Sam at Meat.
>
> I had thought it strange that, in all the flashes back to that night, never once did I recall Sam actually penetrating me. I don't make that distinction to make me feel better about what happened. There's no question that my behavior broke vows. I'm only saying that actual coitus with Sam is something that I would not have voluntarily omitted, if you know what I mean... remorse aside, of course. Back when I lost my virginity to Sam, I had only experienced Joshua and him first-hand, so to speak. Having seen what I had seen, I supposed that the Greek sculptors were either modest, their models were cold, or that they were on the unfortunate end of the genetic pool. I'd learn later that I'd just encountered two fine male specimens out of the gate.
>
> Anyhow...
>
> To understand what happened with Sam that night, I need to explain what happened during dinner. My table turned out to be a wretched hive of scum and villainy. There was the one person who wouldn't stop asking about my "DINK lifestyle" with

questions like, "But who is going to take care of you in your old age?" That led to "reassuring" statements about how, "scientific advancements make late-in-life gestation much safer than it has been in years past," and, "how lucky you are that the clock doesn't tick as loudly as it once did."

At least the soup course was good—a potato-leek chowder generous with onions and garlic. Strategically eaten, it occupied my mouth during any but those rare occasions when my participation in dinner conversation was absolutely required.

Somehow, the topic turned to pets—dogs, generally, and then Frank and Lloyd, specifically. One person thought they had been named after the two *Dumb and Dumber* guys, for crying out loud. The same jerk who was procreation-fixated started in again, asking if the dogs were substitutes for the children I wished I had.

Then, it got worse. Another person asks me, "Why Pit Bulls? Why not some sweet, lovable dogs, instead of animals bred for violence?" I am not sure if my reaction would draw your praise or your reprimand, Colette. I have seen you hold it together under harder circumstances, and I have seen you go off under easier ones. You always seem to know what is called for. Professionally, I usually know this line, but it is a learned skill that I never seem to apply in my personal life. Since that night was a strange mix of professional and personal, my odds of getting it right were even at best.

I did well at first. I explained that Pits are among the last dogs to be rescued from shelters because of irrational fears built up by skewed, lazy, even falsified, reporting. I explained that the dogs people lump together in the Pit Bull category aren't all the same. Rather, there are a category with several breeds who have similar characteristics. I elaborated, saying that "Pit Bull" has become journalistic, legalistic shorthand for dogs caught in virtually any violent situation.

"Characteristics? Characteristics like the propensity for vicious attacks," someone else joked, with a smug tone that made me want to viciously attack.

I held it together, though. "Pits are abandoned more than any other breed, usually by people who intend to do harm with them but discard them when they find they're not violent enough for their evil purposes. Pit Bulls' loving hearts are just too big—they're too compassionate, too eager to please. Both of my dogs were found neglected and alone. They are the 'least of these' among all domesticated animals, and are among the smartest and most loyal."

Thank God Sam showed up just then, because I could see that a retort was coming, and my hackles were rising in response. He'd traded his black tuxedo jacket for a server's white one. "Are you the woman who ordered the vegan plate, ma'am?" he said from over my shoulder.

Before I had the chance to castigate him for calling me ma'am, I noticed the wink. "I did?" I responded with confusion.

Sam set a generous kale and quinoa salad before me. As he did so, he imperceptibly brushed my shoulder and whispered, "Hold up. You can bear this. I am here."

From that point on, the night became a game. The salad, with bits of fig, pineapple, and cranberries was not only vibrant and delectable, but also ample compared to the artistically plated entrees served to the rest. On each plate, others were served an absurdly anemic sea scallop atop a humble puddle of risotto, flanked by two small bundles of white asparagus tied with a ribbon of shaved parsnip.

Even the dessert for the rest of the table was white—fondant-iced petit fours—but not mine. "To maintain the ruse," Sam whispered as if in collusion. He held a tray of four truffles dusted, each, with cocoa powder, pistachios, coconut, and sea salt. I think the lead architect's jaw dropped. "I didn't think chocolate was vegan," was said almost incoherently.

Before I had the chance to bumble through an answer, Sam chimed in. "These have no dairy. It's a coconut cream base. They're also gluten-free, have no hydrogenated oils, and contain no artificial flavors, additives, or sweeteners." Sam was laying it on thick.

I thought back; even the wine for the evening was special. Sam brought out a yummy Zinfandel instead of the staid Sauvignon Blanc bottle on the table. "The chef and sommelier agree this is the more proper pairing for your meal," he said. While the rest poured their own for the evening, I never saw the bottom of my glass, courtesy of Sam.

The awards presentation itself was largely unremarkable. My table had been pretty liberal with their Sauvignon Blanc consumption, and the design principal gave a perfectly forgettable yet entirely conceited speech, supposedly on behalf of the team. I stood in back and nodded politely, modestly accepting the perfunctory praise of the Laboratory and me as its mute spokesperson.

There was little left to the event after the parade of awardees had concluded and, being a weeknight, people scurried for the door. The design principal left promptly upon returning to the table, not even waiting for the other presentations, stumbling a bit while navigating through the sea of tables toward the door. I hoped the drives home for my fellow attendees weren't going to be long ones.

The evening had still been lovely, all things considered, and I didn't want it to end. I really didn't know what to do next, though, being out of touch and out of practice when it came to late-night downtown entertainment. I continued to write.

> Something had obviously been passing between Sam and me all evening long. I couldn't tell for sure, but from a momentary glance, I thought that my procreation- and violence-obsessed table companions had even picked up on it, but I didn't pay them any mind.
>
> In any case, I should have left. I hadn't told Sam that I was staying downtown. So far as he knew, I had been here for the banquet and was already on my way home.
>
> There he was, though, pacing beside the coat check, his anxiousness uncharacteristic. He saw me, and his familiar ease returned momentarily. "Heading out?" he asked.
>
> He beamed when I told him I was staying at the hotel. "You are? Oh, we are going to have a date. A proper grown-up date. Don't say no."

I stopped writing for a moment, trying to remember. I did resist; I was sure of that.

I stammered. "What? But I… can't."

"You can, Manny. I'm only talking about a walk. Come on. Let's hang out. Perfectly harmless. What? I'm losing out to HBO and your mini-bar? Do this. You and me. For old times. No expectations. Just…"

"Okay."

"What?"

"Okay!" I laughed. "Where and when?"

"Fantastic! Okay," he said boyishly, "I have to finish up in back. I'll meet you at the bar in an hour. Be ready to be dazzled. Twenty years have done wonders for my courtly ways." He kissed my hand and almost sprinted down the hallway before I had the chance to renege.

I continued writing.

> I own everything that happened that night. Sam had been exceedingly kind through dinner, but I had full control over my response to his kindness. Wine was free-flowing, but for a cup to be refilled its contents must be drunk first. More than anything, I had let myself get caught up in the spirit of the coquettish game—the chase, the tease, and the dare. When I returned to my room, I upped the stakes. I let down my hair and applied my perfume, which I had hastily thrown in my bag.

There were fewer and fewer places I'd felt like wearing my favorite perfume anymore, I thought to myself. Before Henry's birthday the week before, I hadn't worn it in months—maybe a year. It had begun to run low, and I had no means to replace it. The woman who had sold it to my dad's old shop had made it in her home. When I returned to buy more, it was out of stock, and the store closed not long afterward.

Anyhow, I looked myself over. I didn't want to be too forward or obvious about having changed, but I was feeling brazen. Knowing Sam, he might call me on it and make fun of me. For whatever notion I had of what the evening was going to entail, I didn't want childish behavior to be a part of it.

That's when I got the naughty idea.

Inhibitions are a good thing, Colette. There are times and places to go on dates with boys while not wearing panties, but this was neither the time nor the place. I know that now. I knew that then, but something possessed me to ignore it anyway. I wriggled out of the Spanx, looking in the mirror to examine my altered profile. Structurally, I couldn't tell.

Could I discern any difference otherwise? I felt very different. The soon-to-be Lonely Brazilian felt as if she were alone on stage in a single hard-focused spotlight. I was a second away from wriggling back into the Spanx, or at least grabbing the panties I'd worn on the train, when I dared myself not to. Somehow, in that moment, it seemed like a good story was in the making.

I walked down to the bar and took a seat. Before I had the chance to put down my clutch, a bartender stood before me with a drink. "Sam described you but didn't do you justice. He said to let you order anything you wanted, but to have you start with this."

He told me that it was a sidecar, explaining that it is made with Cognac, Cointreau, and lemon, after I asked. I wondered what had made Sam pick something like that, but I was glad. The wine and champagne portion of the evening had passed.

He was dressed in his black tuxedo again, and he beamed as I watched him walk in. "I see you got my drink. Have you had one before?"

"No, and I wonder how you chose it."

"I'll tell you while you come with me. The hotel doesn't like the staff to hang around in uniform, even if they are this debonair."

I asked him if I'd need a coat, when he whipped his long black wool coat from his opposite arm. "I'll be fine. This doesn't set off that dress as it should, but it's starting to flurry. If we want to walk, sacrifices will need to be made."

I finished my drink, set the cocktail glass on the bar, and hooked my hand in his offered arm. Sam and I said goodbye to the bartender, and we walked toward the lobby and out onto Columbus Drive. "The sidecar will go a long way in keeping me warm, too," I said as we walked. "Why did you choose that cocktail?"

"The sidecar is elegant and feminine without the cloying, fruity nonsense. It's you, Mandelyn. I thought, if you hadn't had one before, then you should."

"I think I have a new drink," I told him.

"Well, good, and now you'll think of me whenever you drink it." I shuddered a bit in response. "I hope that's not a bad thing. I know what drink associations are like. Everyone within fifty miles of Weston knew that Nik Ziegel was a Malört man. As if I needed another reason to be scared shitless by your dad. I'm glad that drink preferences aren't genetic."

> We walked throughout Millennium Park. We walked along the Bicentennial garden promenade, across the BP bridge, down through the Lurie Garden, up the Nichols Bridgeway to the Modern Wing, and back to Pritzker Pavilion. By then, the Great Lawn, shadow-crosshatched by the soaring tubular trellis, was covered with a thin, unblemished sheet of satin snow.

It really was beautiful. "Your courting has benefitted more from Mayor Daley's administration than simple time passing alone," I told him. We had spoken very little as we walked, but I had no complaint.

"I should apologize for not putting more of my A-game moves to work, but I can't," he said. "I'm a little awestruck. I've taken vacationing friends and relatives through this place a dozen times, but it's always been during the day, in the summertime. It's sensational, of course, but it's crowded and touristy. It's an entirely different place to me tonight. It's like it's here for just you and me."

"It is breathtaking."

"Well, you are breathtaking, but this is pretty great, too."

We continued our walk around the Bean, already topped by a fractured whitecap of snow over the polished stainless arch. We circled it, walking to look out over the ice rink in the plaza. The rink had officially closed hours earlier, but a lone rogue skater was tempting fate by practicing single axels and toe loops, oblivious to the new voyeurs.

"Hot chocolate would be the only thing I'd add to this moment to make it perfect," I said.

"I can think of one more thing I'd add," Sam whispered. I looked up to see what it would be. "If I don't do this, I'll regret the missed opportunity for the rest of our lives."

> As I told you, he kissed me. His lurid study of my features was divided between my eyes and my mouth. When it happened, I could see what wonders twenty years had had upon his courtly ways. I've had kisses that made my stomach flip, kisses that made my inner thighs ache, and kisses that warmed my heart, but I'd never had a kiss utterly buckle my knees before. The world completely disappeared as he dipped me slightly, only in part to accommodate my dizzy sway. Past and present and future became immaterial. My flesh rose and prickled as a breeze came in from over the lake, and I ran my hands under his tuxedo jacket as protection against it. When we finally drew apart, he asked, "Now, how about some hot chocolate?" I nodded before burying myself into his embrace.

Rather than offer his arm again, he draped it over my shoulder, hand resting on my clavicle. I kept my arm beneath his jacket, slung low around his waist, and I nestled my head into the hollow of his shoulder. Suspense was slowly building—that confounding combination of expectation and mystery that is at the root of almost all the world's misdeeds, and I was succumbing to its allure.

We headed back to the hotel in silence. The night sounds of the city washed over us; the engines and dog barks and sirens were our conversation.

> When we returned to the hotel, he ordered the hot chocolates with suave urgency. Their scent alone was heady and exotic. Each of us with mugs in hand, he motioned to the elevators. "There's something you should see. Are you done with the cold, or will you indulge just one more excursion?"
>
> "I'm in your hands," I said, a phrase that Sam would have made a joke about on any other day. As it was, I was only stating the obvious.

He waved his badge over a sensor inside the elevator, then he pressed the button for the third floor. I held my steaming mug in both hands, trying to let the warmth settle the tremble of my fingers. I wasn't the least bit cold. Sam took a cautious sip of his and released a guttural response as it warmed his throat.

The elevator opened to the podium roof garden. "Only employees are allowed out here after ten o'clock," he noted. "We're alone."

Even if it had been open to the public, I reasoned that few, if any, people would have had interest in roaming the grounds at what was now after one in the morning. It was easy to see what the gardens would resemble snowless and in the daylight, but the landscape that night appeared barren. Beyond a berm, however, Sam led me to a fire pit encircled by sumptuously upholstered loveseats. I sat facing Sam, with my back to the tower, and, leaving my shoes on the ground, drew my feet up beneath me, my knees stacked underneath my skirt.

Finally taking a sip of the cooled chocolate, I emitted my own animal groan of approval. "Is that Frangelico?"

"And bourbon," Sam said between sips of his own. "So, did I do it?"

"Do what?" I giggled.

"I wanted to find a place just secluded enough that, if anyone were to see us, it wouldn't offend their sensibilities to watch for a moment with a bit of covetous envy."

"It depends on what you're planning," I said. My tremble returned.

"Not as much as I have in mind for later. Do you want me to let you know my entire agenda?"

"Now that you've put it that way, I do."

"First, I want to warm you. Actually make the heat rise in you. There's a reason you're shivering, and it doesn't have anything to do with the temperature outside."

I took a longer sip of the chocolate, feeling the burn of the alcohol augment its ambient temperature as it traveled into me.

"I want the friction of my hands on your shoulder blades to make your trembling subside." He finished his cup and set it beside the fire. "And I want to possess you, ferociously…" He paused to see how I reacted. "No resistance, I take it?"

We sat for a long time, talking, laughing, and flirting. After a while, he took my half-consumed drink and set it beside his on the table. He swept me onto his lap, and I cried out in surprise. His opposite arm cradled my knees as his left wrapped around my waist and beneath the coat, open to allow his hand to grip my shoulder as I held him about his neck. After several moments in our embrace, he removed his hand from under my legs, stroking the top of my thigh over the skirt before daring to explore further. I'd forgotten, until that moment, about the nylons and what would have otherwise lain between me and his ranging hand. He reached the lace band on my left leg, travelled upward over my hip, and then loosened his embrace to look me in the eye.

"What is this?" he asked. "Why didn't you tell me?"
"I didn't suppose it was pertinent."
"Information like this is always pertinent."
"I thought it'd be my secret."
"You'll have a few more secrets after tonight, I'm afraid."
"I'm not afraid," I said as I put my lips to his.

The taste of Frangelico, dark chocolate, and bourbon mingled with the scent of my frankincense and myrrh, yielding an exhilarating mélange. Absolutely possessed, I swiveled to sit astride him. He withdrew his hand from my skirt and placed both of his hands at the small of my back.

"What else do you want to do with me tonight?" I asked.

"I want to bathe you," he responded, and the slightly incredulous look that I felt on my face didn't daunt him. "I want to wash your hair. I want to feel your slick skin under my fingers."

At this point, I started to wonder what exactly crossed the line between sharing scandalous details with a friend and outright pornography. I closed my laptop for a moment as I allowed myself to continue the story in my head. After the debacle at Meat, nothing like what happened that night at Aqua was ever going to happen with him again. What was the harm in reminiscing?

I remembered my half-hummed, half-moaned assent to Sam as he relocated his hands, gripping my naked buttocks and beginning to guide a slow, sliding grind against his thick, responsive shaft.

"I want to press my chest against your back," he continued. "I want to slide my hands down your obliques and over your hip bones, onto your taut stomach, and then pull you toward me. I want you to feel my cock rise against the ridge of your ass while I whisper into your ear about how great you feel. I want to make you moan just out of anticipation before I go any further.

"My left hand would glide upward to trace the curve of your breast and roll your nipple under my palm. My right would tease at your cleft—only tease—as I'd bend to gain better advantage, my left knee against the hollow of yours, my right a firm foundation as you lean further against me."

My heart was pounding while I only recollected the scene as the flight continued somewhere over the Heartland. "You clearly have this well thought through," I said breathily before leaning into his ear. "Let's go get to it."

After a swift elevator ride, during which Sam lifted me and pressed me against the wall as I wrapped my legs around him, we took a handsy trip down the hallway to my corner room. I was ravenous by this point, entirely detached from reality. I fumbled with his tie and the tuxedo shirt buttons for a moment before Sam broke away.

"Let me do it," he laughed, affecting an amusing, complicated strip tease, leaving his boxers as his only remaining clothing as I sat on the corner of the bed and watched.

"Now you," he said, crooking his finger to call me to himself. I rose, stumbling toward him slowly and with an added hip sway that I hoped had the intended effect. Sam took me by the shoulders and, to my surprise, turned me around. He grasped the zipper of my dress and sedulously slid it from nape to tailbone. The sheath fell from my shoulders into a pile of silk on the floor. With continued assiduousness, he released the clasp of my black lace bra. "Turn to me," he said, and I did. With a single finger, he brushed each strap from my shoulders and guided each from my arms.

For a moment, he simply stared, eyes darting from my décolletage to my navel, from the hollow of my neck to my feet, still in those beautiful shoes. From the lacy nylon band on my leg, to my cleft, to my eyes. Finally, when he spoke, his voice cracked a bit. "Come with me," he beckoned, offering me a hand and leading me to the shower.

We began just as he'd described. He lowered the nylons, helped me step out of the shoes, and, just as the water became warm, shed his boxers. He stepped into the shower and offered a hand for me to join him. The lighting was dim, and everything felt ethereal. The sensuousness was impossibly unreal. It was when I grasped for him that the mood changed. I stroked him, the water and the lather escalating my fervor more than the moment yet warranted. I soon lost all control, eagerly massaging as I clasped and caressed. Looking back, I could tell, even in my altered state, that I'd changed the momentum of the evening with my aggressiveness. I ignored my intuition, however, kneeling to take him into my mouth. I started slowly, and perhaps I might have restored the tone of our interlude. Soon, I took him deep, using my hands at the root of him to complete each stroke. His hands were in my hair, gathering it in handfuls, and, leaning against the shower wall, he let his head roll as he moaned.

It was when I quickened my pace that he called my name, but not in the way that anyone wants to be called to in such a moment. At first, it was with mild apprehension that he called, almost in a question, "Mandelyn?" I hummed in response. His second attempt was more flat. "Mandelyn. Slow down, baby."

I flicked my naughtiest glare up to his eyes. "I want you, Sam. I want you inside me," I told him. "I want to ride you. I want it deep in me. I want…"

"Whoa, whoa… easy," Sam said. "Come here." He helped me stand up, then embraced me. "I don't know, Mandelyn," he whispered into my hair.

"Come on, you obviously want it. I want you in me unsheathed. I need to feel that explosion in me."

Coming back to reality, in the fuselage somewhere over Nebraska or Kansas, weeks after the portentous night, I stopped the film roll in my mind. From that point forward, my recollection of the evening relied upon Sam's angry, untoward account. As much as I tried to pretend that his outrage had been about seeing me with Dante, wondering about Brett, and finding out about Henry, I couldn't pretend anymore. For whatever that night had been about for either of us, I had somehow cheated the both of us out of what it could have been: a sweet, if salacious, indiscretion—yes, to be regretted, possibly confessed, certainly atoned for, but, hopefully, someday, forgiven. It could have been that act of closure Sam had sought after his years of pining, and it could have cured my downward-spiraling melancholic nostalgia. Now, not only had I committed my sins, but I'd also destroyed a lifelong friendship in the process.

I felt entirely different than I had when I had begun to write Colette. I felt amorphous, helpless, and plainly unworthy. In that moment, I wasn't sure I was ever worthy of Sam's friendship, Colette's, or anyone else's.

I reopened the letter to finish it.

> You pretty much know the rest. Shower grinding, including a reasonably successful blowjob, followed by bedroom gymnastics that took us to dawn. Not bad for a Thursday night, especially considering what a shitstorm Friday turned out to be. *C'est la vie*, right?
>
> Merry Christmas, Col. I'll write again if I have the chance in Sedona. Otherwise, we're due for another GNO when I get back.
>
> Love,
>
> M

20

The rest of the flight was uneventful, as was the short layover in Phoenix. The connecting flight to Flagstaff felt a little indulgent, compared to the more logical option of driving to Sedona. A two-hour drive in the Chicago suburbs might have been on the longer side of acceptable but certainly not unusual. As it was, the lower altitude of the commuter aircraft made what amounted to a forty-five-minute aerial tour absolutely worth it.

We took off flying westward, following I-10, the radio tower-studded South Mountain range on our port side and the odd squares of green, irrigated land patches resembling a circuit board below. We tipped starboard over the oddly swirling, concentric circles of subdivisions arranged around the Sun City area golf courses, continued over Lake Pleasant, and flew northward, following I-17, the Agua Fria River and its riparian forests, the desert, mesas, and mountains spread like a tapestry below.

I was still fascinated, glued to the window like a kid on her first flight; my eyes couldn't get enough of the terra cotta and sage of the landscape, the jagged cliffs, and the snaking lines of rivers that weaved among and sliced through them. I'd flown over the Rockies before, so I had some context from which I should have recognized or anticipated the ochres and reds coming into view. I still reacted as if I were completely unprepared. Colors became saturated. The mossy greens transitioned to evergreens and emeralds. The hills were ablaze, making the white of the snow-capped peaks that much more startling and mesmerizing.

My seatmate tapped my shoulder. "First time here?" she asked.

"Do you ever get used to this?" I asked, nodding.

"I haven't yet. I don't think you ever do. Makes you see your place in the world in a whole new way."

"You said it," I marveled.

Flagstaff Pulliam Field is smaller than the county airport that contractors, government officials, and scientists use when visiting the Laboratory. There is only one runway—all that's really necessary for a facility with a single commercial carrier. The timber-trussed roof, fieldstone fireplace, and substantial number of beers on tap at the restaurant lend the airport a more lodge-like ambiance than that of a concourse.

Within minutes of landing, I picked up the Jeep I'd reserved online. I had no intention of true off-roading. I hated when Dante had four-wheeled in the ditches and unplanted fields outside of town, and I'd nearly vomited and passed out as a passenger through the foothills of the Aravalli range outside of Jaipur. I wanted to get out and see what was off the beaten paths in Sedona, but I didn't want to risk being stranded anywhere alone, either.

The woman at the rental counter advised that I stop at the Oak Creek Vista Overlook station to get my Red Rock Country pass, which I would need to park at the trailheads. "Besides," the woman said, "it'll let you prepare for the switchbacks. Do yourself a favor and shift to lower gear." I couldn't tell if she was being figurative or literal.

I drove over the intersection with I-17 and headed south down 89A with the windows open and the San Francisco peaks visible in my rear view mirror until I took the first long curve along the two-lane road. The scenery, otherwise, was nondescript at first; I could have been anywhere. The elk crossing signs, distinguishable from the typical deer crossing signs by the exaggerated antlers, were a novelty. The cairn-resembling fence posts lining the way would have been just as common a sight in Wisconsin or Kentucky, however, and power lines strung everywhere further detracted from any sense of real wilderness. Apart from the snow-frosted tips of the Ponderosa and Pinyon pines, nothing of the grandeur I had experienced while flying over this area was evident on the ground.

The sky had been cloudless during my flights, but a few large, lazy cumuli rolled in as I drove, though there appeared to be no threat of rain. My ears popped, and I realized that I had been on a descent for the last five miles. The ground beside the road was becoming rockier, more boulder-strewn, and the drop off the east side grew deep enough to merit the occasional guardrail. Even when I saw the sign warning of a seven percent grade ahead, I still didn't perceive any threat of danger. A sign indicating that I was on the "Sedona Oak Creek Scenic Road" elicited a scoffing, stifled cackle.

A sign warning "Rough Road Next 11 Miles" was on my right, but the entrance sign for Oak Creek Vista Overlook was on my left. I turned, taking the driveway up an embankment that paralleled the road I'd left below. I parked, purchased my park passes in the visitor's center, and went out to venture around a bit.

~ ~ ~ ~ ~ ~ ~

She shouldn't have. She knew that. It wasn't smart, mature, or logical. Maybe she was curious and had no ill intention when she looked through the files and saw his address. Zara only wanted to see Hank's house to get a better picture of what he was all about.

Of the homes in his neighborhood—a mix of modestly sized, well-kept Victorians, Italianates, Craftsmen, Foursquares, and farmhouses—the Bevrijden house was of the last variety. It had been thoughtfully expanded, occupying most of the lot. It sat beside an alley which, as she could see while driving through, provided access to the garage. Between the house and the addition, there was a courtyard, through which she could make out someone who she guessed must have been Hank. He was playing with two dogs. She could see a tennis ball being thrown as it arced into her sight line over the fence.

On a second drive around the house, she could see that there wasn't a Christmas tree inside. No decorations were hung outside or evident inside, in stark contrast to the other festively trimmed houses in the neighborhood. That was rather strange, knowing that he was, by what she could determine, a reasonably ardent Catholic. She had presumed that, as a bachelor—not to mention a successful, busy one—he might have neither the time nor inclination to decorate for the season.

As she went on her way, Zara reminded herself to pick up some apples for the office. She decided that picking up a bag of apples of the same variety Hank had been eating on the train that day would be a nice gesture. It had looked delicious.

~ ~ ~ ~ ~ ~ ~

On my way down the path, I saw an interpretive display meant to convey something grand. "The canyon rim is home to a dazzling array of life," it read. While I had to admit that I was somewhat intrigued by the mountain lion, gopher snake, and tarantula that were indicated as native species, I was less than dazzled by the mundane, familiar species from home: nuthatches, squirrels, red-tailed hawks, chipmunks, skunks, and coyotes. I was trying to be more mirthful and less cynical, but I was struggling to be impressed.

I walked toward the canyon, passing the various vendors displaying jewelry, dream catchers, guide books, and other souvenirs. With each step, I was feeling an increasingly palpable effect from the altitude. The sign at the visitor's center said that the elevation was sixty-four hundred feet. Leaning over the stone wall at the canyon's edge and looking into the precipice, I wobbled a little. The drop to the creek bed below felt every bit of that distance down to sea level.

As I stood in awe of the view, I began to feel a little light-headed. A curious sensation began to stir within me. I felt as if I were being whisked aloft by winds swirling up, around, and almost through me, although I couldn't feel any actual breeze against my skin. I almost felt high, not in the sense of elevation, nor in a chemically-induced sense. I felt like I had at concerts, after inspiring speeches, or… what was most accurate? After those rare church services that actually strike the soul.

I felt the way I did as a child, when I'd pray and knew my prayer had been received.

I was tired, obviously. I was hungry, too, I realized while shaking my head to clear the bizarre sensations. I'd been awake since well before dawn and hadn't eaten anything substantial since dinner the night before. It was just after eleven, although my body felt as if it were well into the afternoon. Looking down at the roadway into the canyon— seeing the hairpin turns that lay between me, my cabin, and a meal—I sighed. "It has to be a thousand feet down from here," I said aloud to myself.

"Just short of that, actually—just over half the height of your Sears Tower," a voice explained from behind me.

"My Sears Tower?" I slurred as I turned to see a lovely, tanned face, deeply creased but serene, framed by long, pure white flowing hair. I admired the turquoise and umber geometric patterns on her serape.

"It's only about eight hundred feet down from here to the end of the switchbacks," she said. "You'll descend another twelve hundred feet before you reach town."

"How did you know I was from Chicago?" I asked.

"Your accent, my dear. How else would you suppose?" She smiled wisely.

"Where are you from? I mean… is your nation near here?" I asked.

"I'm from Detroit," she said, sounding amused. At once, I felt myopic and stupid. "Don't worry, dear. People have been asking me that all day. I bought this from a hippie at Slide Rock. This isn't Midwest-cold, but forty-five in the morning is still pretty chilly."

"I'm sorry. I just assumed."

"It's fine, my lovely. Tell me, dear, did you just arrive?"

"I did." I wanted to ask if that was also something she could tell by looking at me, but, having already put one foot in my mouth, I resisted.

"Just remember that, to truly experience Sedona, you have to open your mind," she intoned.

"Thank you. I will," was the only thing I could manage in reply.

"Follow the road below into town, and heed the warning signs. Follow their instructions, and your journey will be a smooth one."

If she didn't want to be mistaken for a mystic, I thought, she could stop phrasing simple conversation to sound like prophesy.

"Mind how the schisms along the fault lines in this valley created this massive rift. It was not just the tributary that carved the divide. Respect the power of the perennial stream that survives even as it meanders through the high desert."

"Got it. Thanks, ma'am. You've been very helpful. Merry Christmas." I extended my hand to thank her and signal my intention to end the odd conversation. She took my hand in both of hers, and before I could dissuade her, she kissed it gently. "Embrace the wondrous gifts of this magical season," she practically chanted.

"You bet I will. You do the same!" I exclaimed with unintentionally phony enthusiasm while I retracted my hand.

As I walked back toward the Jeep, I looked up and saw a hawk floating in aimless spirals over the canyon. The woman called from behind me. "She's riding the upflow vortex, you know."

"Oh… yeah? Wild." I hoped that the way I had said that hadn't been too depreciative or sarcastic. I had no reason to insult her, no matter how eerie the whole encounter had been. As I passed the vendor displays on my way back, I fought the urge to stop, wanting to get my trip into the abyss under way as soon as possible.

As I drove on, I did take the woman's instructions to heart. I was glad to have admired the cliffs before viewing them from behind the wheel. The drive required total focus through the near 180-degree turns that folded in upon one another like a digestive tract. The speed limits were not the casual suggestion dismissed on typical highways; rather, they were serious advisories to be ignored at travelers' peril. The roadway wasn't one to be merely driven, but conquered and survived.

Vegetation became more dense and diverse as I descended. Clusters of hackberry and cottonwood joined the pine trees. It was only after I had passed the third one that I was sure I also saw some mulberry bushes, too. As Colette had mentioned, cedar, cypress, and sycamore became more prominent, as well. Soon, juniper was everywhere, and the resulting fragrance was as transporting as it was transfixing.

The resort was well north of Sedona, about halfway between Flagstaff and the city. The condo was just a short walk from the main house. The decor was expectedly Southwestern, with knotty pine furniture, Mexican tile, and geometric woven tapestries on the walls. There was a fireplace in the bedroom and a hot tub on the deck. There was a full kitchen: refrigerator, stovetop, microwave, and dishwasher, along with cooking implements, utensils, and dishes.

After freshening up and getting a quick bite in the café, I was ready to explore. I'd assembled something of an itinerary in the week since the Muon g-2 event but tried, per Colette's suggestion, to leave enough leeway in my schedule to improvise. Spontaneity was not my strong suit, however. With five days in the area, before I would take a day to drive to Mom's via Route 66 (or, as much of it as I could find without veering too far from I-40), I had allocated enough time to hike the major trails and see the top sites.

If I cut straight across town, I thought I could still make it out west to the Palatki Heritage Site for a few hours.

It was supposedly the off-season, but traffic in town was still significant. With a turn through the second traffic circle and a few miles' drive through residential and commercial areas, I was on my way out of town, red rock fading to a silver-grey sheen, with yucca, live oak, and agave comprising the sparse vegetation. In the silvery landscape, further bleached by the afternoon sun, I almost missed my unmarked turn. "There but for the grace of GPS go I," I thought to myself.

As it turned out, I arrived only an hour before closing time, having underestimated how long it'd take to traverse the unpaved roads northward from the highway—roads that were rocky and dusty despite the patches of melting snow. The drive was half the fun, actually. I felt bold and capable as I gave the four-wheel drive a decent workout.

I checked in at the Willard house, a small dwelling built by the eponymous homesteader in the 1920s. It had been converted to a guard station and gift shop. The docent inside gave a brief but detailed orientation to the small assembled group, describing the history of the cliff dwellings, grotto, petroglyphs, and pictographs. He provided all of us with walking sticks to help navigate the trails, and then sent us on our way.

We scattered to investigate the artifacts. The site was thought to be up to 12,000 years old. I spotted a few small lizards crawling upon the walls of dwellings built within caves. The grotto, further into the valley, was my favorite. The water inside reflected undulating light onto the walls, and the inhabitants had represented the radiating ripples in their artwork. Crude, abstract likenesses of animals and sacred-seeming symbols were interspersed among the human representations. I imagined the stories the carvings and drawings depicted, and I became particularly enamored with the Kokopelli figures. To commemorate my first day, I selected a simple silver cuff bracelet engraved with its image at the gift shop before I left.

On the drive back to town, the images from the websites came into view. I saw signs for the entrances to Red Rock State Park, with

Cathedral Rock off to the south. Past that, I could make out Bell Rock on the horizon. In town, I saw the places to turn for Amitabha Stupa, with Sugar Loaf and Thunder Mountain on the northern side. Munds Mountain loomed beyond. The colors across the skyline intensified as the sun continued to set.

I decided to visit the Tlaquepaque Arts and Crafts Village. Knowing that tempting dinner options lay ahead, and not wanting to overindulge, I stopped at a grocery store first, stocking up on half a dozen eggs, some produce, some drinks, and some snacks, including a bag of dried mulberries. I stashed what needed to stay cold in the small ice chest I bought, reasoning that the rest would be fine in the car, given the cool evening temperature. I made a snack of the mulberries and some nuts as I drove through the traffic circles and down the hill on 179 toward Tlaquepaque.

Each shop and gallery at Tlaquepaque was more charming than the last, with plenty of sculptures and paintings, but also a wide array of jewelry, apparel, textiles, home goods, and holiday decorations to peruse. I bought a leather-bound handmade paper journal at a stationery store, admiring the fine handiwork and discovering that the artisan was also the shopkeeper. I was glad to have taken the edge off my afternoon hunger, as there were also plenty of sweet shops calling my name.

Each plaza and calle in the Village, clearly beautiful at any time of year, was further adorned for the season with garlands over the archways and pots of poinsettias circling the fountains. Twinkling lights, coming alive as dusk fell, wrapped the trunks of the sycamore trees, decorated the branches of potted bushes, and hung from one balcony to the next.

I knew that I was probably missing a spectacular sunset, but I forgave myself for the omission as I chose, instead, to continue conversation with a woman named Eshe, the owner of an outdoor sporting goods store. We had begun by discussing the relative merits of her hiking boots compared to my gym shoes. My cross-trainers had served me well enough at Palatki, but she insisted my experiences on other hikes would be greatly enhanced with more appropriate footwear. I asked to be shown the pair in my size that she thought would be best-suited to the current weather and the hikes I'd described.

As I tried on the boots she'd brought out, she advised that I skip Grasshopper Point, which was better-suited for a summer visit, and add a trip to Devil's Bridge at sunrise. She let me know that the traffic circle I'd kept referring to as such was known locally as the Y, and that the touristy shopping area north on 89A was known as Uptown. She recommended I try to get a meal at The Cowboy Club there, saying that John Wayne, Elvis Presley, and others had been frequent diners while in town filming westerns in the 1950s and 60s.

"Are you here to check out the vortexes, then?" Eshe asked. "I assume you are, since you described all the places they're located."

"Vortexes? Isn't the plural of 'vortex,' 'vortices?'"

"Don't say that to a local unless you want to get an eye roll back in return. In Sedona, for some reason, they're called vortexes. So, no, I take it. That's still cool."

"What's still cool? What are vortexes?" I'd seen the word a few times while planning my trip, but I hadn't ever seen them properly described.

"Some people say that there are these spirals of energy that are emitted from specific spots around Sedona—well, not just here but around the world. We supposedly have a concentration of them here. People don't just flock to Sedona because of the pretty rocks. They can get their fill of that up at the Grand Canyon, up in Utah, or over in Nevada."

"Sounds like science fiction," I told her, trying to remember whether my mom had mentioned vortexes before.

"Maybe," Eshe responded. "Tell me, where all have you been today?"

"Well, after I checked in to my condo, I drove to Palatki, spent about an hour there, then came here."

"Did you stop at the Overlook station for your RRC pass?"

"Oh, right, yes. I walked around there for a bit. I looked out into the canyon for a while before driving down."

"Anything weird happen there?"

I was starting to get the ill feeling I'd get when friends told ghost stories at the Girls' School cemetery. "I don't know. What qualifies as weird? There was this odd old woman who sounded like an oracle, even though I think she was just warning me to take the turns slowly on the way down the hill."

"Did you see any birds?"

"One," I said with trepidation. "A hawk. It was circling like it was looking for prey."

"It was riding the upflow vortex," Eshe said matter-of-factly. "Did you feel anything?"

I was officially starting to freak out. "I guess I felt a little light-headed, but I had just landed after two flights, I had very little sleep, and I hadn't eaten in hours. Altitude sickness, jet lag, insomnia, and low blood sugar would make anyone feel weird."

"Did you feel happy, though?"

My silence was her answer.

"You weren't that tired or hungry, and it's high up there, but not that high. You felt the vortex."

Appreciating my doubt and apprehension, she changed the subject, complimenting my bracelet. "It's, like, actual jewelry, not the junk people pawn off as Hopi when it's actually made in China. So, you know the story of the Lalenhoya?"

"The what?"

"You thought it was a Kokopelli, right?"

"It's not?"

"They're basically the same thing. No one's ever been able to tell me the difference. I've only heard it called Lalenhoya around here. So, do you know the story of the Kokopelli?"

I was embarrassed to be wearing a symbol without having any idea of its meaning. I admitted that I didn't.

"Well, let me explain it this way. Are you looking to get knocked up?"

Still stunned from the previous topic of conversation, I deflected the question as best I could as I withdrew my hand from hers. "Not today, at least!" I said with a nervous titter.

"Well, watch out, then. Homeboy's a Casanova. He runs around seducing women with his music and fertilizing them when they sleep." Eshe boxed up the shoes as she continued. "That hump in his back carries seed. Not seeds," she said, lengthening the plural S. "Seed," she said, with emphasis on the D.

I took the box from her as I laughed. "I may not be safe from tornadoes of swirling energy, but I'm pretty sure I won't be impregnated by a fairy tale creature, at least for the time being. It's a funny story, though."

"Don't say you haven't been warned. Kokopelli's a trickster. Brother's good at heart, but his means can seem malicious."

"Consider me warned. Thanks for all your help, Eshe." I smiled, genuinely shaking her hand in thanks. I paid for the shoes and headed out into the sparkling Patio de las Campanas.

From study in school, I was no stranger to all manner of myth and legend. From visits to Albuquerque, I'd seen first-hand that storytelling customs were stronger in the American West than just about anywhere else in the developed parts of the world. I just hadn't anticipated confronting the fact this vividly on my first day in Sedona.

As I walked past the chapel at the end of the line of shops, I wondered at its incongruity—a church that couldn't have seated more than forty in the middle of an open-air mall. The doors were open, and a service was under way. Carolers were singing "What Child is This?" in a round, amidst the glow of candlelight. I slowed my pace to spy on the gathering. My heart felt full.

21

Sunday: Vacation Day #2

The next morning, I woke up famished. I had returned to my room well after dark the night before, but I wasn't the least bit tired. I sat in the hot tub for a while and enjoyed the stars. Then, I started a fire once I came back inside. Before I went to bed, I checked my email. After sorting through the spam, I had four actual messages: two from Morgan, one from CVC, and one from Joshua.

I hadn't written to Morgan since the night after the Muon g-2 event and the showdown at Meat. I had been succinct in recounting the events, having already given Colette the play-by-play over panang curry and chicken satay. I hadn't really wanted to rehash it yet again.

Apparently, Morgan was a hypocrite when it came to brevity. On Wednesday, I got this:

> This is an alarming development, made more alarming by a lack of detail you have demonstrated a pattern for providing. Please describe the circumstances that led to your altercation.

On Thursday afternoon, Morgan wrote:

> Cessation of journal-response with your CVC counselor without prior notice may constitute grounds for engaging the emergency contact listed on your enrollment form. Please contact Chevalier Virtual Counseling at your earliest convenience.

On Friday evening, I received this:

> Ms. Mandelyn K. Ziegel,
> You are, herewith, informed that, per policy as described in the Chevalier Virtual Counseling (CVC) Waiver of Indemnification,

signed by yourself, the addressee of this message, you have been found in violation of the CVC Terms of Agreement. In accordance with aforementioned policy, Mr. Henry I. Bevrijden, Emergency Contact identified at the time of enrollment, was alerted by Dr. Riley Chevalier, MD, having been compelled by said Terms to inform Mr. Bevrijden of said violation. Furthermore, having made such report and gaining assurance of the subject's sound mental state, Dr. Chevalier hereby severs affiliation between Ms. M. Ziegel and CVC and considers any former relationship between such entities to be concluded and terminated.

Sincerely,

Dr. Riley Chevalier, MD

I got the gist of what had occurred on the first read-through, but I read it a second time just to marvel at the absurdly obtuse legalese. During the third review, my reaction evolved from one of anger to one of relief. I had gained a certain degree of insight from my journals to Morgan, but I felt as if I should finish the job on my own. This did not, however, put aside the fact that Henry had been contacted. I couldn't just let that go unacknowledged, but I was too chicken to call him.

I opted to text: Sorry about the CVC call

He responded immediately: NP. Heads up B4 U leave town next time, tho?

I hadn't thought about it until just that moment; I hadn't explicitly let Henry know about my trip, just that I needed him to see to the dogs until after the holidays. With the commotion of the Muon g-2 event and the aftermath, in the office and otherwise, it'd slipped my mind to tell him any more. We had barely talked about my possible holiday travel to Albuquerque during our phone conversation just before Thanksgiving, but I'd hung up on him and we hadn't talked since.

I wrote: Sounds like you covered for me. Thx

He wrote: Y. Did I lie?

I always read Y as "Why" before translating the text-speak to "Yes." I responded: I'm OK

A few minutes passed before I got Henry's response: Good :) Enjoy ABQ. Say Hi 2 Nadja 4 me

This was another decision—whether to tell Henry about where I really was. On the one hand, I could have fallen and broken my neck

RELEASE

while hiking. Someone besides Colette should have known my whereabouts. On the other hand, my mom knew I was here, too. A text, which I'd received from her on the drive back from Tlaquepaque, reminded me yet again, "UR welcome 2 ABQ early if U want… LMK." I decided that reporting to Henry like I was late for curfew negated the supposed benefit of vacationing alone.

    I texted back a simple, "K," to Henry, an "ETA still 12/22," to Mom, and, putting my phone aside, I opened Joshua's email.

    M,

        I feel awful. I owe you my deepest apologies. When you called last month to tell me about you and Sam and your separation from Henry, I wasn't there for you. Honestly, I was a little taken aback, but you needed a confidant, not judgment.

        For one thing, I shouldn't have been so surprised that what happened, happened with Sam. I withheld my gut reaction, but my silence was probably just as hurtful. I haven't spoken to Sam in years. Sometimes I regret that, but it sounds like he's become someone I don't need to have in my life. After the ugly things he said to you that night, I don't think he needs to be in your life, either—not that I'm telling you what to do. That's just my opinion.

        For another thing, I was still pretty upset by the way Henry talked to me the night of your birthday dinner. After thinking about it a little, I can see that he had a hard day at work and was trying his best not to let his bad mood spoil the occasion. I know how I would react if someone I worked for exploited my homosexuality for his professional gain; it would be with far less dignity and class than he maintained that night, considering. The fact that Henry's firm is subverting a system meant to empower disadvantaged enterprises is despicable. He is more than entitled to be outraged.

        For yet another thing, I felt guilty for pushing your buttons that night and making you tell your India story. I'm so sorry about all I said about the eggshells and not doing your best. That was a shitty thing to tell someone at any time, let alone you and at your birthday party. Who am I to tell someone they're failing the world by not living up to their potential? Seen a certain way, my whole career might seem like a series of sellouts—first med school, then leaving my research team behind and going corporate. I was going to cure cancer. Now my work amounts to little more than enabling gluttony by making a pill that snakes out people's internal plumbing.

I do have the love of a good man, though. So do you, in Henry. Reynard doesn't care whether my name is in the NEJM, JAMA, AJPE, or JAPhA. He cares if I care; he's happy if I'm happy; and he challenges me in ways that help me achieve. If my achievements get recognition other than his, I am that much more grateful. If, on the other hand, I came home tomorrow and told him I wanted to join the circus, he'd throw me a clown-themed party and rent a pony for rides up and down the streets of Boystown. Such is the nature of our unconditional love.

If I can encourage you to do one thing, please think back to how you and Henry were before Theodore. I can't imagine what a tragedy like that would do to me, and I hope I never know. My greatest fear is, if anything like that happened to Rey and me, that we would be too proud to ask for the help and support of the people who care about us. Notice that I didn't say, "I fear not being strong enough to face it." I know I'm not. I don't think that Reynard is strong enough on his own, either. I don't even think the two of us are strong enough to get each other through something like that without added intervention. Sometimes, strength is admitting when you need reinforcements.

I always thought you were gutsy and ambitious, a pretty brave person for sticking up for others and going after what you wanted in life. Henry told me something on your wedding day that I'll never forget, though. "She's more than that. She's courageous. A brave person does something noble without calculating the risks. Mandelyn perceives, assesses, and summons the fortitude to do what must be done." Until I heard him say that, I didn't know if he really had my full approval (He's a tough read, if you haven't noticed), but he won me over that day and then some.

You guys are opposites in so many ways, but you have the same core values where it counts. One of the things you have in common may be your downfall, though, unless you use your courage to rise above this weakness you share: you're both too damned independent. You're too proud.

Maybe I shouldn't call your independence and Henry's a weakness. Who am I to judge what is weak and what is strong? It's as bad as passing judgment on what is right and what is wrong. Of course there are clear-cut vices, wicked compulsions, and evil temptations. I'm not talking about those. I'm talking about the perversion, misdirection, and excessive application of what, when properly engaged, would otherwise be a virtue. I'm talking about what happens when self-respect becomes pride, when bravery becomes stubborn foolhardiness, freedom becomes irresponsibility, or independence becomes isolation. Those are the things not meant for mortal judgment.

Remember what you said to me that afternoon at the windmill—that you were never my girl, and that I was never your guy? You said it like it was a good thing, and it sounded good at the time, but I thought about it over the years and came to an epiphany. That's no way to be in union with another soul. If independence in that sense is a good thing, then why bother partnering up at all?

There's something to be said for two heads being better than one, and for one person compensating for the other's shortcomings and vice versa, but marriage, when it works, can be so much more than that. Two halves making a whole isn't really love; it's codependence—a transactional relationship that weakens both participants by excluding the involvement of the divine. At best, it's symbiosis; at worst, it's parasite and host.

What I'm talking about is the synergy that occurs when two people, though human and flawed, follow their hearts, choose with their minds, succumb with their bodies, and demonstrate with all three their devotion—thereby attracting and harnessing an energy between them that yields a greater sum than its parts.

The line from *The Little Prince* by Antoine de Saint-Exupéry goes, "It is only with the heart that one can see rightly; what is essential is invisible to the eye." That gets pretty close to the point I'm trying to make. I don't even know if our hearts alone can understand the purpose or the ways to live and love rightly, but it's through the vulnerability we reveal to one another, through deciding to open our hearts to another, that the real potential is revealed. Then, it is incumbent upon us to act—to let the energy of love fill these vessels we've been granted and let it manifest in a better world.

Invulnerability is an illusion. Not only will a chink in the armor be found sooner or later, but what protects you from the horrible also protects you from the wonderful. You've shown courage to stand firm against life's challenges, but it's the tree that bends with the wind, that yields to the storm, that thrives. I know you have the courage to be vulnerable.

That's what I think, anyway. Take it for what it's worth. In the meantime,

I love you,

J

I read his letter several times before going to bed, and I read it again that morning while scrambling eggs, chopping an avocado, brewing coffee, and toasting bread. I had a different reaction each time I read it. That passage about vulnerability and opening our hearts? It was touching, to be sure, but I didn't know how to take the first step. The tangle of thoughts I'd fallen asleep with hadn't unraveled overnight; by morning, if anything, they'd grown and become more knotted.

The sunrise hike to Devil's Bridge would be just the thing to clear my head. As I took the turn off of Dry Creek Road, I was glad again for the four-wheel drive. The path was even rockier and dustier than the previous day's path.

From the end of the road, it was supposed to be only a mile hike in. A rust-brown sign marked the entrance to "Trail 120," the zero a circular hole through the metal plate. I was surprised that no one else appeared to be there. I had promised myself that I wouldn't go anyplace that felt unsafe if I had the least concern.

RELEASE

The dim but sufficient sunlight rose, and the flat, wide path narrowed and steepened with each passing step. About three-quarters of the way in, the path forked. If I went to the left, I'd end up at the base of the bridge; if I went to the right, I'd end up at the top. I went right. The ledge on my left was damp from the snowmelt sweating from the rock. Yucca and prickly pear lined the trail on the right. As I ascended, I was glad that Eshe had talked me into my new hiking boots. Even though the rocks on the final ascent formed a crude set of stairs, the extra grip of the boots was reassuring.

As I arrived at the top and circled the edge of the cliff, I could see why this trail was on every must-see list. It was breathtaking, delicate without feeling the least bit unstable. The bridge itself was wider than it appeared in pictures. The flat, smooth surface down the center was at least six feet wide, with the entire bridge's width more than twice that. I crossed, turning around when I arrived at the opposite side to take in the view over Brins Mesa, with my view of the sun framed by Steamboat Rock to the south and Wilson Mountain to the north.

I rested, seated cross-legged in a clear area on the opposite side of the bridge. I tried closing my eyes but that made me a little dizzy. I felt as if I should pray. I concentrated. With Joshua's letter on my mind, I felt that praying for strength or courage wasn't quite right. Wisdom? Clarity? Then, it came to me.

"God, as I sit here and contemplate Your majesty, I am overwhelmed with gratitude for the privilege of being here and seeing this with my own eyes. Thank You for Colette and her suggestion that I travel here, the Laboratory for granting my vacation request with so little warning, and for the people who You've put on my path during my journey so far.

"Thank You for Joshua, and even Morgan, for the support they have provided and the ideas they have given me to contemplate. I want to understand what the reason could be for my flaws and my shortcomings. I want to understand what possible use they could have. Most of all, I want to know what practical good could come of the havoc I have caused by my reckless, selfish hedonism.

"Keep Henry near to You. I love him, God. I've done a horrible job of demonstrating that—for a long time, really—and I've done an especially bad job of honoring my commitment to him. I'm undeserving of his affection or his kindness. Please help me find a way back to him, if that is Your will, and help me to see what I can do to…"

I paused. What did I want? Restore our bond? Let him be happy again? Be happy again myself?

"Help me see what I can do to rekindle the divine energy that once existed between us. Allow my journey to continue safely, and let it be an instrument to reveal Your will for me. In Jesus' name, Amen."

I remained seated and still while I continued to watch the sun ascend. The shadows receded with each passing minute. It was when I heard the voices of other hikers down below that I finally rose, returned over the bridge, and made my way back down.

~ ~ ~ ~ ~ ~ ~

Zara found opportunities throughout her days at work to walk past Hank's door—opportunities that weren't all that difficult to invent, really, given the layout of the office.

His office was rather spartan—the polished cement floors, glass and bamboo countertops, cream-colored walls, and linen-wrapped bulletin boards all relatively barren compared to those of other offices. Facing the doorway from a spot on the credenza behind where Henry sat, there was a framed picture of two Pit Bulls, along with the requisite rolls and stacks of drawings. No stray paper, pencil, or paper clip lay on his work surface, however. The only items on the table were his oversized monitor, a wireless mouse and keyboard, and a picture frame, facing away from the doorway; Zara didn't dare go inside to see whose face was displayed.

One other personal effect sat alone: a miniature baseball glove, a ball sitting inside it. On the baseball was a white knitted hat. There wasn't any mistaking it. Zara had no doubt in her mind that it had been made by the woman she knew from the train.

~ ~ ~ ~ ~ ~ ~

When I got back to the Jeep, I pulled a bottle of kombucha from the cooler, and I unpacked an apple-almond butter sandwich and some carrot sticks from the bag I'd put together the night before. It was only eight forty-five, but I'd been up for so long, it felt later than that.

RELEASE

I needed to head back toward town if I wanted to make it in time for the meditation at Kunzang Palyul Chöling in Peace Park.

I had been to stupas twice before: the That Foun Stupa at the ruins of Wat Piawat temple in Muang Khoun, and another in the ancient city of Viratnagar. Dante and I had visited Viratnagar on our way from New Delhi toward Jaipur. We had traveled for twenty-two hours the day before—an eight-hour flight from Chicago, a six-hour layover in Amsterdam, and another eight-hour flight which, with the time change, constituted three calendar days—Friday afternoon to just after midnight Sunday morning. We had gotten a hotel, slept (and not-slept) off our jet lag during the day, and gone out for dinner that night. We awoke early Monday and hired a car for the three-hour drive south. We lost track of time while exploring Beejak-ki-Pahar, the excavated circular Mauryan stupa at Viratnagar that was comprised of lime-plastered panels interspersed with octagonal wood pillars.

We did little investigation, devoting most of our time to looking for the next corner or niche in which we could make out. By the time we arrived in Jaipur, I was thoroughly disoriented, retaining little if any recollection of anything learned about Buddhism or the prehistoric times of Mahabharata.

I hardly felt as if I was on my way to a sacred shrine as I pulled into the residential neighborhood. While I still found the adobe homes and pebble stone yards to be charming curiosities, they were unremarkable in any other respect. I turned onto Pueblo Trail off Andante Drive, made an immediate right onto the gravel path, headed up the hill and around the corner, then parked.

As I walked the pathway upward toward the stupa, the color of the sky began to change, or at least that's the best way I can describe my altered state of mind. I didn't realize that I had been squinting. The sky was clear and bright, but the tension in my face had less to do with shielding my eyes from any glare and more to do with force of habit. My cheeks settled into their right position, and my frown relaxed into an easy smile.

At first, I saw the rectangular prayer flags—red, blue, yellow, purple, and green, some with frayed edges, others less worn—strung like pennants in four directions outward from the top of the Amitabha

Stupa, which was in a clearing at the center of the space. Other strings of prayer flags lined the perimeter of the clearing, as well.

The stupa was more than thirty feet tall. The pedestal alone was more than twice my height. While I stood admiring its scale, I started to remember some terminology from my time in Jaipur and Muang Khoun. Four square slabs stacked upon the pedestal represented the Brahmavihara—the Four Immeasurables of benevolence, compassion, empathy, and equanimity. On top of the slabs was a squat, vat-shaped bumpa. A doorway on its side, adorned with a faceplate of gilded swirls and leaves, faced eastward. Inside the bumpa sat the bronze Amitabha Buddha, seated upon a lotus and glistening in the sun. A spire built of bronze discs of diminishing sizes, stacked like coins, sat above that, with the crowning sun and moon jewel shining at the pinnacle.

To fully appreciate the stupa, I started to walk toward the viewing shelter off to the right. Inside, a man sat cross-legged on the floor, despite the available white chairs just behind him. He silently raised his hand to me, and I stopped. Without protest or the least bit of animosity, he motioned, pointing behind me, and circling his finger to indicate that I should approach the shelter from the opposite direction. I turned about, walking clockwise around the stupa. As I walked, I noticed the benches on each side of the stupa, or were they altars of a sort? Polished stones, seashells, small figures, pictures, coins, candles, slips of paper, and other memorabilia were scattered over each. As I reached the twelve o'clock position, I straightened my path toward the structure, but the man inside raised his hand again, motioning with the same unperturbed disposition for me to continue my walk. I continued and made a third circle at his final, unspoken, gestured suggestion. As I approached the third time, he smiled more broadly and waved me in.

I sat, cross-legged, in the fashion of my companion. He might have been my age, though it was hard to tell through the long, densely matted dreadlocks and bedraggled, wiry beard. We sat in silence as I lifted my eyes toward the Buddha.

I don't have a solid opinion on the casual mingling of the words different religious use to describe prayer and meditation. I struggle with the fact that Buddhists don't acknowledge a Creator deity, but I had developed a profound respect for the Buddhist traditions and practices

I had observed in India, Laos, and on a few other occasions over the years. There are probably as many Buddhist hypocrites in the world as Christian ones, but I've encountered far fewer of the former than the latter. When all's said and done, I believe that people who actively cherish and cultivate mindfulness, truth, and peace are okay by me.

A meditation session, the main reason for my visit, would begin in a few minutes at the building down the hill. I sat and gazed in admiration at the stupa's geometry and handiwork, sought quiet and calm within myself, listened to the wind chimes, and decided this is the place I was supposed to be.

There are actually two stupas in Peace Park, as I found out. To the east, I could see a stupa about as tall as me. I walked down to see it, circumambulating before taking my seat at a weathered bench of wrought iron and wood, my left leg extended, my right folded underneath me, and I reclined, my shoulder blades against the seat back.

The gold-leafed image in relief on the bumpa was less detailed than the Buddha inside the Amitabha Stupa, but something was immediately clear. This was the image of a woman, and a shapely one at that. I was confounded, but I was also delighted. I smiled wryly, nodding as if in cahoots with my compatriot of the moment.

Suddenly, I was overtaken by the recollection of my morning picnic with Sam at Aqua. I felt whisked away bodily with a force sweeping up from my core. I shut my eyes to block the vision, but it only became more vivid. I looked down and saw his hands on my knees. I saw my right hand as I placed it over his left, and watched as he drew his hands away. I looked up and saw Sam's dubious smile. "I didn't know how serious that pedestal was," he said.

That vision whisked away as if in a cloud of smoke above a fire. A vision of Dante took its place. I was sitting shoeless on Zara's threadbare couch in my pinstriped suit. "You need to integrate your head, heart, and body in order to figure out what it is you really want in this life, where it is, and how to get it," he said.

I forced my eyes open and shook my head to make the present come back into focus. Instead, I was pulled further back in time. My right hip ached, and the bench beneath me became a hospital bed, the seat back a fibrous pillow. I looked to my right and saw Henry. "You can do this. We can do this. I believe in you. I believe in us."

I was crying as I pulled my leg out from under me, and, with my elbows on my knees and my face in my hands, I sobbed, shoulders shaking as I gasped for air.

Someone rested hands on my shoulders from behind. I should have been startled, but I was too absorbed in my sobs. As the moments passed, I felt weight drain from me. Eventually, I regained enough cognizance to reestablish a regular breathing pattern. After taking several deep breaths, the hands left my shoulders, and I turned to see who had crossed behind me to the left. It was the man from the shelter above.

Almost inaudibly, he whispered to me, "That's the White Tara. She expresses maternal compassion and offers healing to beings who are hurt or wounded. You're going to be okay." As silently as he had arrived, he completed his circle, returned to the path and, turning, walked down the hill.

I looked back at the image of the White Tara, blinking slowly to clear my eyes. The sun glared, reflected from the image, making it as difficult to maintain my gaze as it would have been to stare at the sun. I could feel her light on my face; I felt healed by its brilliance—healing I had not requested; healing for which I had not realized my need.

I sat for a long time on a level of consciousness I hadn't ever achieved before. I'd felt close to it before—during yoga classes, during memoria, or during "the silent prayers of those gathered here today." This state felt more sincere, however. More ardent. It was as if all of my synapses were alight, but instead of frenetic electricity shooting among them, there was a steady glow that emanated from within them.

Nothing in particular pulled me or guided me back from that state of mind. In time, I rose from the bench, completed my own circle around the White Tara Stupa, and then I returned to my car.

~ ~ ~ ~ ~ ~ ~

As I drove away from Peace Park, I felt fantastic—happy, invigorated, and eager for the physicality of an aggressive hike. I had planned to spend the afternoon at Thunder Mountain, getting around Sugar Loaf,

Capitol Butte, Coffeepot Rock and Chimney Rock for as long as my body would allow me.

Being alone, I was smart enough to attempt little more than some minor bouldering near the well-traveled trails. The hiking boots were my best allies as I pushed through what, as I later charted on a map, took me more than ten miles up and down through rough terrain. Every new shoe, however, has its limits. My feet were pounding, but what really started to do me in was my aching back. It was after four o'clock before I finally made it back to the car. I could already feel my hamstrings and calves beginning to seize.

If I was going to enjoy the rest of my trip, I would need to get the lactic acid out of my muscles. When I got back to my car, I called the resort. If I hurried, they said, I could still catch the last bodywork appointment of the day.

My therapist, as it turned out, was named Stanley. I have no idea why I found his name amusing. I'd never had a man give me a massage—at least, not in a therapeutic, professional context. I hoped, as I changed into my robe and filled out the paperwork, that Stanley would be cute, but not too cute. Just as quickly as I had the thought, however, I chastised myself for it.

In a sense, I got what I'd hoped for. As Stanley introduced himself, I decided he looked like the guy who'd work on my car or pick up my garbage. He was easily twenty-five years my senior, judging by the deep-set lines on his face, but his burly, barrel-chested stature radiated health and joviality. When he introduced himself, I flashed back to the conversation I'd had with the old woman at the Overlook, only the shoe was on the other foot.

"Are you from Chicago?" I asked.

"Bridgeport. How did you know that?"

"Your accent. It's not like I'm psychic."

"Ha. Yeah. You can take the guy out of the South Side, but you can't take the South Side out of the guy," he said, sounding something like a cross between Mayor Daley and Elwood Blues. I knew I was in good hands.

"So, what would you like to work on?" he asked kindly as he reviewed my screening forms.

"Oh, nothing in particular. I've been out hiking all day and started to feel a little sore. I wanted to get ahead of it before I was laid up for the rest of my trip."

"Where'd you go?"

"I went out to Devil's Bridge for the sunrise, stopped at Peace Park for a bit, and then spent the rest of the day at Thunder Mountain."

"Nice. Alright, there's something you should know about my bodywork philosophy. I believe in a holistic approach. Body, mind, and spirit, so to speak. You're here in Sedona alone, am I right?"

"I am." I gave Stanley the benefit of the doubt, assuming that either he had been told by the receptionist that my name was by itself on the room record, or that he had seen it himself as he logged my appointment in the system.

"Everyone who comes to Sedona has something they're working on. You don't have to give me the whole story—just the CliffsNotes version. Is there anything on your mind or troubling your soul that might be affecting you physically?"

"You're good, Stanley." I supposed that what he said was true. I bet everyone who ended up on Stanley's table had a story to tell. "My husband and I are… separated. I'm sorting out what I want for the future of our relationship, I guess."

"Fair enough," Stanley said. "I have one more question for you. Are you comfortable with the fact that I'm a guy?"

"Sure," I answered, almost too quickly.

"It's okay if you're not. We can talk it out if you want, or I can get my associate, Julie, if you're hesitant. No offense taken in the least. I just like to put my clients' minds at ease so they can relax. Is there anything you want to ask before we begin?"

"I mean, the massages I've had before have been from women. I never really thought about it one way or another. You seem like good people, though, Stanley. I'm okay."

He took me back to the room and left while I got situated, dimming the lights and turning on some dreamy, atmospheric music as he stepped outside the door. As I lay there with my head in the cradle and scanning my body for tightness and tension, I tried to remember how long it had been since my last massage. Had it been more than a year? Two?

Then, I remembered. Henry had bought a massage for me as a birthday present just a few weeks after I had begun my work at the Laboratory. I was overdue.

Stanley knocked lightly and came into the room. He prepared his hands with oil before he began. He was as capable as his substantial forearms and biceps had made him appear to be. He sought out the adhesions beneath my shoulder blades and up and down my lumbar. I never lost sight of the fact that it was a man working on me, but any trace of apprehension I might have had about the situation vanished entirely within minutes. That comfort level continued, even as he worked down through my hamstrings and calves.

Then, he spoke. "If there's anything you want to talk about while you're here, feel free. My Martha and I have been together for more than thirty years. She's stuck with me through thick and thin. I'm no shrink, but I'm a good listener."

"The fact that you're not a shrink is a point in your favor. Bet you hear some wild stories in here."

"We store our emotions in our bodies, Mandelyn. When they told us that in school, I rolled my eyes, but, turns out, it's an absolute fact. Massage unearths more than just soreness and stiffness. It's a great way to loosen and rid yourself of the mental and emotional garbage you're holding onto for no useful purpose. It's toxic to keep that stuff all bottled up."

"It's funny you say that. I had a cleansing little meltdown this morning at the White Tara Stupa. Cried my eyes out—came from out of nowhere."

"Up at Peace Park, right? Had some unexpected memories crop up, I take it?"

"Is there some sort of municipal ordinance that requires all Sedona residents to be so intuitive?" I wondered aloud. I hadn't meant to, and I hoped I hadn't offended Stanley, but he laughed. "So happens I did. How did you know that?" I asked. "Don't go telling me that it was a vortex that stirred me up."

"Nope, I won't say that. Some of the folks here say that the whole city's a vortex. Me, I don't buy it. I'm not saying there aren't some weird pieces of real estate around here. People tell me some goofy shit about this spot or that one. It's a little too much to be just a coincidence. Too many similarities, you know? Most of the time, though, it's that a view's so beautiful that an emotional reaction's inevitable, right? You'd have to be made of stone not to be moved by what you saw on your hikes today, for instance."

Stanley's bodywork incorporated a few different techniques I hadn't experienced before. It was just as much a physical therapy or chiropractic session as it was a massage. He pulled on my legs, adjusting how my femurs fit into my hip sockets and realigning the joints up and down my leg. He flexed and extended my foot, rotating each ankle with equal amounts of gentleness and authority.

"As for what happened between you and Tara, that's a different situation, as I see it," he continued. "Meditation's a curious thing. It's different from prayer, or, at least, it's different from how most people pray. I should have asked, Mandelyn, is religious talk off-limits? I don't want to turn this into a sermon if that's not your cup of tea."

"You're good so far. I'll let you know if you range out of bounds."

"I'll know before you do, my dear. Your body's an open book. You know you even gesture with your toes when you talk? You some kind of actress, or public speaker, or something?"

"Something like that," I laughed. "Anyway, what were you saying about Tara and meditation?"

"Yeah, right. First, tell me this: how do you pray?"

"I don't know. it's not at all like my husband does it. He's Catholic. There's not a lot of leeway with their approach. A lot of recitation and response, but it's what he knows, and it works for him, I guess. My way's... I don't know... more conversational, maybe? I thank God for what I have, ask for the things that others need, and then ask Him to show me the way—give me what I need to do what He wants me to do, that sort of thing."

"Well, dear, you've got it figured out better than most. There'd be a lot fewer unanswered prayers if more people prayed like you. The asking part of a prayer isn't about what you think you want. It's about asking to be made ready for what He's got in store.

"So most people talk at God when they pray," Stanley continued, "but they don't spend a lot of time listening for what He has to say in reply. A lot of people have their earthly conversations in the same way, come to think of it, and that's a pity. Meditation—it's more like an invitation. It's like saying, 'Alright, God, I'm gonna let you have the floor. I'm going to sit down over here and, if you've got something to say, I'm all ears. If you want, feel free to tidy up the place while you're at it. It's all up to you.'"

"I've never heard it explained that way," I said. "You make a lot of sense. I'm not sure what that has to do with me blubbering to a gilded image of a woman on the side of an adobe vat, though."

"I'm gonna leave that to the Buddhists to explain. Yeah, what happened to you up there this morning could have happened anywhere, I think, but the right setting and the right frame of mind go a long way to making it easier, you know what I mean? Bet you felt pretty great after all was said and done, huh?"

"I felt fantastic, actually. Maybe almost too good. I went right to Thunder Mountain and climbed the crap out of the trails up there… excuse my language."

"You're talking to a veteran of the Chicago Department of Streets and Sanitation—asking that your language be excused? Please, dear. There ain't nothing you can say that'll melt my ears. Just keep the Lord's name sacred, and you're A-okay with me."

I giggled. "You've got it, Stanley."

"I don't think you're sore from hiking, Mandelyn. I think you're sore from letting go of whatever it was that got out of you this morning. I can tell you worked it hard on the trails, but you're a fit woman. This isn't muscle exhaustion. It's emotional exhaustion."

"You can tell all that from my calves?"

"Your shoulders, actually. Bet these babies spend an awful lot of time up by your ears, am I right?"

"More than I'd like, that's for sure."

"Maybe your days of leaning into doorframes and squeezing the meat over your clavicles to release your trapezius muscles are coming to an end."

"Man, here's hoping."

"Ready to flip over?"

I was. Stanley held the sheet between himself and me as I turned over and resettled myself on the table before he continued.

"There's something I'd like to do, but I want to make sure it's okay, first. You ticklish?"

"Not really. My intercostals can be a little touchy."

"I can't tell whether you had an issue with your liver, your guts, or your lady parts, but whatever happened here has you all knotted up. Abdominal massage can be a tricky business if you're not up for it. Are you alright with me giving it a try?"

"Sure, Stanley." I was glad he hadn't asked me to explain what it was to which the knotting-up could be attributed.

"Now, you let me know the second you begin to hesitate. If you feel even the least bit odd, you say the word."

"Alright," I said.

He stood on my right side, starting just below my ribcage. His touch was sure, more aggressive than I had anticipated, and, while unusual, also really marvelous. He worked clockwise across my belly, down my left oblique, and across the area that a T'ai Chi laoshī who led a workshop I'd taken referred to as the Xia Dantian.

Stanley, as if he knew what I was thinking about, confirmed my recollection. "In Qigong practice, this is the energy center associated with sexuality, physical power, and vitality. Makes sense, right? It is where your Qi resides, your life force, as they say. If it sits still here, it stagnates. The idea is to let it flow between here, your Zhong Dantian—that's where your emotions reside, and your Shang Dantian—in your brain, the center for your spiritual self. Basically, it comes down to keeping the Qi flowing between the three. You into yoga at all?"

"I'm not one of those who calls herself a yogi. I pick up a class now and then. I did a little T'ai Chi in college, though. I know about Qi, and I remember learning about Dantians and energy flow. Chakras, third eye, heart center—it all kind of sounds the same to me."

"Different terms, same ideas. Cultures throughout time, all over the world—they all have different names and different explanations, but it all comes down to basically the same ideas, don't you agree?"

"You are an enigma, Stanley, and an absolute delight."

"Be sure to put that on the comment card, dear."

RELEASE

I smiled as he continued to work his way around to where he had begun.

The hour passed as if it'd been timed with a board game hourglass. Stanley finished with my head, gently pulling to elongate my neck, rotating it to the left and to the right, and tilting it toward each ear, pressing against my opposite shoulder as a counter-stretch.

"Take your time getting up. What do you have planned for the rest of your day?"

"I was thinking about going somewhere to see the sunset."

"You have to go to the Airport Mesa. It's bar-none the best place around to watch it. When you're out there, don't spend all your time looking west. Look to the east, and watch what the setting sun does to the rocks. You'll never see anything like it anywhere else in the world."

"Alright, I will." I went to shake Stanley's hand, but he bent over me and gave me a hug that reminded me of how my dad would do it when he put me to bed as a child. I almost expected Stanley to tell me good night and warn me not to let the bedbugs bite.

"You're a good woman, Mandelyn," he said. "I know things will work out for you. You've just gotta let 'em. Don't stand in their way."

"I will. I mean—I won't, I guess. I… you know what I mean."

"I sure do. Oh, and one more thing. Even though your man prays along with everyone else in church, that don't mean that's the only place he does it. Don't sell the guy short."

As I left the spa and walked back to my room, I was practically levitating, liberated from more than just the stiffness that had brought me in. I felt celestial. I felt free.

~ ~ ~ ~ ~ ~ ~

Airport Mesa was easy enough to find, just south of Uptown. The woman at the front desk told me to follow the signs for Sunrise Service to the Masonic Lodge Memorial Cross, but to pull off to the side of the road about halfway up and hike up the closer of the two mounts. When I arrived, I could see why. The mesa was teeming with tourists—families, mostly, with dogs and small children milling around, but also amorous couples and only the occasional loner like me.

I took the trail clockwise around the base and reached the top without much effort at all, although I was glad to have grabbed my water bottle from the car at the last moment. I almost had the place to myself, the few others already there all respecting one another's solitude. From my vantage point, I had a 360-degree view of the valley. Schuerman and Doe Mountains framed my view to the west, with the Cockscomb in between, but Stanley's advice to take all of it in was wise. To the north, I could see where I had already explored. To the south, I could see where I planned to visit the next day: Red Rock Crossing and Cathedral Rock. I hoped to have time to make it to the Munds Wagon trails and Bell Rock, to the east, in the afternoon, before returning to Chapel of the Holy Cross to attend the Taizé prayer service at five o'clock.

If I dedicated the rest of my life to trying, I couldn't do the Sedona sunset justice in words. Thousands of people have attempted it, and many of the descriptions I have read have gotten close. As dusk evolved to twilight, the titian, copper, and russet of the rocks were draped with the azure, cerulean, and heliotrope of the sky, and the stars began to burst forth as magnificently as fireworks.

I thought about what Stanley had said about beauty evoking an emotional response. I could feel the colors of the sky with all my senses—in my ears, on my tongue, and in my core. I wanted to cry out, not in tears but in exaltation. I felt like I had in school, before big volleyball games or debate tournaments. I felt electrified yet focused, like my chest and my belly were filled with white-hot coals, heat radiating out through my fingertips. I raised my hands to the sky, dropped my head back, and began to spin around. Soon, I realized I was alone on the mount and the sun had almost vanished. Composing myself just enough to keep my footing in the enclosing darkness, I made my way back to my car and headed back to town.

As I drove eastward, a gnawing growl emanated from my belly. In my post-massage bliss, I'd entirely forgotten to eat dinner. It wasn't too late to return to my room and cook something up, but I didn't want to go back to the condo and end the day just yet. I remembered a an ice cream shop in Tlaquepaque, the perfect treat at the end of a wondrous day.

I parked and practically skipped along the calles, almost blindsiding Eshe as she came around a corner. Floating in my delirium, I gave her a bear hug, clearly taking her by surprise.

"Thank you, Eshe! Thank you so much for all your help yesterday! I can't tell you how wonderful my day has been!"

"Where have you come from, girl," she laughed, "and what have you gotten into?"

"I've been everywhere, Eshe. I started the day at Devil's Bridge, and I am ending it on top of the world!" I sang as I danced.

Eshe extracted herself from my grasp, amused but also somewhat concerned. "I'm happy for you, for real, but seriously—where exactly have you just come from?"

"The sunset—oh, the sunset! I took some advice and went to the Airport Mesa. I knew it'd be pretty, but it absolutely changed my life!"

"Changed your life, huh? Okay. Were you on top of the mesa or on one of the mounts below?"

"The closer mount, just…"

"…over the edge from the end of the runway. Right. You got swept up in a vortex, girl."

"Huh? Wait, what?" I was confused, a little disappointed that I might not be able to attribute all of my elation to the sunset alone.

"The throngs of tourists up above—bet you couldn't hear them once you got to the top of the hill."

"No. I didn't even think about them."

"And the few people who were around you—couldn't hear 'em, either, right?"

"They were all as quiet as I was."

"They probably were, but not because they were solemn or respectful. They were in it, too." Eshe was serious but unalarmed.

"Can I buy you some ice cream?" I asked. "If this is what vortexes do, I need you to tell me more about them."

"Sure thing. I'll lead the way. God knows where you'll end up, left to your own devices."

We walked into the shop, ordered with little contemplation, paid, and took seats outside the cafe. She had ordered a scoop of honey-whiskey, and I had ordered dragonfruit.

"So here it is," Eshe began. "Everyone has both a masculine and a feminine side, but everyone always talks about them as if they're opposites. That's ridiculous. If they were opposites of one another, having both would cause each one to cancel the other out.

"Of the two, masculine's the easier to describe. Basically, it's strength, which, of course, means something different to everyone. It's not just whether you can bench or squat. It's more like… fortitude, with vacillation as its opposite."

"So, weakness, basically," I added.

"Not exactly. It's like dullness, timidity, indecisiveness… It's apathy, really."

"Okay," I said, processing what she had to say as I continued coming off my sunset high.

"The feminine—well, no surprise here—it's more complicated. Let's wrap it up by saying that it's a measure of goodness, with evil as its opposite."

"Sounds a little too simple to me."

"It always does, until you dig into it a little further. There aren't a lot of absolutes in this world. Think about the atrocities carried out in God's name, or consider the economic inequalities and environmental destruction caused by visionary industrialists and even well-intentioned protectionists. That's what I mean by evil. All it takes is one perversion of a noble goal to turn it on its head. Again, it's not about boys and girls."

"Fair enough," I agreed.

"So the masculine thrives on self-respect, and the feminine thrives on respect for others. Too much masculinity, and you become a narcissistic egomaniac. Let the feminine side overtake you, and you put yourself last, exhaust your resources, and lose your identity."

"Don't have to look too far to see examples of that. Just visit any preschool drop-off line."

Eshe laughed. "Or any boardroom, cubicle, farm field, construction site, or manufacturing plant. Men can lose themselves in service to others, too. I'm not saying that hormones and anatomy don't play a role in gender identity. I'm saying that the motivations that leave housewives bereft of purpose after children leave the nest are the same ones that keep some people—men, women, no difference—at work all hours, surrendering unused vacation days, and finding themselves at the ends of careers that were good on paper, without any idea what to do with the rest of their lives."

"So it's not just a woman's work that is never done."

"Exactly."

"So what does any of this have to do with vortexes?"

"If you believe what they say, there are two kinds of vortexes. Some people say that there are 'complex' vortexes, too, but put that aside for a moment. There are upflow vortexes, and there are inflow vortexes. Upflow vortexes are masculine, electric. You have experienced two upflow vortexes, one at the Overlook and the one at Airport Mesa tonight. How did the way you felt at those two places feel the same to you?"

I had to think before answering. "That's hard to say. I was in different states of mind when I was at each of them. But when I was leaving each one, I felt sort of spacey—happy, unburdened, lighter."

"Straight up. Or actually, upward in a spiral. Upward vortexes sweep you out from the inside. They take away what's burdening you and raise you to a higher plane. They connect you to the divine."

"At the Overlook, I felt the way I feel at church, like at Christmas. Reverent, you know? Calm and warmed. At the airport tonight, I felt like I was at a tent revival. I was fired-up—electrified."

"I saw. If you believe what I'm telling you, then the Overlook felt different because there's also a lateral vortex there. It's one of the complex ones I mentioned. Lateral vortexes supposedly allow you to see the future."

"Alright. I was with you up to now, but the future? Seriously?"

"Some people swear that they see specific, clear visions of possible futures before them, but most people only get impressions. It's fair to say that, based on how you felt, you have calm and reverence in your future."

"That does sound nice," I said. "So, what else? What's supposedly going on at an inflow vortex?"

"Like it sounds, inflow is introspective. It's magnetic, feminine empowerment. You're supposed to feel grounded, like you can harness your wisdom and sensibilities as you contemplate mysteries, set goals, and select among the choices before you."

Eshe finished her ice cream before changing the subject. "Where are you going tomorrow?"

"Southeast, toward Red Rock and Cathedral Rock. Maybe Munds Wagon Trail if there's time before the Chapel of the Holy Cross Taizé prayer service at five."

"Girl, if you fit all that in, you're going to need a prayer service by the end. That's a lot of hiking. What about getting a bike? Munds, especially—it's spread-out but it's not that steep if you stay on the main paths. I'd do that if I were you."

"Thanks for the tip," I said.

"I need to fly. Take it easy tomorrow, okay? You're channeling a lot of energy through your system on that schedule. Don't go doing too much and blowing a circuit. Go with the flow—for real. Thanks for the ice cream. Check back and let me know how it goes, okay?" Eshe gave me a business card and gave me a hug.

"I sure will. Thanks for everything," I said.

I tried to remember a time when I'd had more intentional, benevolent, platonic physical contact from more people in a single day before this one. "I need more days like today," I said to myself. "Every day should be a little bit more like this one."

22

Monday: Vacation Day #3

I was smart to do some planning fireside before I went to sleep. The idea of exploring Sedona by mountain bike added a new, fun element to what had already been an extraordinary vacation. It expanded the area that I would be able to cover, and I'd see things from a different point of view. If I had a month in which to do nothing but investigate every Sedona rock, canyon, and stream, I still wouldn't scratch the surface. A year would barely begin to do it justice. At least this would help.

I hadn't ridden anything but my old reliable Schwinn road bike for ages, so the idea of traversing the gravel and smooth rock of trails like the ones I'd already seen was, admittedly, a little nerve-wracking. I decided that the trails east of town seemed to be the most level. If I could manage those, I'd take the bike to the area around Red Rock State Park, Crescent Moon Ranch, or Cathedral Rock on Wednesday. I'd spend my last day in town at Boynton Canyon and Long Canyon Mesa, and visit the West Fork Trail at sunrise, before heading out of town.

For whatever middling credence I gave Eshe's lesson on the power of vortexes, I supposed this itinerary would give me equal exposure to the upflow and inflow varieties. Inflow vortexes seemed to occur most often in canyons; upflows, as I could confirm, are usually located on mesas and mountains. Today's plan included one of each, plus, according to some sources but not others, a complex vortex at the chapel.

I started the morning with a mixed-green omelette. I was jonesing for cheese, which I'd omitted from my purchases out of haughtiness, and some hot sauce, which I'd just plain forgotten. I did indulge in two cups of coffee with sugar and cream. I packed my ice chest, grabbed my gym bag (Having left it behind the previous day, I was towel- and antiperspirant-less after Thunder Mountain; I learned the lesson not to do that again.) and headed to the bike shop.

The experience at the bike shop, while entertaining, was also an exercise in faith and tolerance. Stoners come in two varieties: the totally trustworthy and the totally untrustworthy. The guys who ran this shop, I decided, were not actually high, as I had first suspected, but perpetually stoked, living their passion as mountain biking evangelists. Totally trustworthy, I decided. After one of them studied me with a wizened eye that rivaled Garrick Ollivander's, I was set up with a Trek Rumblefish 29er whose tires had been "full-on Slimed," whatever that meant. I thought that the entire staff was as excited for my day as I was, if not more so.

I'd mapped a twenty-mile loop, which I could easily curtail if I'd bitten off more than I could chew. With the exception of the upward climb along the Munds Wagon Trail toward the Cow Pies, the Carousel, and the Schnebly Hill Vista, there was little variance in elevation where I'd be riding, and the trails appeared to be well-traveled. I'd play the day by ear, with the Taizé prayer service the only event driving my schedule.

I parked at the Mystic trailhead and took the bike down from the borrowed truck-mounted rack. I stopped for a moment, debating for the last time whether I was taking it too easy by not taking Chicken Point and Broken Arrow around the opposite side of the Twin Buttes. I reasoned that, to reach the other destinations I'd prioritized, I'd have to compromise a bit on the rigor of the overall journey.

Mystic Trail was rather straight and unshaded. Taking the Pigtail Trail alternate to skirt the butte more closely, I quickly reached the residential area just off of 179. Taking that, I rode north and turned right into the next neighborhood. I took the road to the point where the pavement ended and picked up the trailhead for Margs Draw. I crossed washes and passed what appeared to be a dry waterfall along the way, with Grayback Rock, Capitol Butte, Wilson Mountain, and Steamboat Rock—all becoming increasingly familiar landmarks—coming into view.

At the base of Camel Head, the trail curved, bringing Snoopy Rock into frame. The name hadn't made any sense to me until that moment.

RELEASE

I had been looking for his face in profile, but it was when I saw him lying as if on top of his doghouse that the picture finally clicked.

Continuing for about another mile, I reached Schnebly Hill Road. My Schwinn would have been sufficient for the trail up to that point, but I knew, looking uphill, that things were about to change. I paused in the parking area for the Huckaby trailhead, drank some water, and mentally prepared.

The four miles ahead rolled upward and down, but mostly upward. The trail and the adjacent roadway snaked along the side of an old creek bed. As I continued upward, I could see more evidence of the fading snow. Patches remained off the side of the trail, and in some areas, the melt and refreeze left sheets of ice that were, thankfully, easily avoided.

The Cow Pies were about halfway up the hill. I chose to check them out on my return trip from the Vista. When I reached the Carousel, I finally stopped to catch my breath and drink more water. Here, I found the sedimentary lines to be particularly unusual. Among the familiar ferrous sandstone layers, there were layers of limestone. Time had worn the surfaces quite differently, leaving the limestone in jagged outcroppings that I supposed were what someone once thought looked like animals. I didn't see the resemblance.

I continued on, sufficiently impressed but relatively unmoved compared to the previous day's kvelling. I started to feel the burn in my quads as I arrived at the Vista, but it was more than worth it. Between the green of the Oak Creek Valley, the vibrant blue of the sky, and the red of the rock, the rods and cones of my retinae were getting a thorough workout. It made me wish for a better camera. As I had been throughout my trip, I snapped pictures with my phone, sending a few choice ones to Colette and my mom to keep them up to speed.

It was then that I noticed the time. How was it already past noon? I'd left the bike shop at seven-thirty, and I'd left the car by eight. The ride to the Huckaby trailhead had to have been less than an hour, and if the ride up the hill had taken even twice that, it still wouldn't be much past eleven. I'd need to get a move on. I put my phone away, took a last slug of water, and got back on the bike.

After circling the Carousel, I left the trail and found my way up onto the aptly but unfortunately named Cow Pies. I hadn't been able to tell, either from the vantage point above the Carousel or as I'd passed before, that the site was littered with new-age paraphernalia. There were stones arranged in concentric circles, overlapping circles, and circles divided into four segments. There were multiple cairns, most about the perimeters of the evaporated vernal pools that formed shallow indentations in the otherwise even surface. There were slips and scrolls of paper wedged between some of the stones—prayers, no doubt. The last straw was a discarded plastic water bottle with an Om symbol emblazoned on its side, the ink fading under the Arizona sun.

"This," I thought, "is the reason hippies drive people bonkers."

I supposed that, if I was going to try and draw any benefit from the supposed inflow vortex, I ought to get to it. I looked to the horizon to choose the best view. I chose to gaze westward toward the last edge of Mitten Ridge. I sat down cross-legged; then, thinking back to the bizarre events at Peace Park, I repositioned my knees beneath me, my haunches on my heels.

I took a few purposeful breaths and tried to center myself. What was it that Eshe had said? Inflow vortexes were magnetic, feminine—a means to harness wisdom and solve problems. I could be here all day, trying to decide which problem was the one on which to focus first. I rested my hands on my thighs and continued trying to center and regulate my breath.

Nothing was coming. I wondered whether I couldn't feel anything because, at the other two sites, I hadn't been aware of whatever magic with which they were supposedly imbued. I wondered if, because I was already a little out-of-sorts at each of the two other locations, I was somehow more susceptible to the vortex power. Maybe I wasn't getting an answer because I wasn't asking a question.

Maybe it wasn't working because Eshe had fed me a line of straight-up new-age bullshit.

My regulated breath was becoming something more like a series of exasperated sighs. If something didn't happen soon, I was going to leave, so that the otherwise beautiful views I'd seen would be retained as happy memories, not ones of frustration for having been sold a bill of goods—being taken in hook, line, and sinker.

If I really wanted to give this vortex a chance, I needed to come up with a specific question. I thought about the couple of times that Sam, Joshua, and I had played with a Ouija board on rainy summer afternoons. I never liked it. It felt fake at best, evil at worst. I hated trying to come up with questions to ask, eventually coming up with just one: "When will the Cubs finally win the World Series?" The heart-shaped planchette with the little circular window didn't move a hair. The game became a lot less fun after that.

I finally came up with a question, however vague. "What do I need to do to be happy?" I queried aloud. I sat and waited. I felt nothing.

I decided to give it one last try, making my question more specific. "What exactly do I need to do next to move closer to happiness, vortex? Hmm?"

I sat still for about another fifteen seconds. Just as I had surrendered and leaned forward, placing my palms on the ground to press myself up, I heard it. It wasn't the booming voice of God. It wasn't booming at all. It was, however, a deep voice, somewhat gravelly, but sincere and kind. I heard two words.

"Forgive, Mandy."

I froze, there on my hands and knees. I waited to hear it again, but I didn't need to. I felt it.

"Daddy?" I asked aloud. "Forgive who? For what?" I was the one in the wrong. I was the one who had screwed up.

I heard Dante's voice: "Do you think you worked through that grief in the right way?"

I heard Colette: "You know how they say that, 'It's never about what it's about?' Baby, there's gotta be more to this. I get that there are straws, and that there are camels' backs... but what is it, really? What is really going on?"

I heard Sam: "You're no muse, Mandelyn. You are not some irresistible nymph or goddess. For Christ's sake... you're a succubus. Worse; you are nothing but a simple, resistible, whore."

Then, it got worse. I heard Henry. His voice repeated in my head, slowly at first, accelerating to rapid-fire. "Fine." "Busy." "It's complicated." "Don't worry." "I already took care of it." "I wondered whether it was me you couldn't stand, or yourself. Thank you for solving that mystery." I could hear his sighs interspersed with the growing cacophony.

I shook my head violently. Still on my hands and knees, I probably resembled a dog. The voices paused. I rested my head on the ground, prostrate, in child's pose. Then, it came again, only this time it was my own voice I heard.

"Don't tell me I shouldn't feel guilty, and don't tell me I didn't fail. No one is ever going to tell me that I didn't have a part to play in what happened, and that I failed to fulfill some feminine obligation as a result."

I couldn't take it anymore. I screamed. It was primal. Alien. Vile. Supernatural. Unending.

The voices stopped. "Okay, I get it," I said aloud. "I get it."

~ ~ ~ ~ ~ ~ ~

Why I didn't careen into the Bear Wallow canyon or wipe out into the brush is anyone's guess. I tore down the hill in a rage, utterly depleted. I took the road instead of the trail, which, while it was windier and required me to dodge the Jeep tours, at least lacked the unstable pebbles and soil of the alternative. I made it back to my car by one-forty-five. I downed an entire bottle of kombucha, pounded several handfuls of nuts and berries, and scarfed down an apple nearly whole.

I had three hours before the prayer service. I didn't want to sit in my car or in the chapel for all that time, and I knew I wouldn't go back out again if I returned to the condo. I got back on my bike and headed out to make the round trip to Bell Rock and Courthouse Butte. I took the Chapel Trail southeast, cutting back southwest on the Little Horse Trail before joining the Bell Rock Pathway. I covered the three-mile trek in less than an hour.

If anything could take my mind off hearing voices, it was the view before me.

You would think that the red rock skyline would grow commonplace after three days, but that wasn't the case at all. If anything, it became more awe-inspiring. For the first days, it was colors and shapes—earth and sky, but it was more than the forms or appearances that made it magnificent. The Sedona landscape could not have occurred through evolution alone. Evolution is adaptation. How could a landscape like that be better-suited for sustaining life than whatever preceded it? Does it, in fact, have a predecessor? Was Sedona originally created to look as it does today?

Of course, it wasn't. Water and wind had eroded it. Glaciers had carved it. Dinosaurs had roamed it. Maybe that was the reason it staggered my mind: the fact that, unlike cities and farmland—with their parallel and perpendicular lines, with their structures, utilities, and conveyances—land in the West still looks like it has for eons, even after withstanding the onslaught of nature. Considering the speed with which everything else in human existence changes appearance, Sedona looks essentially the same. Contemplating the views in Sedona turns the human concept of time on its ear. No army of humans could create a fraction of that landscape, even if they had one hundred lifetimes to do so. Looking at the majesty, it was clear to me that there is a God, and He transcends any concept of mortal time.

Even so, feeling all Biblical and humble, I still had fear and anger in my heart. I knew that the list of those I should forgive was substantial, but what about the forgiveness due to me? I knew that forgiveness doesn't work that way—I'm not *that* self-centered or naive. I also knew that the scales weren't in my favor. I only had control over myself—my emotions, my well-being. It was the same old refrain. I knew I needed to make some changes; I just didn't know where to start.

Then, it occurred to me. I skidded to a stop at the base of Bell Rock, astounded by the idea that flashed through my head. "How could I be so…?" I didn't say the word "stupid" out loud, but I felt it. "Make a damned list. For crying out loud."

The trek around Bell Rock and Courthouse Butte was five miles. If I really slammed it, I could probably make it around and back in time, but that wasn't my reason for being there. I got off my bike and began to hike into the saddle between the rocks. Reaching a boulder of a reasonable size, I stopped, turned, faced northward, and sat down. I got out my phone, opened my dictation app, and began.

"My father, for leaving too soon and not taking care of his health."

I had not expected those words to come out of my mouth. As with any good brainstorm, I let them keep coming.

"My mother, for leaving town—running away from her memories and abandoning Henry and me.

"All my girlfriends from when I was a kid, for leaving town and promising to keep in touch but never doing so for long.

"Joshua, for not realizing who he was any sooner, so that both of us could have spent a little more of our youth and adolescence forming deeper friendships with other people.

"My seventh-grade gym teachers, who implanted an Amazonian body image in my brain while I was still so impressionable, and that rotten principal who backed them up instead of castigating them.

"Guidance counselors and professors, who could have told me to venture out of my comfort zone, especially when classes bored me and I didn't read the writing on the wall when internships disappointed me.

"My heritage, for having so many starchy, fried foods in its cuisine, and my genetics, for making it damn easy to put on pounds and damn difficult to shed them."

That was a joke, or at least it was meant to be. I continued.

"Dante, for letting some fantasy he'd constructed take priority over allowing a genuine connection happen between us.

"Sam, for seducing me in a scheme to work through his own demented perversions, and then projecting his degradations on me when his Madonna turned out to be a whore."

That got a little nasty. I paused before continuing.

"And Henry…"

I stopped. I looked over the list. This wasn't a list of forgivenesses. It was a list of grievances. I thought about Festivus, that ridiculous holiday born from a *Seinfeld* episode that had, oddly, become almost a real-life thing, but I promptly shut it out of my mind and chose to focus.

In every situation I had just described, I had a part to play, if not in its occurrence itself, then in how I chose to perceive it. Did I really blame my dad for dying or hold onto any negativity about his death? Did I resent Joshua for not coming out on a schedule convenient for me? How vapid and selfish could I possibly be? Clearly, I needed some help with this whole concept of actual forgiveness.

It was a quarter after three, enough time to get back to my car and clean up a bit before the service. I looked skyward. I had Cathedral Rock

RELEASE

in my left peripheral vision, Bell Rock above me, Courthouse Butte to my right, and, though I couldn't see it from this vantage point, my toes pointed toward the chapel. Vortexes or no, I felt as if I was in the right place to get the assistance I required.

~ ~ ~ ~ ~ ~ ~

The sun gleamed down from the glass surrounding the chapel cross as I was propelled toward it, along the last leg of my ride. Choosing the more direct path that paralleled the highway before diverting onto residential streets, I made it back with enough time to clean up a bit and take a look around the grounds before the service would begin. Inside the Jeep, I contorted in the cramped backseat to change from my dusty, sweaty clothes into a simple t-shirt dress and flats. Refreshed, rehydrated, and sufficiently fed, I started my walk up the suspended serpentine walkway that led from the parking lot below.

Statues of angels and saints were placed all throughout the property. As the path veered closer to the rocks, there was this sign: "We are so old and fragile. Please don't hurt us by climbing on us. And just take our picture, no pieces of us. The Rocks. Thanks!"

Closer to the entrance, the path was lined with wide, low benches. Groups of people were taking pictures of one another, each selecting the perfect backdrop from the many within the panoramic vista. The storefront-glazed entrance, while more austere than I had expected, was deeply framed in a trapezoidal adobe shape, heavily studded with limestone and basalt pebbles. A large circular water feature, planters full of moss roses with little waterfalls cascading between them, was beside the entrance. A sign in one planter said, "Please don't pick us. We're smiling at God."

On the ground outside the door, there was a mosaic dove with red-tipped wings and tail. Within the entrance, there were plaques and signs explaining the history of the chapel's construction, including ones denoting the landmark status and the American Institute of Architects Award of Honor bestowed in 1957.

As I had understood it, the chapel had been designed by Marguerite Brunswig Staude, a student of Frank Lloyd Wright, but that wasn't really the whole story. A sculptor and philanthropist, Staude had been inspired by the streamlined, modern takes of the Art Deco, Bauhaus,

International, and Prairie schools of architecture. She believed that, "God can be worshipped as a contemporary—bringing Him closer to Earth and every one of us." Her sketches impressed Lloyd Wright, son of Frank Lloyd Wright, when she showed them to him before World War II. After the war, she remounted her efforts to build the project, but her concept had evolved. She incorporated newer elements that diverted from the concept the younger Wright had originally embraced. Staude sought a different architect who would champion the new iteration, commissioning the firm of Ashen+Allen in San Francisco. Choosing a site for the chapel that was within the jurisdiction of the National Park Service, she enlisted the help of her friend, Senator Barry Goldwater, and lobbied the Secretary of the Interior to get the necessary permissions. The project was built in fewer than eighteen months at a cost of $300,000, about $2.5 million in today's dollars.

The interior was smaller than I had expected. Just inside the door to the right, there was a guest book with the names of people who had come to visit from around the globe. Above the prayer book was a painting of Jesus walking along a creek within a canyon. In the sanctuary, which was only denoted as separate from the narthex by tables set with small sculptures and candlesticks of hammered iron, there were only seven pairs of backless benches to serve as pews, with shallow benches lining each wall. The Stations of the Cross were set above the backs of the benches—no depictions, only simple roman numerals made of railroad spikes. Above, on each wall, primitive-style tapestries were hung, one depicting Moses, the other depicting Saint Michael.

Beside the altar on each side were rows upon rows of votive candles in red glasses, more than three-quarters of which were lit, flames flickering though I could detect no breeze in the room. A cross that had been crafted of wrought iron, in a way that resembled gnarled branches or vines, stood to the right of the altar. Above it was an uplit bronze visage of Jesus, in an Incan style, mounted upon a circular frame, the negative space between each quartered segment of the circle creating a cross, geometric patterns within each quadrant adding visual interest. To the left was a glass plaque honoring Marguerite Brunswig Staude and her husband. An evergreen garland was laid across the altar, presumably a seasonal decoration.

RELEASE

Embracing the wisdom of Truvy Jones, I had long ago decided that, "God don't care which church you go to, as long as you show up." While I had never felt the spirit move me to convert to Catholicism, I attended mass with greater regularity than most practicing adults did. During the early years of our relationship, Henry and I had been what the more devout in the Holy Name congregation called "Creasters," the ones who only showed up on Christmas and Easter. After Theodore died, Henry began attending services every week, first at the more convenient Assumption church on Illinois Street, then at Saint Patrick after we moved. For a long time, I went with him—more as a matter of not wanting to sit home alone feeling guilty or lazy than genuine reverence.

Not taking communion was easy to explain to the rare inquisitor, but in truth, I don't know if I would have taken it if it had been allowed. I felt, if not out of favor with the church, then certainly out of step. Some homilies were touching or moving, but services left me wanting most of the time. I didn't care for how readings were specifically assigned by the Vatican, gamboling around from one book to the next as if someone had either outright cherry-picked passages or had just opened pages at random and dropped his finger on this verse or another. Even with my inconsistent religious education and skipping out on Methodist Confirmation, I still felt as if I had a better command of the Bible than most of my fellow Catholic parishioners. My attendance had dwindled in the last year or so, as my despondence had grown.

Growing up, we attended a United Methodist church on the major holidays and a handful of times in between. For my parents, church was a matter that landed somewhere between honoring their own childhood traditions and keeping up appearances with the local community. We took part in our fair share of clothing drives, spaghetti dinners, and CROP walks. I attended Vacation Bible School all the way through fifth grade. We generally gave up the same things for Lent year after year: Coca-Cola for me, chocolate for my mom, and fast food for my dad. We went to several Friday fish fries during Lent, although that was more a matter of social occasion than one of fasting or sacrifice.

I was glad I had taken a seat in the chapel instead of milling around for much longer, although I could have spent hours reflecting on any of the artwork in the narthex. A choir of six or eight, accompanied by a guitarist, began to assemble there, which was a cue to the regular attendees that the service was about to begin. The visitors followed their lead; soon the pews were packed shoulder to shoulder. I sat on the aisle on the right-hand side, three pews from the front.

The guitarist began to play a plaintive tune, and after a verse a chant-like song began:

> *Nada te turbe, nada te espante;*
> *todo se pasa, Dios no se muda.*
> *La paciencia todo lo alcanza.*
> *Quien a Dios tiene nada le falta*
> *solo Dios basta.*

A woman rose and stood beside the right side of the altar and bade us welcome before leading us in the recitation of Psalm 103. Unlike the excerpted readings at masses, the entire Psalm was recited. As hard as I tried to concentrate on every word, I drifted in and out of alert attention, but several phrases resonated with me, this one above all:

> *He does not treat us as our sins deserve or repay us*
> *according to our iniquities.*
> *For as high as the heavens are above the earth, so great is*
> *His love for those who fear Him;*
> *as far as the east is from the west, so far has He removed*
> *our transgressions from us.*

After a brief contemplative pause, the woman announced, "A reading from the Letter of Saint Paul to the Ephesians." She began to read; the passage that meant the most to me was:

> *Then we will no longer be infants, tossed back and forth*
> *by the waves, and blown here and there by every*
> *wind of teaching and by the cunning and craftiness of*
> *people in their deceitful scheming. Instead, speaking*
> *the truth in love, we will grow to become in every*
> *respect the mature body of Him who is the head, that*
> *is, Christ. From Him the whole body, joined and held*
> *together by every supporting ligament, grows and*
> *builds itself up in love, as each part does its work.*

RELEASE

> *So I tell you this, and insist on it in the Lord, that you must no longer live as the Gentiles do, in the futility of their thinking. They are darkened in their understanding and separated from the life of God because of the ignorance that is in them due to the hardening of their hearts. Having lost all sensitivity, they have given themselves over to sensuality so as to indulge in every kind of impurity, and they are full of greed.*

As the guitarist began to play, the reader turned to the altar and lit a candle. The choir began to sing "Be Still" by Sarah McSweeney.

> *Be still and fill up with my peace...*
> *With my peace.*
> *Be still and be comforted, be comforted within me.*
> *I am with you now... I am with You now...*
> *I am with... you... now.*
> *Be still and know I am God. I give you peace.*
> *Be still and be comforted, be comforted within me.*
> *Be comforted*
>> *be comforted*
>> *be comforted*
>> *be comforted*
>> *within me.*
> *I am with you now. I am with You now.*
> *I am with... you... now.*
> *I am with you now. I am with You now.*
> *I am with... you... now.*

Afterward, there was silence. Ten solid minutes of silence, as it turned out. I hadn't ever been in any organized event, worship service or otherwise, when this much intentional silence was allowed.

I was wrung-out. Tabula rasa. I had tried, as I read and listened, to catalog the phrases that resonated most, but I lost track, words and phrases swirling in my mind. "Redeems your life from the pit..." That was good to hear. "Satisfied your desires with good things so that your youth is renewed..." Who doesn't want that? "He does not treat us as our sins deserve..." Thank God! "As far as the east is from the west, so far has He removed our transgressions from us." Let's hope so.

Then, the tougher ones to hear, like: "I urge you to live a life worthy of the calling you have received." "...You must no longer live as the Gentiles do… Having lost all sensitivity, they have given themselves over to sensuality so as to indulge in every kind of impurity, and they are full of greed." I could vouch for that.

And the clincher: "Get rid of all bitterness, rage and anger, brawling and slander, along with every form of malice. Be kind and compassionate to one another, forgiving each other, just as in Christ God forgave you."

Yikes. I wanted to retrieve my list to see if there were some opportunities to do just that. Maybe not the toughies to start—some low-hanging fruit, maybe? Even in silence, I couldn't resist the easy, if not totally irreverent, Adam and Eve pun.

I knew that whipping out my cell phone would be the epitome of gauche. I ran through the list mentally. My dad. Why would I start the list with him, of all people?

"Daddy," I prayed silently, "I miss you every day, but the anger I have about your leaving won't bring you back. If anything, it separates me from enjoying your spirit in my life. I'm grateful for the time we had together, and I forgive you, both for what was in your power and for that which was not in your control."

That did feel good. I wanted more time to reflect on my mom and her reason for being on the list, so I moved on to an easier one. "Auld acquaintance. Surely we served some role in one another's lives, and I was equally at fault for our losing touch. I trust that, if there's any way in which I can be of some purpose in your lives again in the future, then our paths will cross again."

Not bad. I was under no false pretense that others on the list would be this easy, but I felt more clear-headed, knowing the list was going in the right direction. How about another?

"To the gym teachers—and the coaches, for that matter. It was a different time, to an extent, and your intentions were good, if your methods were not. Challenges and adversities made me into the athlete and person I am today—agile, resilient, gutsy, and collaborative.

"And as for the guidance counselors and professors who could have been better at guidance, counseling, or professing? I need to take ownership of that situation. I knew how I felt when I came back to school junior year, but I didn't tell anyone. Under the guise of being independent, I didn't admit what I saw as a failing on my part, when what I should have done was redirected my path, sought assistance and mentorship, taken a class in anything outside my major. I could have gone pre-law with my debate experience and very little change to my class schedule. Just a class in criminal justice, business, law, political science, or economics would have helped. Heck, I did Dante's accounting homework on more than a few occasions. Something might have clicked.

"I'm at peace with how things have turned out, and holding onto resentment serves no one. I give it up and let it go."

Something occurred to me. While I didn't know how long the silence would last, I knew that the service was only scheduled for thirty minutes. I thought about what Stanley had said about most prayers being about talking at God, not listening. I put my mental list aside. "Here I am, Lord," I mouthed silently. Then, I sat in stillness, listening.

The choir began an a capella chant:

> "O Lord, hear our prayer. O Lord, hear our prayer.
> When I call, answer me.
> O Lord, hear our prayer, come and listen to me."

Several intercessions were read, with the same appeal sung in response. Then, the choir continued to sing. Individuals began to rise. I hadn't noticed, but the cross had been laid down upon the floor in front of the altar. Standing before the assembly, a minister handed a candle to each person who approached. Upon lighting it, each person set it at a spot beside the cross. This proceeded for the next ten minutes, maybe longer.

I managed to whisper a question to the person beside me. "Who can go forward?"

The response was simple. "Anyone with a prayer."

I rose. I walked to the altar. I took a candle. It was lit. I knelt. I set the candle down beside the left hand of Jesus. I lowered my head. I rose, and I returned to my seat.

My prayer was that I could find a way to forgive the one person I had omitted from the list.

I prayed for the courage to forgive myself.

23

Tuesday: Vacation Day #4

The sun set as the Taizé service concluded. Before heading back to the resort, I returned the bike. I had two days left before my drive to Albuquerque, and I wanted to spend them taking in quality, not quantity. I wanted to spend them in quiet contemplation, not rushing around. Besides, my legs and my ass were already beginning to ache.

I was nearly out of groceries, having used everything but half the greens, a few slices of bread, the almond butter, most of the kefir, and the mulberries. I didn't want to derail my good habits of the last several days, but I was sick of eggs. I made a deal with myself that if I'd pick up some stuff to make a salad for dinner and a decent granola for my last two mornings, then I'd hit a greasy spoon for breakfast before heading out to the trails.

I decided to spend my day at Buddha Beach. I mapped the route, checked emails, read a couple of stories in the Alice Munro I had brought, and went to sleep.

The greasy spoon did not disappoint. The country ham with red-eye gravy, a buttermilk biscuit, fried okra, a big glass of orange juice, and too much coffee would stick to my ribs enough that an almond butter sandwich, an apple, the rest of the nuts and berries, and the last bottle of kombucha should be sufficient to get me through to dinner.

Buddha Beach sits in the shadow of Cathedral Rock at a bend in Oak Creek. The cairns built by visitors number into the hundreds, but they didn't bother me the way that the few at the Cow Pies had. Depending on who you asked, the vortexes here were supposed to occur somewhere between this spot and the saddles between the spires of Cathedral Rock. If I decided I needed to work my legs at some time during the day, I supposed I would hike up to investigate, but I was perfectly pleased by how I felt while I was at the water's edge. People came and went on their travels up and down Oak Creek, and a few stopped to take pictures or build a cairn of their own, but I had the place to myself, for the most part.

I took out the journal I'd bought my first night in town. Having reexamined the list I made the afternoon before, I knew that most of what I had to do would take more than a silent prayer. I would let my writing go where it wanted to go, where it needed to go. Maybe it'd take the form of a journal entry, or it could be a poem to read and contemplate. Maybe it'd be a letter. Maybe I would send it; maybe I wouldn't. Maybe I'd write gibberish notes that I'd use to talk things through with someone in person. I was looking forward to seeing where this work would take me.

It would be better to address my mom in person, I decided. I hadn't suffered much when she put distance between herself and Weston. I had always wanted to ask her, though, why she felt as if she had to go. That was easy enough to discover. I would ask her about it when I got to Albuquerque.

Neither had I suffered for the time I had spent with Joshua. Having read his letter yet again, I felt the opposite. My issue wasn't with finding more friends, it was treasuring the ones I had. Job one: Be a Better Friend. Since the fall, at the very least, and probably going back long before that, I'd been a selfish friend. I'd asked the ones I was genuinely in touch with—a number I could count on one hand—about their lives once for every five times I'd been asked how I was doing, maybe ten. I made a third as many phone calls as I received, and sent half as many texts. I couldn't remember the last time I had written a letter-length email that wasn't for work purposes, and it'd been years since I had written one on paper. I only had good, long conversations with people when I was in crisis or on special occasions. I had allowed greeting cards and cut-and-paste electronic communications to supplant genuine communication.

Conversely, I felt more connected to romcom, sitcom, and "reality" television characters than to people in real life. Why? Because they were there to give to me, without making any demands of their own. I'd told

RELEASE

Sam that I wasn't ready to give up on the fantasies I had created during my childhood. I still wasn't; they'd only evolved.

I'd think about Sam later. Instead, I started writing Joshua a letter.

> J,
>
> At another time, I might have responded to your email quickly, to say that there's no need to apologize. I've learned a little bit about regret, apologies, and forgiveness during my time in Sedona, however. You deserve the closure that comes from expressing your feelings, and I heard you loud and clear. I just want you to know that I'm not offended by anything that happened in November. We're cool.
>
> I never thought that much about the life cycle of asking for and receiving forgiveness. Apologizing is a big step toward feeling whole again, even if forgiveness isn't granted. It's the giving of forgiveness, even voluntarily giving it without being asked — maybe especially so — where the magic happens. It's not a transaction, an "I ask for this, you give me that" scenario. Forgiveness liberates you from the weight of a wrong done upon you — a wrong that continues, with your permission, to burden you. Ask for forgiveness from, or give it directly to, the person who has committed the wrong, and it is all the more powerful, but 'giving it up to the Lord' has its power, too.
>
> It is only with this caveat that I can forgive you: I forgive you because you want to be forgiven.
>
> Alright... It's not exactly true that I didn't take offense to what you said at Next. It's just that it didn't take me long to get over it when I admitted to myself that everything you said at the restaurant was

true. What you said about the eggshells and losing my conviction was especially true. Combined with what you said in your beautiful letter, I can see as clear as day what I have to do. It is going to be the hardest thing I have had to do in my life, which—Henry was right—isn't necessarily saying much. Mine has been an easy, privileged existence.

People joke about first-world problems. At the root of that is the faulty tool with which we measure our relative fortune and challenge. My challenges are not a big deal, in the grand scheme, but they are a big deal to me. I hope they're still important to Henry. They're important to you, too; knowing that means so much to me.

I met someone here in Sedona who gave me a new perspective on the meanings of femininity and masculinity. She talked about how the two aspects aren't at cross-purposes, the way most people make them out to be. Whenever I've faced hardships, I've responded by turning inward—becoming rigid and isolating myself. I did this in the name of self-preservation, self-respect, and strength. These are all masculine traits, even though there's nothing about any of those behaviors that has anything to do with gender. I didn't grow a penis during any of my life's trials. Not even a little bit.

When I look back on those times in my life—when you and I broke up, when things got out of control with Dante and me in college, when Theodore died, or when things soured for me professionally downtown—I don't have a lot of detailed memories. It's like I was only half-there. I allowed my masculinity to take

RELEASE

control and denied the power of my femininity. What I've learned is that it doesn't have to be either-or. The best people in the world cultivate both. They rotate their crops—vary what they plant in their garden.

Looking back on how things were before with Henry, like you suggested, isn't going to be the best course of action. He and I have to find our way forward from this point. It's not about rekindling a fire, but creating one anew. I need to ask Henry to forgive me, and I need to forgive him, too. We're standing in each other's ways on our paths toward happiness, which may continue together or may part, but no one's going anywhere without resolving this impasse.

I love you, my friend. I'm so fortunate to have you in my life. — M

P.S. You're not a sellout. Cholesterol was a large part of my father's undoing. He didn't have the best diet, but he was one of the healthiest people I've ever known, when you account for his mind and his spirit. Succeed with your project, and you could save hundreds of thousands of others from the same fate. Don't join the circus.

I stretched out on the ground, exhilarated. I extended my hands out above me and flexed each leg, trying to open space between every joint in my body. I tensed and relaxed muscle groups, each in turn, squeezing out the stagnant blood to let the positivity flow through me.

Carefully, I tested the three pages, which I had covered with writing on the front and back, to see if I could remove them from the journal. I planned to send the letter to Joshua that night, if I had been able to get to the post office in time.

Next… Dante. I didn't hold any animosity toward him, either. Whatever amount I had was purged the night we spent together. "When the sun rises in a few hours, you have a job to do and so do I, and neither of us can be of any further help to the other," he said.

Was any further contact, especially so soon, a selfish act on my part?

I thought of Dante's other words that night. "Me, I need to deconstruct the internal masquerade I've created and learn to be vulnerable. What you said, about how the descriptions of the types of women I meet—that they apply just as easily to men, to myself? You're right. I am heartsick and disillusioned. I need to cure that; trying to be more vulnerable is a step in the right direction."

I wasn't choosing to distance myself from Dante, exactly. I was giving him the space in which to transcend, evolve. Whatever there had been between Dante and me had served its purpose in his life and mine. Rick and Ilsa would always have Paris; Dante and I would always have Jaipur. As a friend, I would never leave him, but where we were going, we could not follow each other. What we had to do, we couldn't be any part of for the other.

If anything, I owed him a debt of gratitude, which I gave to him in a moment of silent meditation.

Three people left: Sam, Henry, and me. I'd managed to pick off the easy marks, leaving the ones for which I would have to dig deep. I needed to take a break before starting in. I had parked at the Cathedral trailhead, but my hike to Buddha Beach had essentially amounted to following Back O Beyond Road to the end and then following Oak Creek down to the beach. I forged my way toward the Templeton Trail. The climb up the switchbacks felt auspicious; it symbolized my return from the descent that had brought me to this point.

I had to stop at the top of the ridge to catch my breath, drink some water, and rest. As beautiful as my time at the beach had been, I did not want to go back down the way I had come. With another inhalation, I realized that I didn't need to go back. Everything I needed was here with me. I'd left nothing behind. Here I was, ready to press on.

As I continued up and into Cathedral Rock, I felt what had become a familiar surge of energy. I still don't how I feel about my sensitivity to the vortex energy. It goes against any logic or science I have ever known.

RELEASE

I wonder how many other times I had felt that inexplicable sensation and attributed it to something else. The energy is real, though. I can't deny it any more.

I arrived at a spot that was as good as any, which was to say that it was equal in its magnificence to any that preceded or would likely follow it. I ate my apple, got out my journal, and began.

> Sam,
>
> What happened between us makes me want to cry. We took our history for granted, choosing to use each other instead of confide in, trust, and rely upon one another to satisfy whatever needs we brought to each other that night. There's always been a potent magic between you and me, which, instead of respecting, we unleashed to disastrous ends.
>
> You seduced me as part of some game that I have stopped trying to understand, but I was a willing participant, baiting you once I realized the match was under way. For my part, I was careless with you and even more careless with myself, not calculating the risks before diving in.
>
> I'm still working on forgiving myself for the part I had to play in what happened, and, with or without your consent, I forgive you for the part you played. I won't let the degrading, horrible things you called me afterward hold any further sway over my self-worth. If it matters to you, the information you were working with was inaccurate and your perceptions were off-base, but I am not compelled to justify myself or dissuade you from whatever you have come to think of me.
>
> I owe you an apology, in fact, for something else. Even without you telling me how you had put me on

a pedestal, I knew, or had a clear enough idea of how you felt about me back when we were young. I feel as if, maybe, you hid behind the clearly ill-destined romance between Joshua and me, instead of revealing your true feelings for me and letting the chips fall where they may. For my part, I was pleased to have your doting attention without any of the responsibility or consequence.

I couldn't have told you that Joshua was gay, but I knew on some level, and I think you knew, too. To your credit, you were a good friend to him, which is no small thing, considering that times were different back then.

It's entirely possible that I'm projecting my thoughts and actions onto you, so please don't think that I'm putting words in your mouth. I am not seeking an apology, regardless. I know what I did diminished you. I hope you can forgive me.

I don't know what the future holds for you and me. I am willing to bet that we've served the purpose that each of us could serve for the other in this lifetime. If that is the case, I can be at peace with that. I wish you the best. If you and I have reason to cross paths again, I know our wisdom, good sense, and self-respect will prevail.

Love,

M

It was nearing four o'clock. I would get back, eat dinner, and spend the evening on the deck in the hot tub or inside by the fire, dedicating the rest of my waking hours to getting my thoughts together about Henry.

24

New Year's Eve, nine years earlier

Mary, Susana, and Bethany had come to Chicago to celebrate New Year's. I hadn't seen them since I had moved back to Chicago more a year earlier, so I was happy and excited to let them stay at my apartment when Mary brought up the idea of a long weekend visit. None of us had been all that close in school, brought together as volleyball teammates during those years but having little else in common. If anything, we'd become closer because of Mary, queen of the email forward, who had kept us all in touch, a kind of twenty-first century town crier.

Each of us had stayed around Des Moines after school while transitioning from college life to adulthood. Mary and Ben married immediately after college, and they both went to work at Pioneer. When a job opened up for Ben in Denison, they moved to the smaller town out west, taking both of them closer to home. After she had given birth to her daughter, Daisy, she didn't return to work. Susana, a year behind Mary and me and home from California for the holidays, was staying with her parents in Davenport. Bethany, two years behind us in school and graduating just before I moved back to Chicago, went to Drake for law school. Mary had picked up the other two on the way across on I-80.

Of the three, Susana was the one with whom I had most closely identified. Also taking a break after senior year, she had stumbled around from one retail job to the next, logging time at a department store makeup counter, a jewelry store, and a lingerie shop before she was discovered by a model scout. She moved to Los Angeles and found herself with steady work in print ads for everything from toothpaste to home electronics. She and I had seen advertising from the inside, albeit from two very different points of view.

Leading up to the weekend, everyone seemed to have different expectations for New Year's night. Mary, with a toddler at home, was the one most in need of a night out. She had researched the places to see and be seen in Chicago that still felt "normal," deciding that we needed to spend the evening bar-hopping on Division Street. Bethany was being a stick in the mud, worrying about being tired for the drive home on New Year's Day and the studying she needed to do before classes resumed. She wanted to go out for dinner and return to my apartment to hang out for the rest of the night. Susana had a list of clubs that modeling friends had told her about, and she never missed a chance to tell us about the ones where she said we'd have VIP access.

I had a lot to balance. I had no interest in bass-thumping techno music or hauling from crowded bar to crowded bar, paying covers. I didn't want to stay in, either. I took a risk, saying that I, being the only local, had the best line on something that would please everyone, and I convinced everyone to trust me with the plans.

After hitting the requisite tourist staples throughout the weekend, we took it easy around my apartment the morning of New Year's Eve. Through an indie label connection from my time on college radio, I was able to get tickets to the Flaming Lips show, with Wheat as the opening band. We got ready late in the afternoon, snacking as we preened, and got to Cabaret Metro when the doors opened. As it turned out, Susana wasn't the only one with VIP access. The friend, who'd been with Sugar Free records before they collapsed earlier that year, had made the jump to Aware and was working with Wheat on a collaborative major-label release with Columbia, due to come out in the next year. He set us up with roped-off balcony area access and promised to get us backstage after the show. I hoped that it was chill enough for Bethany, cool enough for Mary, and inside enough for Susana.

I wasn't entirely successful, as it became increasingly clear through the night. Bethany was having a nice enough time, it seemed, although she immersed herself in Wheat and didn't really socialize. She decided to take a cab back to my apartment during the break between acts. Mary really tried to keep up, but she, too, was done early and rode with Bethany back to my place.

Susana, on the other hand, was having a marvelous time. Someone recognized her from a contact lens ad, and she was swept into a horde of gawkers who kept her supplied with drinks and attention. I found myself alone by the time the Flaming Lips began.

Fortunately, being alone meant that I could get caught up in the music without paying much attention to anyone else's needs. It was an amazing show from the moment they took the stage. In addition to the requisite lights, smoke, and balloons, there were giant screens flashing myriad hallucinogenic images.

I had been a deep admirer of the band from well before their resurgent popularity that year. I must have aired every track from the *Clouds Taste Metallic* album at least twice when I was in school, so when they started out with "Lightning Strikes the Postman," I screamed with delight. It's a curious song, upbeat-sounding with a driving beat, but the lyrics are decidedly melancholic, about love and fate, miscommunications and squandered opportunities.

My screams drew the attention of a guy leaning on the railing just on the other side of the velvet rope. I gave him a cavalier smile and shrugged in non-apology, and he smirked in reply.

"Not just a bandwagon fan. That's great," he shouted.

"Middling, not hard-core," I shouted in reply.

Every time I go to a concert, I reprimand myself for not going more often. Nothing beats live music—watching artists create and interpret their work right before your eyes, letting it invade you, and sharing that common experience with the crowd.

The song ended, leading right into "Fight Test," a song about choosing what's worth fighting for. The way I always hear it, the person in the song has chosen not to fight, presumingly letting his adversary win. Who is the adversary, though? Is it a competing suitor for the one he loves, or is the object of his affections, in fact, the adversary? By ceding the choice, he loses, regardless. No one ever accused the Flaming Lips of writing bubble-gum pop lyrics, but they are real and they are pure.

The man on the other side of the velvet rope was clearly alone. It wasn't just that he was by himself, and not just that he wasn't looking around to keep tabs on anyone returning, but that he had a reaction, similar to the one I'd had for "Lightning," for this song. It was genuine, impetuous, and guileless—an uninhibited reaction of someone not the least bit concerned about making an impression on anyone around him.

"Alone on New Year's Eve?" I shouted at my neighbor.

"Beholden to no one," he replied. "Tough to keep track of a group at a show, anyway."

"I hear that. Two friends bailed after Wheat wrapped, and the third…" I motioned in Susana's direction.

"Like Scarlett at the Wilkes' picnic," he observed.

"That's about right," I laughed.

"What Floyd tune do you think they'll play?" he asked.

"It's not a lock, you know," I said.

"Wayne's a huge fan. I'm betting on 'Jugband Blues.'"

We didn't get the chance to shake on it before "Lucifer Sam" began.

"Good thing we didn't shake on it. I was totally going to call 'Lucifer Sam,'" I said.

"Sure you were," he smiled.

"I'm Mandelyn," I said, reaching over the rope to shake his hand.

"Magdalene, like Mary?"

"Man-Deh-Lynn."

"Mandolin?" he asked, air-strumming to pantomime the instrument.

"Closer," I surrendered.

"I would but this rope's in our way," he joked.

I smiled and, unhooking it, stepped out from the private party.

"Better?"

"A lot. I'm Henry."

The crowd cheered as "Lucifer Sam" concluded, but then lost it, collectively, with the opening chords of "Yoshimi Battles the Pink Robots Pt. 1."

"Things are about to get trippy," Henry said.

"About to?" I asked.

By this time, a parade of inflatable mascots and a menagerie of animal-costumed dancers had emerged and spread throughout the crowd. We swayed to the music, confidants among a crowd of increasingly ecstatic devotees, two sociological witnesses to the escalating Dionysian merriment below.

"It's almost a little cultish," I observed.

"When in Rome, I guess," Henry said.
"But we're in Wrigleyville."
"Hard to tell the difference sometimes," he said.
"True," I replied.
"First Flaming Lips show?" he asked.
"Yeah," I answered.
"Just wait till midnight."
"How many have you seen?" I asked.
"This is my first, too," he said. "I've just heard."

We didn't have to wait long. Coming out of "Yoshimi," the screens changed to midnight countdowns. Wayne was waxing philosophical about the band's love for the fans and the wonders that the last year had brought, but it was tough to hear him over the crowd's delirium. They began to play "Auld Lang Syne," and the crowd slowly chimed in.

"We're likely the only people here who aren't tripping balls or stoned," Henry noted.
"Speak for yourself," I joked.
"Really?" he asked.
"Kidding… dumb joke," I replied.
"I was going to say… You seemed like you had your head about you. Didn't want to feel like I was taking advantage."
"What do you mean?"
"I'm kissing you at midnight," he said.
"Oh, you are, are you?"
"It's good luck. Did you have any other commitments to keep?"
"I guess I can oblige," I grinned.

As the last thirty seconds passed, he took my hands in his. We counted down the last minutes of the year as we looked into one another's eyes and drew together. The sensation between us was electric, like a magnetic field spiraling around us, dimming and blurring anything outside our shared atmosphere. At midnight, the ceiling exploded with hundreds of balloons, but we were oblivious to that and all the rest as we met.

At once, all that had come before that moment in time felt intentional, consequential, fated, as if an ancient truth had surfaced as a result of our union. This wasn't amalgamation; it was alchemy—transformative, a restoration of what we were always meant to be. The word "destiny" had never meant anything to me before that moment, but the definitions in my heart were all being rewritten as he gathered me into himself. This kiss was not lustful or disorienting. I felt centered, purposeful, and entirely alive. I didn't feel lost; I felt found—not by him, or even by me. I felt actualized, sentient for the first time in my life.

As we finally parted, I could feel his smile against my lips. I searched his eyes for corroboration—some evidence that I wasn't alone with the feelings alight inside me. The fire in his eyes was his testimony.

A gong was struck. "Race for the Prize" began.

"I don't know this one," I managed to say.

"Nothing I knew before this moment has any real significance to me right now," Henry said.

I could feel the mile-wide smile across my face. "I know."

"Happy New Year," said Henry.

"To the best one yet," I replied.

We continued to stand, searching each other's eyes for an indeterminate amount of time. Confetti accumulated shallowly at our feet. It appeared to be inches deep on the main floor below.

"Do you want a drink?" I finally managed to say. "I should introduce you to my friend."

"Sure," said Henry.

I reached behind my back to unhook the rope, and we both stepped inside. "In the Morning of the Magicians" had begun. The ponderings of the song—wondering about the meanings of love and hate, about whether any of it matters, still resonatate with me to this day.

I got two cups of water from the bar and handed one to Henry. Without any awkwardness, neither of us seemed to know exactly what to say. The sheepish smiles we exchanged were the permission we required to let the wordless exchanges be enough.

I saw Susana against the wall beside the ladies' bathroom door. The scene was too familiar. She was embroiled in a close-quarters exchange with a grungy, wild-haired man in a studded leather jacket and ratty acid-washed jeans. His right hand was beside her head as he leaned into her face, his left a wagging finger of castigation. For a girl who typically had her pick of the lot, Susana often managed to end up with the outliers, the dark-horse rebels, and the jerks.

I sank from my cloud as "She Don't Use Jelly" began to play. Of their entire catalogue, it was among their most popular songs, but it didn't rank as a personal favorite of mine. In any case, I was distracted, considering my options to help Susana when the repugnance leaned in to kiss her. She weaved to avoid the incoming filth, but he grabbed her chin, intent on infestation.

I'd seen enough and knew what to do. Tapping Henry on the arm to let him know my direction, I headed over toward my friend. Insinuating myself in between the two, I acknowledged the vermin and whispered into Susana's ear.

"I like your friend. Boy's got moves," I said sardonically.

"I'm in kind of a jam," she whispered in reply. "He came across as intense, but it turned kind of creepy all of a sudden."

"Seems so," I said, still in her ear. I turned around. "Who's your friend?" I asked over my shoulder to Susana.

"Rolf, this is Mandelyn."

"Charmed," I said. "Is that like the Nazi in *The Sound of Music* or the piano-playing Muppet dog?"

"Move along, bitch," he said with a thick Scandinavian accent. "You interrupted our conversation."

"Oh, dear. See, I have this New Year's resolution not to let anyone call me that this year. You're the one who'll need to move along."

"Come on, man," Henry said to Rolf from behind him.

"This don't involve you, Chalky," he said, snarling in Henry's direction.

I'll never know what possessed me. I kneed Rolf right in the groin, which buckled him. I met his falling frame halfway down with a right uppercut that caught him in his left cheekbone. Something fell out of Rolf's jacket pocket as he doubled over. For no reason I could articulate, I bent down and picked it up off the floor, stuffing it in my pocket. Commotion ensued as Henry rushed Susana and me into the bathroom and onlookers rushed in to part the two men. Security men swarmed in an instant, but the crowd was on Henry's side, vouching for him as a defender of "those chicks who were just talking to that punk Viking dude." The crowd cheered as they hauled Rolf down the stairs and out the door. Susana and I poked our heads out to see the last of the tumult die down. Wayne even seemed to acknowledge the disturbance from the stage below, with typical blissful mirth. "Come on. I love you guys. Let love rule this year, eh? All we have is now, after all, you know?"

The band began to play "All We Have is Now." The lyrics about meeting a man from the future, about something seemingly illogical being proven true, hit me squarely. Many of the songs in the set that night seemed to score the evening like we were characters in a movie. I ignored the lines about the bleak predictions the man from the future foretells. He explains how all we have is now and how we're not going to make it; that we were never meant to be, and to just enjoy the now.

"Is it just me," Henry asked us, "or has this whole night's set felt prophetic, or what?"

"Like our soundtrack," I half-agreed.

"I want to go," Susana mumbled, embarrassed. "Sorry, guys. That whole thing just kind of blew it for me. You should stay, though. I'll get a cab."

"No!" I objected. "The garbage is thrown out. Stay."

"They didn't even play the one song of theirs that I know," Susana said.

"The concert isn't over," Henry added.

As if on cue, their current hit, "Do You Realize," began. If you don't know the song, you have to look it up. It's a wonder, possibly the most romantic song, ever, at least for me.

We stood transfixed. Susana straightened up as we watched the balloons continue to float, fall, and rebound. Henry took my right hand. I put my left arm over Susana's shoulder. We stayed for the rest of the show. At the end of the night, Henry and I walked Susana down to Addison Street in search of a cab, passing Yak-Zies, Bernie's, and Casey Moran's, all still hopping, before walking past the McDonald's in the shadow of Wrigley Field. Once she was on her way, we looked at each other.

"My friend who got us the tickets said he'd get us backstage if we wanted. You game?"

"Absolutely, I am. Lead the way."

Our experience backstage was kind of a bust. The bands seemed really personable, especially considering that they'd just finished up a combined three-plus-hour show. It was just unbearably crowded. The shuffling of people to and fro was more of a hassle than a privilege.

As I put my hands in my pockets, I found whatever it was that had fallen out of Rolf's pocket. I pulled it out. It was a baggie, lined along the bottom edge with what appeared to be a heavy dime's worth of marijuana, and a little orange box—Zig-Zag rolling papers. Not knowing what else to do, I nudged Henry with my elbow and showed it to him. His eyes bugged out.

"Rolf's," I said in lighthearted defense. "You smoke?"

"Not really. You?" Henry responded.

I took no issue with pot. I'd passed on it all through school, not wanting to get caught and thrown off my team, or worse. Opportunities abounded at the brew pub, too, of course, but most of the frequent smokers were a clique unto themselves, which diminished the overall appeal.

"Never had quite the right opportunity, I guess," I finally answered.

"What do you say—to the victor go the spoils?"

"What, here?" I asked.

"Probably not the best, even though I'm sure it wouldn't draw attention."

"True. Where's your place?" I asked.

"South, near IIT."

"Ugh. That's far. My fire escape's pretty secluded. We could go there. I'm nearby—Lawrence and Magnolia."

We talked into the morning, hours after the two joints were long since exhausted. Faith and politics, work and school, fears and dreams. We touched with innocent affection—a brush here, an assurance there. The new moon rose that morning.

This is the place in the story where I ought to try and capture the intense conversation we had that night. It was the kind of conversation that happens between two people at exactly the right place, in the right time, under the right circumstances. That'd be nice, don't you think? You know how it feels when everyone says the right thing… the brilliant thing… the honest thing… when no one has any self-consciousness or pretentions?

I've captured sunsets and first kisses. Breakups and breakdowns. Racism and sexism and poverty. Extravagance and vanity and greed and corruption. Good sex and bad sex. Seized opportunities and opportunities missed. Challenges met, failed, struggled through, and conquered. Seductions. Laughter. Friendships. And loss, of others and of self.

Instead of trying to tell you what was said that night, I want you to imagine your own best conversation. Remember your walk with your best friend in the middle of the night. The talk with your new lover as you lay together, intertwined under Egyptian cotton sateen. The last lucid talk you had with a grandparent. That feeling that everything might just have the potential to be right with the world, somehow; that, for whatever else was happening, someone actually knew the real you. Understood you. Was entranced and amazed by you. And that you knew, understood, and were entranced and amazed by that person in turn. That feeling.

25

Wednesday: Vacation Day #5

    I finished writing sometime in the early-morning hours, nearly filling the journal. I decided, as I finally closed the book and lay down, that I was done in Sedona. I would go to West Fork at dawn for one more hike, and then I would head out of town. I'd reach Albuquerque by mid-afternoon if I didn't make any stops; early evening if I did.

    I had snacked as I worked into the night, so I wasn't all that hungry by morning. The last of the almond butter, bread, kefir and granola, and coffee would get me through the hike. I'd snack in the car and pick something up for lunch along the way, in Winslow or Gallup.

    I checked out and drove north toward the trailhead. After parking, I walked through the relic apple and cherry orchards and past the foundations and chimneys that remained of Mayhew's Lodge. A homespun tourist destination that had been renovated and expanded over its lifespan from the 1920s to the 1960s, it was where several actors, including Clark Gable and Jimmy Stewart, had stayed while in town to shoot westerns. It had burned to the ground in 1980; arson was suspected.

    Of any of my hikes in Sedona, this was the only one on which I'd wished I was visiting at a different time of year. The trees, while beautiful in their barren starkness against the sky and the red rock cliffs, are probably something to behold, full of leaves in the summer or fall, winds rustling through them, complementing the gurgle of the shallow creek. There are other reasons I should return—to see Boynton Canyon, Grasshopper Point, Slide Rock, and Crescent Moon Ranch, just to name a few. I might have to get back to Sedona someday.

If I drew any intuition from the lateral vortex supposedly at this site, it was the confirmation that it was my time to move on. Sedona had done wonders for me, but it was time to take that wondrousness out in to the world. There was just one more thing to do.

Heading just far enough from the trail to make a cairn that would not obstruct other hikers' views, I found a glen of ivy. I set the letter that I'd written to Sam on the ground. I stacked stones upon it, then I stood, stepped back, and regarded my work. After satisfying myself of the cairn's relative integrity, I turned, walked out of the canyon, got in the Jeep, and drove away.

~ ~ ~ ~ ~ ~ ~

Colette scheduled the meeting with Hank Bevrijden as soon as she saw his firm's press release about him. His was a firm she had always wanted to contact. The leadership was sensible, they produced serviceable designs and well-coordinated documents, they collaborated amicably with engineers and contractors, and they were especially well-known for their customer service. While all of that was admirable and rarer with every passing year, none of it differentiated them enough to get them into federal teaming arrangements. Now that they would also be able to help prime firms meet diversity requirements, it was time to start making some introductions.

There was little information to be found on the firm's website that Colette could use for pre-meeting research. The site's design was far more slick and sophisticated than their portfolio justified. Hank's marketing angle, she thought, should be one about identifying challenges and devising practical solutions, not a play for conceptual design.

Colette sat in the lobby, a bright, open, modern space which was, again, unexpected, given her perceptions of the firm's staid reputation. She fluffed her hair and tried to ignore the fact that the receptionist, a brooding yet striking woman—Italian, she thought—was staring at her, glancing away whenever Colette would try to catch her in the act.

As he approached her, Colette was struck by one undeniable fact: Hank was hot. This didn't make any specific difference to her at nine o'clock on a Wednesday morning, but it did take the sting off of the two-hour Eisenhower commute.

As he showed her around the office, she knew she shouldn't wonder but couldn't help it. What *was* Hank, exactly? He'd checked the African-American box on the application, but there was more to his look than that. She thought Spanish at first, with the light eyes and caramel skin, but he was particularly tall and more broadly built than any Spaniard she'd ever met. His last name sounded like something from the Eastern Bloc—maybe that was it? She was fascinated and distracted, but she told herself to shake it off.

"So, how long have you been here?" Colette asked as they looked out over the Chicago River and Michigan Avenue.

"Just two years. We picked up the space for well below market value. I don't think they'd want me to say the word 'vulture,' but…"

"No, not that," Colette laughed. "I mean…"

"Oh, the firm. They were founded when the principals left their former company, just after the recession bottomed out in '82."

"No, Hank, you! When did you join the firm?"

Now it was Hank's turn to smile. "Right after I finished my Master's at IIT. I was with Antonosov and Colson for an internship through my final year, but they didn't choose to keep me on."

"Their loss. Nobody likes those guys!" Colette exclaimed. "Look at what you've built here. I know that this place basically subsisted for two decades, only managing to double in the years since you came on board. At A and C, you'd be just another cog until you were fifty."

"It is nice to stand out, I guess," Hank replied.

"And now you're President of a new subsidiary. But why go MBE/DBE now? This office is sustaining its volume, it seems. How many do you have on staff?"

"They have twenty-one—or, I guess they had twenty-one. We're still sorting out how the staff will separate into the two companies. Our founders and the new board would like to see us expand, now that the worst of the recession is hopefully behind us."

"You and every other outfit in town. You know what makes you different?"

"Melanin?"

Colette was unflustered by his attempt at self-deprecation. "Honesty. I love it. No. There are plenty of crappy companies with horrible reputations who fall back on their gender or ethnicity instead of earning their work. You're in an elite group of professionals, Hank. You have an established reputation in your wheelhouse markets. You deserve more, and you're doing what it takes to get a toe hold. Some people do it by talent acquisition, others do it by lobbying, and others yet do it by buying it with bargain-basement fees. If you're going to be any one of those kinds of firms, I can't help you."

"We're not."

"Good. I didn't think so. So, I have to ask. What's your heritage?"

"I'm Dutch," Hank said without any apparent irony.

"You identified as African-American on your applications. I'm not trying to be nosy. I just need to know what story to tell. If I'm going to represent you to other firms, I need the details, not just the surface-level stuff."

"Alright. I'm Sint Maartener by my paternal grandmother, Netherlands Dutch by my paternal grandfather, Cape Verdean by my maternal grandfather, who immigrated to Rotterdam, and Dutch-American by my maternal grandmother."

"That's quite a melting pot," Colette marveled.

"Tell me about it. I was raised by my mother on the south side of Milwaukee. I got out as quickly as I could and didn't look back."

"That's so sad," Colette said. "That you felt like you had to get out, I mean."

"I suppose. I had a lot of respect for the hard work that my mother did to keep the two of us fed and clothed, but she had her own battles to fight. Nothing with drugs, alcohol, or anything like that. Just sad, you know. Bitter and tired. I knew if I stayed, I'd be pulled under, too."

"You went to Iowa State and got a degree in Architecture, turned right around and got your Master's from IIT."

"I started at MATC—Milwaukee Area Technical College—while I worked as a laborer. I worked through undergrad in a factory in Ames, and I put the money aside. I delivered pizzas when I moved to Chicago, but mostly I lived off savings and racked up more student loan debt."

"And a dual M.S. in Architecture and Civil/Environmental Engineering."

"Took me four years instead of three, but it's been worth it."

"Overachieve much, Hank?"

He smiled.

Colette motioned to the picture of the dogs on the credenza. "My friend has two rescue Pit Bulls. Are yours rescue?"

He looked cheerfully at the picture over his shoulder. "They are. Frank and Lloyd," he said.

"What did you say?"

He chuckled. "After the architect. Really original, I know."

"My girlfriend's dogs are named Frank and Lloyd."

Hank and Colette stared at each other for a moment, calculating.

"Is this your friend?" Hank held up his wedding photo.

"Holy shit. You're Henry."

"Col? I always assumed you were named Colleen, or Nicole maybe."

"I always assumed you were named Ziegel."

"That's Mandelyn's family name. She wanted to keep it after her dad died."

"She'd mentioned you were an engineer. I always assumed you were related to the Lab, somehow."

"Nope."

"And you're very tan in that picture. I've seen that picture. You look like Denzel in that one, but you look like Channing Tatum sitting here in front of me."

"Channing Tatum?"

"*Public Enemies*? *Stop-Loss*? Trust me; it's a compliment."

"I guess that's better than being compared to A-Rod or Tiger." Hank was clearly flustered.

Colette was still trying to figure out how she hadn't known this small-world connection. "What's with Hank? Mandelyn calls you Henry."

"The guys in the office called me Hank when I started here, because there was already another Henry. It stuck."

"Holy shit," Colette said, astonished.

"Yeah," he agreed.

"Small world."

"You said it."

"So…" Colette found herself in the highly unusual position of not knowing what to say. "How are you?"

"Have you heard from her?" he asked carefully.

"I've gotten texts. Pictures of Sedona, mostly. I think she's driving to Albuquerque today or tomorrow."

"Can I see them? The pictures?"

"I guess so. It's all rocks and trees and sunsets, really."

Colette handed her phone to Henry. He flipped through the pictures, scanning back through them in reverse before handing the phone back across the table.

"She loves you, you know. I just think she's lost track of how to show you so."

Henry sat silently for a moment, contemplating.

"So this is Theodore's," Colette stated more than asked, motioning to the ball and glove.

"They were going to be. The hat is his."

"Henry, is there anything I can do?"

"I just wish she'd call."

"She's been writing in a journal, she said. She went to meditate at a Buddhist shrine of some sort, and she attended a service at Chapel of the Holy Cross."

"That's Catholic, right?" Henry asked.

"I think so."

"I've tried to call her, and I know the service is terrible out there," Henry said.

"Maybe that's why she hasn't called."

"Maybe," Henry sighed.

Colette couldn't tell for sure, but she thought Henry looked a little bleary-eyed and choked-up. "Look, we can talk more another time. I should let you get back to your day. I've already taken too much of your time."

"Your presentation—we didn't even get to what you came here to do," Henry said.

RELEASE

"I think maybe I did, even though neither of us knew it. Don't worry, Henry—or Hank. Whatever. I'm a closer," she said with an entirely chaste wink. "I'll be in touch again."

Colette showed herself out of the office and, glancing around for a place where she could go to calm her nerves, she headed off to recollect herself before the rest of her day's appointments.

~ ~ ~ ~ ~ ~ ~

I took 89A into Flagstaff, picked up Milton Road, and bore right onto Route 66 until it merged with the interstate east of town. I felt as if I was betraying my father's muscle car legacy, but the first portion of my experience with America's Highway wasn't doing it for me. I knew that much of I-40 wasn't directly on the original alignment, but it was close enough to approximate the view, which was desolate—overcast, flat, and bleak. I took the Two Guns exit and saw what remained of some original pavement, but I didn't entertain the idea of driving it, since it was rockier than the trails I'd taken to Palatki or up to Devil's Bridge. I drove past Standin' On The Corner Park in Winslow, and I got off the interstate to take Main Street through Joseph City and past the Jackrabbit Trading Post, but nothing I saw was really living up to the hype.

The upside was that I was making excellent time. At a quick lunch stop in Holbrook, near Wigwam Village, I got the advice to take 180 southeast out of town and to pick up the southern entrance to the Petrified National Forest. I'd drive through the Rainbow Forest, along Puerco Ridge to the Painted Desert, around the loop road past the lookout points, see the famous Painted Desert Inn, and rejoin I-40 at the opposite end. Without stops, it would only add about an hour to the trip. I decided to take the scenic route.

The skyline began to take on a little more variety at this point, although there was nothing on the horizon that excited me about the drive ahead. Mesas, buttes, and plateaus rose from the horizon like so many suburban skyscrapers. At the turn into the park, signs, each more gaudy than the last, advertised "T-shirts 3 for $10," "Free Petrified Wood," "Navajo Blankets $4," "Kachina Treasures," and the like. I was beginning to regret the decision to prolong my travels.

What I found inside the park, however, was pretty astonishing. The landscape was lunar in places, Martian in others. The iridescent, massive petrified trees glistened in the icy blue sunlight. Unlike the timelessness I had felt in Sedona, the long-fallen trees and eroded badlands were a metaphor of impermanence. I'd never felt smaller or less significant, as if my existence were hardly a punctuation mark on a page, in a volume, of a set of books, in a library of every book ever written. Yet somehow, accepting these feelings gave me a sense of calm and resolve. I was reminded of Psalm 23:

> *The Lord is my shepherd; I shall not want.*
> *He maketh me to lie down in green pastures: he leadeth me beside the still waters.*
> *He restoreth my soul: he leadeth me in the paths of righteousness for his name's sake.*
> *Yea, though I walk through the valley of the shadow of death, I will fear no evil: for thou art with me; thy rod and thy staff they comfort me.*

I was also reminded of a promise I had made to myself the night before. I needed to call Henry.

~ ~ ~ ~ ~ ~ ~

He hadn't gotten anything done all day. With the recent reorganization, he had spent more time away from design matters than he had in his entire adult life. Contractual agreements, business models, and marketing plans had nearly blinded him, as much because of their small print as because of their astounding banality. Reading and editing yet another document after Colette left in such a hurry that morning seemed like an impossibility. He yearned for a structural challenge to resolve, not another SWOT analysis to study.

He took another bite of the honeycrisp apple, the third that he'd had in as many days. Zara had brought them to the office on Monday, a feat made more challenging because she'd had to haul them in what appeared to be a gunnysack over her left shoulder all the way around Wacker Drive. By the time they reached LaSalle, he had offered to carry it for her. While it was an offer made in earnest, he hadn't supposed that she would take him up on it. His lower back still ached.

Just then, Zara poked her head in the doorway. "Is now a good time?" she asked.

"As good a time as any. The archaic language in this commitment agreement isn't going to get any older if I look away for a moment. What's up?"

"I saw that you're off for the next few days. I wanted to make sure I had the chance to say Merry Christmas to you."

"Well, Merry Christmas, fellow commuter. I'm glad you came on board with us this year."

"I'm on board during auspicious times, I think. You're going places, Hank."

"Yeah, to the optometrist. It's funny that our profession awards design excellence by burying high achievers in spreadsheets and prospect lists."

Zara seemed to find this disproportionately funny, but it was nice to be found humorous.

"Do you have any plans for the holidays?" he asked her.

"I'll go back to Iowa for the weekend. I got out of it over Thanksgiving, but I promised family that I'd be back at least for the two days."

"What part of the state?"

"Des Moines, which is just as exciting as it sounds."

"Oh, yeah? I…" Henry began, but Zara interrupted him.

"I wanted to give you something. You made a comment about it, so I thought I'd go back into the studio and make you a little something."

She handed him a gift bag festooned with tissue paper and curled ribbons. Drawing all of that back, he reached in to find a candle in a glass.

"I used to make them for a living, along with perfumes, incenses, lotions, oils, and stuff."

Before Henry had inhaled, he was already transported. He could hear the Flaming Lips, see her smile, feel her hand on his forearm. He could see her breath in the cold morning of New Year's Day, feel their legs intertwined as they sat on the fire escape, his head abuzz and unlocked. He could hear her applaud and her father whistle through two fingers at his graduation. He could taste dinners and kisses, feel embraces and touches, hear laughter—giggles, cackles, even snorts.

He could see her on their wedding day. And his heart sank. "What have I done?" he asked himself.

"Is something wrong, Hank? I hope it doesn't come on too strong," Zara said.

Hank spoke slowly. "Is there any chance you ever sold to a shop in Weston?"

Zara seemed bewildered. "I did. It's been years. I had a… good friendship with the owner. He was my *simpatico*, but we had a parting of ways. He died not long afterward." Zara looked aside, out the windows across from Hank's office, wistfully.

"God's Gift," he said to himself.

"What?" Zara asked. "I couldn't hear you."

"I have to go," Hank said, rising abruptly, crossing to the rack in the corner for his coat and hat. Attempting in the next beat to disguise his urgency, he turned to Zara. "Thank you for this. It's exactly what I needed. Merry Christmas," he said, giving her a firm handshake, brushing past her as she remained, immovable, in the doorway.

His phone rang as soon as he was out of earshot. Zara had been away from her desk for more than ten minutes. She wondered how many other calls had bounced to the auto-attendant, callers left to route their own calls directly. It was very important to ownership that all calls be received by a live voice.

She crossed behind Hank's desk to make a degree of amends, answering the call on the fourth ring. "SJG Bev-ridden, this is Zara," she stuttered, straightening her throat. The new firm name was a mouthful.

"Who?" said the voice on the other end of the line.

"Zara, ma'am,"

There was a pause before the voice, static-garbled, said, "No, not you. What firm?"

"Oh, they just had us start answering his calls that way last week. You've reached the phone of Hank Bev-ridden. Can I be of assistance?"

"Well, first of all, you're mispronouncing it. It's bear-FRY-den. Second, can you let me know where Henry might be or how I might reach him?"

"Hank has left for the holiday, I believe," Zara guessed.

It was hard to tell, but Zara heard what she thought was an exasperated sigh. "You don't know for sure?"

"He left just a few moments ago, and he's… I'm sorry. I don't know who you are."

Another exasperated sigh. "I am Mandelyn Ziegel. I'm his wife. Would you please put me through to Henry's voice mail?"

Perfunctorily, Zara responded, "Yes, of course, Ms… Ziegel."

The woman at her condo the week before had introduced herself as Delyn, but Dante had called her Ziegel through the early morning hours. She had to be the same person. Zara had written off the coincidence of it also being Nik's last name, trying to convince herself that the name was more common than it really was, in fact.

If there had been any doubt of the connection, the picture before her made everything clear. In it, the two of them were radiant. So, Hank was married to Nik Ziegel's daughter. But if that was the case, where was his ring?

~ ~ ~ ~ ~ ~ ~

"Henry, it's Mandelyn. Look, it took me all week to get the courage up to call you. I was awake most of the night, writing to you. Well, I was writing about you, but also to you. I was writing about us. There's so much I want to say, but I don't think my signal is very strong. The light's fading here, too. I need to get on the road. I'll call you tomorrow, when I…" I remembered that I hadn't ever made my location known to him. "… when I wake up tomorrow morning. Hopefully, I'll catch you. I love you, Henry. Goodbye."

It was three o'clock. With any luck, I'd be able to take 118, the original Route 66 alignment, from the state line through Defiance and on to Gallup before dusk fell. The terrain would become more mountainous as I approached the Continental Divide. I didn't want to find myself too far off-course after dark.

At the exit for 118, I happened upon the Yellowhorse Trading Post. I might have driven right by, except that I had a taste for beef jerky. My mom always said that the best beef jerky in the Southwest is at the roadside stands, not in the stores, just like boiled peanuts in the South and fruit in the Southeast.

I was never much of a souvenir-buyer, which meant that this place was not my scene. I did a cursory search around the store to see if there was anything of genuine value that I might want to bring to my mom for Christmas. She was never one for trinkets, holding a general disdain for anything outside of my father's core business, and a particular disapproval of the curios he stocked in order to draw new customers. "If a lady wants to buy cigars, a pipe, tobacco, that's great. But what does that have to do with collectibles, which are called that because they do nothing but collect dust? Statuettes with no artistic consideration, snow globes, picture frames, magnets, and key chains—ugh. And perfumes, candles, lotions, and oils, now?"

I discovered a sign while looking around the shop's outer edges.

<u>Hozho</u>
The nature of the universe, as the Navajo understand it, is expressed:

Sa'ah naaghai bik'eh hozho
This phrase exemplifies a model of balance in living:
Static Male and Active Female
Father Sky and Mother Earth
All is impermanent; creation is its own artistry: therein lies its beauty

May the wisdom of age bring you into harmony with the beauty of existence.

The Navajo paradigm of Hozho seemed to mirror my mom's philosophy and mine. My mom did like Native American jewelry, and the store's collection of artisan-crafted pieces was among the most beautiful I'd seen throughout my trip. I found a sterling silver bracelet with three sugilite stones for her. I also chose some malachite earrings for Colette, a spiral brooch for Eshe, matching turquoise tie tacks for Joshua and Reynard, and a pair of lapis-coral-jet-cobbled inlay cufflinks for Henry. I had the bracelet gift-wrapped, and I shipped the earrings, brooch, and tie tacks, enclosing the latter with Joshua's letter and scribbling brief thanks and wishes of holiday cheer for the others. I would hold on to the cufflinks, hoping that I would have the occasion to give them to Henry in person, one way or another.

26

I pulled up to Mom's northeast-side townhouse, beneath the Sandia Mountains, just after eight o'clock. It was fun to surprise her; I am not sure if George felt the same way. I had clearly interrupted a date, or, at the very least, his attempt to fabricate one from a contrived circumstance. They hadn't been home for long, judging from the coats they were still wearing and the keys in George's hand. I offered to call the car rental place to see if I would be able to get a lift back if I dropped off the Jeep that night, but my mom volunteered George for the task.

So there I was, making small talk with a seventy-year-old retired biology teacher from Omaha as we drove back to the townhouse. I carried most of the conversation, giving nothing but the most superficial account of my trip. He dropped me off without coming inside, a relief to me as well as Mom.

"He's very sweet, just a little wishy-washy," she said. "He is new in town and still getting his social bearings. Speaking of which, are you tired, or do you have it in you to stay up and start telling me about your travels, dear?"

"What do my travels have to do with social bearings?"

"Oh, I just meant bearings, in general, I guess. Wasn't that the whole idea behind going to Sedona? To find your bearings?"

"When you put it that way, I guess so," I said. "Just let me unpack and change into pajamas."

"You have pajamas?"

"I do… Well, a t-shirt and a pair of yoga pants. It's a little creepy that you know to ask that."

"Honey, you've been a naked sleeper for as long as I've known you."

"Wow," was all I could manage to say, laughing, before going back to the spare room.

The antique furniture set I'd had since birth filled the room. After I changed, I checked under the side rail of the four-post bed to see if the note I'd tucked into the slats was still there. I checked every time I visited. Yep, still in place.

> *To be opened twenty years from today*
> *ONLY by Ms. Mandelyn Katharine Ziegel*
> *NO EXCEPTIONS!!*

Violating my own warning, I supposed that I was finally close enough to the date to open the letter. I honestly couldn't remember what I had written.

> *December 31*
>
> *Dear M,*
>
> *Hello, future Me! It's hard to see a whole TWENTY YEARS in the future, but on this New Year's Eve, I'm feeling like this year's resolutions should go farther into the future than they have in years before. Here and now is pretty good (as you probably remember). I've got my early acceptance to college, my second semester classes aren't going to be too hard, and once Debate is done in the spring, I can coast if I want to and still be fine for the fall.*
>
> *The guidance counselors tell us to always be setting goals and striving toward new achievements, so I am going to write down the kinds of things I think I want in the years to come. I'm sure that stuff will change as I get older, but at least I'll have an idea of where to start. If anything, this will be hilarious to read when I'm more than twice as old as I am now (that hardly seems possible!).*

RELEASE

1. I want to graduate from college with honors. Tassels and Latin words after a name are cool.
2. I want to leave some legacy at college, like an award that gets my name on a plaque somewhere.
3. I want to meet my husband and be engaged before I graduate.
4. I want to have my family early so that I am not too old to have a life after my kids—a boy and a girl—are grown.
5. I want to have the kind of job that lets me make good money but also still have a life.
6. I want a hot car, like a 1965 Ford Falcon Futura convertible, original blue, that my dad and I can restore.
7. I want to be an urban pioneer in an up-and-coming neighborhood, like Ukrainian Village or Bucktown.
8. I want to keep up with volleyball after college, like on a league.
9. I want to stay life-long friends with my volleyball girls and my debate buddies!
10. I hope that you aren't that grey or wrinkled yet, and that you don't have as many chin hairs as Grammy or Aunt Marcy.

That's enough for now. Stay awesome, and good luck!

Love,

M

For crying out loud, I thought. How self-absorbed was I back then? I was just as taken aback by how little my goals were going to truly challenge me, as I was by how vapid and flimsy the foundation was on which they were based, as well as by how few of them I had actually accomplished.

I'd give myself a break on 1 and 2. I think I was trying to be cute by quantifying my general goals of working hard and winning by tying them to something tangible. Still, I had achieved only one out of two. As for 3, it was a different time, in which life's priorities changed in an instant. I knew plenty of people like me who had changed their plans for domesticity after a month at college.

I skipped consideration of the ridiculous 4, dwelling instead on the insipid 5. Who sets out to be mediocre like that? I knew that part of what had been behind my thought process was my dad's mid-life crisis and corporate exodus, but really? Where might I have been by now if I hadn't hedged my bet from the get-go? Still, I was batting .400, having failed 4 but achieved 5, whatever path I took to get to that point.

The car, 6, hadn't happened, and I didn't regret it, either. A fifty-year-old ragtop wasn't the least bit practical with two dogs and winter driving conditions. That wish had more to do with spending more time with my dad than the car itself. As for 7, I had lived in Ukrainian Village, albeit after moving in with Henry. Uptown, my first neighborhood, wasn't exactly sunshine and rainbows at the time, so I still counted that as a goal achieved. I chalked up my win rate as five-ish out of seven.

Of 8, 9, and 10, it was fail, fail, and… succeed, at least most days. Six-ish out of ten was still above even. None of it meant very much, though. Where was anything related to a strong faith, service to others, or a life without regrets? How did the most important people in my life find the person who had written this list "courageous?"

My mom came into the room, slowly but without knocking. "I wondered if you had found that," she said.

"You knew it was there?"

"We took the bed apart to move it here, so sure. I didn't open it, though. Anything interesting?"

"How spoiled was I?"

"Pretty spoiled," she laughed. "You were the only child of two reasonably successful parents, raised in an ivory tower among people just as fortunate and even less exposed to the world than yourself. You felt as if you understood the world because of all the diverse, international contract workers and consultants, maybe, but you never saw poverty, famine, violence—struggle of any kind, really, until you sought it out for yourself."

"My idea of urban pioneering was getting an apartment in Bucktown."

"I wish you had. If you'd bought there when you moved back to Chicago, you could have retired on the sale of it."

"Not quite, but I know what you mean. I've done just fine, regardless," I sighed.

"Are you kidding? Better than fine! I'm so proud of you. My friends are sick of me bragging about you."

"My job is to hype when other people create and discover great things. I don't create or discover anything of my own. What do I contribute?"

"I'm not going to let you feel sorry for yourself for leaving advertising. What did you create there? Artificial need. You manufactured want. You created diversion and distraction. Honey, if you were digging ditches or cleaning streets, I'd be proud of you if you were living your passion, but I'm far more pleased with your place in the world than I was before."

"I have a fallback job, Mom. I gave up—threw in the towel."

"You are the voice of the humble and inhibited—the promoter of rock stars in the world of theoretical physics. You work among geniuses every day—people who have dedicated their lives to discovering the nature and origins of the universe. You can't write a better job description than that, and no one I know is better suited to doing it."

I smiled. "I never thought about it that way."

"Now come out and sit with me. Tell me what you discovered during your vision quest," she said.

We talked late into the evening. Basically, I downloaded every last detail of my trip as raw data. Exhaustion began to set in before either of us could really sort the information or draw any conclusions.

Resolving to sort it all out in the morning over Frontier cinnamon rolls, she told me about the plan for the day. It would begin early with a hot yoga class, which I was entirely receptive to after my day-long drive. After breakfast, we would head to the Open Space Visitor's Center to be part of this year's Solstice Mandala creation.

In honor of the solstice, several of my mom's SF friends were participating in the creation of a mandala, a 90-foot-wide mural on the ground, an offering to the indigenous and migratory wildlife, a symbol of the turning of the seasons, and a tribute to the rebirth of the sun—with a schematized representation of the cosmos. It seemed like as reasonable a celebration as any.

"Mandalas carry on the spirit of Navajo and Tibetan sand paintings. We'll use corn, millet, sunflower seeds, alfalfa, and other grains. The birds will eat from the mandala, and what's left will compost as the creation fades away," my mom explained.

Next, we would go to Old Town to do a little shopping before indulging in the rite of green chile-laden foods and sopapillas. In the evening, we would attend a Wheel Walk. The confused look on my face drew my mom to explain.

"*Iul* is the Norse word for 'wheel,' from which we derive the word for Yule, the festival celebrating the light returning after the darkest hour. The wheel, or labyrinth, represents life's trinities. Wheels take all kinds of forms, depending on the culture from which the traditions are derived. The path of the wheel we will follow winds through three spirals. Traveling the path is meant to bring your spirit back into balance, allowing the full power of their interplay to restore your own connectivity to the world."

In a lighthearted way, I sort of wished that the universe would just shut up once it had made its point.

~ ~ ~ ~ ~ ~ ~

The yoga class was everything I needed it to be. It included a plank sequence that somehow resulted in side crow, a *prasarita* component that rolled into *skandasana*, and an open-hearted half-moon variation that launched into birds of paradise as the peak pose. After twists and plow pose, *savasana* included a cool forehead towel infused with bergamot and lime oils.

I almost felt guilty about the cinnamon roll we ate afterward. Almost. Every city has its favorite, you know. Ours in Chicago is Ann Sather's, hands-down, but nothing compares to the one at Frontier.

It was clear that Mom had thoughts to share, but she didn't intend to come right out with them. That was never her style. She had a way of making you follow her logical path to its inevitable conclusion, making you feel as if what you wanted to know was inside you all along.

"So, do you think that your apprehension about having a baby is at the root of your disconnection from Henry?" she began.

"I don't know if it's that simple, but it's a big part of the puzzle, yeah."

"Is it birthing a child or raising a child that fuels your fear?"

"The gestating, really," I said.

"Have you talked about adoption?"

"I haven't had the nerve to bring up the subject."

"Why are you afraid of talking to Henry about things like this?" she asked. "Wouldn't it be better to know how he feels than to endlessly wonder?"

"I want to want to have a baby with Henry. I just can't imagine failing again."

"Every doctor confirmed that what happened before couldn't have been predicted, almost never happens, and doesn't have any bearing on the possibility of it happening again."

"But I'm four years older now," I protested. "I was high-risk because of age back then. My odds of success diminish every day."

"Your complication was not age-related. In every other respect, you're healthier than most people, even those ten or fifteen years younger than you."

"It's not my head I need to convince."

"You don't think Henry trusts you, do you?" she asked. "And not just with a baby."

"There's no good reason he should."

"'Faith is confidence in what we hope for and assurance about what we do not see.'"

"Hebrews 11. I know," I said.

"Do you? Do you have the faith to believe that Theodore's passing happened for a reason?"

"Who's to say that the reason wasn't to prevent me from trying to conceive again?"

"The foolishness of presumption. Where would you be if I'd reached a similar conclusion?"

That stopped me in my tracks. It took me a moment to figure out what she was saying. "What do you mean?" I asked stupidly.

"Did you ever find it odd that you were an only child?"

"Not particularly."

"I think that's because you sensed you were meant to be," she reasoned. "You are here, however, because I chose to rise above my fear, garner my own courage, and… try again."

I felt all the muscles in my face slacken as I processed what Mom was saying. "You lost a baby?"

"Sebastian."

I could feel my eyes welling, and I glanced around the room to ward off tears. I took both of Mom's hands in mine, swallowed hard, and finally managed to ask, "Why didn't you tell me?"

"When it comes to processing grief, you don't exactly come from good stock. I didn't think that interjecting my own flawed experiences into your situation would do anything but derail you."

"But what about when I was a child? I never even heard his name. I've never seen a picture."

"Do you have pictures of Theodore?"

"A few," I admitted. Henry had wanted more, but I barely allowed the few to be taken. I thought it was morbid to take pictures of a dead baby.

"Do you have them on display?"

"They're in an album on a shelf in my bedside table."

"Like mother, like daughter," she said.

"Where is he?"

"In the Calvary Church graveyard."

"In your hometown? Why there, not here?" I asked.

"We still lived there when he died. We intended to stay, but I wasn't coping very well. Your father thought that if we got a fresh start somewhere new, we could be happy again. That's why we moved to Weston."

"Why Weston?"

She smiled. "When we visited Weston, it felt like home—and also completely different from home at the same time."

I didn't know how to ask the next question, exactly. "Did it work? Were you happy?"

"Baby, I've led a life of good fortune, comfort, and privilege. I have few regrets. I have you, I have my family, and I have a wonderful network of friends now. It took a long time to get to this place in my life, and whatever it took for me to get here has been worth it."

"You didn't answer my question."

"But I did. Was there instant gratification? Was it all highs and no lows? Was it all safety and no risk? No disappointments, failures, or devastations? Of course not," she said. "A life like that is not a life lived."

I sat still and thought for a moment. "You weren't happy for a long time, were you?"

"Not for a long time," she echoed.

"You didn't really have many friends in Weston, did you? Of your own, I mean—not just Daddy's friends' wives, clients, or my friends' parents?"

"Not really."

"You didn't go out very often," I said.

"Nope, except when…"

"Except when it came to me and fulfilling obligations."

"You've got it."

"So when Daddy died…"

"I realized it was 'go' time." Mom smiled again. "I didn't have anyone to live vicariously through anymore. You had a life of your own, between your work and your growing relationship with Henry, and Nik's passing cleared my slate. That is one of my few regrets—that I let his passing make my decision for me—for not deciding for myself to be fully alive again. It's not that I would have left if I'd learned that lesson sooner. It's that I would have conscientiously made the choice to be happy, or gotten help toward being happy, instead of drifting along, month to month, year to year, waiting for the direction of my life to be determined for me."

"That's why you didn't stay in Weston or move back to Iowa."

"That's the reason. It's like praying and church. You don't have to be in any certain place to bow your head, but it sure makes it easier if you have the right surroundings. I needed the right surroundings to start anew."

"Why Albuquerque, then?" I asked. "You could have gone anywhere."

"I think that'll be easier to explain once you see the mandala. Come on; it's time to go."

~ ~ ~ ~ ~ ~ ~

When we arrived, people were already setting out bags and barrels of red, yellow, white, green, blue, and black seeds. Others were using hoes and shovels to outline the area I presumed would be our canvas. George was there, along with other SF friends to whom I was graciously introduced. I was hugged several times, and I was told things like, "I feel as if I already know you," "You truly are your mother's daughter," "I've heard so much about you," and the like.

I was taken aback by the age range of those gathered for the event. There were a few toddlers, several school-aged children and teenagers, on up to men and women who could have been my grandparents. The common thread was that everyone was happily busy.

It wasn't long before a few leaders stepped forward and displayed the plan the group had devised. They gave simple instructions, such as to walk lightly over the mandala to keep from scattering the seed already laid, to respect the work of others, and to patiently help one another, especially the newcomers. They had general guiding principles, but the final piece was everyone's creation.

Work proceeded methodically and rapidly, with surprisingly little conversation. Everyone was of like mind, purpose-driven and resolute. It was like watching ants build a hill. When the piece was finished two hours later, the collage of stars, spirals and chevron stripes was something to behold.

It was shocking, then, that as we were finishing, flocks of sandhill cranes and Canada geese began to arrive and feast, as if on schedule. I was reminded of how seagulls started to swarm over Wrigley Field during the bottom of the ninth inning of day games. They, like the cranes and geese, innately knew that the banquet was imminent. "Why isn't anyone disturbed or upset about the flocks?" I asked Mom. "I mean, I understand why the adults aren't too bothered, but you'd think that the kids would be mad that their work is being destroyed."

"If anything, I understand the children's serenity more than that of the adults. Children make mudpies, wildflower bouquets, sandcastles, jack-o-lanterns, and snowmen. Their art is in the creation, not its endurance. The process is its own reward. Adults forget this, which is why they so rarely make any of those things on their own. Some of them pick it up again when they have children to make them with together, but most don't bother to take the time."

I had to think hard to remember the last time I had made any of those things. "Like Hozho," I mumbled.

"And circle gets the square! Did you learn about that during your travels?" Mom asked.

"That and so many other things," I replied.

"Can't wait to hear more. Are you ready for Old Town?" Mom asked.

"Actually, what if we saved that for Friday? I sort of want to rest before the walk tonight. Besides, Old Town is our Christmas Eve tradition."

"Tradition, even without..."

"Maybe especially without. The fact is that he isn't here, Mom. I don't want to cede ownership of our tradition to Henry. It's yours and mine."

"Fair enough," she said, somewhat aloof. "I could use a disco nap myself."

"Mom, seriously?"

"What? You didn't think that was your generation's idea, did you?"

Once we got home, I lay down, thoroughly exhausted. Before I drifted off to sleep, I did two things. First, I texted Henry: Enjoying ABQ. Wish you were here.

Then, I reached into my makeup bag, retrieved my ring, and put it back on. With or without him here, I wanted to believe, at least for the night, that we could be together once again.

~ ~ ~ ~ ~ ~ ~

Mom woke me in time enough to get ready, eat a sandwich she'd prepared, and make the walk to the Elena Gallegos Double Shelter Amphitheater. It was only about two miles from her place, but it took us most of an hour to get there because of the climb into the foothills. It wasn't a walk I was looking forward to making back in the dark, but Mom assured me that we would be able to get a ride back with someone.

With a beautiful view of the valley below, a path descending from a massive picnic enclosure at the top of the site led to benches arranged on either side of an aisle, the edges of which were lined with weathered, squared timbers. The benches faced a large fire pit, nearly six feet in diameter, surrounded with flagstone wide about its perimeter. The sun was setting as we approached, and the fire was lit. Three circles—or, as I realized on closer examination, spirals—were mapped around the fire with a dull-glowing tape. Several people were milling about, making last-minute adjustments.

We took our seats as others began to arrive. Soon, a stout, cherry-cheeked woman in a long white robe stepped forward to indicate that we were about to begin.

"Good evening, everyone. I'm so pleased that you have chosen to celebrate the Winter Solstice with us here this evening. For those of you who haven't been with us before, I have a little history and background to share as we begin.

"The best way to start is by talking about the significance of the triskelion, which is among the most enigmatic of the ancient symbols. It is predominantly Celtic in origin, but similar images appear in cultures throughout all of Europe and Asia, from as early as 3000 B.C. These three interlocking spirals represent the perpetual cyclical momentum of progress toward understanding life's trinities, which, depending on who you ask, could be father-son-holy spirit, life-death-rebirth, mind-spirit-body, power-intellect-love, past-present-future, mother-father-child—the list goes on and on.

"Let me be clear: ours is not a pagan ritual. It is a blend of multiple cultures' celebrations, recognizing that this day has astronomical significance, literally and symbolically. The Earth has reached the turning point. From here, each day forward will be brighter and longer; the daylight of each new day will be a little stronger."

That sounded nice, I thought, literally and symbolically.

"The winter solstice occurs on the longest night of the year," she continued. "At night, we mortals dream. This is a time to reflect upon and celebrate the important things in life and to look forward to a wonderful year to come. Not all dreams are happy ones, of course. winter solstice can be a time to revisit the dark times that haunt us, tapping into our wisdom and intuition to relinquish the detrimental power past wrongs still hold.

"In darkness, there is also chaos—strife, loneliness, and confusion. As hard as we try to force order upon the chaos of our lives, we finally learn to accept this fact: it is from chaos that beauty and order can emerge, if we are alert to the signs. When mired in chaos, we have the choice to either deny it and hide from it, or we can explore it, seek to understand it, and use what we learn to shape new perceptions.

"At this time, I would ask everyone to stand and gather with us around the bonfire," she said.

I got the feeling that I was one of only a few newcomers, or perhaps the only one. As I'd glanced around at the faces of my fellow solstice celebrants, I had seen a lot of serene faces and nodding heads. I hadn't seen George, but I recognized others from the mandala-building earlier.

"Is this when the animal sacrifice begins?" I asked Mom.

"Shhhh," she hushed, although unstirred. "Trust me. You'll enjoy this more if you appreciate it for what it is, instead of resisting it or judging it."

I nodded to begrudgingly agree.

The woman in white continued. "The triskelion is fashioned about our bonfire; it is reminiscent of the 'oculus mundi,' the eye of the world through which our forbearers believed we could see our divinity and that divinity could see us. Misunderstandings are at the root of much of our suffering. To truly see and to be seen requires both courage and vulnerability. The seed cast upon unbroken earth will not set root. We must trust the dormant seeds unto the earth, where they will absorb its warmth, germinate, and, in their time, grow and flourish.

"We welcome the dawn, but rather than ceding power to the interim darkness, we harness this fire to symbolize our potential to master chaos. In the night, we allow ourselves to wonder at the stars we cannot see during the brilliance of day. The moon, reflecting the sun's light, is the promise that the sun, in its due course, will return.

"Where is the drum circle?" I whispered to Mom.

"You've got me there. They used to have one, but it did kind of weird us all out. It made it a little too intense."

"I imagine," I replied.

"Many people associate the winter season with death," the woman continued. "Solstice is a time to anticipate rebirth. We trust that the returning heat, like that of the fire, will decimate impurities and strengthen that which is righteous and true: clay will be hardened; metal will be annealed; good plants will thrive as weeds wither away.

"Our predecessors from cultural traditions far and wide celebrated the visions that were awakened during winter solstice through music and dance. We now invite you to walk the triskelion about the bonfire. If you are so moved, feel free to dance or sing. Walk the first spiral to celebrate your past. Gather strength from what you've learned on your journey to surmount the impediments that may lie before you."

She paused for a moment to let the first of the walkers begin. As the first reached the intersection leading toward the second spiral, she continued.

"Once you enter the second spiral, use your walk to recommit to your life's mission. Regard how you feel in this moment without judgment or evaluation. Honor your presence in the here and now."

I was next in line after Mom stepped onto the spiral path, which turned inward toward each spiral's center before turning to head back out again.

The woman continued. "As you depart from the second spiral and enter the third, take this time to imagine your future, discover your visions, be your own poet, be your own muse. Kindle, stoke, or tend your inner fire as your place along life's path demands."

I had to admit that the guided meditation in motion was soothing in its reflectivity, the prompts proving to calm and direct my thoughts.

"As you walk, cultivate aura. Everything you perceive anticipates reciprocation. To sense the aura of another empowers that aura. Aura exuded and unrequited is diminished. Do not just look—see. Do not just hear—listen. Do not just touch—feel. Participate. Engage. Transform.

Transcend. Journey. Dare to see the infinite around you. Embrace your liberation."

Her final prompts concluded as the last member of the group stepped off of the third spiral.

"Now, if we can all evenly surround the perimeter of the fire, we will conclude our celebration." We did as she asked.

"If you wish to know the secrets of the universe, think in terms of vibration, frequency, and energy. Take what you need from our gathering here tonight. Leave behind that which you have purposely shed. Know that the precepts we contemplate tonight are here for you to revisit at any time you need them. Significance is afoot. Be ready. Happy Winter Solstice, Merry Christmas, and the best of new years to each and every one of you."

I was surprised at the brevity of the celebration, but I was alight with all of what had been conveyed. The assembly began to drift up the hill, to the shelter where cider was being served.

"So, what did you think?" Mom asked.

"That was lovely," I answered. "The perfect capstone to my journey. She summed up a lot of what I discovered along the way."

"Did you catch the bit about vibration, frequency, and energy?"

"Yeah, that part did seem a bit incongruent with the tone of all the rest. Was that something said by the Dalai Lama?"

"Nikola Tesla, actually."

I laughed at how everything truly came full circle, or, rather, how the strange loop seemed to be circling, allowing me to make the quantum leap to the next plane. I let faith and science work together. Philosophy, physics, and psychology. None benefited from placing them in opposition, working at cross-purposes, I thought to myself.

"The question is, then, what lies ahead?" I asked my mom.

"That is the question, isn't it?" she asked in return. "That is the question."

Before I went to bed that night, I checked my phone. Henry hadn't texted back. Maybe he had finally gotten tired of waiting for me to come home and beg to be taken back.

Maybe I should stop hiding behind texts and just call him.

27

Christmas Eve

I slept in and awoke to the scent of glühwein already on the stove. I started the day with two sizable mugs of it and ample servings of stollen. I gave my Christmas present to Mom over breakfast. She protested that she hadn't intended and would not give me her present until the evening, but she accepted my gift under my persistence. She wore the bracelet with a simple navy sweater dress and a chunky sugilite pendant that I'd forgotten she owned. I hadn't seen it in a while, but she used to wear it constantly around the time I returned to Chicago.

The day before, we had prepared the Christmas feast. The kartoffelsalat and sauerkraut were in the fridge. The cheese was cubed for fondue to go with the weisswurst, the main course. We baked lebkuchen for dessert. We decorated the tree and decked the halls to finish the day, using all of the old ornaments we cherished and reminiscing over the stories each brought to mind.

Heading out to Old Town for our long-anticipated lunch, we planned to stay through the evening, until our throats would be sore from singing carols and our bellies would be full of biscochito and hot chocolate.

At La Placita, we each got a cup of the green chile stew, and we split an order of chiles rellenos and an order of the mole chicken enchiladas to make a combo no restaurant, mysteriously, ever seems to put on a menu. Our conversation was dappled with moans of pleasure, only occasionally emitted at an appropriate volume.

"Did you buy any jewelry for yourself on your trip?" Mom asked as we ate.

"Just a bracelet on the first day."

"This one?" Mom removed the bracelet from her purse and set it on the table.

"Why did you bring that here?"

"I wanted to ask you about it. Why aren't you wearing it? It's beautiful, and it is a souvenir of your time in Sedona."

"I was a little thrown when I found out what the symbol on it meant, so I thought I'd stick to buying jewelry for others."

"Did you know that these stones," she said, motioning to her bracelet, "represent and empower spiritual love and wisdom?"

I sighed. "Does everything have to mean something?"

"I guess it depends on what you want to believe," she replied. "Everything, scientifically speaking, has energy and vibration. There are plenty of people who will tell you that energy is perceptible if you sensitize yourself to it. Many of those people call that energy 'aura.' Whatever you call it, there is no such thing as a truly inanimate object."

"I can respect that point of view, but what I have a hard time believing is that objects, like crystals and stones, have auras, to use your word, with specific, useful powers."

"I'm not disagreeing with you, but I have two thoughts on that. For one, who would have supposed that the most powerful antibiotic of its time would have been discovered oozing from bread mold, or that tetrahydrocannabinol would be the panacea we know it to be today. Powerful, medicinal properties can be found in the strangest of places."

"What is that? Tetrahydro..." I asked.

"It's THC, dear. It's found in cannabis. It's marijuana... You know, pot?"

"I know what pot is!" Glancing around self-consciously, I made an effort to lower my voice. "For crying out loud," I whispered.

"Well, I'm not always so sure about what you know. You've turned out to be quite the lily-white ivory tower idealist, sweetheart. I didn't realize I'd raised you to see the world through such stark, strict definitions."

"Are you saying I'm uptight?"

"Well, I'm not saying that..."

"You are!"

"When was the last time you smoked a joint?" she asked.

"What does that have to do with whether I'm uptight or not?"

"It'd be a helpful indicator."

"I don't smoke because it's illegal," I insisted. "I don't smoke because I work for the federal government."

"You don't think people who work for the federal government smoke pot?"

"Not if they like their jobs."

"You don't especially like your job."

"I don't want to lose it over weed."

"We'd be in a better state of affairs if more federal workers did light up."

She had a point.

"You're not even going to ask me when I lit up last?" she asked.

"Last? Oh, man… I don't want to know…"

She interrupted me. "…the afternoon before you got to town. It's the reason George brought me home. I wasn't quite right to drive."

"Ugh… you were high the night I got to town?"

"I guess the Visine, a shower, and a good tooth-brushing concealed the evidence. Not that I'm ashamed. I just didn't suppose the other night was the right time to discuss it."

"And now is?" I wondered aloud to myself. "How did we get so far off-track? What was the other reason you think crystals have magical powers?" I asked, hoping to change the subject.

"I never said 'magical,' but to answer your question, the other is psychological."

I made a noise of disgust. "I'd rather talk about smoking pot."

"Really?" She seemed only too eager.

"No! Can we not talk about psychology, though?"

I was given a momentary reprieve when the waitress returned to see if there was anything else we wanted to order. We placed an order for the sopapillas, even though we were both already stuffed.

"I know. I know all about your aversion," my mom assured me. "All I'm talking about is the placebo effect. If people feel better, whether it be luckier, or stronger, or healthier, or more peaceful, because of stones, lucky pennies, wishbones, four-leaf clovers, or anything else—how is that any different than medicine? What's the harm in that?"

"Nothing, I suppose, so long as such belief doesn't cross over to worship. I can't stand idly by if I witness misguided idolatry."

"What do you suppose is the extent of your responsibility in that arena?" Mom asked.

"I haven't given it that much thought. I don't cross paths with a lot of crystal-worshippers."

"How about this, then: why don't you want to wear this bracelet? What's the symbol on it that bothers you so much?"

"It's a Kokopelli."

"And you don't want to find yourself with a magical bun in the oven."

When the sopapillas arrived, I was reminded once again of why the simple delicacies shouldn't be ordered anywhere but Albuquerque. The baseball-sized, air-filled pillows of dough only rise properly at high elevations. I bit the corner off of one and began to fill it with honey. "So you know what it is, obviously. No, it's not that. Well, I don't want to get magically pregnant, of course." I laughed, but Mom remained straight-faced. "I don't want to wear an image that someone might misconstrue."

"This could be an exhausting conversation if we take it to its logical end. We could talk about the hypocrisy of your attributing negative connotations to objects but denying the attribution of positive connotations to others. We could talk about the co-opting of symbols and the distortion of their meanings across ages and cultures. We'd never get anywhere. I'm saying wear the bracelet or don't. My point is this: 'Start where you are. Use what you have. Do what you can.'"

The quotation was one of Mom's favorites. Teddy Roosevelt was the first person to make the point, but it was better stated by Arthur Ashe. Two more different people there never were.

"Better yet," she continued, "remember Matthew 7: 'Judge not, that ye be not judged. For with what judgment ye judge, ye...'"

"I know, I know. It's funny. In the last two months, I've heard, cited, and contemplated more quotations, especially of scripture, than I have in the last thirty years."

"All while in the midst of adultery, separation, professional crisis, vortexes, and meditation."

"What's your point, Mom?"

"Whatever's brought you to this point has brought you here for a reason. Listen to the universe. It's trying to talk to you."

"I'll get right on that as soon as my husband responds to my texts."

"This has almost nothing to do with Henry. You need to have faith, regardless of what comes."

"I'm trying."

"I know." She put her hand over mine, gave it a squeeze, then picked it up and kissed my palm like she had always done when I was small. On cue, I put it to my cheek.

"Can I completely change the subject?" she asked.

"Please. Absolutely," I begged.

"What is that fragrance you're wearing?"

"I got it at Dad's shop, not long before he died."

"I thought so. *God's Gift*, right?"

"That's the one."

"I've been thinking about something. I never considered telling you this until the other night, when you were telling me about Dante and Sam. The woman who sold those perfumes, oils, lotions, and candles at the shop? She and Niklaus were lovers."

I almost choked on my sopapilla.

"That's how I learned about the supposed powers of the sugilite," Mom continued, not missing a beat. "It's supposed to bring light and love to matters requiring forgiveness, protect the soul from emotional trauma, and alleviate disappointment, hostility, and spiritual despair."

"*That's* how you…" I finally managed to put a few words together, but I didn't really know how to continue, considering my synapses were exploding and spinning like Catherine wheels. "*That's* how you learned about the powers of some purple stones? Talk about burying the lede, Mom."

"Believe me, I prayed for assistance during that period in my life. I also drank and medicated for a time, to get me through. The former worked; the latter didn't. Still, when I learned about the supposed powers of the sugilite, I used one—this one—as an amulet, something to fortify me while I did what I needed to do."

"Which was what, Mom?"

"Confront Nik. And that's why I bring this up. I have no desire to disparage your father or his memory. Nik repented for what he did, living out the rest of his days, however few, as a tribute to his love for me. And I was able to forgive him, eventually. You know what made all of that possible?"

"Please don't say the sugilite," I moaned.

"No. Conversation. You harbor animosity against Henry and against yourself. I can see it. Henry has animosity, too. When you see him, you have to have that hard conversation."

"I know. And you're right about the animosity. I wrote all about it while I was in Sedona. When I see him, I'll be ready."

"Is that what's in your leather-bound journal there?"

"That's right."

"Good," Mom said as she smiled. "I'm glad. Do you want my amulet, too?"

"It couldn't hurt." I took it from her and began to hook the clasp at the nape of my neck while I continued. "I've worn this fragrance on every special occasion since I bought it, including my wedding. You never said anything."

"I know. Let's just say I'm not the biggest fan."

I picked up the bracelet and put it on before we left the restaurant.

~ ~ ~ ~ ~ ~ ~ ~

We milled around Old Town, often hand in hand or arm in arm, absorbing the sites and the culture as luminarias were set in place on every curbside, walkway, fence line, and roof top. We walked all the way up San Felipe, weaving our way through the courtyards off the street before taking Charlevoix to Romero, circling through the various shops and galleries on our way back southward.

I learned that there was a specific term—*en plein air*—for paintings created outdoors, and that it wasn't until the mid-19th century, when oil paints in tubes became available and French box easels were invented, that the pastime became popular. We tried on hats; Mom talked me out of a bowler but approved of a wool cloche. One gallery owner talked with us at length about photogravure printmaking; another talked about the extraordinary *trompe l'oeil* on display; a third described the encaustic painting process. We admired dozens of Zuni fetishes, storyteller figurines, kachina dolls, and santos wood carvings. I resisted the urge, but finally surrendered and bought a large chile ristra to hang on Mom's kitchen wall.

It was dusk when we crossed the main plaza. As we passed the gazebo, I heard him call my name. I froze for a moment before turning around.

"I supposed you'd come through here sooner or later," he said.

"I… think that San Felipe de Neri is still selling hot chocolate," Mom said, taking the bag with the ristra from my wrist.

"Did you know about this?"

"I only hoped. Merry Christmas, Mandy." She hugged my suddenly nerve-stiffened frame, then touched the sugilite amulet at my solar plexus before turning to walk away. As she approached the church, I could make out George under the entrance archway, waiting for her. She looked back over her shoulder before proceeding, her arm around him, his hand draped over her shoulder.

I turned back to Henry. There he was, leaning against the newel post beside the staircase into the gazebo. Carolers inside were milling around, presumably on a break.

"Merry Christmas, Henry," I said.

He smiled, warmly but tentatively. "It's good to see you."

A warm feeling came over me. I rushed toward him and leapt into his arms, dropping the journal at his feet as I flung my arms around his neck. He buried his face in my neck as he wrapped his arms around the small of my back.

"There's a lot we need to talk about," I whispered in his ear.

"I know," he replied.

I loosened my grasp a bit, letting my feet reach the ground. "That's as good a place as any to start," I said. "'I know' has to be one of the most infuriating things anyone can hear. It's condescending, like a note of congratulations that I finally reached your enlightened state."

"Okay…" Henry wondered. "I can be more sensitive to my use of those words, if you can admit that it's really just a figure of speech." He spoke carefully. "I was just agreeing with you."

"I can do that," I said, mirroring his methodical tone, "but I need you to know that your words, gestures, and expressions are all I have to go by when I'm trying to communicate with you. If I can't rely on the meaning of your words, that removes a big part of the equation."

"Are we doing this right here? Is this talk really happening right now?" he asked.

"I guess it is," I said.

"There are Christmas carolers and *Flamenco* dancers."

"They're *Folklórico* dancers, actually. *Flamenco* is Spanish—Andalucían, actually."

"*Folklórico*, then. It can be hard to talk to you, sometimes, when you dwell on every last detail. I'm not saying it's a bad thing to be as smart as you are, but you knew what I meant. It's a little busy here, that's all."

I had to agree with the absurdity of our surroundings. "I'll just add the setting for this scene to the list of things that haven't turned out the way I thought they would."

Just then, a strolling mariachi band began to play "Oh Come, All Ye Faithful," drowning us out.

"Can we sit down, at least?" he asked, shouting. "This might take a while."

"The rest of our lives, I think," I hollered in reply.

"I am available that long," he said, taking my hands in his. He squeezed them resolutely, and then searched over my shoulder. "How about over there?" he asked, pointing to one of the wrought-iron benches along the sidewalk.

"A little too *Forrest Gump*."

"Alright… how about over there by the cannons?" Two large replicas of cannons, like those buried and left behind as the Confederate troops retreated from the area, stood beside San Felipe Street.

"I hope the metaphor doesn't hold, but sure," I said.

We walked over to sit beneath the cottonwood trees, somewhat away from the park paths.

"I like that you surprised me," I said. "Coming to Albuquerque, I mean. Did Mom know you were coming?"

"She stopped begging about a week ago, when I told her to stop. I'd been asking her to stop for at least a week prior, but I finally insisted last Tuesday."

"Last Tuesday… That was the day I spent at Buddha Beach and Cathedral Rock."

"I mean the Tuesday before that. The day after your open house."

"Grand opening," I corrected.

"That's it, again—right there. You knew what I meant."

"Alright, alright. Last Tuesday."

"Last Tuesday I told Nadja I wasn't coming and to stop asking. It's the day I took off my wedding ring and gave up all but my very last hope for us."

I hadn't noticed that he wasn't wearing his ring until just then. The sight of his bare finger stunned me. Were we breaking up? "I don't know whether to ask why you were still thinking about coming, what made you decide you weren't, or what made you change your mind."

"I was still thinking about coming because you are my wife. We are family, and we should be together for the holidays. I wasn't sure if I should come, because I didn't want to intrude, especially after you yelled at me on the phone that day—about talking with your mom."

"And what made you decide not to come? What made you take off your ring? I'm still wearing mine, you know."

"You weren't that night. I don't want to talk about that, yet. What have you been doing, Mandelyn? Except for your notes about the dogs at home, I haven't heard from you in weeks, and then after you left, almost nothing at all."

"I've been getting out of my own head, Henry. I was doing the kind of self-reflection you can't do without some solitude and perspective. I hiked a lot, and I meditated. I prayed; I wrote. I found some balance, made some discoveries, and came to some conclusions."

"I've heard Sedona can be helpful with things like that."

"How did you know I was in Sedona?"

"Your credit card statements. I saw everything."

The look I gave him must have burned holes in his face.

"I wasn't tracking you. The charges download to the home accounting software every night. I supposed you knew I knew. Why would you even want to keep that a secret from me?"

"Step back a minute. I want to talk about our finances. I have no idea where we stand. None. I don't know what kind of debt we have on the house. I don't even know if we're still paying your student loans. I don't know what our credit card limits are, whether we have anything in reserve, or what's budgeted. I know nothing."

"I have all of that plainly organized. I can show you all of that. All you have to do is ask."

"I shouldn't have to ask, Henry. I should just know. That information should be shared freely. That's my money, too. My livelihood. My future."

"You can open the program any time you want."

"You've been handling our money in that program since a month after I moved in with you. Back then, I kept my books on my check register and in an expandable file. I had rent, an electric bill, a phone bill, and a rolling balance on two credit cards. I'm a smart woman, but I don't know how to navigate that program, especially with how complicated our finances must be now, with profit-sharing, 401Ks, TSPs, mortgages, stocks… I asked you time and time again for some sort of report—for you to make some sense of things, and you always said you'd get to it at some point that never came. I finally gave up."

"I can respect that. I can. What I can't do is intuit that, Mandelyn. I haven't kept score, but I know there are several things I asked you to do over the years that you didn't do, either. I didn't realize it was that big a deal to you. I supposed you trusted that everything's fine, and it is."

"Alright. When we get home, I want you to work up a presentation. Do we have money set aside to vacation at all?"

"Do you need to go on another vacation?"

"Vacation isn't something you need. Wait, you know what? Change that. It's something I am going to need, going forward. We always used to talk about the places we wanted to go and the things we wanted to do and see, but we haven't even begun to scratch anything off the list. After this week, I don't think I can go back to just wishing and hoping to tackle that list someday in the undefined distant future. My heart felt full during my time in Sedona. I feel alive again: recharged, focused, and invigorated. I can get that feeling from a night at the theater, or from a concert, or from a trip to a museum, but it's fleeting. We don't even do much of that other stuff I just listed, either. That needs to change, too."

"We don't have money specifically set aside for vacationing, but we have the flexibility to allocate more toward entertainment."

"I'm not talking about entertainment. This isn't about diversion or escape. I'm talking about memory-making, inspiration, and, literally, expanding our horizons. I'm talking about exploration and discovery. Hell, it can be some volunteering or charity work. I'm talking about having a life."

"Like you did in India, I guess. With Dante."

I gritted my teeth. "If you have something to say, why don't you just come out with it?"

"How is he?" he asked bitterly.

"He's fine, I guess. I wouldn't exactly know."

"Were you in Sedona with him?"

"I was in Sedona alone. Why would you think otherwise?"

"Why wasn't there a hotel charge? Why didn't you send any pictures to Colette, except of the scenery? Why didn't you contact me at all for the entire time you were gone?"

That was a lot to unpack. "Wow. All that from someone who wasn't tracking my every move. There wasn't a hotel charge because I stayed at a condo where Col's friend has a place. I didn't send any other pictures because I was alone and selfies are narcissistic. I didn't contact you because phone service varied from awful to nonexistent in the places where I spent most of my time, and I was busy, Henry, doing the very thing you sent me out to do."

"I saw you with him. The night of the grand opening. That was him, right? Dark, sexy Southern Italian frat boy? That's the night I took off my ring."

"What? Where?"

"Meat. I was sitting by the door. There was a moment that I thought you saw me, but it turned out it was Sam and some other guy who drew your attention instead. How is Sam, by the way? While I'm thinking about it, am I the only man in your life that you haven't beaten up?"

I inhaled through my nose and exhaled through my mouth. "I want to say this simply and slowly, so there is no confusion. I hadn't seen or heard from Dante since I moved back to Chicago from Iowa. I'd seen him twice or three times, tops, since college graduation. He came to hear the lecture. I didn't know he was going to be there, and he didn't know that I worked for the Lab. What you saw that night was a pair of friends catching up. We talked about old times and discussed science. We dredged up some old pain, sorted out some things, and found some closure."

"Fine. What prompted you to throw your left hook into Sam's jaw?"

"He said some incredibly vulgar, hurtful things that I wasn't going to stand for."

"He apologized to me, you know?"

"What? Why? When?"

"That night. I followed him out. Him and that other guy. Brett, was it? Sam was a little out-of-sorts. He wasn't making a lot of sense, but yeah. He said he was sorry while I was trying to see if you'd done any permanent damage to his face."

"What exactly did he say?"

"You really gave him a shot, I think. I couldn't really tell, but it sounded like he said something like, 'I'm sorry I was the honeysuckle in your garden.' Does that make any sense to you?"

"It does. Sam is of no concern to me now. He's a part of my past, and I have no desire to resurrect memories of him ever again."

"You've known him since you were barely out of diapers, Mandelyn. What happened between the two of you?"

I gulped, steeling myself to give the answer I'd prepared. "Henry, I made a terrible mistake. He seduced me and I let him. I played right along. I was drunk when it happened, but I make no excuses. He told me that he'd always had feelings for me, and rather than dismiss what he said, I delighted in it. He lavished me with attention, and instead of pushing him away…"

"What exactly did you do, Mandelyn?" His voice was calm, unwavering, but altogether different from the way he had sounded the night he released me. He was studying me, intent upon understanding.

"There are so many ways I'm ashamed of what happened, Henry. The fact is that I don't know what I did, exactly. I blacked out. Sam told me that night, when you saw the two of us at Meat, that it was a lot less, physically, than I had thought. I'm not saying that what I did or didn't do doesn't matter. Of course it does. The betrayal happened the moment I suspected that his intentions, or even his desires, were anything but platonic, and I didn't walk away.

"I don't expect your forgiveness. I am still working on forgiving myself. I came to the conclusion in Sedona, though, that I need your forgiveness and my own if we are going to make it, you and me. I'm so sorry, Henry. Regardless of what happens with us, I hope you can find it within yourself to forgive me."

Henry looked away. "I'm going to need some time. I heard everything you said. It shouldn't even be as shocking as I'm finding it, if I'm being honest with myself. I was the one who sent you out. This was a possibility. I have a question for you, though," he said, looking back at me. "Had you always thought about Sam that way? I mean, I knew he was your first, from that CVC stuff."

"I didn't, Henry. I swear. After Homecoming, each of us was pulled in a different direction. Well, that's not exactly true. I turned away, throwing myself into volleyball, debate, my classes—to the point that I stopped considering his whereabouts, his thoughts, or his feelings with any more intensity or regularity than I would consider those of a longtime acquaintance. We'd have our banter here and there over the years, but it was over between us, so far as I was concerned, until I conjured the nostalgia for him while writing about it to Morgan."

"I knew I hated that program," he grumbled.

"You can feel however you want about CVC. Maybe it was a misguided attempt to sort out my confusion and despair, but the confusion and despair were real, Henry. I told you I was drunk the night all this happened with Sam, but there's one more thing I have to tell you: It happened the night before you released me."

"It happened at the Architectural Celebration?"

"Well, after. During and after. The seduction, I mean. That began at dinner."

Henry was silent for a long time. "I never completely gave up on you, but I got pretty close. My faith in you had been diminishing for a long time. That doesn't make what happened okay, of course. I'm devastated. But… my distance from you, my indifference towards you—that left the door open, didn't it?"

"Henry…"

"You pushed it wide open, or let it be pushed, but the way I treated you left your heart vulnerable, didn't it?"

"Henry, you bear no responsibility for what I've done to you. I wanted to blame you, but in the end, the fault is all mine."

"Is that what this is? Is this the end?" he asked.

"I don't want it to be."

"Neither do I."

We hugged fiercely. We had that kind of embrace where you retract and reset your arms, grappling for a tighter hold. The rush over my skin felt terrifying, like I would burst into flames, or at least into choking sobs of tears, but neither occurred. "I love you. It's not easy, but I love you so very much."

"It's not easy to love you, either," he said.

We finally parted. Darkness had fallen fully by that time and, unbeknownst to us, the luminarias had been lit all around us. The flickering glow obscured the view of anything beyond the gentle light that encapsulated us.

"How did you get here, by the way? Or when?" I asked him.

"Earlier today. Before noon. George picked me up from the airport."

I laughed at the part George had to play in all of this. "And he dropped you off here?" I asked. "He could have coordinated with my mom. We could have been having this talk all day."

"But this is where I wanted to see you, and I wanted you to come to me. I didn't mind waiting, or even setting up the circumstances so it was likely to happen, but when it came down to it, I wanted this to happen on its own. Besides," he said, rising, "this is where I wanted us to dance. Will you dance with me?"

"Dance? Here?"

"Here."

"But there's so much more we need to talk about."

"There will always be more we need to talk about. I thought I was out of things to talk to you about, but this afternoon's made me realize that I'd only run out of the safe, polite, appropriate topics."

"I'm almost never safe, polite, or appropriate," I joked.

"I know. I loved that about you from the moment we met. You're impetuous and lighthearted. I thought I had to be the serious one in order for you to retain those qualities. All I ever wanted to do after that New Year's Day was take care of you."

I finally rose. "I never needed taking care of. Well, that's not true. I'll tell you what: if I dance with you, can we keep talking?"

"That's the best deal I've ever heard."

I put my hand in his, and he drew me close. The carolers had concluded their performance somewhere in the time we'd been sitting together, but the mariachi band was playing "Oh, Holy Night" somewhere in the distance. We swayed.

I started. "Without you, after Theodore passed, I wouldn't have survived. I don't think I properly thanked you for that."

"I never needed your thanks," he replied. "Caring for you in that time was my outlet, my way of enduring."

"I think I knew that, which is why I let it continue long after I really felt that it was necessary. I enabled your coping mechanism and masked my needs in the process. Instead of drinking, doing something reckless, or just withdrawing…"

"I did a lot of that, too," he joked.

"You coddled me. You still coddle me, and for a long time I played the part of someone who needed to be coddled. We both fell into roles instead of being our genuine selves."

"I'm a man. It's my job to protect you."

"Coddling isn't protection. And protection may be a masculine instinct, but it isn't strictly male. Try taking a bear cub away from its mother."

"Did you do that on one of your hikes in Sedona?"

I laughed. "You know what I mean. Strength and courage, caring and nurturing—these things have nothing to do with gender, but our dumb society has categorized them as if they were. We're in desperate need of new vocabulary."

"Well, between the two of us, that task is on you. Not because you're a woman, but because you're eminently better-suited."

"I can't argue with you there. Am I making my point, though?"

"Stop coddling you. Got it."

"When you're mad, get mad. When you disagree with me, argue. When you have a secret, tell me. When there's something that'll be hard for you to explain to me, you have to try, and through it all, you have to trust that I am strong enough, smart enough, and mature enough to handle it."

"I hate my job, Mandelyn. How's that for a complicated secret?"

"Oh. Well, go ahead and jump right in."

"I hate what my role has become. I never should have accepted the partners' offer. If I were to start my own firm, I want to do it on my own terms, not as a front for some shady scheme."

"I believe in you. I've always believed in you. Don't you know that?"

"I'm not sure I always did. With every accolade or promotion I've received, you seemed more astounded, or impressed, than just proud. It's like you had the bar of your expectations for me set pretty low."

"I never wanted you to feel as if I expected anything from you, as if my love for you was contingent upon your achievements."

"See, when you put it that way, it sounds really wonderful, but sometimes it feels as if your Type A drive was reserved for your success alone. I want you to make me want to be the best version of myself, not in place of my own ambition or sense of self-worth, but as a supplement to them. There's only so much I can accomplish alone, and my reserves sometimes run low."

"You present this façade to the world, Henry, that seems impenetrable. No one who knows you thinks anything could stand in your way."

"That's fine for the world to believe, I guess, but I need you to know the truth. I'm only human, Mand."

"To know that, really know that and not just believe it because you're saying so, you need to have this kind of vulnerability with me all the time," I said. "If I promise to be more sensitive, can you be more forthright about your needs?"

"It's not as much about lifting my spirits when I'm down," he said. "It's about knocking me back to reality when my head swells, keeping me on my toes, and making me think. I want to grow with you. I don't want to continue just subsisting like we have. I can't contemplate a forever like that."

"I guess I've done a little coddling of my own," I realized.

"That's another way of thinking about it, sure."

"Then I hate your job, too," I admitted. "I've hated it for a long time. Everything you do for that firm is out of step with who you are and who you have the potential to be. I thought I was being supportive all this time by not saying so before now."

"For two reasonably intelligent people who should know better, we kind of suck at this, you know?"

"It's a wonder we made it this far," I joked. "We'll figure it out," I continued, "whether you rescind acceptance of your contract, start your own practice, or whatever other option is out there for you. As long as we're revealing things we should have been saying all along, I also resent your job for another reason. It looks so glamorous, with the downtown office, the suits, the meetings, the credentials, the authority. I never admitted it, but taking the job at the Lab felt like giving in—like surrendering."

"I knew that. Even I could see that."

"I don't mean that I surrendered in the competition with my peers. I mean that I conceded the rat race to you."

"Me?" he asked.

"It's like what you're saying about being kept on your toes. When you got promoted, I wanted to get promoted. When you won a new project, I wanted to win a new plum assignment. When you won an award, I wanted to win one. Pretty dumb, huh?"

"Not at all. It explains a lot. So what, do you hate your job, too?"

"No. I didn't realize it until this trip, but I love my job. I just don't love how I've been doing it. I half-ass it. Until the Muon g-2 event, I phoned it in. There's so much more work to be done, and massive unrealized potential for my colleagues and myself if I just have at it."

"Well, great. I'm glad you feel that way." Henry looked aside, then, in a way that made me think he wasn't telling the whole story.

"What? What else were you about to say?" I asked.

"You have an entire journal that you wrote about this. I just dropped a pretty heavy piece of news on you, which you handled beautifully, by the way. It's your turn. Go."

"I don't know. With all the big issues already on the table or out of the way, the rest of what I wrote is pretty silly. I'll let you read it, of course, if you want to. It's little things."

"Name one."

"Okay... I want you to initiate sex more often."

"Easy. I can do that," he laughed.

"No, I mean really. Let me describe the dynamic between us, as I see it, and tell me if you agree. You're always telling me how hot you think it is that I'm so easily turned on by you. Then, when we're together, you're so giving. You're a very selfless lover."

"I'm waiting to hear what the problem is with this."

"The way you've got it drawn, I'm this easy, eager girl who always wants it, and it's your responsibility to give it to me whenever and wherever I please."

"I know you're not easy. I cherish you."

"That's kind of the trouble. I mean… I know this sounds crazy. Maybe I'm being too picky, but what I'm trying to say is that, if I didn't initiate sex, we'd almost never have it. I want you to be the eager one, the aggressor, at least sometimes. I want you to show me that you want it and that you intend to get it. I want you to take me. I don't always want to be the seducer. I want to be seduced."

"Wow. I wonder if I'm the first guy in the history of the world who's heard his wife say that."

"I couldn't say. Precedent makes very little difference to me."

"I mean, here I was, supposing that I was treating my wife with honor and esteem, when all along she wanted to be hunted, taken down, and dominated."

"Is that what I do to you?"

"No! But I'm a man. I'm the known quantity. I'm the sure bet. What man out there wants less sex than he's getting? The woman is the limiting factor, at least for any man that respects women."

"I'm not talking about disrespect. Sex is not degrading, at least in the manner in which it happens between you and me. It's making love. That phrase always sounded so hokey to me until I was with you. It comes back to trust and vulnerability, Henry. If you want something from me, you should go for it. If you ask me to do something, I'll almost definitely say yes."

"Almost?"

"I reserve the right to consider requests before acceptance, and I reserve the right to negotiate, but that's part of what keeps the mystery alive, isn't it?"

"This could get interesting."

"I hope so. Col talked me into a Brazilian wax." When I said that, Henry's eyes popped. "It's high time I took it out for a proper spin," I said.

We kissed, carefully at first, but with a building passion inappropriate for two middle-aged people in the midst of a busy plaza on the eve of Jesus' birth, but neither of us seemed to care.

When we finally parted, we continued to sway as Henry spoke again. "Speaking of Colette, I finally met her. Small world, it turns out. She scheduled a meeting with my office right after the press release about the new firm. Why didn't you mention the line of work she's in before?"

"You don't like to talk about marketing, you and she operated in different sectors, and she and I don't talk a lot about our professional lives. We're sort of each other's respite from that. She's become a good friend, though. I should have introduced the two of you long before now."

"I owe her a follow-up meeting, at least. When we made the connection between the three of us, we were both a little unsettled. You have a good friend in her. Reminded me that I need to get out there and develop that personal network you're always bugging me about."

"Just get out there. Join a gym. Get a new bike and go cycling like you used to, before you got rid of your old one. Get out your camera and go shoot like you used to. Friends will follow, and you'll discover new passions and try new things."

"I hope none of those new things involve genital waxing, not that I'm not intrigued about it on your account. When did she talk you into that?"

"Thanksgiving."

"Just like the pilgrims." He gave me another kiss, this one decidedly more lascivious.

"What was that about the honeysuckle, after all?" Henry asked once he'd finished, whispering in my ear.

I drew back to explain. "It's a seemingly desirable plant, but it is really an insidious weed. Better to pluck it from the garden than be fooled by its allure. Speaking of which…" I steadied myself before continuing. "I want you to beware of Zara, your receptionist. I don't trust her. I trust you, but guard your heart, okay?"

"How did you…? I mean, what do you know about Zara?"

"What do *you* know about her?"

"I think she made your favorite perfume, for one."

"Ex-favorite perfume. It's got an association with it now that I don't want to be reminded of again."

"Then you really aren't going to like the candle she gave me for Christmas."

"Why is she giving you gifts?"

"We talked for the first time last week. We were on the train. Even though she's been in the office since the summer, I don't think I ever even said hello. During our first conversation, she confided that she's a recovering alcoholic. That seemed like a rather intimate thing to share in a first conversation, but I think she's had a hard go of it these last several years—hasn't had many people in whom she could confide. I complimented her perfume, innocently enough, I thought, but there was something odd about her... I don't know if I'm using this word the right way. Her aura? Her aura began to bother me. On Wednesday, she gave me the candle—just after Colette left the office, actually. As soon as I smelled it, everything clicked. It smelled like you. I asked her whether she used to make products for your dad's shop, and I'm telling you—it was clear as day—she had this look of... heartache. Painful longing. It was clear that..."

"Nik and Zara were lovers. My mother told me this morning."

"Merry Christmas to you," he joked, however darkly.

"I know." I laughed with him. "But really, it's better that I know. I put my dad on a pedestal my whole life, especially since his passing. I spent some time thinking about choosing to see, or, in this case remembering, only the good in people—choosing to acknowledge only the good in someone, shaping reality to the point of distorting it. It's a dangerous game. Choosing to only see the light doesn't make the darkness go away. It's only by shining the light in the darkness that it fades. Niklaus Ziegel was human—flawed, fallible, and in some ways just pitiful. Despite all of that, he loved me. My mother actually forgave him, and he worked every last day of his life to rise above his transgressions. Those are powerful lessons that aren't accessible from him if I picture him as a saint. I'm grateful.

"Speaking of gratitude," I continued, "where did you spend Thanksgiving?"

"At Joshua and Reynard's. Without the dogs, I was like that sad divorced dad without his kids for the holidays."

"I miss Frank and Lloyd so much. I can't wait to get home." I shook out my shoulders and adjusted the tone of my voice to be more business-like. "Alright," I said, "is there anything else you want to talk about right now? It's getting late. Are you tired? And where is your luggage?" I kept asking questions, because Henry was shuffling his foot, glancing around anxiously, hemming and hawing. "Are George and Nadja watching us from somewhere for a cue to come back?"

"I want kids, Mandelyn," he blurted out to interrupt me.

Of course. We had to talk about that. "One child, at least," he continued. "I know how you feel about being pregnant again. We can talk about options…"

"I want one, too," I interrupted. "You're right; we can talk about options, but my carrying our child is the top option on my list."

Henry gave me a curious smile, like he couldn't quite believe what I was saying.

"I was afraid for a long, long time, Henry, but I finally found the root of my fear. It was trust. An utter lack of trust, and of confidence, and of self-esteem. I didn't think you'd trust me to keep another baby safe. I didn't trust myself to prevent… it… from happening again, and my entire self-worth got wrapped up in whether or not I could bear children…"

"That's ridiculous, Mand…"

"Let me finish. I know it's ridiculous, but the greatest lack of trust I had was in God, Henry. I couldn't fathom a reason He'd let something like that happen to a child, let alone to you and me. The only reason I could ever discern was that I wasn't meant to bear children. What I finally figured out, though, was that I was presuming to know the will of God, even in the face of all the evidence that my presumption was wrong. I couldn't promise you a healthy child or a complication-free pregnancy, so the best thing I could do was eliminate the risk of the alternative.

"I still can't promise anything, Henry. Not a healthy child, or a healthy marriage, but I can promise to do everything I can to make it so and to have faith in God for the rest. That's what I've come to take as the meaning of this little guy." I held up my wrist and showed him the bracelet.

"What is that?" he asked, examining the engraving.

"It's a Kokopelli. He's a fertility deity of the Hopi people. I didn't know that when I bought it. I haven't worn it since. My mom brought it out with us today, so I wore it. Talking with you this afternoon has made me look at this and think of Theodore, wanting us to give him a brother or sister to keep an eye on things down here on his behalf."

"Then that's how I will think of the Kokopelli, too," Henry said, reaching into his pocket and retrieving his ring. "Maybe I'll update this with an engraving of my own."

"I think that's a wonderful idea."

"I also want to read this journal of yours," he said. "Sounds like you've come up with all kinds of brilliance and wisdom during your journey."

"It's not all brilliant. Some of it is bullshit. But some of it is pretty good."

Henry smiled. "That's life, after all, don't you think?"

The End

ACKNOWLEDGEMENTS

I'm glad that an author gets to write her thank-yous for readers to peruse them at leisure. This is much better than scrambling up an aisle, pulling a list from the décolletage of my haute couture, and barking everyone's name like an auctioneer, music rising to play me off the stage. My academic foundation is largely theatrical, so, naturally, I've played out *that* scenario about a thousand times. While I imagine it, I'm usually holding a shampoo bottle in my hand instead of a statuette, and suds are dripping down my forehead. This stings considerably less than that.

Speaking chronologically, I, naturally, have to thank my parents first. Even with my weird friends (yes, we were weird—still are—and I wouldn't have had it any other way) and wide-ranging aspirations, Sharon and Dave were never anything but thoroughly supportive of me, even when support took the form of constructively talking me out of absurd paths toward frivolous, harrowing ends.

Maht Wells gets the next nod, chronologically, because he told me about NaNoWriMo, the catalyst for this extraordinary journey. We've weaved in and out of one another's lives across three decades now, Maht and me, and always for good reason. For that, I am truly grateful.

Shelly Flowers is the first person to whom I confessed my plot. She whisked my kids away during prime writing hours, responded to inane blurts and questions without once wondering (to me, anyway) from whence any new tangent or brainstorm might have originated, and contributing key "what if" questions to the discussions in order to spur me on. Her guidance on psychiatry and quantum entanglement were the linchpins of this whole operation. Clearly, *Release* would not have been written the way it was—quite possibly, it would not have been written at all—without our talks, calls, texts, and emails. I'm glad,

ACKNOWLEDGEMENTS

too, that God had her carry half of our set of twins. Between the two of them, we've got it covered, A to Z, Sassy.

I owe enormous gratitude to Joanie Davies. In 2010, she proposed the formation of our mother-daughter book club, whose regular meetings ever since have transformed the loose associations among its members into cherished friendships. When I announced that I was participating in NaNoWriMo, she eagerly, continually asked after my progress. She celebrated each revelation, encouraged me through challenges, patiently listened to all my rants, and helped me remember what (and who) is truly important and… not. When I was wondering what my next step should be after finishing the first draft, it was Joanie who suggested that our book club workshop the manuscript (mothers only). The voice, pitch, and pace of Release is what it is because of the hours of meetings, together with the equally wise and empathetic Lisa Bertagna and Joanne Fledderman, when we hashed through Every Last Aspect of the story. After the meetings and subsequent revisions, Joanie lovingly, laboriously edited the new draft. She edited the book club questions, as well. She's an astounding fount of information about literature from the pulpiest to the most erudite, she's got a new marketing idea each time I talk to her, and, each time I see her, she has a bag of hand-me-downs from her daughters to give to my own.

The passages in Sedona and Albuquerque, the references to Jaipur and Muang Khoun, and the chapters at "the Department of Energy Laboratory in the western Chicago suburbs" wouldn't be right without the insight of Priya Adiraju, Lisa Verploegh, and particularly Sarah Marie McSweeney, whose song, *Be Still*, is a revelation. Learn more about Sarah Marie's work at operamantra.com. The yoga sequence in Chapter 26 closely resembles one created by Allison Bagby, who, with Kelin Holmes, motivated my practice when I needed it most. Thank you also, to Laoshī Laurince D. McElroy for your help with the passages describing bodywork and martial arts; your insight made the difference between research and truth. More information about Laurince can be found at watertigertaichi.com.

When it came to workshopping the updated novel, Shelly came through, again, roping in Darlene Flowers, Elisabeth Chambers, Joan Chambers, Lauren Noble, Marcy Chambers, Shannon Chambers,

ACKNOWLEDGEMENTS

and Sharon Zirves for the wild ride. Not that my own club pulled any punches (I don't tend to consort with punch-pullers), but the ladies I met in May, related to one another by blood or marriage, and each one as strong as the next, offered revelatory, targeted, constructive, and boisterous feedback. It was brazen and unvarnished, yet the great debates that broke out indicated clear direction, not conflicting advice or ambivalent opinion. It was often occurring all at once, I should add; it was hard to know where to look and listen sometimes. This book club/family is a crew accustomed to speaking in shorthand, anticipating each other's thoughts, and finishing each other's sentences. The interactions among mothers and daughters, between in-laws and sisters, and across generations was one aspect of the awesomeness, but I don't want to reduce their dynamic to that of a feisty family trope. For their diversity as well as what they have in common, these women were the first insight I had to the full breadth of my readership. The only common thread: No shrinking violets need apply.

After months of seeking the representation of a literary agent, and after determining that independent publishing was the right path forward, I fortuitously met Craig Park, FSMPS, Assoc. AIA. After Mexican food and several margaritas, he and I talked writing and publishing. Over the summer months, he patiently walked me through all manner of independent publishing minutia and nuance before making a well-reasoned proposal that he advised I not take, in favor of going solo. A more seasoned marketer, generous advisor, or warm-hearted Renaissance Man is tough to find. I'm glad I did. craigpark.com

Lindsay Megahed is my magnificently talented, hilarious, and overall badass neighbor. As if that's not enough, she's also a successful commercial artist, she's got mad parenting skills, and her husband and kids are straight-up awesome. All that, and she also designed the cover of *Release*. God, it's beautiful—perfectly elegant and exceptionally multifaceted. It's seemingly straightforward and light, but hauntingly complex the longer you look at it. lindsaymegahed.com

I first contacted Marcia Heroux Pounds in 2010, following up on a HARO request in which she was seeking people to interview for her book, *I Found a Job!* Her been-there-done-that insights about the publishing industry rounded out my marketing program. This proves,

ACKNOWLEDGEMENTS

once again, that it's smart to build and maintain professional connections with good people, no matter how seemingly distant or inexplicably "useful."

Speaking of marketing, I have to thank Amanda Feeley, proprietress of Esscentual Alchemy, natural perfumier... People, I can't even. I've known this lady since college. She's a classically trained lyric coloratura, but she's no Johnny-one-note. After reading the book, she agreed to fashion *God's Gift*, the fragrance described in the novel. Actually, before that, she gave the story such heartwarming, encouraging praise, I still look back at it every few days to motivate me when I'm feeling down or daunted. The work she's creating will actually yield two perfumes: *God's Gift: Seduction* and *God's Gift: Redemption*. As of this printing, plans are in the works to co-promote the fragrance and the novel, opening avenues to new customers for us both. Her website is: esscentualalchemy.mysupadupa.com.

Also, let me tell you about Bobby Moynihan and Ashley Whitney at Tiesta Tea. Small-world interactions really do yield amazing results. My daughters' girl scout troop leader, now good friend, Joyce Moynihan, was proudly sharing news of her son's burgeoning venture with fellow childhood friends. Without that mom-bragging, I wouldn't have known how to reach out to Bobby. In another cooperative marketing arrangement, I'm working with Tiesta to fashion a set of teas that will deepen the experience that readers, especially book club members, have with he book, while also introducing Tiesta brand to new customers nationwide. Win-win, as the marketing cliché goes. tiestatea.com

I thank Nick Kokonas, co-owner of Next Restaurant; Dr. Sonat Birnecker Hart, President of Koval Distillery; and Jim Moorhouse, an owner of Aleman Brewing. Each of these three do their respective spheres of the Chicago culinary scene proud. Patronize their establishments and drink their potables. *Release* is not set in Chicago without the sights and sounds beyond Navy Pier and the Mag Mile, people. Get out in the neighborhoods. See local shows. Scour the museums. Eat. Drink. Be Merry.

Along those same lines, thank you, Jim DeRogatis, for writing "Extraordinary Pucker for Fans" on January 2, 2003 for the *Chicago Sun-Times*. It was this article that provided substantive background for

ACKNOWLEDGEMENTS

the goings on while Mandelyn and Henry met in the balcony above.

Speaking of work in the background, I'm so pleased to be working with Barbara J. Sabel, C.P.A. and Seth Sabel of BJS & Associates, Ltd., my link to whom is the lovely Amy Sabel. Through Barb and Seth, I established Noon Key Productions LLC. If ever there is a grown-up moment, it's the one in which you lock in your FEIN. Walking them through my right-brained flights of fancy and getting their left-brained approval gave me such peace of mind about this little pipe dream enterprise actually having potential.

Jane McAdams, Owner of Beaumont Hardy Editing, is my editor. The experience of receiving my edited manuscript and reviewing the changes was like going on a job interview—one that you think you've nailed until you look in the mirror afterward and see spinach in your teeth. Though we've only interacted virtually, she's the friend who tactfully pulled me aside and told me there was spinach in my teeth before I smiled at one more person. I need as many people like this in my life as possible; I eat a lot of spinach, and I smile quite a bit, too. Thank you, Jane. beaumonthardy.com

Thanks to the beta readers, frequent inquirers, and providers of advice and encouragement not mentioned above, including but not limited to Julie Olszowka-Widmer, Amanda Lamerato Kelly, Jennifer Jarvis, Michaellyn Carlucci, Pamela McGowan, Brie Yaksic, Kathy Contreras, Abigail Breitenbach, Katherine VanLandingham, Marcia Hilger, Sue Binder, Stacey Forde, Kate Niemiec, Kristin Binder, Jennifer Verploegh, and everyone else who read, liked, shared, friended, followed, or favorited.

Finally, I thank my most treasured *Release* readers—my sister, Erin Hardy and my husband, Tom—and my wonderful girls. Tom and Erin are both very busy people whose hobbies don't usually include reading, but they championed and continue to champion this story and its characters—even better than me, sometimes. Together with F, Z, L, and T, this team kept me motivated when I faltered, focused when I wavered, confident when I was daunted, and humble when I needed to be reminded. Erin, always the cheerleader, and Tom, keenly and honestly wise—together with my dear daughters—keep my head, heart, and soul in balance. I love you. Thank you.

BOOK CLUB DISCUSSION QUESTIONS

1. Did you like the characters in Release? Who was your favorite character and why? Who was your least favorite character? How did your impressions of the main characters change throughout the novel?

2. Is Mandelyn a likable character? Can you relate to her or any of her experiences?

3. In Chapter 1, Mandelyn mentions that, "the straw that broke the camel's back" was Henry's re-washing of the sour cream container for recycling. Have you had any seemingly innocent, but completely exasperating incidents similar to this? What's your "sour cream container" story?

4. Mandelyn reluctantly participates in the CVC program. Mandelyn says, "Psychiatrists are useless. You're the only shrink I'll ever need," referring to Collette. Do you share Mandelyn's views on modern psychotherapy? Would you consider participating in a program like CVC? Do you think Morgan was a man or woman?

5. "Over the years, I have grown, matured in the face of life's challenges. Henry is exactly the same person as he was the day we met. Nothing fazes him. I don't know why that bothers me. It just does." Discuss emotional maturity and the benefits of holding firm stances vs. impressionable flexibility. How much do you think Henry's mother, his economic roots, or other aspects of his upbringing shaped his outlook, for better or for worse, especially when it comes to romance and intimacy?

6. How would you feel in Mandelyn's shoes about Joshua's revelation that he is gay? Is her anger justified?

7. Events at work put Henry in a bad mood for their outing at Next. Why does Joshua try to stir things up by bringing up Mandelyn's trip to India? Is Joshua out of line? Was Mandelyn truly "fired up" upon her return from the trip or simply lovesick over Dante?

BOOK CLUB DISCUSSION QUESTIONS

8. For being as surprised as she was that Dante knew so much about her, Mandelyn seems to know—or think she knows—a lot about Dante. How much do our assumptions and preconceived notions about people feed into our interaction with them once a real introduction's made? What was your first impression of Dante? What do you make of Dante's artwork, or his room decor in general?

9. How important are the traditional romantic gestures and acts of chivalry? Do you empathize with Mandelyn when she says, "You don't know what it's like to be in a marriage where opened doors, or dedicated songs, or chocolates, or flowers, or handholding, or… touching?! Where none of that happens anymore. You don't know how starved I've become for any hint of affection, and you don't know how hard it is to resist taking the… the kindness, the most innocent of gestures, and, and making it into something it's not." Do you agree or disagree with Sam, "The guy who opens your doors, or dedicates songs to you on the radio, or sends you chocolates? That's seduction, Mandelyn. That's artifice. It's the protocol for gaining panty access. The guy who does that may love you, but love has nothing to do with any of those moves. They're moves, Mandelyn. You do understand that, right?"

10. In Chapter 14, Colette and Mandelyn have a long discussion about submitting "to one another out reverence for Christ" vs. woman submitting to their husbands. Collette states, "The worst relationships of all are the ones where one person subjugates themselves to the other without reciprocation, with one person stalwart and the other just hanging on. Submissive behavior from both people is the key to successful relationships." What does she mean by that?

11. Masculinity and femininity are discussed throughout the book. While at the Palmer House, Collette discusses gender roles past and present and how the evolution of feminism has ruined generations of men "confusing them by teaching them to exhibit the very characteristics we spent a generation degrading." Do you agree

BOOK CLUB DISCUSSION QUESTIONS

with Collette? Later in Sedona, Eshe tells Mandelyn, "Everyone has both a masculine and feminine side, but everyone always talks about them as if they are opposites. That's ridiculous. If they were opposites of one another, having them both would cancel one other out, so you'd really have neither." Is this the same thing that Collette was expressing? Do you think we need to balance our masculine and feminine selves or should we embrace one or the other based on our sex?

12. Do you agree that heartbreak barely exists anymore because no one allows themselves to be vulnerable enough to let it happen? Does behavior like this leave people perpetually heartsick instead?

13. If there are degrees of infidelity, which is worse: what happened with Morgan, Sam, or Dante? When Mandelyn tells Sam, "What happened last night…I have never done that. I haven't ever been unfaithful to Henry," is that true? Later, Mandelyn tells Henry that "nothing happened between Dante and me." Is that true?

14. Mandelyn presents herself as a skeptical person with strong beliefs in science. She isn't deeply devout and doesn't believe in psychotherapy. When she arrives in Sedona, she says that the vortexes "sound like science fiction." Within a few days she is embracing the vortexes and the stupas. What happened? Have you ever been to the places mentioned in the book? Have you ever had an experience similar to those Mandelyn had in Sedona?

15. Did you like the ending? What did you think of Henry showing up unexpectedly? Did Henry and Mandelyn resolve their problems satisfactorily? Will they be happier now?

ABOUT THE AUTHOR

Hope is a former professional mascot, signmaker, thespian, and school teacher; the common thread among these is a passion for illuminating common yet complex issues in accessible yet unusual ways. With a degree in theatre arts, communications, and English from Simpson College, she performed, taught, directed, and coached in Iowa before returning to her Chicago area roots.

With more than fifteen years of experience in professional services marketing, Hope ghost-writes and by-lines articles by day. By night, she volunteers her time and opinions far too easily and laughs really obnoxiously. She serves at the pleasure of her Alpha Chi Omega alumnae chapter, the local Panhellenic society, her children's school association, and the Society for Marketing Professional Services. Hope also manages to practice hatha yoga intermittently and run 5K races poorly. She and her husband are raising four daughters who are convinced they are the modern incarnation of the March family.

CPSIA information can be obtained at www.ICGtesting.com
Printed in the USA
LVOW12s0505081114

412656LV00006B/6/P